Body
Heat

Body *Heat*

SUSAN FOX

BRAVA

KENSINGTON PUBLISHING CORP.

www.kensingtonbooks.com

BRAVA BOOKS are published by

Kensington Publishing Corp.
119 West 40th Street
New York, NY 10018

All Kensington titles, imprints, and distributed lines are available at special quantity discounts for bulk purchases for sales promotions, premiums, fund-raising, educational, or institutional use.

Special book excerpts or customized printings can also be created to fit specific needs. For details, write or phone the office of the Kensington special sales manager: Kensington Publishing Corp., 119 West 40th Street, New York, NY 10018, attn: Special Sales Department; phone 1-800-221-2647.

BRAVA and the B logo are Reg. U.S. Pat. & TM Off.

ISBN-13: 978-0-7582-7480-9
ISBN-10: 0-7582-7480-7

First Kensington Trade Paperback Printing: December 2012

10 9 8 7 6 5 4 3 2 1

Printed in the United States of America

AUTHOR'S NOTE

I know it's an unconventional choice to set a sexy romance in a senior citizens' residential facility, but Cherry Lane is perfect for this story. Heroine Maura Mahoney, an accountant raised by elderly, academic adoptive parents, is in her comfort zone dealing with numbers and seniors. But as romance readers know, comfort zones exist to be shaken up, and who better to do that than Jesse Blue? The bad boy, sentenced to do community service under Maura's supervision, is her worst nightmare. He's also exactly what she needs to make her let down her hair and discover her passionate, unconventional side. Jesse, too, has lessons to learn, and who better to teach him than a woman who's way out of his league, plus a handful of meddlesome elders?

I had so much fun teaching Maura and Jesse the lessons—and giving them the sexy romance!—they both so deserve. I hope you enjoy reading their story.

Thanks so much to the people who helped turn *Body Heat* into a real live book: Audrey LaFehr and Martin Biro at Kensington, Emily Sylvan Kim at Prospect Agency, and my critique group: Michelle Hancock, Betty Allan, and Nazima Ali.

I love sharing my stories with my readers and I love hearing from you. You can e-mail me at susan@susan lyons.ca or contact me through my website at www.susan fox.ca where you'll also find excerpts, behind-the-scenes notes, recipes, a monthly contest, my newsletter, and other goodies. You can also find me on Facebook at facebook .com/SusanLyonsFox.

Chapter 1

"Whatever else happens today," Maura murmured to herself as she clicked the SEND icon on her screen, "this is a great beginning to my thirtieth birthday." She smiled with pure satisfaction and stretched back in her office chair. Cherry Lane's tax filings were done, and now she'd turn to the budget—and prepare one that was so brilliant it would blow the Board of Directors out of the water and they'd offer her the promotion she craved, from accountant at the seniors residential facility to general manager.

Maybe then her adoptive parents would stop pressuring her about being an underachiever.

Thinking of Agnes and Timothy, her mind leaped ahead to the end of the day, and her birthday dinner. They wouldn't dare bring a man, would they? That was the other area in which she failed to meet up to their expectations. She could hear Agnes's voice in her head: *A girl shouldn't marry too young, Maura, but nor should she marry too late.*

For the last two or three years, her parents had been introducing her to men—men *they* were perfectly compatible with. They assumed the same would be true for her.

And it should have been. It really should. After all, she'd been raised by a history prof and an archaeology prof—her real dad's aunt and uncle—since her birth parents died when she was six. Maura was most comfortable with intellectual types like the colleagues Agnes and Timothy tried to match her up with.

Yes, comfortable. A little bored. Definitely not excited. The reality was, she'd never dated a man who excited her. Was she crazy to wish for that? Had her brain been warped by the movies and TV shows that were her secret vice? Her adoptive parents had banned them from the house: *They're trash, a complete waste of time—the intellectual equivalent of white sugar, and equally unhealthy.*

Maura did stay away from junk food, but she was well and truly addicted to junk entertainment.

As for men, it was probably impossible to find one who was compatible with boring, introverted her, and who also excited her. Much less was excited by her. No, she couldn't imagine that happening.

Likely, she was doomed to be single. "And that's just *fine.*" Yes, a part of her longed for romance, love, a home and children, but not all women were designed for that kind of life.

She'd never been the typical girl, and now she wasn't the typical woman. So what if she chose to celebrate her birthday by coming in early on a Saturday to finish up the year-end tax filings and start on the budget? So what if she got her thrills from accurate, disciplined figures, neat and tidy and controlled, supplemented in the evening by clicking on the TV and indulging in her guilty pleasure? So what if she hung out with senior citizens rather than people her own age?

She'd built a life around the things that made her happy. She'd come to terms with that, and so would her parents, even though the thought of disappointing them in even the tiniest way sent an acidic twinge through her stomach.

She owed them everything. But for them, she'd have gone into the dreaded "system" when her parents were killed in a car accident.

She was deliberating whether to call and confirm that it would be just the three of them for dinner tonight, when the phone rang.

"Cherry Lane," she answered. "Maura Mahoney speaking."

"Maura, thank heavens." It was Louise Michaels, the human resources manager. "I'm so glad you're working today."

"Hi, Louise. I came in to finish up the tax filings. Things were too busy yesterday to focus on them." Two weeks ago, Cherry Lane's general manager had suffered a heart attack and, though he would be all right, he'd taken early retirement. Louise and Maura had agreed to fill in until a replacement was chosen. Then, two days ago, Louise and her husband had received a surprise call saying they could adopt if they did it right now, and Maura'd agreed to cover for her as well. Not only had Maura's workload increased, but some of the added duties were stressful. She was much more comfortable with numbers than with HR work, yet she had to work on her people skills if she wanted that promotion to general manager.

"How are things going with the expectant mom?" Maura asked.

"Really well, but no labor pains yet. Don and I are so impatient, we have to keep reminding ourselves to breathe."

"I bet." Maura smiled, happy for them. They were such a terrific couple, so beautifully compatible, and they'd give a wonderful, loving home to their new baby. She felt a momentary twinge of envy, then reminded herself that she was perfectly happy with her own life.

"Brittany, the mom, is totally committed to adoption. She wants to get back to being a teenager. Same with her boyfriend."

"That's great." It would be horrible for Louise and Don if the girl changed her mind about putting her baby up for adoption.

"But that's not why I called," Louise said, her voice going brisk. "I forgot to tell you something."

Maura clicked her pen open. "Shoot." While she used computers for most of her work, there was something satisfying about task lists written in notepads.

"Don't kill me for this."

"Uh . . ."

"There's a young man coming in—"

"Maura?" another female voice broke in.

Maura lost the rest of what Louise was saying as she peered over the top of her reading glasses at Gracie, the young redheaded receptionist, who stood in her doorway. "Louise, hang on a minute. Gracie, is it urgent?"

"Sorry, I didn't realize you were on the phone. But there's a Mr. Adamson here. Something about community service?" Gracie widened her already huge eyes.

What on earth? "Community service?"

"He arranged it with Louise Michaels?" A question, not a statement, and Gracie's mobile features formed a comic "don't kill the messenger" expression.

The receptionist reminded Maura of the *I Love Lucy* Lucille Ball, and her expression made Maura smile momentarily. Into the phone, she said, "Community service, Louise?"

"That's what I called about. Sorry, I know it's not the kind of thing you like doing."

Maura reminded herself that she should welcome any opportunity to develop her people skills and impress the Board of Directors. All the same . . . "We've never done that before. This person's a criminal? Aren't you concerned we'll be putting our seniors at risk?"

"I don't think that'll be an issue," Louise said, "and this young man deserves—" She broke off, and Maura heard excited voices in the background.

"She's in labor!" Louise screeched, then there was a click, followed by silence.

Slowly, Maura hung up. She gazed across the room at Gracie. "The good news is that Louise's baby is on the way." On her own birthday, though she was too private a person to share that information with co-workers. "The bad news is, I guess we're stuck with community service." A juvenile delinquent at Cherry Lane. *Aagh!* Louise really had too soft a heart. Tilting her head, Maura eyed Gracie. "How scruffy is he?"

"Not." She shook her head vigorously, curls bouncing. "Like, seriously. He's wearing a suit and tie. Good smile, too. Want me to bring him in?"

"No." She didn't want a petty criminal in her office. "I'll meet him out front."

"I'll tell him you'll be right out." Gracie hurried away.

Maura groaned. So much for digging into the budget. Now she'd have to dream up some kind of community service and supervise a young troublemaker.

What had this boy done? He hadn't been sent to juvenile detention, so his offense couldn't have been too serious. She guessed Louise had been about to say that the kid deserved a chance, which probably was true. It didn't mean Maura had to like it, though.

She stuffed her reading glasses in the pocket of her tailored dove gray shirt, then picked up her notepad and pen. Steeling herself, she strode out of the office. Though she felt the familiar trepidation at meeting a stranger, this boy would never see her nervousness. As a scared, lonely child taken in by middle-aged academics, she had mastered poise at an early age. *Act mature, never act childish, and don't let people know you're afraid or vulnerable,* Agnes and Timothy had counseled.

Maura hadn't learned the kind of social skills that built close friendships—her adoptive parents' own relationships were based on academic connections—but at least no one saw her insecurity. She'd even, for the most part, managed to control the tendency to blush that went along with her Irish coloring.

As she walked into the reception area, a figure standing near the front door turned to face her. Her first thought was of the young Ron Howard.

The boy who stood near the front door was Richie Cunningham from *Happy Days,* right down to the ingratiating smile and reddish-blond hair, close to her own hair color. Maybe this wasn't going to be so awful. What was the worst he could have done? Shoplifted a can of beer because he hadn't hit the legal drinking age?

"Mr. Adamson?"

"Barry. And you're Ms. Mahoney?"

He mispronounced her name, as most people did. "It's Ma-honey." She was darned if she'd give a delinquent her first name, no matter how cute his smile.

"Sorry." He nodded and mumbled, "Think of bees, honey, Mahoney," then gave her another of those sweet grins. "It's my trick for remembering things."

"I'm filling in for Ms. Michaels while she's on leave. I gather you're going to be doing community service with us."

His eyebrows flew up and he gave a hoot of laughter. "Not me! You thought it was me? No, I'm Jesse's lawyer. I know Louise through Toastmasters and she was kind enough to arrange this."

A lawyer? So he must be in his mid to late twenties, though he didn't look old enough to have finished high school. Her shoulders sagged. She'd known he was too good to be true. Why hadn't Louise remembered this earlier, so Maura could have read the file? *Always be prepared,* her parents had counseled. Being caught off guard made her seriously anxious. "Where's your client?"

He glanced at his watch. "Should be here any minute, and—"

The roar of a motorcycle engine cut him off. Maura glanced through the door, open as usual when the weather permitted.

A huge, shiny black bike pulled into the parking lot.

The bad feeling was back, in full force. A juvenile delinquent on a motorcycle, wearing a black leather jacket. Like Marlon Brando, in that film where bikers terrorized a little town. *The Wild One. Double-aagh.* Why did this have to happen on her birthday?

The machine pulled to a stop under one of the flowering cherry trees that gave the place its name.

The rider slung his right leg over the bike and got off. A breeze stirred the tree and a drift of pale pink blossoms fluttered down, onto his leather shoulders.

"Let me guess," she said wryly.

"That's Jesse. Jesse Blue." Barry Adamson stepped through the open door and Maura followed, jaw firm and head held high.

The bike rider's back was to them. He stretched, and Maura realized how big he was. Well over six feet, with broad shoulders and lean, jean-clad hips. The build of a man, not a teenager.

His head was hidden by a black helmet so shiny it reflected the light. Lazily, he reached up, unfastened the helmet, and pulled it off. As he leaned forward to hook the helmet over a handlebar, cherry petals drifted to the ground like delicate flakes of pink snow. Then he stood tall, legs apart, and ran his fingers through the wavy black hair that fell to his shoulders. Finally, he turned to face his welcoming party.

Oh yes, this was Marlon Brando, James Dean, Russell Crowe, all the bad boys come to life. *To my life!* She was going to kill Louise. She doubted this man's crime was shoplifting beer. Possession of drugs, perhaps? Car—or motorcycle—theft? A brawl in a bar?

She gripped her notebook tightly as Richie Cunningham went down the steps to meet Marlon Brando. The men shook hands, the biker dwarfing the lawyer. Then they walked toward her and she got her first good look at Jesse Blue.

He was a gypsy. A rugged gypsy with bronzed skin, winged eyebrows, a craggy nose, and full, sensual lips. He even had a gold earring: a small hoop in his left ear. The longish wavy hair would have looked feminine on another man, but not on Jesse Blue. He was the single most masculine creature she'd ever seen in her life. She felt a fizz in her blood, a tingle low in her belly. The kind of feelings that—to date—she'd only experienced when watching sexy actors in sensual love scenes. *Triple-aagh!* She definitely wasn't herself today. Is this what being thirty—and incontrovertibly single—did to a woman?

Standing beside the boyish lawyer, Jesse looked close to her own age, and his face said he'd seen things she wouldn't dare even imagine. His eyes were slitted against the sun and she couldn't tell their color. Nor could she understand why she was curious.

He was studying her from head to toe in a lazy, insolent way that brushed tingly heat across her skin. It startled her as much as it offended her, and she felt color—that embarrassing color she tried so hard to control—flush her cheeks. She wasn't used to a man looking at her like that. A guy like Jesse couldn't be interested in a plain, tailored woman like her—not that she wanted him to be—so in all likelihood he was trying to throw her off balance. Little did he know, she'd been off balance since the moment she first heard of his existence, not to mention laid eyes on him.

Speaking of laying eyes, she realized she was still examining his features, trying to figure out if he was Native American or maybe Hispanic, wondering exactly what ethnic mix had combined to form that strikingly male face.

She firmed her jaw again and narrowed her eyes. He was an offender and she was the boss here. He'd do well to remember it.

So would she.

Jesse squinted through a dazzle of sunshine to see the woman who stood in the doorway. The woman who controlled his future. This lame-ass community service thing was fucked up. But he had to admit, it was way less fucked up than doing jail time.

And hell, he'd done what he had to do to protect Consuela, and now he would take the consequences like a man. With any luck, this supervisor person would give him a few straightforward chores and leave him alone to get on with them.

As he walked toward the porch, his first impression was of height. She had to be around five ten, only four inches shorter than he was.

He mounted the steps, the overhang cut the sun, and he saw the woman fully. Awareness rippled through him, and an unexpected throb of arousal.

She was lean, that ritzy leanness that verged on skinniness but never got too close. Oh, yeah, she had curves. His gaze lingered on small, high breasts and gently rounded hips as he scanned her from head to toe. Boring shoes and plain clothes—a tailored shirt and pants. Kind of classy, but

Jesus, they were gray. What woman under the age of eighty wore gray?

How old was this one? She could be a few years older than his own twenty-seven, or a few years younger. Her kind of poise and elegance made it hard to tell. He didn't have much experience with classy women like this—and what he had told him to steer clear.

His gaze returned to her face, guessing from her coloring that she was Irish. Framed by pulled-back reddish-gold hair, her features were flawless. If she wore makeup, it was just a touch to darken brows, lashes, and lips. The flush on those ivory cheekbones was all her own, as much as the freckles that dusted them.

Her eyes were incredible, somewhere between blue and green. He'd seen that color in Hawaii the time he went there on holiday.

And then, saving the best for last, there was her mouth. Fuck, what a mouth. It was one of those wide, lush ones that got a man hard just thinking what she might do with it.

She reminded him of someone, in a good way. Who was it? In the crowd he hung out with—mostly other construction workers and their girls—he didn't see women like this. An actress maybe?

Her brows arched and suddenly he knew who she looked like: a lingerie model he'd seen on the cover of one of his friend Consuela's Victoria's Secret catalogs. Oh, the clothing was way different—the model's dynamite body was barely covered by sexy scraps of black silk and lace—but the women had the same vibe. Elegant, yet lush, and totally self-contained. Both had hair pulled back in a knot, calling attention to every perfect feature of a classic face. Gorgeous eyes, though the model wore glasses, thin-framed ones that magnified rather than disguised those stunning eyes. Somehow, all that prim-and-proper stuff that should've been a turn-off actually had the opposite effect. The advertising folks knew what they were doing.

Thank Christ his new boss didn't wear glasses. Already, Jesse's temperature was climbing and his dick thickening as he tried to imagine what lay under all that buttoned-up clothing.

Stick to your own kind, he reminded himself. The couple times he'd forgotten that rule, he'd ended up feeling like crap.

Not only was Miss Priss his supervisor on this community-service gig, but he knew all about her type. She was way too good for him and she damned well knew it. Even if she was attracted to him—and lots of gals were—she'd consider it slumming. She'd view him as a charity case, try to make him over, the way Nancy, a nurse he'd once dated, had done. Or, worse, she'd act like that rich bitch Sybil: treat him as her dirty little secret, good enough to fuck in private but not to acknowledge in public.

He wasn't letting himself in for any more of that shit. Yeah, it'd be best for both of them if the ice queen stayed frozen. She was his boss. That's all it would ever be.

"Jesse? Jesse!" Barry Adamson's sharp voice broke through his thoughts.

Jesse focused on him and absorbed his lawyer's narrow-eyed glare before Barry turned back to the woman. "Ms. Mahoney, this is Jesse Blue."

Mahoney? My honey? Now there was a wet-dream of a name. All soft and warm on the tongue. Although the lady looked straightlaced as they came, he'd bet there were parts of her that were plenty soft and warm to taste.

Honey. Creamed honey, honey that melted and dissolved when it got warm. What did it take to make Ms. Mahoney turn to liquid honey? And what would she taste like when she did?

He swallowed and his blood heated further.

"Mr. Blue," she said crisply.

No honey was melting now. The lady with the warm name and pink cheeks had a voice that dripped icicles. She held a notebook in one hand and didn't offer him the other. She'd have read his file; she knew what he'd done. Wasn't going to sully her delicate flesh by touching him.

He flexed his fists. The cuts and bruises had healed, but the memory'd barely faded. As a kid, he'd been a brawler, out of frustration and anger, but as an adult he'd learned better. All the same, it had felt good, smashing Pollan's nose, crunching his cheekbones, breaking his ribs. With every blow, he'd imagined the way Pollan had beaten up on Consuela. Yeah, Jesse had gotten revenge for Con. More importantly, he'd done his best to make sure she and Juanito would be safe. If it took breaking bones to do it, then—

"Mr. Blue?" she said again, warily this time, taking a step backward.

What had shown on his face to make her react that way? Barry shot him another warning glare.

Time to shape up. He had to get along with his new boss or he'd be spending time in a jail cell. "Good morning." He gave the woman his best smile, the one that always made women smile back.

This one didn't. Her eyes widened, then she glanced away, addressing a spot over his shoulder. "I'm the accountant and acting human resources manager at Cherry Lane. I'll be supervising your community service." Her tone said she resented every moment of this.

Her and him both.

Barry said, "I'll leave you to work out the details with Jesse, Ms. Mahoney. You've got all the information you need, in Louise's file?"

Her jaw tightened and Jesse guessed she was envisioning his less than stellar file. "I'll call you if I need anything, Mr. Adamson."

"Barry, remember?" He flashed that boyish grin of his. It seemed Jesse's lawyer found his new boss plenty attractive, too. Barry fished his wallet out of a pants pocket and pulled out a card, which Ms. Mahoney took carefully, her fingers not touching the lawyer's.

Jesse gave an amused snort. Looked like even the hotshot kid lawyer wasn't good enough for her.

Barry shot him another glare. "There's a lot invested in making this work out."

Jesse'd already learned that the lawyer wasn't much for subtlety, which was part of why the two of them got along. Jesse straightened up and stuck out his hand. Barry'd gotten him a better deal than he'd any right to hope for, and he'd better knuckle down and get serious. "Thanks. It'll work."

His lawyer pumped his hand, beaming. "Sure it will. You and Ms. Mahoney are going to get along just great."

Jesse barely managed to suppress another snort.

Chapter 2

Maura studied Jesse Blue as he watched his lawyer walk away. Brown, his eyes were brown. Hazel, really. Tawny. A lion's eyes.

Then he turned to her. "What's the plan?"

Plan. As if she had a plan. As if she'd known about him coming, read his file, and prepared a plan. *The surest path to success is a thoroughly thought-out plan,* her parents had emphasized. Maura lived her life by that sensible rule, and it always worked for her.

In retrospect, it had been foolish to bluff with Barry Adamson. She should simply have asked for a copy of the file, but she hated looking anything other than perfectly in control.

The file must be in Louise's office. Until she found it, she had to come up with something to keep the biker gypsy occupied. She reminded herself that she was the boss. All she needed was a plan.

Maura glanced at him dubiously. Normally, she hated being so tall, but now she hated being shorter and having to look up to him. She hated how big and muscular he was, and she was troubled by that scary expression she'd seen on his face, almost like he was contemplating doing violence to someone. Not that she had any experience with violence. The very idea nauseated her.

But of course this man couldn't be violent, or Louise would never have agreed to take him on. And thinking of Louise, that reminded her that the HR manager often had students at Cherry Lane doing volunteer work. Maura snapped her fingers. "You can read to our residents. Some of them are blind or have failing vision and—"

"No." He didn't say it aggressively; it was just one flat word.

It stopped her cold and she didn't have a clue how to respond. She should exert her authority. But now she realized that of course she didn't want this insolent James Dean punk mingling with the residents. Even if he wasn't actually dangerous, he'd been in trouble with the law.

While she was trying to think of some other chore he could do in isolation—her own version of solitary confinement—he said, in that same level tone, "I'm good with my hands."

Her gaze flew to those hands. Large, brown, strong-looking. There were a few scrapes but his hands were nicely shaped, with long fingers. Very masculine hands, the kind she'd rarely if ever seen. Oh, yes, she could just imagine what those hands might be good for. Long fingers stroking, caressing; the gentle abrasion of calluses against tender flesh—

No! Good God, what was she thinking? "You mean, things like carpentry?" she asked quickly.

Humor glinted in his eyes. Oh, no. Had he guessed what she was thinking? Probably. Most women likely had the same reaction.

She glared at him, annoyed he would assume she was a typical female. Annoyed at herself for responding like one.

"Yeah," he said. "Things like that. My day job's construction, and I'm good at fixing stuff. Carpentry, plumbing, wiring." His voice was deep, with a touch of gravel that matched up perfectly with his craggy features and sensual mouth.

She forced herself to focus on what he'd said. There were lots of things that needed fixing: the cracked tile in Mrs. Jenssen's bathroom, Ms. Montoya's perennially dripping tap, and half a dozen more repairs that their lazy maintenance man hadn't gotten around to. But she didn't trust this man in the residents' apartments.

"Gardening," he said grimly, and again she got the uncomfortable feeling he'd read her mind.

"Gardening . . ." The courtyard was a disaster. There'd been discussions—some daydreaming about a pool and fountain—but that was way beyond their current budget. Cherry Lane wasn't a luxury facility, which was one of the things she loved about it. They kept their rates affordable for most seniors, so had to pinch pennies. Maybe Jesse Blue could plant some flowers to brighten the place up. That shouldn't cost too much, and the residents would enjoy the improved view.

Tawny eyes studied her. She felt too exposed and reached into her pocket for the glasses she used for reading and computer work. When they were perched on her nose she felt more confident, even though they did interfere with her distance vision.

The motorcycle man looked startled. Did she look that dreadful in her glasses? She reached up to whip them off, then gave a little growl. Why should she care how she looked to Jesse Blue? She wasn't his kind of woman. Never would be and certainly didn't want to be. Besides, as her adoptive mother Agnes had taught her: *Vanity is frivolous and egotistical.*

He peeled off his leather jacket and cleared his throat. "Warm out here."

Rather than gape at the muscles stretching his black

T-shirt, she wrote his name in her notebook, then *Court-yard garden.* "Come with me," she ordered.

He slung the jacket over his shoulder, hooked on one finger. Was he trying to look cool or did it just come naturally? His T-shirt wasn't new, but it was clean and respectable. If you could count anything as respectable when it revealed broad shoulders, a solidly muscled chest and slim waist, and well-shaped dark arms covered in a skim of black hair.

Okay, so maybe she'd gaped a little—enough to memorize an image—before she'd focused on her notebook. The man looked downright rugged. It wasn't a look she was used to, or comfortable with. Not in real life. The fact that she found it attractive made her even less comfortable.

How perverse that, when she dated men who were perfect for her, she was far less attracted than she was to this stranger who was pretty much her worst nightmare. Her hormones were definitely out of kilter.

She led Jesse through the lobby, ignoring Gracie and a couple of the older women who were sitting on a couch. The truth was, she couldn't make out anyone's features anyhow, what with the distortion caused by her stupid reading glasses.

She opened the courtyard door and walked out, forgetting there was a step. She lurched and would have fallen, but a strong hand caught her under the elbow, steadying her. That firm grip shocked her, making her skin sizzle under the silk of her blouse. She yanked away with a muttered, "Thanks."

Okay, she was a klutz, but the damned glasses made it worse. She pulled them off and stabbed them back in her pocket. She gestured around her. "The city takes care of the boulevard out front, but the courtyard needs work." It was an understatement, she realized now. Her office had a courtyard window, but when was the last time she'd taken a good look out here? The ground was covered with scrubby grass which no one had watered yet this spring. There were a couple of lovely cherry trees in full bloom, but the half dozen other shrubs were in sorry shape.

"Uh-huh," he said.

A man of few words. Not her favorite kind. She liked the intellectual type, articulate men who spoke in full sentences. Of course some of those sentences were the length of entire paragraphs, and she found herself drifting off in the middle—

"Nice trees." His voice broke into her thoughts. "But the rest is bad. Gloomy view for the old folks."

She raised her brows, surprised he'd spoken again, even more surprised he would think about the effect on the residents. "Yes, it is. We've discussed improving it, even talked about a pool and a miniature waterfall, but unfortunately we don't have the funds."

"I can do that."

"You can do what?"

"That. Pool, waterfall. Flowers, shrubs. Little Japanese maple over the pool."

He gazed up at the sky, then down again, and gestured to a corner. "Morning sun falls there. Put in a sitting area with a few chairs, couple of little tables for coffee. That cherry tree'll break the sun." He waved to the opposite corner. "Same kind of thing there, for the afternoon. They like to sit outside, right?"

The sudden spate of loquaciousness left her gaping. "I . . . I guess so." When the weather was nice, residents often perched on the wooden benches by the front door.

He pointed toward the units that surrounded the courtyard. "No balconies. Lots of open windows. They like fresh air."

She squinted at him. He was observant and almost . . . considerate.

Or maybe he was a thief and he was casing the joint, planning to steal precious treasures from people in the last years of their lives. "Yes, well," she said, "that's all very ambitious." He clearly hadn't paid attention to what she'd said about lack of funding. "Can you think on a smaller scale?"

He grinned. It was so quick she almost missed it, but that sudden flash of white teeth in his dark face made her heart stutter.

"Fix up the lawn and shrubs," he said. "Flower borders around the edge."

"What would be involved?" She tried to ignore her racing pulse and sound businesslike.

He cocked a skeptical eyebrow, but in truth she wasn't having him on, or testing him. She'd grown up in Agnes and Timothy's roomy condominium, now lived in her own small one, and hadn't done an hour of gardening in her life. She was an indoors person. She gave him her best steely-eyed glare, and his eyebrow went down.

"A few tools," he said. "I gotta dig through this grass for the borders, turn over the soil. Fertilizer, maybe some peat. Depends how bad the soil is. Buy some flowers and plant them. Grass seed and fertilizer for the lawn."

"Lawn." She frowned at the scruffy grass.

"It can be saved. Gotta buy a sprinkler."

"We have one." She was sure she'd seen one last summer, out in this courtyard. Gracie might know where it was.

"Yeah?" He glanced pointedly at the dismal grass.

She hated feeling defensive. She wasn't in charge of the stupid garden. The old general manager really hadn't been very efficient. Hmm. If she was responsible for getting the courtyard in better shape, it would win her brownie points with the Board when it came to winning the promotion. She waved a hand toward the scrubby bushes. "What about those? Can they be saved, too?"

"Sure. Pruning, fertilizer." He glanced at her. "Water."

She ground her teeth.

He went on. "You got a couple of nice rhodos, lilac, japonica."

Lilac was a name she recognized, and she guessed rhodos were rhododendron. As for japonica, she didn't have a clue. Maybe she should be taking notes. She put on her glasses, clicked her pen, and wrote the first two names, then paused. "How do you spell japonica?"

When he didn't answer, she glanced up.

He was frowning at her.

She glared back. So she didn't know how to spell the name of some exotic plant. It didn't mean she was stupid.

"The way it sounds," he said.

"Oh. And the flowering trees are cherry, right?"

"Yup."

She wrote it down. He might be too darned sexy for her peace of mind and purely frustrating to communicate with, but maybe they'd get a nice garden out of this arrangement. "You know a fair bit about this."

He shrugged. "I work construction. See a lot of gardens go in. I've helped out on some jobs."

"How long will it take?"

"Dunno."

Annoyed, she clicked the top on her pen. "Can you give me an estimate?"

"Dunno until I start. See what the soil's like. Guess my *estimate* would be two, three days."

"That's all? And you're here today, then . . ." How many days of community service was he required to put in? She longed for Louise's file.

"Yeah, tomorrow, too. Weekends, and some weekday evenings. But not Mondays or Fridays."

She noted that down. What did he do on Monday and Friday nights? A standing date with a special girlfriend? No, this man wasn't likely to have just one name in his little black book or little black BlackBerry, or wherever else he kept such information. He had a definite "play the field" look, and she was darned sure he had no trouble finding women. Women who lacked refinement and taste, of course. Women who just wanted a gorgeous male animal to get naked with and—

"You got a problem with that?" he asked.

Aagh again! Where were these ridiculous thoughts coming from? Turning thirty must have had a bizarre effect on her hormones. She clicked her pen again. "No, those times will be fine. Start on the garden this weekend, and if it takes longer than that, you can finish during the evenings next week." By then she'd have read his file, know how long he'd be working at Cherry Lane, and have figured out what other tasks were safe to assign him. She'd have a plan. Maura peeled off her glasses.

" 'Kay." He moved restlessly, as if he'd stood too long in one spot. "Need to buy the stuff. Gotta borrow a car. You got an account somewhere, or you going to give me cash?"

In your dreams, Mr. Blue. Sure, she was going to hand over car keys and cash to a criminal. She heaved an exasperated sigh. "I'll drive you."

He looked her up and down in that cheeky way he had. "I figured."

Now that she thought about it, she wasn't keen to get into a car with him. Not until she'd read his file, seen him work. Decided if she could feel safe with him.

She glanced up at all of that smoldering male sexuality and realized that "safe" wasn't a word she'd likely ever use

with reference to Jesse Blue. But at least she wanted to reassure herself he wasn't likely to do anything violent. Or
start using—or even dealing—drugs. Or steal her car.
"Not today," she said abruptly.

Great, now what was she going to do? Did Cherry Lane
own any garden tools? If not, there was a home supply
store in the mall across the street. "Stay here," she ordered.

She left him in the courtyard, locking the door from the
inside, and hurried to the reception desk. Gracie beamed
excitedly at her, but Maura spoke first. "We've got a sprinkler, don't we? And some garden tools? Any idea where
they might be?"

"Maybe the janitor's storage room? But wow, isn't that
guy a total hottie?"

She frowned discouragingly. "I'll check the storage
room."

There, in a back corner, she found a dusty sprinkler attached to a knotted hose, plus—thank God—a collection
of dirt-encrusted tools.

She tucked her pad and pen into her pocket alongside
her glasses and picked up the sprinkler and hose. Holding
them at arm's length, she hurried back, and Gracie jumped
up to open the courtyard door for her.

"Ooh, would you just look at that," the younger
woman purred. "Yummy." She gazed outside with the expression of a dessert-lover staring in the window of a cup-
cake shop.

Maura glanced out. Jesse was sprawled on the nicest-
looking patch of grass, on his back, arms crossed behind
his head. His T-shirt pulled tight across his torso, accentu-
ating a spectacular chest and flat stomach. He'd said he was
a construction worker, so no wonder he was strong and
well-developed. Completely unlike the professorial types
her parents socialized with, and tried to match-make her
with. Of course for her, brains were far more important

than brawn. Compatibility was what mattered, if a relationship was to last.

Jesse shifted and stretched, like a big, lazy cat. She had to admit that brawn, in the form stretched out in front of her, was really quite nice to look at. Nice enough to prompt disconcerting physical heat and tingles.

Her mouth opened in a silent "oh" of enlightenment. She had a physical, hormonal reaction to Jesse—and likely it was because he was such a physical person. Her body, and that biological clock she'd read about but never been particularly aware of in herself, was ticking. It was urging her body to mate, even though her mind knew that qualities other than physical perfection were far more important to her.

Good. She'd worked things out logically, and now she could get on with her job. She glanced at Gracie. "Isn't there something you should be doing?"

"Oops, sorry." Those big blue eyes seemed a little dazed as she turned them on Maura. "I was just thinking, there's that rule, right, about not dating other staff here?"

A rule that was frequently ignored, Maura knew, but that was Louise's problem. No, wait, Louise was away, so it was Maura's problem. "Yes, there is," she said firmly.

"But, like, this guy's not staff. Right? He's here on some community service thing."

"Uh . . . No, technically he's not staff. But Gracie, community service means he's been in trouble with the law. Surely it wouldn't be wise to date a man like that."

Those blue eyes sparkled mischievously. "That just gives him an edge, that whole bad-boy thing. I'd rather have fun than be"—she held up her hands and made quotation marks in the air—" 'wise.' "

"Gracie, if you aren't wise about dating, you could get hurt." How well Maura knew that, from her experience in grade twelve with Troy Offenbacher.

"I'm resilient. 'Sides, with a guy like him, a girl would be crazy to think long-term. I can't see him being into that. But I bet he could show a girl a good time." She licked her lips. "If you know what I mean."

Sex. She meant sex. Maura shook her head, bemused. In the year that Gracie'd been at Cherry Lane, they'd never had this kind of talk. Never really talked about anything other than work. What a peculiar day this was turning out to be. "We both need to get to work," she said briskly.

"So you're saying there's no rule against it, right? If he and I, like, hit it off?" She giggled. "Or get it on?"

In her head, Maura reviewed the HR policy that she'd brushed up on when she took over Louise's job. "No, no actual rule," she said reluctantly. Why did the idea of Gracie and Jesse getting together trouble her? They were young, attractive, and it seemed Gracie was savvy enough to look out for herself.

Frowning, Maura stepped down into the courtyard and walked over to Jesse. "I found the sprinkler," she announced unnecessarily, bending to place her burden on the ground.

He stretched again, which had the effect of banishing her frown and raising her blood pressure a few degrees, then curled to his feet in a long, continuous, cat-like motion.

Shoving his hands in his jeans pockets, he stared down at the disreputable-looking equipment. "Let's see if it works." He hunkered down to work the knots out of the hose.

She watched, fascinated at the deftness of those large hands.

He glanced up. "Edger?"

"Edger?" she echoed, the word not ringing any bells.

Edger—presumably from "to edge." Ah. "Oh, tools. We've got some." She could haul the whole kit and kaboodle out to the garden, but she'd end up filthy. Better, on balance, to let him inside, under her supervision. "You'll have to come look."

"Get the sprinkler going first," he said. "Easier to dig when the ground's damp."

That made sense, so she waited as he set up the sprinkler in one corner and attached the hose to a tap. Lazy sprays of water arced back and forth. It was pretty, the way the droplets sparkled in the sun. Caught in the simple spell, she watched, smiling.

"Tools?"

Damn him, he'd snuck up on her. The man walked like a panther: sleek and powerful and deadly silent. A black panther, in that muscle-hugging T-shirt. Lion eyes, panther movements. Dangerous beasts, both. "Right, tools. Come this way."

She felt clumsy as she minced along in her low-heeled pumps beside the smooth-strolling panther. It crossed her mind that, with a man as tall as Jesse, she might actually wear real heels. Ever since suffering beanpole jokes as a kid, when she'd been taller than all the boys in class, she'd dressed to minimize her height.

As they passed a window, she caught a glimpse of her reflection and winced. In higher heels she'd be even more the beanpole.

When the two of them passed the reception desk, Gracie called out a bright, "Good morning!"

Jesse flashed her a sexy grin and said, "Mornin'."

Maura ground her teeth and wished Louise was there to deal with all of this. But no, if she wanted to be general manager, Maura had to be able to handle people situations as well as numbers. This was good experience.

She and Jesse walked past a couple of curious seniors, then Jesse followed her into the storage room. The small room seemed to shrink.

"Mph," he said when he saw the tool collection.

"Do we have what you need?" She leaned against the door frame, keeping her distance.

"Edger, mattock, shovel, fork. Yup." He separated out the tools as he spoke.

She gazed dubiously at the collection of dangerous-looking implements. The one he called a mattock was particularly nasty. One blow would cave in someone's head. Though she had trouble picturing Jesse Blue as a shoplifter, she sure hoped his crime was something equally nonviolent.

"Need pruning shears," he said. "Can buy those when we get the flowers."

She put on her glasses and turned to a new page in her book. Heading it "To Buy," she said, "All right, pruning shears. And you said fertilizer, didn't you? What else? Any particular kinds of flowers?"

"Decide when I see them."

"I can leave the list with you today. You can add anything you think of."

"No need."

Now what the heck did that mean? He wouldn't be adding anything? Or he'd remember?

He scrounged out a couple of metal spikes, a hammer, and a ball of thick cord.

"What are those for?" she asked nervously, half in and half out of the door.

"Straight lines."

Oh, right. That was supposed to make perfect sense, was it?

She followed him back to the courtyard to make sure he didn't take any detours, like to steal anything or to flirt

with Gracie. He dropped the tools and studied the sprinkler. His thumbs were hooked in belt loops and his hands
hung downward, pointing toward the tantalizing bulge at
the juncture of his thighs.

She clicked her pen in frustration—mostly at herself for
noticing such things. "I'll leave you to it then."

He glanced up as if he'd forgotten her existence. "Sure."

Jesse watched his new boss walk away, her back ramrod
straight. Her hips swayed just a little, sexy but not trashy.
Jesus, when she first put those glasses on, it had been his
lingerie fantasy come to life. Now, if she'd only unbutton
a couple of buttons at her neck. Not too many. He didn't
want his fantasy woman to be like the gals he hung out
with, with their big tits exploding out of their low-cut
necklines.

A fantasy woman had to be different. Unattainable. A
temptress who promised with subtlety. He needed Ms.
Mahoney to be unattainable, or he'd be in real big trouble.
He had to make this community service thing work.

Not only was there the whole jail issue, but no way was
he getting involved with another snotty bitch who'd treat
him like crap. Was his new boss one of those? He was
good at reading people—had to be, with the life he'd
lived—but he couldn't figure her out yet. Mostly, it
seemed like he disgusted her, but then there were those
blushes. And was that glasses-on, glasses-off thing just a
habit, or a sexy tease? Was she attracted to him, too?

He watched her approach the low step where she'd almost fallen. He'd gripped that fine-boned elbow for just a
moment before she jerked away. Nope, he figured she
wasn't attracted. And maybe she was going to treat him
like crap, all high and mighty.

She tripped slightly again as she mounted the step. Was
she self-conscious, guessing he was watching? Or was it

the funny little half-inch heels on her shoes? Seemed to him, a woman ought to dress for either comfort or sex.

Ms. Mahoney obviously had a different idea.

She closed the courtyard door firmly.

He glanced around, feeling caged by the surrounding walls, and reminded himself he was here because he'd kept his best friend, Con, safe. Besides, this was—or could be— a garden. He liked gardens, had a knack for making things grow. It was a lot of hard work, but that never bothered him, and there was a kind of peace in it. A landscape gardener he'd worked for had said it was Zen.

That was the same guy who'd said Jesse had a talent for it, that he should go back to school and study landscape design. Yeah, like hell he would. Guy like him, who hadn't even finished grade ten. He might have street smarts, but he sure didn't have school ones.

Besides, there was nothing wrong with good solid blue collar work. He liked his construction job, liked building and fixing things, worked for a great boss. His lips quirked wryly. His real boss actually respected him. Didn't seem that was going to happen with Ms. Mahoney.

And it sure as hell wouldn't if he stood around daydreaming rather than getting to work. Thank God she hadn't pushed when he'd said "no" to reading aloud. He'd ended up with a job he could ace, if he knuckled down and got to it.

He turned his attention to the garden, assessing the sunlight, the lay of the land, the trees and shrubs that were already there. A picture began to form in his head. No, he wasn't going to do straight line borders after all. Ms. Mahoney probably liked things all neat and ordered, but even though this courtyard was a square-edged box, it was a garden and not a cage. It needed shapes that were more free-form. He'd build a place where those old folks could come and relax.

He moved the sprinkler so it would get the ground behind him, then he dug the edger into the newly watered
ground. The tool could use sharpening, but it'd do.

He glanced down at his jeans. So much for wearing his
best pair, like Barry'd told him. Should've worn his oldest
clothes. But Barry had wanted him to make a good first
impression.

Usually, he did with women. His type of women. Ms.
Mahoney was the other type. Not much chance that he, as
a person, would impress her. But his work would.

The edger went in again, cutting through overgrown
grass. This wasn't the fun part, but it was easy, steady work,
and he was getting the feel of the garden.

Wouldn't mind getting the feel of Ms. Mahoney,
though. The thought crept into his mind and he shoved it
away. Stupid. A really stupid idea. And, while he might be
dumb about school-type stuff, he wasn't dumb when it
came to people. He might make one mistake, like with
Nurse Nancy or Snotty Sybil, but he wouldn't repeat it.

Maura retreated to her office, fighting a tension
headache. She searched through the pile of files Louise
had passed on to her, confirmed that there was nothing related to Jesse Blue, and buzzed for Gracie to come see her.

A moment later, the young woman popped through her
doorway, face bright. "The closer you get, the better he
looks, right?"

"Gracie, that's not appropriate," she snapped.

Her excited expression crumpled. "Oh, man, sorry. I
just meant— No, I mean, you're right. Of course you're
right."

Maura felt guilty for taking her annoyance out on the
girl. She really was terrible with people, at least those under the age of fifty. It wasn't that she didn't like them; she
just wasn't as comfortable with them as with figures.

"Sorry," she muttered. "I shouldn't have snapped at you. But we do both need to focus on work. Can I get you to do something?"

"Sure."

As well as handling the reception desk, Gracie often assisted Louise and had authorization to deal with confidential HR files. Maura handed her the key to Louise's locked file cabinets. "You know the HR files better than I do. Would you hunt for the file on this . . . person. His name's Jesse Blue, his lawyer is Barry Adamson, or it might be under something like 'community service.' "

Gracie brightened. "I'll look right now. What d'you figure he did? It's gotta be something sexy, right? Like, oh, street racing or something."

She really was irrepressible. An annoying quality. "Street racing endangers lives," Maura said sharply. "Honestly, Gracie, I don't think breaking the law—any kind of breaking the law—is sexy."

Looking chastened again, the girl hurried away.

"I'm right," Maura muttered to herself. "I know I'm right." But maybe she shouldn't have phrased it so abruptly. She slapped her glasses on and surveyed her desk. "What was I doing?" Oh, yes, she'd finished the tax filings.

That thrill of control and satisfaction was a thing of the past.

She pulled up the spreadsheet for the budget she'd been looking forward to working on, but found it difficult to concentrate. There was a disturbing stranger at Cherry Lane and she was responsible for him. She shot glances out her window, which faced the courtyard.

Good with his hands, yes. The speed of light, no. He didn't seem to have it in him to rush. His movements were economical, she'd give him that, but he was as slow as—

Damn it, he was as slow as she was being with this budget.

She turned back to her computer with fierce determination. There was a Board meeting Friday afternoon and she wanted to present a perfect budget, with all the backup figures and analysis. The directors had advertised for the general manager position and résumés would be coming in. She was the only internal applicant. Louise had prioritized family over career advancement, and Neil, the resident services manager, loved his job and wanted to stay with it. Maura should have an edge over external applicants, and she had a master's in Business Administration as well as her accounting diploma, but she had to make sure that every single thing she did was flawless.

Engrossed in work, it was a while before she looked out again. She must have really lost track of time because Jesse had moved the sprinkler and was halfway through digging one of the borders. A very meandering border, rather than the neat straight line she'd envisioned—and sure enough, he wasn't using the cord and spikes he'd brought from the tool room. Honestly!

She tilted her head, caught up in the way he moved. It was hard work, she could see that. He stabbed the edger into the unyielding ground, stuck a foot on the top, and seemed to be throwing his whole body weight into levering the tip into the soil. He had his back to her and muscles bulged in his shoulders and upper arms, under his black T-shirt. He did have the most incredible build . . .

A fact that was completely irrelevant. What mattered was that he was a hard worker.

She glanced at the practical gold watch on her left wrist, then frowned out the window. His slow movements were deceptive; he'd accomplished far more than she would have thought possible.

As she watched, Fred Dykstra, one of the residents, strolled into the courtyard. His arthritis mustn't be too bad today, because he barely used his cane. The elderly man watched Jesse for a few minutes, then said something. Jesse looked up, answered, then rested his hands on his edger and seemed to be settling in for a conversation.

He was supposed to be working, not chatting to residents. Ordinarily, it was good for the seniors to have social contact with people from outside Cherry Lane, but this wasn't a high school volunteer or one of the university students from the animal-assisted therapy program. This was a petty criminal doing community service.

She groaned and headed out to intervene.

Chapter 3

As Maura approached the two men, she heard Mr. Dykstra saying, "Yessir, it was back in the late forties. She was an Indian, red and racy and—"

"Fred?" she broke in. Good God, was he talking about some youthful sexual experiences? And in downright racist language, in front of Jesse Blue, who she guessed was at least partially Native American.

Fred Dykstra beamed at her. His faded blue eyes were full of life. "I was just telling young Jesse about my bike. His Harley's a fine specimen, but I had this old Indian Chief."

"An Indian is a motorcycle?"

She heard a snort of laughter and glanced at Jesse.

He straightened his face, but she saw the twinkle in his eyes. Obviously he'd realized where her thoughts had been going.

She glared at him. Glaring at Jesse could easily become a habit.

"One of the finest bikes ever made," Fred said, "in my opinion."

"Yeah," Jesse said. "Rode one once, a classic from back before World War Two."

"I used to take my young lady for rides in the country, and she thought I was pretty hot stuff." Fred's elderly face crinkled with smile lines. "Think she married me because of that bike." He shot Jesse a pure "guy" look. "Bet the ladies still go for a man on a bike."

Jesse returned the look. "Been known to happen."

Maura was sure of it. Particularly when the man on the bike was as "hot stuff" as Jesse Blue.

She had come out here to break this up. She still had a lot of concerns about Jesse mixing with the residents, yet she hadn't seen Fred Dykstra so animated in months. She didn't have the heart to drag him inside.

Jesse glanced at her. "You want something, or just visiting?"

"I . . . I'm not visiting, I'm supervising. Didn't you say you were going to use straight lines for the borders? You seem to have wandered off track. Do you need more cord?" Or, she let her tone say, need to remember to use the cord you already have?

Humor lit his eyes again. "Rethought the straight lines. Figure curves are more appealing." He shot a wink in Fred Dykstra's direction.

The old man chuckled and replied promptly, "Some things never change."

Was Jesse joking about her own beanpole figure? She knew the older man wouldn't do that, but she wouldn't put it past Jesse.

"Want the garden to be relaxing, not all disciplined," Jesse said.

Implying that there was such a thing as too much discipline, and that she was an example of that? She was about to snap back about lack of discipline, then thought of the amount of work he'd accomplished. He might not seem like the most disciplined man in the world, but he was a hard worker.

"Jesse's been out here all morning," Fred said. "I bet he could use a cold drink."

And now she felt negligent for not having thought of that herself. Working with people was so not her forté. How did people learn these skills when they didn't come naturally?

"Been drinking out of the tap," Jesse said, "but a cold soda sure would go down fine."

Into her mind flashed a classic commercial she'd seen in a business school class on marketing. It had been for Diet Coke. Women working in an office dashed to the window to watch a hunky construction worker pour a cold drink down his throat. She closed her eyes briefly, the picture clear in her mind . . .

The women in the window, looking out . . .

The man, dark-haired, brown-skinned . . .

Jesse Blue. It was Jesse they were watching.

Jesse she was watching, his bronzed skin sweaty from hard work, his black T-shirt glued to his sculpted shoulders and chest. He lifted the can, muscles flexing. He tilted his head back, that gold earring glinted in the sunshine. When he gulped soda, his throat rippled as he swallowed, then he—

Said "Yo? You okay?"

Her eyes flew open and she saw two concerned male faces. "I'm fine. I just . . . got dizzy for a moment. It's hot out here."

It was warm, not hot, and Jesse's brows lifted skeptically.

Fred said, "You're sure you're all right? You're flushed and starting to sweat."

Hurriedly, she dabbed her brow. Darn it, he was right, and it wasn't from the weak spring sun. "Honestly, I'm fine." To Jesse, she said, "What kind of soda?"

"Whatever you got. Just so long as it's cold and wet."

She stalked away. How could he make simple words like "cold" and "wet" sound sexy? And why couldn't she control her blushing around him?

In the kitchen, she studied the assortment of cold drinks. Why hadn't Jesse named a brand and made this easy for her? She wasn't a soda pop drinker, so she didn't know what these drinks tasted like. Only club soda, which she loved, especially when served with a slice of lime or a splash of cranberry juice. Somehow she didn't think Jesse Blue was a club soda guy.

She could give him a Diet Coke like in the commercial, but that struck her as silly. *Silliness is for little children,* as she'd learned at the age of six.

At random, she pulled a can from the fridge, remembering the discussion in business school. Most of the female students had argued that the commercial wasn't effective marketing because no woman was looking at the drink can, just at the man. She had to agree. She'd never have remembered the product but for the analysis in class.

The beverage she now poured into a tall glass was clear, fizzy, and smelled citrusy. It should be refreshing.

Cold and wet.

She stuck the glass under the ice machine and topped it up. Should she pour another for Fred? No, she didn't want to encourage him to linger.

The glass was so cold she had to switch hands as she walked back to the courtyard. When she handed it to Jesse, being careful not to touch his filthy hand, the glass was sweating. A drop trickled down the outside, wending a slow, curvy path.

Her palm was wet. She didn't want to brush it on her pants and leave a damp patch, so she rubbed it against her other hand.

Jesse lifted the glass, threw back his head, and made the commercial come true. She watched mesmerized as he drank deeply, then drank again. In his neck, muscles moved, his Adam's apple shifted.

Adam's apple. Why had she never wondered about that term? Adam and the apple, the Garden of Eden. Temptation.

A bead of sweat ran down his throat, just as the drop of condensation had trickled down the glass. It moved with painstaking slowness and she held her breath until it touched the neckband of his T-shirt and disappeared.

The Sprite hit the spot, Jesse thought, though a beer would've been better. He finished the drink in a few long swallows, then held the cold glass against one cheek. Ms. Mahoney had gone into another of her trances. The tip of her tongue peeked out between her lips. It ran slowly across her top lip, then the bottom one, almost like she'd been the one to take a drink and now she was catching every last drop.

This gal in her prim-and-proper clothes was one bundle of sexy moves. He was pretty sure they weren't intentional—or at least, she didn't intend to aim them in his direction. If she knew how much she turned him on, would she be shocked? Horrified?

Or, maybe, aroused?

He shifted the glass to his other cheek, then handed it to her. "Thanks. That went down fine." The melting ice cubes clinked together as she took the glass. Her hand was shaking. Because she hated being around him, or was she fighting attraction?

Attraction was a weird thing. Like with his friend Consuela, always being attracted to the wrong kind of guy. Jesse had no business being attracted to Ms. Mahoney, but he was. Okay, that was a fact of life, and he'd deal with it. He might not be much sharper than the pathetic edger and mattock, but at least he knew to keep that crazy attraction under control.

As for his boss, maybe she felt a physical pull, but she'd never give into it. Not with how she looked down her aristocratic nose at him.

"What year's your Harley?" the old guy asked. "She's got a classic look."

Jesse turned to him gratefully. "Nineteen ninety-seven. Called a Heritage Softail Classic." Soft tail. Oh, Lord.

Fortunately, Ms. Mahoney took her own sexy tail back inside.

Jesse hefted the mattock, using it to pry up strips of turf as he listened to Mr. Dykstra talk about his bike and his adventures. From time to time Jesse contributed a word or two, or answered a question about his Harley. After a while, the man—he said to call him Fred—went in.

A nice old guy. It'd been good listening to his memories and seeing how he enjoyed revisiting them.

This community service thing wasn't turning out to be half as fucked-up as he'd feared. At least if his boss stayed out of the way. She was too distracting, in too many ways.

Jesse finished digging the border and stretched the aches out of his back. He sloshed cold water on his face, took a nice long drink out of the hose. Was there a john somewhere around this joint? He'd take a piss under a cherry tree, but he figured Ms. Mahoney would frown on that.

He rinsed his hands under the tap, then went inside.

A tiny, white-haired woman pushing a walker at a snail's pace stopped and turned a sharp-eyed gaze on him. "You're the boy who's been working in the garden."

Boy? It was a long time since he'd felt like a boy. "Yes, ma'am. Jesse Blue."

"I'm Virginia Canfield. I saw you out my window." She offered him a trembling, blue-veined hand.

How about that? Ms. Mahoney might not be willing to touch him, but this old lady had no qualms and it made him feel good. Still, he held up his own hand and warned, "I'm kinda dirty."

"Garden dirt never hurt anyone." She gestured with her hand.

Liking her already, he put his hand in hers as gently as he could, knowing his normal handshake would crush her. "Wonder if you could help me out, Ms. Canfield. Looking for the men's room."

"Down the hall to your left." She pointed.

He nodded his thanks. When he returned she was still there, propped up on her walker.

"It's Mrs. Canfield. I'm old-fashioned. I was married to Elmer for fifty-two years and I was Mrs. Canfield all that time."

"Okay, Mrs. Canfield."

"But please call me Virginia."

"Thanks."

"Will you show me what you're planning for the garden?"

"Sure." He doubted this was part of the job description, but he wasn't going to blow off a white-haired lady who was nice to him. He held the door for her and walked beside her, keeping an eye out as she shuffled the walker across the uneven turf to the bed he'd been digging.

Turned out she'd done a lot of gardening, and she gave him a couple of good ideas.

"I wish I could get down and grub around in the soil with you," she said. "There's nothing so healing as planting things and watching them grow."

"This landscape gardener I knew once, he said it was Zen."

"That's it, exactly." She beamed at him.

At that point, Ms. Mahoney showed up again. Either

she didn't trust him with the seniors, or she didn't want him goofing off to chat. Or, probably, both.

"Oh, Maura dear," Virginia Canfield said, "Jesse and I have been having the most interesting discussion. You've certainly hired us a knowledgeable young man."

Hired. His gaze met Ms. Mahoney's. He shrugged. Her call whether to tell Virginia about his community service. While she decided, he'd think about the name he'd just learned. Maura. For some reason, his mind conjured an image of the ocean. Cool Maura, ocean-eyed Maura. Maura with the soft, warm-honey last name.

"Actually, it was Louise's decision," Maura Mahoney muttered. "I'm sure he knows what he's doing. Now, don't you think we should let him get on with his work?"

"I suppose so. Besides, my legs are getting tired." The elderly face, which had been all perky when they were talking about the garden, drooped. Then she brightened again. "Maura, I was going to bring you this." She reached into the basket on her walker and pulled out a huge hardcover book, struggling with its weight.

The younger woman reached out to take it. "Have you finished? Did you enjoy it?"

"Very much. Thank you so much for loaning it to me. Perhaps we might discuss it one day?"

Maura Mahoney smiled gently, her face soft and caring.

Oh, man, and he'd thought she was gorgeous before.

"Perhaps over tea tomorrow afternoon?" Her voice, too, for the first time, softened around the edges.

If she gave that look, that voice, to a guy . . . Jesse sucked in a breath, battling arousal.

"My dear," the old lady was saying, "that would be delightful. And now I must head in and put my feet up." She held out her hand again, to him. "Such a pleasure meeting you, Jesse."

He clasped her hand, treating it like a delicate flower. "My pleasure, too, Virginia."

She frowned down at his hand. "My boy, you need gloves."

Jesse and Maura walked with her to the door. Once she was safely inside, his boss turned to him. "You called her Virginia." Her voice was crisp again.

"She told me to."

"Hmm. I'm not sure I like you spending so much time socializing with the residents."

He cocked an eyebrow. "Want me to tell them to get lost?"

She made an exasperated sound low in her throat. He'd heard it before. It sounded like a growl, and was damned sexy.

"Don't be rude to them," she said, "but don't encourage them."

"They like having someone new to talk to," he pointed out. Didn't she realize that?

"I *know* that!" Then she sighed. "Yes, they do. Especially Virginia Canfield." Her voice went all warm and husky again, almost like she saw him as a real person, not a garden pest.

It made him bold enough to ask, "Tea tomorrow?"

She smiled, that same soft, sweet smile. "A lot of residents have visitors on Sundays, or go out to family or friends. She has no one. Her husband's dead, her children and grandchildren live in different cities. We often have tea together on Sundays."

"That's nice of you." Did Maura work Sundays, or come in specially to get together with Virginia? For the first time, he was seeing a side of this woman—beyond the snotty boss and his lingerie fantasy—that he might actually like. Which probably wasn't a good idea.

"I'm not doing it to be nice. I enjoy it as much as she

does. She's intelligent, well-educated, well-read. Our conversations are stimulating."

He gestured to the huge book she held. The thing intimidated the hell out of him. "Might try a smaller book
next time."

"What do you mean?"

"It's too heavy for her."

Those stunning eyes widened. "You're right. I never
thought of that. I'd just read it and thought she'd enjoy it,
but I should have bought it in paperback for her."

How about that? She'd said he was right about something. He glanced again at the massive book, which must
have hundreds of pages and millions of words. "You're a
big reader?"

"Oh, yes." Her face glowed. "I just love books." She
shot him a dubious glance. "How about you?"

Books were his definition of hell. He wasn't going to
confess to Maura Mahoney that he had trouble making his
way through a comic book. "I'm more of a movie man
myself. Movies or TV." Never needing much sleep, he
spent lots of middle-of-the-night time in front of the TV.
There were a few classics he'd seen half a dozen times or
more. "Guess that's not your style?"

Nope. Obviously that stuff was way beneath her, because she reacted like he'd made a rude suggestion. Her
cheeks flooded with color and one hand flew to her
throat. "No! Not at all."

That blush was sexy, too, even if it did hide her freckles.

He wondered what she looked like when she was
aroused. Would the heat creep through her body gradu-
ally, or would her cheeks and her breasts flush at the same
time? He glanced down at the sexy rise and fall of female
curves under silky gray fabric.

She crossed her arms across her chest, cradling the book in them, shielding her breasts from his scrutiny. Damn, had she caught him looking?

He glanced away. "Okay if I go across the street and get some food?"

"Is it lunchtime?" She pulled back her sleeve, baring a slender wrist as she checked her watch. "Oh, my, it's almost two o'clock. I hadn't realized. Sorry. Yes, of course. There's a sandwich shop, hamburger place, pizza, fried chicken, Thai, sushi."

She sounded almost like a waitress reciting a menu, and he was tempted to say, "BLT on toasted multi-grain, extra mayo," but figured she wouldn't get the joke. He'd be willing to bet she'd never waitressed, not even to pay her way through college.

"Oh, by the way . . ." She flushed again. "There's a men's room inside, if you want to, uh, wash up."

"Thanks. Virginia showed me."

"Is there anything else you need?" She glanced at his hands, hanging at his sides. "Virginia mentioned gloves."

He shrugged. "I'm okay."

"Let me see," she ordered.

It took him back to a couple of the foster homes he'd lived in, where they'd inspected the kids' hands before they could sit down at the table. He'd mostly always been sent back for a second wash.

Trying not to scowl, he held out his hands. Despite the calluses he'd built up over the years, he had a few blisters.

She winced. "You should have said something. I didn't think . . ." A frown creased her forehead and he guessed she wasn't used to supervising the garden help. "I'll give you money for gloves." She kept staring at his hands.

He was damned sure she rarely saw grime and calluses. Stuffing his hands in his pockets, he said, "I'm okay."

"Don't be ridiculous." Her gaze switched to his face and the frown line deepened. "You may think you're being macho, but I'm not impressed."

"Not trying to impress you." He kind of was, but he wasn't about to let on. He also enjoyed winding her up.

"I didn't mean it that way!"

Those ocean eyes glittered with annoyance and he decided to let her alone. "Gloves would be great. Twenty bucks ought to do it. I'll bring back the change." While she was being semi-civil, he said, "Got a place I can put my jacket? Don't want it to get wet."

"I'll take it."

He retrieved it from the corner where he'd tossed it. "Thanks." He watched to see if she'd treat his prized leather like a dead rat. Instead, she draped it neatly over top of the book with more respect than she'd shown Jesse himself.

She headed in and he waited a moment, then guessed he was supposed to follow. He trailed a few steps behind, down a couple of corridors and into a small room that must be her office. There were filing cabinets and bookshelves laden with binders, everything as orderly as he would expect. No photographs or personal stuff except for an orchid with a spray of vivid purple blossoms. That plant didn't go with her prissy style, but he'd just bet Ms. Warm Honey had a sensual side beneath all those buttons.

Behind her desk was a courtyard window. She could watch him any time she pleased. Fine. He was a hard worker with nothing to hide. Nothing but the fact that she turned him on something fierce.

Her back still to him, she placed the book neatly on a stack of a half dozen atop a cabinet and hung his jacket on the back of a chair, spreading it with gentle fingers, almost caressing it. He imagined those fingers on his own skin, and shivered.

She went behind the desk, turned around, and jumped a foot in the air, pressing her hand to her throat. "I didn't know you were there. You sure walk quietly."

"Sorry. Thought you meant for me to come and get the money."

"I was going to bring it to you."

He shrugged.

She glanced around nervously, making it clear she didn't want him in her office. What did she think? He was going to punch her out? Steal her purse? Rape her?

His jaw clenched and he forced himself to relax it. This woman knew he'd beaten up on Gord Pollan. Made sense she'd be scared. He shouldn't take it personally. He stepped back so he was just outside her door, in the hallway.

Keeping an eye on him, she picked up her phone and punched a button. "Gracie, could you get twenty dollars from petty cash?"

She waited a moment, then said, "Good. I'm going to send Mr. Blue out to you. Would you give it to him, please?"

Another pause. "You're welcome," she muttered dryly.

She directed him to the cute redhead at the reception desk, where he passed a pleasant couple of minutes. Gracie, just like Fred and Virginia, made him feel welcome. She also made it clear she wouldn't say no if he asked her out.

He thought about that as he walked out of the building. She was pretty, curvy, nice, funny. Had curly hair, huge, sparkly eyes, and arched eyebrows like Lucille Ball, his all-time favorite comedienne. Maybe he'd ask her for pizza and a movie one night. If he could only get his mind off Maura Mahoney.

Maura hated movies; he'd bet she hated pizza, too, and she'd think *I Love Lucy* was slapstick and unsophisticated.

Who the hell wanted to be sophisticated anyhow?

Cussing under his breath, Jesse crossed the street in search of a burger.

Now reminded that it was past lunchtime, Maura realized she was hungry. She had a tendency—learned from Agnes and Timothy—to get so involved in a task that she forgot about mundane matters such as meals.

The Cherry Lane dining room closed at two o'clock, so she was too late to join the seniors. Staff at the residential facility were given one meal a day as part of their benefits package, and encouraged to mingle with the residents. The seniors enjoyed a break from each other's company, and Maura truly enjoyed talking to them. Growing up with parents who'd been forty-eight and fifty when they adopted her at age six, she was more at ease with older people. The seniors were the closest thing she had to friends.

She headed for the kitchen and put together a tray with leftover salads, a whole-wheat roll, and a glass of club soda, then returned to her office. As she nibbled, she thought ahead to dinner with her parents. Over the years, they'd always given her a birthday present, but it was rare for the three of them to be together. Agnes, the archaeology prof, was usually away at some dig in the summer, but since she'd turned seventy, she'd been spending less time traveling and was showing a disconcerting tendency to be more domestic and maternal.

Maura realized that, distracted by the unexpected arrival of Jesse Blue, she never had phoned to make sure it would be just the three of them for dinner. She was reaching for the phone when Gracie popped through the doorway.

"Maura, I've been hunting but I can't find Jesse's file anywhere. It's not in any of the filing cabinets under any kind of name that makes sense. I could call Louise, but . . ." She trailed off.

"No, this is her big day, becoming a mom." A pair of

adoptive parents had found out they were pregnant themselves, and backed out on an adoption at the last minute.
Offered the sudden opportunity, Louise and Don had
rushed off to the teenage mom's hometown to bond with
her and be there for the birth. "But if she does happen to
call in, don't forget to ask her about Jesse."

"Not likely I'd forget about him!"

Maura gritted her teeth as Gracie headed off. The girl
ought to have better sense. Jesse Blue was trouble with
a capital T, and that rhymed with B, and that stood for
Blue. She hummed a few bars from *The Music Man,* then
glanced at the leather jacket. Yes, she had a suspicion they
had trouble, right here in Cherry Lane.

She glanced into the courtyard. He had come back, tot-
ing a bag with the McDonald's arches. She shuddered at
the thought of all that cholesterol. He would die young.
She gave a small chuckle. If not of hardening of the arter-
ies, then on that motorcycle. Or maybe he'd continue his
life of crime. Street racing? Was Gracie right about that? It
fit better than shoplifting. And, though street racing was
indeed dangerous, obviously Jesse hadn't hurt anyone or
he'd be in jail rather than sprawling on the grass outside
her window.

He opened the bag and got to work on a hamburger,
accompanying it with French fries and a drink. When he
glanced toward her window, she ducked back.

She picked at her own healthy, boring lunch. Across the
desk, his jacket was a foreign object, all black and masculine
hanging on the spare chair, very much a contrast to the
spray of purple orchids on the bookcase beside it. The plant
had been an impulse buy, one gray day when she'd been
feeling just a touch lonely and depressed. The vivid color
had struck her fancy, as had the exuberance of the tall curving stalk with its dozen blooms, and the shape of the flowers with their butterfly-wing petals and full, pouty mouths.

She wandered over to mist the plant and couldn't resist stroking Jesse's jacket, confirming her earlier impression that it was excellent quality leather. Buttery smooth under her fingers. Just like the couch and chairs in her parents' sitting room. While Timothy didn't care about his surroundings, Agnes, who roughed it on field trips, liked her creature comforts at home. Thanks to a sizable inheritance, she had the money to indulge herself.

Hmm. Maura had been assuming Jesse was poor, but maybe he was a spoiled rich kid, with his expensive leather and his classic motorcycle. Or maybe a woman had bought him the toys. A lover. Maybe a rich older woman. A Mrs. Robinson, sleek and sophisticated and sexy. Smoking a cigarette held in one of those long holders, crooking a finger and beckoning Jesse over for a little afternoon delight.

She glanced into the hallway, checking that it was deserted, then bent to inhale. No cigarette smoke, but yes, of course there was a hint of perfume, more flamboyant than subtle.

She abandoned the Mrs. Robinson scenario and imagined Jesse with a curvy, vivacious blonde draped all over him. The girl would be wearing a skin-tight mini-skirt and a low-cut leopard-print top. In that outfit she'd be all hips and breasts, curly peroxided hair, and a toothpaste-ad smile. Yes, that would be Jesse Blue's type of woman. Her IQ would probably be right around her bra size, and he wouldn't have it any other way. She'd seen the horror on his face when Virginia Canfield handed her *The Time Traveler's Wife,* and when Maura asked if he liked to read.

Grinding her teeth, she went back to her chair and looked at the plate of unfinished food. She shoved it aside and yawned. She shouldn't have stayed up so late, but she'd gotten hooked watching *Rebel Without a Cause.* No wonder she'd been thinking of James Dean this morning. Though there was really very little comparison. Jesse was taller, better built, his voice was deeper, he was definitely more masculine. Sexier.

Had he had an unhappy home life, like Dean's character in the movie?

Guiltily, she remembered that she had out and out lied to Jesse Blue. While she truly believed in honesty, she couldn't confess to being a TV and movie addict. Her parents had raised her to believe such things were a pure waste of time. The television in their house had been solely for watching documentaries and other educational programs, and woe betide her if she ever got caught watching a movie or sitcom. *Maura, find something worthwhile to occupy your time.* Movies were for people like Jesse, who wanted superficial entertainment.

She yawned again, then forced her drooping eyes open and glanced out the window once more. He had finished eating and was lying on his back on the grass. Had he been up late, too? Probably not watching movies by himself. More likely, creating his own sex scenes with some gorgeous female.

He looked so peaceful, lazing in the sun on his lunch break. Like a cat, a giant cat, dozing in a sunny spot. Jesse seemed as natural and unselfconscious as a cat, too.

Maura was never unselfconscious, except when she was absorbed in working with numbers. She was always aware of trying to please people, to impress them, to be accepted. She'd heard that orphans were often like that.

It would be nice to be different. To be like Jesse. To not have to put on a poised façade but to be natural, confident . . .

She studied the man lying on the rough grass . . .

Confident . . . She could imagine being more confident . . .

She could imagine . . .

Chapter 4

This time, when Jesse glanced toward her window, Maura didn't move away. What would he do once he knew she was watching?

He rose in that cat-like way of his, taking his time. He stood, stretched lazily, ran his fingers through those long curls. Then he began to walk. Straight toward her.

She didn't step back from the window. Instead, she reached out and unlatched it. It was a tall window, starting a couple of feet above the floor and stretching almost to the ceiling. When she pushed it open, fresh air streamed in and she smelled the perfume of the cherry trees.

He reached the window and she stood aside. He didn't stop, just vaulted easily over the wooden frame, and suddenly her office was filled with his presence. The smell of earth and male exertion was intoxicating.

Those tawny eyes glowed with fire and, though she'd never seen passion up close and personal, she recognized it from movies. She knew her own eyes were sending the same message.

He reached out a hand and held it beside her cheek, close but not quite touching. Boldly she leaned toward him, fitting herself to the curve of his palm. He smiled then, a quick dazzle of white in his dark face, and caressed her heated skin. That strong, capable hand was unbelievably gentle, absolutely tantalizing. His palm was hot and dry, rough with calluses. It abraded ever so slightly, and she quivered at the sensation.

He slipped his hand away, then returned with one finger, tracing the outside line of her top lip, then her bottom lip.

She trembled.

His finger teased the crease that separated her lips.

Involuntarily, her lips parted.

He gave a rough chuckle, a satisfied masculine sound.

Then he tipped his head down and his lips touched hers, so soft after the roughness of his fingertip. So gentle. It was disarming, from a man so rugged and male. Again she opened to him and he accepted her invitation, slipping his tongue between her lips, exploring, flirting, seducing her own tongue.

She moaned softly. His lips pressed more firmly as he deepened the kiss, quickened the dance.

His arms came around her, one just below her shoulders and one at the base of her spine. Slowly but inexorably he pulled her toward him and she went willingly, her body yearning to learn the feel of his.

Her chest met his, her breasts softening against the cotton of his T-shirt even as her nipples peaked. He eased her hips forward, and she felt the roughness of denim and then, as a shock, the hardness that told her he was fully aroused. From just one kiss with her.

She nestled her hips closer. He pulled his mouth away from hers and groaned, then whispered, "Maura . . ."

"Maura? Ms. Mahoney?"

Gracie's voice penetrated her brain and Maura jerked awake. What? Had she been dozing? Had she actually had a *sex dream*? About Jesse Blue?

Cheeks burning, she swung her chair to face the door. Gracie stood there, looking puzzled. How many times had she called Maura's name?

"Yes, Gracie? Sorry. I was, er, working out some budget scenarios." And now she was lying to Gracie. Turning thirty had warped her entire personality.

"Sorry to interrupt." The redhead made her rueful-apology face again. "Been doing that all day, haven't I? Anyhow, I just wanted to tell you I'm going for the day. Unless you, like, need anything else?"

Need. Maura squeezed her thighs together against an unfamiliar ache. Oh, yeah, she needed something, but Gracie sure couldn't provide it. "No, nothing," she mumbled, cheeks burning. Good God, she'd never felt so . . . hot and wet, so swollen and achy, when she'd made love with the only two boyfriends she'd ever had sex with. Uninspired sex; sex that hadn't given her what she needed, either. Let's face it, her little sex dream, drawn more from movies and books than her own experience, had been sexier than lovemaking with either Bill or Winston.

When Gracie had departed with another quizzical glance, Maura groaned. A sex dream? A little daylight sex fantasy? What was wrong with her? The only time she'd ever before imagined a guy kissing her was back in grade twelve.

Troy Offenbacher, the captain of the debate team. He hadn't been every girl's idea of cute, but she'd admired his brain and those big blue eyes behind wire-rimmed glasses. They'd studied together, she'd fallen in love, and he'd asked her to the prom. She'd bought a dress, got her hair styled, done the whole mani-pedi thing with her girlfriend Sally.

The two of them had giggled and fantasized, her about Troy and Sally about her football-star boyfriend, and for once Maura had felt like a normal teenaged girl rather than the plain, serious one who never fit in. She'd felt pretty. Even desirable. Until the night of the prom, when a cheerleader named Nicki had too much to drink and came onto Troy. Maura guessed it was due to a bet or a mean joke.

Troy didn't give a damn about the reason.

So there was Maura, the girl who worked so hard to avoid being rejected, dumped at her own high school prom by the boy she loved.

Shattered, she'd done something really stupid. She'd let Sally—a girl who definitely had a wild side—convince her that getting drunk would make her feel better. Sally's football hero had a bottle of tequila, and the three of them had gone down to the beach. The police had caught them and, thank God, not pressed charges. But parents had been called.

Maura had received a "we're very disappointed in you" lecture, the kind she hadn't heard since she was ten and Timothy had come home from work with the flu and caught her watching *I Love Lucy* reruns.

A brand-new high school graduate, she'd been grounded for the summer. Not that the grounding mattered, because she was also forbidden from seeing Sally, and Sally had been her only social life. Maura was disappointed in herself, too, and scared by what she'd done, by the way she'd let Sally's wildness overcome her own better judgment. She'd agreed that the girl was a bad influence.

She'd lost her first love and her one-and-only best friend in one fell swoop—and learned that, as Sally would put it, her own judgment sucked big-time.

Maura gave a snort of disgust and shook her head. The past. Why was she even thinking about this?

A glance into the garden, where Jesse was now hard at work, reminded her. She'd been thinking about sexy fantasies.

How completely ridiculous to have them about Jesse. He was edgy and crude, hated books, and was a petty criminal. He was the opposite of what she wanted in a man.

Even if that weren't true, and she was insane enough to be interested in him, he was way too handsome and sexy to ever be attracted to a woman like her. There were a couple of times she'd wondered if he was checking her out, but if so, it was just a natural male instinct to look at breasts and hips. It wasn't attraction. If geeky Troy had blown her off for a cheerleader, she'd never stand a chance with Jesse. Not that she wanted one. She definitely didn't.

Oh, Lord, why on earth was she having wicked thoughts about him?

Wicked thoughts. Her lips twisted in a smile. The phrase was pure Sally. The two of them had really had fun to-gether in grade twelve, when Sally's wealthy parents had moved her from public school to the Wilton Academy in hopes of settling her down and making her apply herself, academically.

Maura had helped her with schoolwork, but it wasn't in Sally to settle down. She'd unsettled Maura, bringing out a side of her she'd barely known existed.

Sally hadn't been bad. Just irreverent and a little reck-less. Maybe, Maura now thought, she shouldn't have been so quick to go along with Agnes and Timothy when they'd forbidden her to see Sally again. Maybe kids should be allowed to make some mistakes and learn from them, not have to behave perfectly all the time.

The man she was staring at out the window had made a mistake, too, doing whatever had landed him in court. Did he view it that way himself, and intend to learn from it? Hopefully so.

He pulled up the bottom of his T-shirt and used it to fan

himself, giving Maura a tantalizing glimpse of a brown six-pack.

She felt like fanning herself, too, and she wasn't even out in the sun, much less doing hard physical labor.

He got back to work and she kept watching. No, she wasn't fantasizing, she was supervising. By now she'd figured out his method. He used the edger to cut a curving line, either at random or following some pattern in his head. Then he used the wicked-looking mattock to peel up strips of turf. When that was done, he shoveled soil onto the lawn and broke it up with the fork. Finally he put the turf back, with the grass side down, and piled the soil on top. It was clever and efficient, she had to admit. He was basically swapping soil for grass, with nothing left over to dispose of.

He leaned over to drink out of the hose, letting water splash his face and down his front. She wondered if he would take the T-shirt off. She doubted her blood pressure could take it, yet she was sorry when he didn't.

Above and behind Jesse, another window opened. Mrs. Rudnicki rested her arms on the sill and gazed down into the garden. Maura would bet a month's pay that she and Sophie Rudnicki weren't the only females watching the show.

She forced herself back to work. Across from her, the leather jacket was a constant, disturbing reminder of the new male presence in her life. The purple orchid flowers arched toward it, their full mouths opening in sexy smiles.

Sex. Now even her orchid plant was making her think of sex. This was ridiculous.

By the end of the afternoon, Maura's shoulders and neck ached from tension. She'd have gone home for a relaxing bath before her birthday dinner if she hadn't had to supervise Jesse.

Of course, if she hadn't had to supervise Jesse, she wouldn't be tense and stressed.

No bath, no change of clothes, but there was one thing she could do to make herself feel better. She pulled open her bottom drawer and took out her hairbrush. She removed the pins that held her hair in its neat knot and let it tumble free, halfway down her back. Rotating her swivel chair to face a bookcase, she leaned back in the chair and lifted her legs to rest her feet on the second shelf.

Maura began to brush. A hundred long, slow strokes. When she was little, before her parents died, her mom brushed Maura's hair this way. Later, when Agnes and Timothy took her in, no one had brushed her hair for her. She'd done it herself, her small hands growing larger and more deft over the years.

Now, this was still a favorite method of relaxing. She'd even been known to exceed the hundred strokes.

Jesse flipped the last strip of turf back into the new border and shoveled soil on top of it. He stretched aching shoulders, then tidied up his tools and washed up, using the courtyard tap. That was three borders ready to plant. Tomorrow, he and the boss-lady could go shopping for supplies. If she could force herself to get into a car with him.

Probably should check in with her, because she was supposed to keep track of his hours. Besides, she had his jacket.

He locked the courtyard door behind him and saw that there was a different woman at the receptionist's desk now—a sturdy woman with gray-streaked brown hair. She studied him without warmth. "You're Jesse Blue. Gracie told me about you."

When she didn't go on to give him her name, he flashed her a cocky smile. "Pleased to meet you."

She hmphed.

"I'm supposed to check in with Ms. Mahoney," he said. "I know the way."

Her eyes narrowed, but she said, "Fine."

Jesse strolled down the hallway. It was past six o'clock, and obviously his boss was still there or the nameless receptionist would have told him. Did Maura Mahoney always work Saturdays, or was she only doing it so she could supervise him? If so, he owed her.

He didn't like owing people.

When he stepped into the doorway of the office, Jesse froze in place. She was seated behind her desk but had swiveled her chair so she was facing away from him.

Long hair streamed over the back of the chair, gleaming under the overhead light. The length, the color, the shininess stunned him. He tried to find a name for the color, somewhere between blond and red. The best he could come up with was copper-bronze.

Her right hand lifted lazily, holding a hairbrush. She stroked through her hair from crown to ends, tilting her head slightly as she did. He couldn't see her face, but he'd bet it wore an expression of sheer pleasure.

What she was doing—the simple act of brushing her hair—was one of the most sensual things he'd ever seen. He could imagine her naked in bed: that creamy skin, the vibrant hair flowing over her shoulders and down her chest. Almost hiding her breasts, but not quite. Allowing the slightest glimpse here and there. Perhaps a nipple peeking out, growing hard as she became aware of his scrutiny.

And speaking of growing hard . . . He took a silent step backward, out the doorway, suddenly realizing he had a hard-on.

Grateful no one else was in the corridor, he paced up and down, trying to think of anything but the ice queen with the honey-dripping name. Mahoney. My honey. He wondered how many men had called her that. He guessed not many. She'd be picky about the men she allowed into her life. Lawyers and doctors, probably. No calloused-hand laborers for her.

Ruthlessly, he forced her out of his mind and instead thought about how busy his schedule was going to be for the next few weeks as he juggled his regular job, this community service work, and the kids' pickup basketball games he coached a couple of nights a week.

His body under control, he strode back down the corridor. His plan was to knock on the door before he took a look at her, but temptation got the better of him. Just one quick glance . . .

He froze with his hand fisted in the air near the door frame. She had stopped brushing and was rotating her neck.

Damn but he wanted to bury his face in that gleaming curtain of hair. Inhale the aroma, burrow through silky strands to her soft, vulnerable nape. Kiss her there, touch his tongue to her skin. She would tremble and he'd kiss his way around to her ear. He'd already seen what fine-shaped, delicate ears she had.

He must have made a sound, because she suddenly spun around.

"Oh!" she gasped, and color flooded her cheeks.

"Sorry." Hurriedly he jammed his fists into his jeans pockets, stretching the fabric away from his body to hide his physical response.

But maybe she'd already seen. Why else would she be blushing like that?

God, but she looked fine with her hair down. Her face was softer, more approachable. Of course all that rosy color helped, too.

"You startled me." She dropped the brush like a hot potato and gathered her hair in both hands, pulling it back firmly from her face, twisting it behind her head.

He watched, thinking she looked pretty fine that way, too. She had one of those Hepburn faces. Skinning back the hair only emphasized the strength of the face. Her fine features were more like Audrey's than Katharine's, but the set of her jaw reminded him of Katharine playing Rosie in *The African Queen*. And that glare she'd summoned up was pure Rosie, disapproving of crude old Charlie Allnut.

Not that Jesse and Maura Mahoney were going to end up like Rosie and Charlie, that was for sure. But man, what it would be like to take the pins out of all that hair, to have it tumble down over his hands, his face. To have her lean over his naked body, all those fiery silk strands brushing his—

Whoa! Trying to look casual, he grabbed his jacket off a chair and draped it over his arm to hide his lower body.

"You're done?" she asked.

More like done in, by her sensuality. "For the day." His voice rasped low in his throat. "When do you want me tomorrow?"

The hot flush had begun to recede but now came back in a wave.

Want me. Damn, he'd said "want me." And that's how she'd heard it. And she was blushing, not glaring.

Nope. Now she was glaring.

If the ice queen really was attracted to him, she hated herself for it. That was good, he told himself. He wasn't about to hook up with another Sybil, who'd screw him as her dirty little secret.

Fantasies about long hair and taut nipples aside, Jesse knew his boss was out of his league, just as much as she did. Plenty of women found him attractive, liked his company, didn't play fucked-up games. He never had a problem getting a date if he wanted one.

"Shall we say nine to five tomorrow." She made it more of a statement than a question. "Unless you go to church on Sundays?" Her arched eyebrows told him she figured there was slight chance of that.

"Not much of a churchgoer. Don't let me hold you up, if you want to go."

She shook her head. "I don't attend church." She didn't meet his eyes; her gaze was higher and quite intent. "You have . . ."

"What?"

"In your hair. The cherry tree . . ."

Quickly he shook his head and a pale pink flower, one perfect cherry blossom, fell to her desk. Damn, he'd been walking around with a flower in his hair. That must have given her a laugh.

"Tomorrow, then," he said abruptly, and strode out of her office and down the hall.

"Wait!" Her heels clacked behind him. Probably wanted to make sure he didn't make any stops along the way to the exit. She'd made it clear she didn't trust him with her precious old folks.

He stopped and swung around, so abruptly she almost crashed into him. "What?" he demanded.

Her nostrils flared and her whole body quivered a little. "I just . . . I, uh . . ."

She was so close, if he reached out he could tug her into his arms. So close, he could see the slight tremble of her full bottom lip. A lip that begged to be kissed.

"Jesse, you're working late." A male voice made Jesse start, and swing around.

Fred Dykstra was walking from the elevator together with an attractive woman who had brown skin and short, very curly gray hair. Fred wore tailored khakis and a blazer, and the woman had on one of those dresses that buttoned down the front, patterned with swirly pink flowers.

"Just finished for the day," Jesse said. Needing to get away from Maura and that irresistible urge to kiss her, he went to meet them.

Heel clacks told him Maura was following.

"I'd like you to meet Lizzie Gilmore," Fred said. "Lizzie, this is Jesse Blue, the young man I was telling you about. I'll show you his bike when we go out."

"Pleased to meet you," the woman said, extending a hand.

It was sturdier than his gardening pal Virginia's, so he gave it a firm squeeze. "Me, too."

"You two are going out?" Maura asked, sounding surprised.

The older woman nodded, her brown eyes bright. "We're going across the street to a movie. They're showing *Eat Pray Love* and I've never seen it."

Jesse knew the movie complex across the street. It was an independent, run by a billionaire who loved movies and didn't care about making a profit. The five cinemas, each a different size, showed everything from old classics to the latest blockbusters. He guessed it came in handy for the Cherry Lane folks, and bet the owner had great rates for seniors.

"*Eat Pray Love,* huh?" Not his favorite, but he guessed it made a good date movie.

"We must be off," Fred said, kinking his elbow toward his lady friend. She slipped her hand through it and they moved away.

Maura shook her head bemusedly. "He's been yearning after her for months now," she murmured. "How did he get up the courage to ask her out?"

He sensed it wasn't a question directed to him. In fact,

he figured she'd pretty much forgotten he was around. "I'll be going."

"Oh!" She turned toward him, and he could tell he'd been right from the way the color rose to her cheeks. She was sure a blusher, this lady, but he still hadn't worked out whether it was sexy thoughts or annoyance that triggered her. Mostly, he figured it was annoyance.

"I'll see you tomorrow then, Jesse," she said in a polite, society-woman voice. The kind of voice that made his skin crawl. "At nine, as we agreed. Please be prompt."

Just to be wicked, he flashed her his best lady-killer grin and put on a husky drawl. "Tomorrow," he said with promise in his voice. Unlike everyone else in this place, she hadn't told him to use her first name, and so he didn't. Instead, when he said, "I'll be looking forward to that, Ms. Mahoney," he let his voice linger caressingly over every syllable of her name, just the way his hands longed to twine themselves in that silky hair and never come out again.

Her cheeks flamed brighter and she turned back into the building, banging her shoulder against the door frame before she strode off.

He chuckled softly, then, whistling, strolled toward his bike. It had been one hell of a day. And this was only the first one of his three-month community service gig.

When Maura heard the bike roar to life, she looked out the window by the door. Jesse, in helmet and jacket, cruised down the block under a canopy of pink blossoms. James Dean and cherry blossoms. Something was wrong with this picture. And something was wrong with her. Had turning thirty transformed her normally sensible body into a mess of raging hormones? She growled with annoyance and turned, to see Nedda, the evening reception-ist, watching her curiously.

"What's he doing here?" the older woman asked brusquely. "Why did we hire him? I asked Gracie, and she just said Louise had done it. Mostly, she was gushing like a teenager."

Maura had never liked Nedda diFazio, who was one of those sour women who derived her greatest pleasure from tattling on others. Still, in the interests of working on her own people skills—not to mention the fact that Nedda's sister was the chairman of the board's wife—she tried to be pleasant. "Gracie's right. Louise made the decision, and I'm sure she had good reasons." Gracie, as Louise's assistant, knew about HR matters, but they were none of Nedda's business.

Earlier, Maura had made a spur-of-the-moment decision, when Virginia Canfield had assumed Jesse was a gardener, and hadn't corrected her. After, Maura had thought it through. Without being able to read Jesse's file, she couldn't know whether the terms of his community service included confidentiality.

"I bet Louise didn't see him," Nedda said darkly. "He looks like trouble."

It was exactly what Maura had first thought—and still believed—but for some reason she found herself saying, "He's a hard worker, and we're going to get a nice garden for the residents."

"Huh." Her tone made it clear she wasn't buying in.

Maura headed back to her office. On her desk lay the blossom that had been in Jesse's hair. She picked it up gently and lifted it to her nose. The scent was amazingly powerful for such a small, delicate thing. It contrasted with the rich musk she'd smelled when she had almost bumped into Jesse. Male sweat, earthy and not at all unpleasant. A foreign smell. The men in her life hadn't been known for sweating. Yet, in her afternoon dream, she'd got the scent amazingly right.

That was the reason she hadn't been able to move, after almost plowing into him. She'd been analyzing the scent. Not fighting the urge to touch his dark skin, to tug his head down to hers, touch her tongue to his lips, and—

Aagh! There she went again. Sexual fantasies? Why, she rarely even read the sex scenes in novels, just skimmed over them the way she did other scenes that she couldn't relate to. What a bizarre day this had been.

Unable to resist, she sniffed the blossom one more time, then tossed it into the wastepaper basket.

She consulted her watch and realized she'd be late for dinner if she didn't leave right now. Fortunately, her adoptive parents' philosophy about clothing was to buy good quality, neutral items, and not fancy, dress-up clothes. They wouldn't criticize her for wearing her office clothes to dinner.

Of course if today's streak of bad luck held, they'd be grilling her about how little she'd achieved by the ripe old age of thirty. On the career front, she'd update them on her efforts to win the promotion, but on the personal, single-at-thirty front, she had nothing to offer.

Oh, drat! She'd never gotten around to calling Agnes to make sure it would be just the three of them.

Chapter 5

When Maura walked into the dining room at her parents' club and saw three heads at their table, she groaned. This was Jesse's fault. If he hadn't kept distracting her, she'd have remembered to phone.

The host who was leading her across the room paused. "Is something wrong, ma'am?"

Great, now she was getting "ma'am" rather than "miss."

"Nothing you can fix," she muttered, forcing a smile and waving to her mother, who had seen her coming.

As Maura reached the table, she was confronted by two men in gray suits, standing.

"Hello, Timothy," she said, giving the portly bald one a quick, formal hug and ignoring the younger man. Maybe if she pretended he wasn't there, he'd go away. She leaned down and touched her cheek to her mother's. "Hello, Agnes." Their family had never been much for physical demonstrations of affection. Or verbal ones, for that matter.

"Happy birthday, Maura." Her mother smiled at her from a face that would have persuaded anyone in their right mind to never go out without sunscreen. "Your gift's out in the car. Don't forget to take it when you leave."

Far be it from her parents to create a public display as

Maura squealed in delight over some dry textbook or pottery shard.

"Maura," Timothy said, "I'd like you to meet Professor Edward Mortimer. He's a visiting lecturer and is considering joining our faculty next year." Her father had semi-retired from teaching to do more research and article-writing, as well as keeping his longtime position on the board of the Wilton Academy where both he and Maura had attended secondary school. But he was still very much attached to his beloved history department, and rare was the day that he didn't spend a few hours at the university.

With a sense of inevitability, Maura turned and assessed her parents' latest offering. She was thirty. Maybe today's awful luck would change and, for once, Agnes and Timothy would have chosen a man who actually appealed to her.

Edward Mortimer was a poster boy for the word "average." He certainly wasn't bad looking, but nor was he handsome. Roughly her age, he had regular features, medium brown hair, and a build that was neither lean nor heavy. She didn't see a single distinguishing feature. He'd make a perfect spy. No one would ever remember seeing him. He'd be the George Smiley type of spy—the character created by John le Carré—not the flashy, unrealistic kind.

She thought of her favorite spies, especially the various 007s. No one had ever topped Sean Connery, in her considered opinion. Pierce Brosnan's Bond was debonair, like Connery's, but didn't have that raw masculine edge, the edge that women went wild for in Daniel Craig. And, no doubt, in Jesse Blue.

She shook her head to clear it. Thank heavens her parents and, presumably, Professor Mortimer, weren't mind readers or they'd be appalled.

"Pleased to meet you," he said, holding out his hand.

She put hers into it. "Likewise." His grip was neither strong nor weak, just . . . average. His skin was neither hot nor cold, and definitely not sweaty. As they both let go, she saw that his hand was slim and pale. No calluses or blisters. Not a hand she could imagine on the handlebar of a motorcycle, or levering a garden tool into the resistant earth. Or tracing the outline of her lips . . .

As they all sat, Edward said, "May I wish you a happy birthday?"

What if I said "no," she wondered mutinously. Instead, the soul of decorum, she murmured, "How kind of you." In her head, she heard Eliza Doolittle dutifully repeating "How kind of you to let me come."

Come? The double meaning resonated in her head. Not that she had any personal experience with the sexy connotation of that word. With Bill and Winston, she'd never achieved orgasm. But she'd just bet Jesse Blue's women *came,* and thanked him for it—but by shrieking their lungs out, not mouthing platitudes.

Edward lifted his water glass and Maura closed her eyes briefly, remembering how Jesse's muscles had flexed and shifted as he drank that glass of soda.

". . . drink?"

Her eyes flew open as she realized her father was asking her a question. She made a guess. "I'd like a glass of red wine, please."

"White might do better," Timothy said, putting down the wine list. "The club has a number of excellent seafood specials tonight. Why don't we get a bottle of the New Zealand chardonnay?"

Why could he never remember that she didn't like chardonnay? She always hated to disagree with her adoptive parents—the only people who'd been willing to take her in when she was orphaned—and risk their disapproval, but tonight was her birthday and it had been a rough day. Despite the acid twinge of guilt tugging at her belly, she said, "White's fine, but I'd rather not have chardonnay."

Edward picked up the wine list and handed it to her. "It's your birthday. You should choose, Maura."

Pleasantly surprised, she beamed at him. Then, of course, she felt the overwhelming pressure of choosing a wine neither of her parents would criticize. Though Agnes and Timothy maintained that they lived frugally and weren't pretentious, the fact was that he'd grown up comfortably well-off and she came from serious money. It showed in a thousand ways, from their choice of wine to their decision to send Maura to the exclusive Wilton Academy.

As the meal progressed, Maura learned that Edward was indeed considerate. He was also intelligent, articulate, and really quite boring as he chatted easily with her parents about the paper Agnes was writing on funerary pits. Her parents would consider him an excellent match for her. He was certainly a good match for them, she thought, suppressing a yawn. He'd fit into the family seamlessly.

So, really, that did make him a good match for her, too. As her parents had always said, *A good marriage is a partnership of equals, based on a solid foundation of similar values and interests.* If the woman was well-bred, well-educated, well-spoken, and not exactly exciting, then those were the qualities she must look for in a mate. Maura couldn't fault their logic; the formula had served both of them well.

What was wrong with her, that she longed for a man who discussed movies rather than archival materials, one who tossed her suggestive winks rather than polite nods? Whose gaze made her pulse race, and sweat break out on her skin?

And why had it taken until today for her to realize this? Had the age of thirty brought this self-knowledge?

Or was it the coming of Jesse Blue?

The other three were still talking happily, and no doubt believed she was listening attentively. The subject wasn't completely uninteresting, but right now she was in complete agreement with Eliza Doolittle, when she'd sung, *Words, words, words, I'm so sick of words.*

Jesse Blue was too short on words. Edward Mortimer, like her parents, was too full of them. Somewhere, there must be a happy medium.

She forced herself to tune into the conversation, and after a few minutes had to struggle to hold back a yawn. She hadn't gotten enough sleep last night; it had been a long day; it was warm in here. She should stop drinking wine. But it was her only pleasure at the moment, so she sipped again. Gazing into her glass, she noted how the pale gold of the wine reflected the glimmer of subdued lights. When she swirled the liquid, it swished in gentle curves, almost hypnotically . . .

It was her birthday and she should be having fun. If she had her choice, what would she like to be doing this very minute? She sipped, and ran her tongue over her lips to catch a stray drop as she stared into the golden liquid and held back another yawn.

An hour ago, she'd been staring, mesmerized, at something very different. When she'd almost bumped into Jesse, she had frozen in place, heat pulsing through her veins. Hypnotized . . .

She sipped again, remembering how she'd stared at his lips . . .

She'd been drawn toward him as if they were magnetic . . .

Maura's tongue ran slowly across . . .

Jesse's lips. They were full, sensual, swollen. Her own body felt swollen, too, ripe with feelings she'd never experienced before, a lush new territory just waiting to be explored. By his strong brown hands.

He cupped her breast through her silk blouse, and the roughness of his skin caught at the delicate fabric. Underneath, her own skin tightened, yearning for the touch of flesh against flesh.

His fingers went to the top button of her blouse, and he slipped it effortlessly through the hole. He parted the sides of the blouse and ran his finger down the flesh he had bared—the base of her neck, that little hollow between her collarbones. She knew he could feel the flutter of her pulse as her heart raced with pleasure.

He undid another button and leaned down to moisten her skin with his tongue. Her breasts strained against the confinement of her bra, longing for him to reach them. But he was drawing this out, tantalizing and torturing her. What would it feel like when his tongue finally touched—

"Maura?" her mother's voice broke in.

She almost dropped the wineglass. What? Where was she? "Yes?" She gazed across the table, aware that color flamed in her cheeks. What was wrong with her? And, come to think of it, how was her mind coming up with sensual details she'd never personally experienced? Maybe she hadn't been skimming those sex scenes as much as she'd thought.

"You were miles away."

If Agnes only knew. "Sorry," Maura said respectfully. "I'm a little tired tonight. It's been a long day."

Respectful. Yes, she'd learned respect in her first months at Agnes and Timothy's house, and now it was a habit.

Not a habit of Jesse Blue's, she'd noticed today. He wasn't out-and-out rude or insolent, but he got his own way. There was a tone—a kind of taunting, teasing tone—she wasn't used to. And the occasional expression in his eyes that she couldn't read, as if maybe he was viewing her with interest. Male interest. When she'd swung around in her chair and found that he'd been watching her brush her hair, his eyes had been glittering, his mouth was slightly open, she'd almost have said his nostrils were flaring.

She shook her head and banished the image. What an idiot she was. He was a man, not a horse, and no doubt he'd been tired and anxious to get away. It was impatience she'd seen, not . . . something else she didn't dare name. Something she wouldn't allow herself to want, not from a man like him.

She looked at three sets of raised eyebrows. "I'm fine, honestly. Please go on with your conversation."

"You've barely said a word," Edward commented. "We've been talking about our work, and now it's your turn. Timothy didn't say what you do."

No, he wouldn't have, because he and Agnes weren't happy about it. Her parents had strongly encouraged her to go into academia, but it was one of the few areas in her life where she couldn't bring herself to respect their wishes. She loved numbers, and was intrigued by the way businesses worked. So, no doctorate for her, just a master's in business admin.

"I'm an accountant at a seniors residential facility," she told him.

"You enjoy it?"

"I do." Her parents couldn't seem to understand that the job at Cherry Lane was perfect for her, letting her indulge her passion for numbers and spend time with seniors she liked and respected. Or, rather, the job had been perfect until today.

"Her talents, and her education, are being wasted," Agnes said. "Fortunately, she has a good chance of becoming the general manager."

"Sounds impressive," Edward commented.

Left to her own unambitious devices, she'd have been quite content in her current job. She only hoped that, if she won the promotion, Agnes and Timothy would finally get over being disappointed in her.

Edward started to say something else to her, but Timothy intervened with a question about some research Edward had been doing, and the three of them were off again.

Maura reflected on her chances at that promotion. If things worked out with Jesse, and a nice garden was created on a minimal budget, that would be a big point in her favor. If Jesse screwed up, though—especially if he did steal something, or drink or do drugs at Cherry Lane—she'd be in serious trouble. Tomorrow, surely she'd locate the file on him and find out exactly what kind of man she was dealing with.

What kind of man . . . She glanced across at nice, average Edward, nodding as he listened to her father. She'd just bet Jesse Blue was having a much more exciting evening than she was. And so was whichever curvy, sexy, vivacious woman he was spending it with.

In bed, Edward would probably be average, and nice. As for Jesse, with that hot body and loads and loads of experience, he'd probably be blow-your-mind good.

Did he make love the way he gardened: slowly and thoroughly, with attention to every detail? What would it feel like to have a man devote his single-minded attention to her body, the way Jesse had tended to that neglected garden?

"Dessert?" a soft voice asked.

"Oh, yes, please," Maura murmured. Whipped cream and Jesse Blue and—

". . . cake and a pear tart."

She came back to reality with a thud. The waiter was looking at her expectantly. What had he said?

Embarrassed, realizing she'd again become the center of attention and Agnes was frowning, she muttered, "The pear tart."

"An excellent choice, madam."

She felt like snapping, *I'm not a madam!* Then she realized how it would sound. What an odd word, with two such different meanings. No one on earth would take uptight Maura for the madam of a, uh, brothel, to use the most polite word she could think of. She remembered Jesse's odd expression the first time she put her glasses on. Maybe it was time to consider getting contact lenses.

She'd bet, whoever Jesse was spending the evening with, the woman didn't wear glasses.

Jesse tested the burgers by pressing the spatula against them gently. "I figure they're done. Whadda ya say, dude?" he asked the eight-year-old boy who watched his every move.

"I say so, too, dude."

"Okay, go tell your ma."

Jesse flipped the burgers onto a plate and turned off the barbecue. He stepped off the balcony and followed Juanito into the tiny apartment, feeling abused muscles protest. It'd been a hell of a long day out there in the blazing sun, and he was beat.

Consuela emerged from the kitchen, looking tousled and pretty in hot-pink shorts and a white crop top. "Juanito, go wash your hands." As her son ran off, she thrust a family-size jar of mayonnaise at Jesse. "I can't get the lid off."

"Con, I gave you one of those thingamajigs."

"I can't find it. 'Sides, it's easier to ask you." She flashed him a dazzling smile and handed him the jar.

"Glad I'm good for something." He twisted the lid off, his blisters making him wince, and handed the jar back. "Mayo doesn't belong on hamburgers."

"I like it."

"Just don't make me eat it."

She went back into the kitchen, and Jesse sat down at the red-top table they'd picked up at the Salvation Army thrift shop. Though he'd had a burger for lunch, these would be better. She'd spread out all the fixings. Ketchup and mustard, tomatoes, lettuce, raw onions. He looked at the onions. Hell, why not? It wasn't like he had a hot date.

Hot. He sure as hell had been hot today, and not just from the sun and exertion . . .

He closed his eyes for a moment . . .

Remembered slugging down that cold soda, then looking at Maura Mahoney's face and heating up all over again . . .

Tiny beads of sweat had pearled on her forehead. Before now, he'd have bet she was too cool a cucumber to ever break a sweat . . .

Was it that hot in the courtyard or did it have something to do with him?

He reached out a finger and swiped it across her forehead, then put it in his mouth, sucking her sweat, tasting the salty tang of her.

Those stunning eyes widened and she gave a tiny gasp.

When he took his finger from his mouth, she reached for his hand. She brought it to her own lush, ripe mouth. Her eyes never leaving his, she took his finger into that sexy mouth, a little bit at a time. Her lips were soft, but they circled him firmly. The inside of her mouth was a hot, warm sheath, enveloping him. She sucked gently, swirling her tongue around his finger. Then she increased the pressure, moving up his finger then down again.

Fucking his finger.

His hard-on craved the touch of her lips and tongue. Wanted her to fuck his dick rather than his finger.

He groaned and felt her lips smile against his finger. She knew she was torturing him. Maura Mahoney, a seductress who could make him come just from sucking on his finger.

She scraped her teeth gently against his sensitive flesh, he groaned again, and she said . . .

"Jesse, what's wrong?"

No, what the fuck? That was Consuela's voice. His eyes flew open and he gaped up at his friend. "Huh?"

"You groaned and had this weird expression on your face. Have you got a stomachache?"

Hurriedly, he shoved his chair farther under the table. If Con glanced at his lap, she'd have no trouble figuring out his problem. "Sore muscles. I worked hard today, over at that seniors place."

"Then you'll be ready for a good meal, hon." She bent and kissed the top of his head. Her breasts—gorgeous, voluptuous ones—were about two inches from his face, but he had no desire to touch them. Con was his buddy. Even though she was most definitely a babe, there'd never been an attraction between them.

Attraction was an odd thing. He and Consuela would be perfect together, and he was just plain crazy about Juanito. But he could no more imagine going to bed with Con than . . . than he could stop imagining touching Maura Mahoney. Having her touch him.

He stifled a groan, relieved when Juanito came and took his seat, and they all began to slather the top halves of their hamburger buns with their favorite combination. He and the boy competed to see who could draw the coolest picture in ketchup and mustard. It was a tradition.

He wondered what the classy Ms. Mahoney was doing tonight. Did she ever eat hamburgers? She was probably into that fancy stuff like truffles and caviar.

Having constructed the perfect burger, he opened wide to take the first bite. And thought of Maura opening those sexy lips wide, wider. But it wasn't a hamburger she was opening wide for . . .

"Jesse?"

He bit down hard. Into bun, meat, and his own finger. "Bloody hell!"

Con shot him a warning look. "Sorry," he muttered. He inspected his finger and decided he'd live, then forced his mind back to present company. He took another bite and smiled at Juanito. "Hey dude, we did a mean job on these. They're way better than Mickey D's."

"They're even better with mayo," Con teased.

Once they'd all taken those first few bites to ward off starvation, she said, "Tell us about the seniors place, Jesse. This was the big first day, right? Your, uh, new part-time job." They hadn't told her son about the assault charge against Jesse, nor his community service. "How did it go?"

"Okay. They've got me cleaning up a rundown garden."

"Great! You're good at that stuff."

"Thanks." He liked how Consuela focused on the positive. She didn't know that he couldn't read properly—he was real good at hiding that—but she did know he wasn't exactly the intellectual type. Yet she never dumped on him for dropping out of school, just gave him credit for the things he was good at.

"What are the people like at this Cherry Lane place?" she asked.

He wasn't going to tell her about Maura Mahoney, because Con picked up on stuff. "I've met a few of the seniors and they're pretty cool."

"Seniors?" Juanito asked. "Like, old people?"

"Yeah, pretty old. And pretty smart. And kind of lonely, too."

Con nodded. "That's sad."

"How come I don't know any old people?" her son asked.

She bit her lip. "We've talked about this. Some kids have grandparents and aunts and uncles, and some don't.

We're just this itty bitty family, you and me." She glanced across the table. "And Jesse."

"But he's not old."

"Thanks," Jesse said. "Now, you figure you got room for another burger?"

Consuela shot him a relieved glance.

The issue of relatives was sensitive. Her stepdad had been an abuser and, when Con's boyfriend Rico knocked her up in twelfth grade, she'd decided things had to change. She said she never wanted to see her abusive step-dad again, and that her mom had to choose between them. Her mom called her an ungrateful little bitch. Con left home and moved in with a girlfriend's family, and a few months later her mom and stepdad moved away. As for Juanito's father, Rico had been another jerk, another abuser. Best thing he'd done was leave Con when she told him she was pregnant. He'd probably never told his parents he had a kid, and Con hadn't, either.

She was pretty smart about most things, but not when it came to men. She kept picking losers, men like her step-dad, Rico, and that supreme asshole Pollan. That thing she did, seeing the best in people, sometimes got her into trouble.

After the three of them polished off the burgers, he and Consuela tidied up while Juanito went to change into pa-jamas. They took bowls of fruit salad over ice cream into the living room and started watching a *Spy Kids* movie on DVD. Jesse sprawled in the big chair with Juanito on the floor leaning against him. Consuela took the couch, half watching the show as she painted her fingernails and toe-nails a bright pinky-red.

It was homey, which Jesse liked a lot. He'd never had much of that as a kid. Still, it was kind of weird, a twenty-seven-year-old guy spending his Saturday nights this way.

He hadn't been dating much, not since he'd beaten up Pollan. Con, with her ex out of her life—hopefully forever this time—was relieved but edgy. It was taking her a while to sort herself out. She said hanging out with Jesse kept her from doing something stupid. It worked for him; he hadn't met a gal who turned his crank in quite a while. Not until today. And his *crank* knew better than to mess with the likes of Maura Mahoney.

He tried to imagine her here in this living room. She'd think Con looked trashy, she'd notice the ice cream Juanito had dribbled on his PJ top, and she'd itch to turn the TV off. As for Jesse, she'd see him for exactly what he was: a big dumb lunk of a physical laborer.

Why the hell was he picturing Maura in this living room? If he was going to bring any woman here, it'd be someone like that pretty redhead, Gracie.

"Okay, kiddo," Con's voice broke into his thoughts as she spoke to her son. "That's your hour of TV. Go brush your teeth and hop into bed." She stopped the DVD.

"It's Saturday," Juanito protested.

"Yup, and that's why you got to stay up this late."

Grumbling, the boy got to his feet and trudged away.

Consuela took the ice cream bowls into the kitchen.

Yeah, homey was good, and there was a part of Jesse that wanted a home and family of his own. He'd never had those things, and it was his own damned fault. He'd always screwed things up, been the dummy, the troublemaker. Yeah, he was older now, but did that mean he'd do any better? So far, he hadn't met a woman who made him want to try. He didn't think Gracie'd be the one, but the two of them could have some fun.

"Need any help?" he called to Con.

"Nah, I'm good."

He hunted through the magazines on the coffee table, wondering if that Victoria's Secret one was still there.

Nope. Probably a good thing. A copy of *National Geographic* reminded him of one of the foster families he'd lived with. They'd encouraged the kids to read it. It was supposed to be educational. Jesse, twelve, had been the oldest. He'd grab the magazine first and look for photos of women with bare boobs, then check out the rest of the pictures. There were some cool things, like shots of space capsules and outer space, photographs taken undersea. It really burned him that his foster brother and sister, who were only eight and nine, could read the damned stories.

It hurt more when they figured out he couldn't, and called him "dummy." Bad enough he got that crap at school; it sucked to get it at home.

He slapped the magazine down on the table. What kind of idiot got to be twenty-seven without knowing how to read?

A moment later, Juanito called, "Jesse, I'm in bed. Come read me a story."

Jeez, was the kid a mind reader? Jesse wandered into the bedroom the boy shared with his mother. Juanito, propped up on pillows in the twin bed by the window, handed Jesse a book.

Recognizing the kid with big glasses, Jesse knew it was a Harry Potter. When Juanito had been little and his books were the kind with big pictures and only five or ten large-print words on a page, Jesse'd read to him. Too bad the boy had graduated to big-kid books. The sight of all those letters jumbled up on the page gave Jesse a headache. "Nah, I'd rather tell you a story."

"Dude, your stories are so cool. Tell me about Robo Kid."

Robo Kid was a character Jesse had made up, who was half human and half android. He spent his nights fighting bad guys and aliens and vampires, and his days pretending he was a normal kid.

Jesse spun another adventure and Juanito listened raptly. Then Jesse whacked the little guy on the shoulder and said good night.

In the living room, Con flicked the television off. "I'm gonna go kiss Juanito good night, but then can I talk to you, Jesse?"

"Sure." He wandered out to the kitchen and screwed the top off one of the beers he'd brought. He came back and settled into his chair.

When she returned and took her own chair, he asked, "What's up?"

"I met this guy."

"Yeah?"

"At the coffee shop at the mall where I work. He's just got a job at the transmission place." Consuela worked at a beauty salon in a strip mall. "He seems nice."

"Uh-huh."

"He asked me out. I don't know what to do."

Jeez. Why didn't she talk to a girlfriend about this stuff? "You wanna go?"

"Yes, but . . ." She fiddled with the edge of her crop top, yanking it down over her brown skin.

"But?"

"How do I know . . ." She rubbed her left arm, where Gord Pollan had broken it a couple of years ago. That was when Con had had that restraining order against him. It had cost the asshole a trip to prison, but even that wasn't enough to stop him.

"How do you know he's not like Pollan? Or your stepdad?"

"Or Juanito's father. Yeah. I know I've got this pattern. I pick that kind of guy. Even if they seem nice at first. Like, Gord seemed really sweet when we first got together."

Jesse sighed. "Didn't the social worker help you with this stuff?"

"Yeah, but I'm still not sure . . ."

"You want me to check him out?"

She came over to hug him. "Hon, you're the best. He asked me out for coffee Monday night. Maybe if I met you after your basketball game . . ."

"Okay. But what about Juanito?"

"Ms. Barzhi next door says he can come over any time. She's lonely 'cause her husband's away on some training course."

"You maybe wanna think about bringing Juanito along. Let this guy know up front you've got a kid. Not to mention a . . . whatever."

"A protector. That's what you are, Jesse. You're my protector. If you hadn't beaten the shit out of Gord, I'd have never been free of him."

"Yeah, well. Listen, I gotta go."

"Hot date?"

"Nah, just tired." A hot date. Hah. And now he was wondering what Maura Mahoney's idea of a hot date was. Champagne and caviar at some ritzy restaurant? Ballroom dancing? He imagined her in some slinky dress, her shoulders bare, a full skirt swishing around those long legs. Her back straight and regal, her partner holding her gently, her hand resting lightly on his shoulder. Not his idea of dancing. No, what worked for him was . . .

He thought about Patrick Swayze and those girls in that old movie *Dirty Dancing,* where the summer staff got all raunchy together. . .

He imagined Maura, dressed all sexy like the girls in that movie . . .

Getting down and dirty on the dance floor . . .

Except her partner wasn't Swayze, it was Jesse.

It was Jesse who had his thigh between her legs, Jesse she was grinding her pelvis against. And she had her hair down. She tossed her head and those red-gold tresses swirled like wildfire.

His hands gripped her waist and she leaned back, laughing, to run both hands through her hair and toss it. Her head swung from side to side as her pelvis made circles against his. Her whole body moved sensually in time to the music. The music was . . .

The theme song from some stupid TV show. Crap.

Consuela had flicked the tube back on. Thank God, or he'd have lost control of his body again.

She glanced at him, her expression kind of beaten down. "Is there even any point dating? I mean, at some point I gotta tell the guy, don't I, Jesse? Tell him I can't have any more kids?" Pollan had done that to her, too, when he got out of prison. "What man's gonna want me?"

Jesse felt guilty as hell for having relied on the law rather than stopping Pollan himself, years earlier than he had. "Jeez, Con, you can't think that way. You and Juanito are great. Any guy'd be damn lucky." He went over and dropped a kiss on the top of her head. "Night. See you Monday."

"Night. And thanks, Jesse. You're the best."

Not hardly. It was his fault Con couldn't have kids.

As Jesse rode home, he thought about stopping for a drink at Low Down. Hang out with the guys, shoot some pool. But then he'd probably settle in for a few more drinks, maybe screw up tomorrow. His lawyer had told him to be careful, and he guessed he ought to listen. If it hadn't been for Barry Adamson, his butt would be cooling in a prison cell right now rather than hugging the leather seat of his Harley.

Riding the bike was great, but there was one thing that would make it even better. A warm, sexy female on behind him. He could just imagine . . .

Arms tight around his waist . . .

Chapter 6

Maura's arms, squeezing him. Her face snuggled into his shoulder. She wasn't wearing a helmet.

Her breasts pressed into his back and she nipped his neck. He didn't have a helmet, either, he realized. His hair blew back in the wind and hers did, too. Even though he was riding the bike, somehow he could see the two of them from the outside, with that flag of fiery hair streaming out behind them like a flame.

Her hands were clasped across his belt. He took one of them and moved it down, spreading it across the front of his fly where he was already hard for her.

She accepted the invitation, pressing tight, sliding her hand up and down. A horn honked and—

"Hey buddy, get a move on before it goes red again!" someone hollered.

He gaped at the light, then gunned it and roared away. Why the fuck couldn't he fantasize about Gracie, not Maura? Tomorrow, maybe he'd see if Gracie felt like seeing a movie. See if she could drive Maura out of his mind.

Back at his apartment, he peeled off his jacket, hung it up, and sank down in his comfy old recliner. He flicked through the movie channels, looking for distraction. Though everything else in his apartment was what Con called "bachelor minimal," his television was a fifty-incher, and state of the art.

He paused, recognizing a scene from *Crazy, Stupid, Love,* the movie that said lucky people have soul mates. Emma Stone looked a little like Maura, with her beautiful face, greenish eyes, and red hair. Except Maura's eyes were more striking and her hair more of a reddish-gold, and silkier . . .

Shit. He flipped channels again and the strains of *Moon River* filled the room. He groaned. Audrey Hepburn. Hell, it seemed that tonight everything was going to remind him of Maura Mahoney.

Crazy, Stupid, Love or *Moon River?* If any of his guy friends caught him watching this shit, he'd never live it down, but the truth was, he liked a good chick flick just as much as action adventure.

Holly Golightly stood on the deserted street outside Tiffany's in her cocktail dress and high-piled hair, drinking her breakfast coffee and munching a croissant, gazing in the window. He had to grin. This movie got to him.

Maybe because they were all losers. The girl who took money from men, the gigolo who lived off an older woman, even the no-name cat. Losers like him, yet together they found, or created, something that mattered. If there was hope for the three of them . . .

He grabbed a beer from the fridge, then sprawled on the couch with his feet up on the coffee table.

Back at her apartment, Maura plunked her autographed copy of *The Search for the Real Nefertiti* on the coffee table. For once her parents had come up with a gift that looked semiinteresting, but tonight she needed—she deserved—lighter fare.

And she knew just what she wanted. In fact, she'd timed her departure from the restaurant around the TV schedule that she'd studied last night. Her birthday had begun happily, and it would end happily, and she'd let the magic of a favorite movie obliterate everything in between.

In the kitchen, she mixed cocoa powder, sugar, and milk in a pan, leaving it on low heat. Then she washed her face, peeled off her work clothes, and slipped into soft cotton pajamas. A couple of giant marshmallows on top of her hot chocolate, and she was ready.

She swung open the doors to the antique wardrobe, revealing the television hidden within. Seconds later, propped up on pillows in bed, she sighed with pleasure at the sight of Holly Golightly outside Tiffany's.

Two hours later, Maura watched through tear-flooded eyes as Holly claimed her no-name cat, then turned to Paul, her eyes telling him that she knew they belonged to each other. The three embraced in the pouring rain, and that New York alley became heaven on earth.

Maura blew her nose prodigiously, then gave a satisfied sigh, clicked off the television, and closed the doors of the wardrobe. Her guilty secret—indulged, then hidden away again.

She brushed her teeth and climbed into bed. What a sweet guy George Peppard's Paul had been. Flawed in the beginning, but he'd become Holly's true friend. He understood Holly's frailties, yet loved her all the same. How could she have helped but fall in love with him, and trust him with her battered heart?

Snuggling down in the covers, Maura yawned. Once, she'd hoped to find a man like that herself. Increasingly, she'd come to believe they only existed in the movies. But oh, wouldn't it be wonderful? Smiling dreamily, she hugged the spare pillow against her . . .

And relived that final scene . . .

It was raining . . . Cold, nasty rain . . .

But Maura didn't mind a bit because warm arms encir-

cled her. Her and her cat. She hugged the cat and Jesse
hugged her. They were a family now, no longer drifting—
or, if they were, they'd do it together. Chasing the same
rainbow's end . . .

She sighed contentedly as Jesse's strength sheltered her
and his body heat counteracted the cold.

"Maura?" Jesse said, his voice husky.

She glanced up. Somehow, magically, it had stopped
raining.

And they were no longer in an alley full of garbage cans.
They were in a park, with lush grass underfoot and cherry
trees flowering overhead.

"It's so beautiful," she murmured.

"You're so beautiful."

He released her and for a moment she felt bereft, but all
he was doing was taking off his leather jacket, tossing it on
the grass. The cat meowed and Maura leaned down to free
it. It twined itself around their ankles, as if it were weav-
ing a spell to keep them together.

Maura gazed at Jesse. "We belong together," she said.
"The three of us."

He leaned toward her, those tawny eyes warm with affection and desire. His mouth captured hers and she
moaned with pleasure. His lips were soft on hers, gentle,
almost teasing. Then his kiss became more intense, and inside her she felt a quickening, a thrill of desire.

A sudden breeze rustled the cherry tree above them,
and a cascade of blossoms drifted down. "Oh, look, Jesse,
it's pink snow."

She captured a blossom that had landed on his shoulder
and held it to her nose. What a sweet, perfect scent.

He reached behind her head and began to take out the
pins that fastened her hair into its elaborate Holly Golightly style. His fingers were deft; he didn't even look to
see what he was doing. Instead he watched her face, occa-

sionally leaning forward to scatter small kisses across her forehead, her nose, her cheeks.

Her lips yearned for him, but he avoided them.

He ran his fingers through her hair, and she realized he had removed the last pin. He leaned over and buried his face in her hair, then, finally, he kissed her lips. It was a quick kiss, only whetting her appetite.

He took her hand, tugged it gently. "Lie down with me."

Vaguely, she wondered where their cat had gone, but then she and Jesse were sinking together to the grass and it was soft, so soft, under her. She sat, leaning back on one hand, reaching the other to touch his cheek. "Jesse . . ."

He gathered a handful of pale pink petals from the grass and scattered them in her hair. "You look like a wood nymph. A princess. Titania."

She gave a blissful sigh. Who would have guessed that Jesse Blue knew *A Midsummer Night's Dream*? That he could be so poetic?

He stretched out beside her and she leaned over him, petals drifting down from her hair. She took that sexy gold earring between her teeth and tugged gently.

He chuckled.

Then she nipped his earlobe and ran her tongue around the inside.

He stopped chuckling and gave a soft groan.

She trailed kisses down his neck and across his Adam's apple. Today, she was the snake, tempting him—though he wasn't putting up much of a fight. His hands were warm on her back, lifting her blouse, insinuating their way underneath. Caressing bare skin and moving up to the fastener of her bra.

He was wearing a black T-shirt and she kissed her way around the neck of it. Then she said, in a seductive growl, "Take it off."

"Only if you do the same."

At that moment his fingers unfastened the clasp of her bra. "I'll . . . think about it," she murmured, suddenly nervous. "You first."

Breathless, she watched as he sat up to strip off the T-shirt. First, he tugged it free from his jeans, then he crossed his arms in front of him, each hand grabbing an edge of the bottom. He began to peel the cloth upward, and she saw a flat, bronzed stomach, then an arching rib cage, then firm muscles, dark curls of hair, small nipples. Everything was so foreign, so very male, so absolutely perfect.

She leaned down to bury her face in his chest, but his hands gripped her shoulders. "Now you."

Her breasts, confined inside her blouse, inside her unhooked bra, were heavy. Aching. For his touch. She might be nervous, but yes, she wanted this. "Unbutton me," she murmured.

Those deft fingers went to the top button of her blouse and he slipped it free, then moved down, one by one. Her blouse separated slightly, and he made no effort to pull the sides apart. It was like he was drawing out the moment, the anticipation.

Then he said, "Take it off, Maura."

With shaky hands she obeyed, easing her way out of the blouse, holding it bundled in front of her for a long moment, then finally tossing it to the floor. She realized they were in bed now, a huge bed with ivory sheets and pillowcases with embroidered edges. She was entranced by the sight of Jesse's dark masculinity against the pristine sheets.

"So beautiful," he murmured.

She glanced down at herself, startled to see that her bra, barely clinging to her breasts now, was a lacy peach-colored one. When had she acquired that? But that thought fled, too, as Jesse reached up to peel the fabric away from her, his hand so brown compared to her pale skin and the pastel fabric.

Her nipples were hard, blatantly inviting him to touch them. And he accepted the invitation. He cupped her breasts in his hands, and she felt the roughness of his skin abrade delicate female flesh, a sensation the likes of which she'd never experienced before.

His eyes were glazed with desire. He opened his mouth and said—

"It's seven o'clock and a beautiful sunny Sunday morning."

Maura jerked awake and slapped at the clock-radio beside her bed. *Aagh!* What the heck was she doing dreaming about Jesse Blue? Dreaming about things she'd never experienced—not even during intercourse—things she must have subconsciously absorbed from movies and books?

And here she was, feeling all swollen and achy and . . . aroused again. She'd turned thirty and suddenly all her female hormones, which had pretty much lain dormant all her life, had kicked into overdrive. Yes, it had to be a hormonal thing, or otherwise surely she'd have felt this way about Bill or Winston. This . . . lust couldn't relate specifically to Jesse Blue. Could it?

But if it had to do with turning thirty, why hadn't she felt the slightest bit of attraction to Edward, the considerate, intelligent man who would dovetail so perfectly into her and her parents' lives?

Disgruntled, she got ready for work. A shower, a quick breakfast in her robe, then she dressed in a tailored taupe skirt, a short-sleeved pale green blouse, and a sage-green cardigan. She chose flat shoes, recalling with a grimace that today she had to go plant shopping with Jesse. How could she face him, after that ridiculous lurid dream?

She could at least postpone the inevitable.

When she arrived at Cherry Lane, she greeted Mingmei, the petite woman at the reception desk. Gracie was off today, so Maura said, "A man named Jesse Blue should be coming in at nine. He's doing some work on the court-yard garden. Louise arranged it. Tell him to go ahead, please, and call me when he arrives." Yesterday, she'd noticed that Jesse didn't wear a watch, and she wondered if he'd be on time—or if he was still tangled up in sweaty sheets with some sexy woman.

At eight fifty, trying to again work on the budget, Maura's gaze flicked to the time display in the bottom corner of her computer screen, and again at eight fifty-three. She jumped when, shortly after that, her phone rang.

Eight fifty-five, she noted, as Ming-mei informed her that Jesse was on his way out to the garden. She also noted that Ming-mei was completely businesslike. There was no gushing à la Gracie, or sour comments as with Nedda.

Being equally businesslike, Maura opened a new spread-sheet and recorded the date and Jesse's arrival time. She frowned over what to enter for yesterday. What kind of supervisor was she? She'd been so off balance that she'd forgotten to keep track of his time, but she did recall it had been around six when he left, so he'd certainly put in his full day.

That task done, she allowed herself to glance out the window, sitting some ways back in her chair in hopes Jesse couldn't see her. He retrieved the tools that he'd tucked neatly under an overhang of the building, and lugged them to where he'd left off work. A moment later, he was busy digging.

Today, he wore work clothes. Disreputable jeans that were so ripped it was a wonder they held together. A gray tank top with tears of its own. The top was tucked into his jeans, but he wasn't wearing a belt as he had yesterday. A sweat band held back his hair. There was no sign of the leather jacket. Today's style was early Rambo. He looked even more the male animal today than yesterday, if such a thing were possible.

She watched for a few minutes, telling herself she was just doing her job as a supervisor, but she kept remembering this morning's dream and comparing the dream image to the man who labored in the garden. Had she underestimated the muscles of his chest? Did he have more or less hair than she'd imagined?

Her cheeks, her whole body, burned. Was it hot in here or what? She peeled off her cardigan and fanned her hand briskly in front of her face.

One thing she knew for sure, Jesse Blue sure as heck wouldn't know who Titania was. She laughed. What an idiotic dream! Even down to the no-name cat and the lacy bra.

She forced her eyes away from Jesse and got going on her budget presentation for the Board meeting.

"Maura," a female voice spoke from the doorway, "please excuse me for interrupting."

She glanced up. "Yes, Ming-mei?"

The receptionist was always so serious and diligent. Maura respected her and recognized a kindred spirit. She wondered if it bothered the young woman that people liked effervescent Gracie better than her. Or did Ming-mei even notice?

"Mrs. Wolchuk is here. She'd like to have another tour."

The woman, in her early seventies Maura recalled, was trying to decide whether the time had come to leave the house she'd lived in for almost fifty years. This would be her third tour of Cherry Lane. Clearly, it was a tough decision, as it was for many seniors.

"Do you have time to show her around?" Maura asked.

"Yes, of course, but she's brought her dog."

Aagh. Cherry Lane allowed pets only in the one room that was used for animal-assisted therapy. While a number of the residents loved animals, many others suffered from allergies. "I'll come talk to her and we'll figure out what to do."

Maura grabbed her cardigan and walked to the reception area with Ming-mei. Mrs. Wolchuk was a fluffy little person with shaggy white hair and a fringed ivory shawl, and her dog was a fluffy little creature, too. They made a cute pair. "It's good to see you again, Mrs. Wolchuk. But I thought you knew, you can't bring your dog here."

"I know I can't if I move here. But it was such a nice day, I walked here, and Boopsy needed the exercise, too." She leaned down to pat the dog, and it looked up at her adoringly, brown bug-eyes peeping out from its mop of hair.

Maura sighed. Louise—or even Gracie—would have known what to do. She glanced at Ming-mei, who shrugged helplessly.

Inspiration struck. "Let's put Boopsy in the courtyard. It's enclosed. There's a gardener working there. Jesse can make sure she . . . he? . . . comes to no harm."

"She," Mrs. Wolchuk said. "That's fine, dear."

"Good. Ming-mei, would you—"

"Ming-mei!" someone called. "Could you come help?"

They all swung around and Maura saw Mr. Chen's daughter struggling to fold up his wheelchair. The middle-aged woman always picked up her dad and took him home for the day on Sundays.

If Maura offered to help, she could avoid Jesse a while longer. *The mature person never shirks responsibility.* Her parents were right. She needed to act like a general manager, not a coward. "You go and help," she told Ming-mei resignedly. "I'll look after Mrs. Wolchuk and Boopsy."

She led the woman and her dog toward the courtyard. Steeling herself, she opened the door and stepped down, turning to steady the woman who followed her. Then she gritted her teeth, straightened her spine, and faced Jesse.

He must not have heard the door open, because he was

bending over, flipping the turf he'd removed and laying it back down, soil side up. She walked closer, admiring the view. He really did have a great backside. The tank top had pulled out of his jeans, baring a patch of brown skin at his waist.

Her fingers twitched restlessly and she laced them firmly together. She shouldn't be noticing Jesse's butt, or that bare skin. "Jesse?"

He froze, then slowly straightened and turned toward her.

"Good morning." She forced herself to look him in the eyes, aware that her cheeks must be bright pink. Maybe he'd just think she was incredibly sensitive to the sun.

He seemed to be avoiding her own eyes as he muttered, "Mornin'." He rubbed a gloved hand across his jaw, leaving a smear of dirt.

Her hand itched to wipe it away, and she clenched her fingers together more tightly. Of course, she told herself, the urge was only because she abhorred mess, not because she wanted to touch his brown skin. She tilted her head toward the visitor. "Mrs. Wolchuk is taking a look at Cherry Lane. I thought we could leave Boopsy out here."

Until she said the dog's name again, she hadn't realized how silly it was.

His eyes met hers for the first time. He raised an eyebrow. "Boopsy." His voice was almost level, but there was a hint of something in it that told her he was suppressing a laugh.

Hearing the ridiculous name spoken in that gravelly voice made her want to chuckle too, but she held it in. "Yes, Boopsy."

"Uh-huh." He studied the dog.

What a mismatched pair they were, the ball of white fluff and the tall, rugged gypsy with his gold earring. Then Jesse squatted down, removed a glove, and held out his hand for the dog to sniff. "Hey, *Boopsy*. Want to hang out with me?"

Each time one of them said the dog's name, Maura's urge to laugh grew stronger. She sensed it was the same with him, and couldn't resist saying, "You take good care of *Boopsy* now."

He made a choked sound, quickly raised one hand to shield his face, and looked up at Maura. His eyes, above the hand, danced with glee.

Glee so infectious that she grinned at him.

His eyes sparkled, and for a long moment their gazes held.

Then Boopsy yapped, demanding attention.

Maura caught her breath, forcing her attention away from Jesse to the dog. Her heart raced. For that little space in time, she'd forgotten who he was—a criminal; a super-hot guy; the person she was supervising—and dropped her guard. And they'd connected. Really connected. In a way she rarely did with people.

It was a small thing, really. Just shared humor over the dog's silly name. It shouldn't feel significant, and yet it did.

That person is not our type. Agnes and Timothy had said it about Sally, and they'd feel even more strongly about Jesse.

Disconcerted, she turned her attention to Mrs. Wolchuk and said briskly, "So you're seriously considering moving to Cherry Lane?"

"Maybe, but I don't know what I'd do without my Boopsy."

Maura, who had never had a pet, couldn't relate personally, but she did sympathize. "How old is she?"

"Nine. She's still got a number of good years."

And yet the dog was old enough that it would be hard to find another home for her if Mrs. Wolchuk moved to Cherry Lane.

"Do you have any pets, dear?" the elderly woman asked.

"I'm not allowed to in the building I live in."

Jesse gave a low snort and Maura glared at him, wondering what his problem was. That moment of connection was clearly a thing of the past—if he'd even felt it in the first place. "Mrs. Wolchuk," she said with saccharine sweetness, "this is Jesse Blue. Jesse, do you have any pets?"

"I'm not home much."

She wrinkled her nose. He probably had a bevy of beauties who invited him over for home-cooked meals in exchange for mind-blowing sex. No, she—not Jesse—was the one who could use a little companionship at home.

Pets take over your life. That was what her parents had said, and they hadn't believed her when she'd sworn that she'd do all the caring-for. Lonely so much of the time in their big apartment, she'd pleaded first for a puppy, then for a kitten. She'd have been willing to compromise on almost anything—a hamster, budgie, even a turtle—but they had never agreed. After a while she'd stopped asking, then even thinking about pets.

It was true that her apartment building didn't allow dogs and cats, but if she wanted, she could have a bird. Perhaps a parrot, a bird that spoke. A voice to greet her when she came home, to fill the empty silence of her apartment. She'd lived so much of her life with silence, and the thought of a voice—even a bird's voice—was appealing.

She shook her head to clear it and returned her attention to Mrs. Wolchuk. "Let's go inside and Ming-mei will give you a tour."

After getting Mrs. Wolchuk set, Maura returned to her office and got on with her work. It was perhaps half an hour later when she glanced out the window to see Boopsy barrel across the grass to Jesse and drop something at his feet. Maura squinted. It was his glove. Jesse picked up the glove and hurled it across the courtyard. The dog took off after it, her furry little legs flying.

Maura chuckled and shook her head. If Jesse Blue got blisters, he couldn't blame it on her.

"How's my Boopsy?" Mrs. Wolchuk, who'd returned to the courtyard looking sad-faced, asked Jesse.

"Happy to see you, from the sounds of it."

The woman leaned down and gathered the barking dog into her arms. Boopsy squirmed excitedly and, as the woman tried to kiss the animal's face, the dog got in a few licks of her own. When Mrs. Wolchuk put her pet back down, Boopsy bounced around on her hind feet.

Jesse smiled. In their case, owner and dog really did look alike. He retrieved his work glove from where the dog had dropped it, straightened, and put it back on. "How'd the tour go?"

A frown tightened the elderly woman's face, but before she could answer, his boss called, "Mrs. Wolchuk?"

He turned, to see her striding toward them. When Maura had first come into the garden this morning, his mind was still so full of last night's wild fantasies that he'd been unable to meet her eye. But then they'd started joking about the dog's name, and she'd become . . . human. Nice. Something had happened between them, and he'd liked it. For that moment before she'd gone all cool and businesslike again.

He liked how she looked, too. She was all buttoned up, but today she wore a skirt that revealed damned fine legs, and her cardigan was the green of aspen leaves.

Man, she was sexy. Consuela's clothes were way tighter, but there was something about the way that sweater just skimmed Maura's breasts. It didn't cling, the neckline wasn't low, yet it left no doubt about the curvy female flesh beneath it.

Oh, Jesus, he was getting hard again.

He dropped to his knees, pulled off his gloves, and ruffled the little dog's fluffy coat. Boopsy gave a pleased yip and licked his hand.

"Did you enjoy your tour?" Maura asked the old lady.

A note of concern in her voice made him look up, and he saw it echoed in her expression.

Mrs. Wolchuk sighed heavily. "This is a nice place, but it's not home. Besides, I'll have to give up Boopsy if I come here. I can't bear it."

"So don't move," Jesse said.

Maura frowned at him, and Mrs. Wolchuk shook her head. "I don't want to, but my house is starting to fall down around me."

Those few words gave him a good idea of the whole picture. Alone in the world, or with kids who couldn't be bothered to help. No money to hire people to fix her house. It was a damned shame. "That's too bad," he muttered.

"It's a fine house," she told him eagerly. "Only a few blocks away. The white one with green trim over on Linden Street. Do you know it?"

When he shook his head, she went on. "I raised two children in that house. Celebrated forty-five anniversaries before Albert passed away. Now it's just Boopsy and me, but it's still home."

Jesse figured that if he ever had a real home, he'd be pretty damned reluctant to give it up, too.

Maybe after work he'd ride by Mrs. Wolchuk's house. See how bad it was. There might be something he could do. On his construction job, scraps of lumber and other odds and ends were often left over. And he had lots of connections in the industry, could get stuff at wholesale prices. He could do the work himself. Like he'd told Maura Mahoney, he was good with his hands.

Mrs. Wolchuk kneeled down beside Jesse, not caring if

her tan pants got grass-stained. She stroked the dog and Boopsy lapped her hand affectionately.

Jesse sat on the grass hugging his knees, watching the two of them. Sure would be nice if the old gal didn't have to part with her dog.

Maura bent down to pat Boopsy. She seemed hesitant at first, then more enthusiastic as the fluffball squirmed happily at her touch. The dog rewarded her with a couple of healthy licks. She jerked her hand back.

"A few dog germs won't kill you," Jesse said softly.

Maura narrowed her eyes and stared at Boopsy. The dog laughed up at her, and Maura gave the dog another cautious pat, staying out of the reach of her tongue.

Jesse shook his head. He'd almost bet she'd never had a pet. Probably too messy and undisciplined for her.

His boss-lady glanced back his way, assessingly. He guessed that lounging on the grass and playing with dogs probably didn't count as community service. "Goin' to need those bedding plants soon," he told her, getting to his feet.

"I'd better head home," Mrs. Wolchuk said. "There's a bingo game and potluck dinner at the Polish Community Center tonight, and I need to make pyrogies." She glanced at Jesse. "If you're looking for good food, come along as my guest. I owe you, for looking after Boopsy."

"You don't owe me," he mumbled as Maura said, "I'm sure Jesse has other plans."

In fact, he'd planned to ask Gracie, the bubbly red-headed receptionist, out tonight, but it turned out she had Sundays and Mondays off.

Maura escorted the old lady to the door of the building, then returned, pulling her notepad and pen from the pocket of her cardigan. She clicked the pen, opened the pad, and handed it to him. "Is there anything you want to add?"

He glanced down at the white page with its blue lines

and her written notes. She had neat handwriting, and if he worked hard at it, he could probably figure out most of these words. But it would take too long, the effort would be too obvious. He handed it back. "Think that's it. Wanna go now?"

Her jaw firmed, and he guessed that being alone with him was pretty much the last thing she wanted. But he was getting to know her. She had a strong sense of duty.

"We'll take the Cherry Lane minivan," she said.

"I'll go wash up. Just be a sec." He headed for the door into the building. He'd expected her to follow, but when he glanced back she was still standing there. For a practical woman, she sure did go off into la-la land on a regular basis.

He yanked off the sweatband that held his hair out of his eyes and stepped through the door.

Maura watched Jesse go, the slanting sun dazzling her eyes, blurring her vision . . .

He was going to wash up. Straightforward words for simple actions. Wash up . . .

He pulled off that Rambo sweatband and . . .

Dark curls tumbled free . . .

He shook them back, and the movement was a strong, proud one. Almost arrogant, yet unselfconscious.

He was standing at the sink now, washing his hands. Squirting on lots of soap, working up a lather, his hands moving sensuously against each other.

He held them under the tap and the suds rinsed away, leaving his skin wet and gleaming, his hands brown and strong. Hands that would fascinate a sculptor or painter.

Hands that would seduce any woman who laid eyes on them.

He leaned over the sink and splashed water on his face, then straightened. Drops tangled in his long eyelashes, ran down his cheeks, dripped off his chin, darkened the gray tank top that was already damp from his sweat. Lit on his shoulders, muscular brown shoulders that flexed as he moved.

He leaned down again and this time splashed water on his hair, soaking it, letting the water sluice over his head. He moaned with pleasure, then ran his hands over his wet hair, squeezing out moisture. He straightened and shook his head, in a lazy, slow motion. Droplets flew out like the spray from the rickety sprinkler in the garden, and he laughed. His laugh was a husky, delighted rumble, and there were sparkly golden lights in his hazel eyes.

His tank top was quite wet now over his shoulders and chest. It clung to his body, highlighting the muscles underneath. Muscles developed through hard work. Lean and sculpted, not the gross, overdeveloped ones of a body builder. Muscles that, if she touched them, would feel—

"You ready?" Jesse called.

Ready? Ready to touch him? No, wait. Maura jolted out of her trance. Good God, she was still standing in the courtyard, and he was at the door, calling to her. She growled with exasperation. She was losing her flipping mind.

It was bad enough to have sensual dreams when she was sound asleep. Having sex fantasies in the middle of a bright, sunny day was simply unacceptable.

As she hurried toward Jesse, she took in the damp hair, face, shoulders. The way the tank top clung to the muscles of his chest. Under it she could see the buds of his nipples, hard against the soft cotton.

Her own nipples tightened in reaction, and she barely managed to hold back a gasp as she forced herself to walk past him. "I'll get the keys and meet you at the front door."

Chapter 7

Her hip bumped the door frame and she rubbed the sore spot absentmindedly as she hurried to her office. This was absurd. She'd never had these kinds of thoughts in her life. Well, not since she was in high school, with Sally egging her on. Wicked thoughts, but even then, they'd been more romantic than explicitly sexual.

Teenagers were supposed to be ruled by hormones, but she hadn't been. In her twenties, she'd had two lovers and barely felt aroused. Now, she was making up for lost time. She'd heard that women reached their sexual peak in their thirties. She had guessed she might be frigid, but maybe not. Maybe she just hadn't reached her peak.

So these strange physical symptoms and sexual fantasies might be perfectly natural. She bit her lip. It would be nice to be able to ask someone. She couldn't imagine talking to Agnes—to think of her adoptive mother and sex in the same breath made her grimace—and definitely not the staid old family doctor. As usual, she'd do her learning from books.

If Sally had still been in her life, she'd have had a friend to ask about this.

No, if Sally had been in her life, her life would be very different from what it was today. Quite possibly, she'd have ended up in jail—or doing community service like Jesse Blue.

The thought gave her pause, and again she wondered what crime the man had committed. Street racing, automobile theft, a brawl? Surely nothing really dangerous or despicable, or Louise would never have agreed to let him work at Cherry Lane. Indecent exposure, like having sex on a public beach? Now that, she could clearly envision . . .

Jesse's brown body, naked against pale sand—

No! No, she absolutely wasn't going to fantasize again.

Where had Louise put the file? Quickly, Maura phoned Ming-mei. "Has Louise called in? Yesterday, it looked like their birth mom was going into labor."

"No, she hasn't. I hope everything's all right."

"So do I. If she does call, would you ask if there's a file on Jesse Blue? I can't find it."

"Of course."

Maura unlocked a desk drawer and took out the Cherry Lane charge card and the keys to the minivan, then grabbed her purse and went to get Jesse.

He was waiting for her outside the main entrance, leaning against a cherry tree. When he saw her coming, he moved toward her, running his hand through his hair. There'd be no stray cherry blossoms today.

She led the way to the minivan, which was equipped for transporting people with wheelchairs. She couldn't imagine sharing her tiny silver Smart Car with Jesse. It would be too close, too intimate.

Awkward in her pencil skirt—why hadn't she worn pants?—she clambered into the driver's seat of the minivan as Jesse vaulted easily into the passenger seat. Even in the roomy van, he took up way too much room. It wasn't that he was huge, just that he was so . . . present. So male and physical.

As she put the van into Drive, she noted his bare arm. He seemed so much more naked today, in the tank top. Not to mention the old jeans. She glanced across, seeing skin peep through a series of rips across his left thigh. He did up his seat belt and shifted position, getting comfortable, wriggling his hips deeper into the seat.

Her eyes traveled up his thigh. The jeans weren't exactly tight but they were snug enough—or he was well endowed enough—that she had a disturbing sense of what lay beneath them. It had been a long time since she'd seen a naked man, but she got the impression Jesse's male equipment was something rather special.

A fact she was sure many women appreciated. It irked her that she was one of them.

"Waitin' for something?" he asked.

Maura dragged her gaze up to meet Jesse's and faked an excuse for her wool-gathering. "I'm trying to decide where to go. There's a nursery out by the big discount food store, isn't there?"

"Not there. I know a place."

Oh, well then. Obviously they'd go to the place *he* knew. Lord but the man could be exasperating.

She jerked the van away from the curb. She rarely drove it, didn't like driving it, and it seemed ten times the size of her car.

Jesse gave her directions and she followed them, feeling self-conscious. On the highway, she settled into the right-hand lane, trying to ignore the cars that zipped past. She always drove just under the speed limit, and today it seemed as if they were crawling. He hadn't asked to drive—not that she'd have let him—but she guessed he was dying to take the wheel and stomp down on the gas pedal. Burn rubber. Yes, he was probably one of those guys who burned rubber. A stupid habit. For some reason, they seemed to think it made them sexy.

Or maybe he wouldn't do that. Maybe he was confident enough of his own sexuality—God knows, he had enough reason to be—that he didn't need to posture about it.

The cell phone rang, from deep inside the purse she'd tossed on the back seat. Few people called her cell, but it might be Ming-mei. Though the girl was diligent, she was much better at soliciting instructions than in using her initiative to find solutions.

"I need to get that." Maura flicked on the right turn signal and pulled hurriedly onto the shoulder of the highway. "Can you grab my bag?"

She shifted into Park and turned toward Jesse. As he handed her the purse, his arm brushed hers, making her jump at the contact even through her sweater.

Her phone was set to go to voice mail after eight rings, so she scrabbled it hurriedly from her bag and answered. "Yes?"

"Hello? Maura?" It was a male voice, one she didn't recognize.

"Yes. Who is this?"

"It's Edward Mortimer. From last night?"

She rolled her eyes at the last bit. Yes, he was the unmemorable perfect spy, but it had only been a few hours ago. "Good morning."

"I wanted to tell you how much I enjoyed meeting you. It was a very pleasant evening, and particularly nice for an out-of-towner to meet someone, uh, nice."

"Thanks. I enjoyed the evening, too." It was only a white lie, and he did seem like a *nice* guy, even if he was unexciting. But then, the same could certainly be said of her.

"I hope you don't mind, but your father gave me your cell number."

Obviously, Timothy figured she would come to no harm in Edward's hands. And, she feared, no great pleasure, either.

Edward was going on, but his words were lost in the roar of a big truck passing far too close. The minivan, sizable though it was, rocked on its wheels.

Jesse was saying something, too, his expression urgent, but she didn't catch his words, either. When the truck had passed, she said to him, "Excuse me?"

Edward's voice in her ear said, "I was saying that—"

"Not you. I was speaking to someone else. Could you hold on a minute, please?"

She frowned at Jesse, who'd been rude enough to interrupt. "What?"

"You shouldn't park here. It's dangerous. We could get sideswiped."

He was right, and she hated that he was right.

She said into the phone, "I'm sorry, Edward, I'm in the middle of something and this isn't a good time. Could you call this afternoon?"

"Oh, I'll only be a minute. There's a lecture tomorrow evening that promises to be quite intriguing."

What part of "this isn't a good time" hadn't he heard?

He went on. "Professor Merrymont from Oxford has done a fascinating bit of research on—"

Another truck roared by, drowning his words and making the minivan shake. Research? He should date her parents. "I can't," she snapped into the phone. "Thanks anyhow." She flipped the phone shut and handed it to Jesse.

"Yikes," he said. "Poor bastard."

She glared at him. "I'd appreciate your not using that language around me."

"I'd appreciate your not endangering my life by parking somewhere you shouldn't, just so you can conduct your busy social life," he snapped back.

She gripped the wheel with both hands, fuming. How

could he have the audacity to suddenly turn articulate, just to criticize her so . . . justifiably!

Maura grimaced. Fair was fair. "You're right." She started the engine, shifted into Drive, and checked on-coming traffic. As she pulled out cautiously, she said, "I'm not used to driving the van. And I thought the call was from Cherry Lane, and I'm in charge so I wanted to an-swer. But I shouldn't have."

"Oh." He sounded surprised and said nothing more for a few seconds. Then, "Sorry I swore."

An apology. How about that? "Apology accepted."

"Shouldn't have commented on your personal life, ei-ther."

Her eyebrows flew up. She'd just stopped at a stop sign so it was safe to turn and study his face.

He gave her a grin and for once it seemed genuine, not cocky.

It disarmed her. As she pulled away from the stop sign she found herself saying, "When you go out on dates, what do you do?" She was sure that other people had more interesting dates than attending academic lectures.

He didn't answer and she glanced toward him. The in-solent, teasing look was back. She replayed her question and gave a little gasp. "I didn't mean . . ." She could guess how his dates ended. With hot sex. There was no way to stop the blush that flamed her cheeks.

He chuckled, a knowing, confident sound.

Quickly she said, "I didn't mean to pry into your per-sonal life, I was just wondering what . . ." She didn't know how to finish that thought.

"What normal folks do on a date?" he asked dryly.

She thought of *Camelot,* of Arthur and Guinevere singing, *"What do the simple folk do?"* Was she coming across as a horrible snob? "Honestly, I didn't mean it that way. It's just, this man I met last night asked me to a lecture, some academic thing, and I'm sure it would be very interesting . . ." It would. An interesting lecture, in the company of a nice man. What more could a woman like her possibly want?

"But it's not every guy's idea of a hot date?"

A hot date? *She* wasn't any guy's idea of a hot date. "Somehow I don't think so."

"What's your idea of a hot date, Ms. Maura Mahoney?" He drawled out her name in that sexy way of his.

Maura gulped, trying to ignore the sultry gravel of his voice. A hot date? Her few-and-far-between dates often did involve lectures, or meals with families and colleagues, and occasionally the symphony. If she could go on the perfect date, what would it be? Drawing inspiration from the movies, she murmured, "Dinner and dancing. Somewhere elegant, with a view. All dressed up. Champagne."

"Caviar and truffles," he suggested.

"Yes!" She was warming to this now, building the image in her head. "Fresh flowers on the table. Live music, maybe a piano and saxophone." She half-closed her eyes, imagined dancing to that music. The only problem was, the man in the tux who swept her around the dance floor was Jesse Blue. How ridiculous. "So, that's mine." And not one she was ever likely to experience anywhere other than in her imagination. "Will you answer my question now?"

"Jeez, my dates are nothin' like that. We'll go see a movie. Go for a ride in the country, on the bike. Have a drink or two. Get a bite to eat, but not at that ritzy place with the champagne and fish eggs. Just, you know, pizza or something." He tugged on the frayed edge of one of the rips on his thigh.

How was she expected to keep her eyes on the road when he did that?

"Guess we got different tastes," he said.

"I guess." But the truth was, the activities he'd suggested sounded like fun. She *loved* pizza, darn it! And she'd never in her life ridden on a motorcycle, but she'd bet it was wild and exciting, sitting behind a man like Jesse, holding on tight as they swept around curves. As for movies, no one even knew she liked them because she'd been too . . . *repressed* to be honest about it. So, because she hated to go to the movies alone, she watched shows on Netflix or one of the TV movie channels.

Popular movies are junk food for the brain, she remembered Agnes saying. And though pizza wasn't junk food, it wasn't exactly health food, either. As for motorcycles, they could be downright dangerous.

She should be glad Edward had invited her to that lecture. The truth was, she rarely got asked out by any man, to do anything. She'd always been the odd one out, the awkward one who couldn't relate to girls her own age, much less boys. The only person who'd ever seen anything special in her was Sally, and look how that had ended up.

"Up there," Jesse said, pointing, diverting her from her depressing thoughts. "See that big green sign?"

"Sunnyside Nursery," she read, turning where he indicated.

When she'd parked in the large lot, they both climbed out and headed for the entrance.

Maura had never been in a garden center before, and she looked around curiously as she followed Jesse. The place bustled with activity and she guessed Sunday was their busiest day. Even so, it felt peaceful with all the greenery and pretty flowers. It smelled wonderful too, a fresh, heady scent.

Jesse led her to a section labeled BEDDING PLANTS, and an image flashed into her mind of ivory sheets and embroidered pillowcases with red rose petals strewn across them. Of a dark, muscular man with longish hair and a gold earring—

She stumbled and knocked against a ceramic pot over-flowing with abundant growth.

Jesse reached out one hand to steady the pot and the other to grip her arm.

Flustered, she pulled away from the seductive warmth of his touch. "I'm a klutz."

Something flashed in his eyes—annoyance? hurt?—before he said, "Yeah," and turned away from her to examine plants.

Not speaking, he moved from one table to the next.

She followed and finally asked, "What shall we get?"

"Plants like this." He gestured to flowers with orange, red, pink, and purple blossoms that were almost fluorescent.

She frowned. "They're awfully bright. How about something more subtle, like these." She pointed to decorous blossoms in white, mauve, and a delicate pale pink.

He snorted disapproval. "Your residents are old, not dead."

"What, exactly, do you mean?" she demanded.

"They don't want funeral flowers. They want something lively."

Just who did he think he was? Huffily, she responded, "I think I know our residents better than you do."

He breathed out air through his nose. "We'll get both."

He moved around confidently, picking up the little black plastic containers and checking the plants. His hands seemed huge next to the delicate blossoms, yet he handled the plants gently. Oh, yes, he was good with his hands . . .

She gulped and drew her mind back to business. "Should we make a list?"

"Nah."

She trailed him, feeling useless, hating being in a situation where she was ignorant. Grudgingly, she said, "You seem to know a lot about this."

He glanced up in surprise and flashed a smile that knocked the breath out of her. "Did some work with a landscape gardener. But it goes back further than that. One of my foster moms worked in a nursery. She took me along on the weekend, let me help out."

He'd said "let" not "made" him help out. Maura suspected most kids would have thought of it as a chore. But this foster child had clearly considered it a privilege to be allowed to assist his foster mother. Just as Maura had felt flattered when Agnes or Timothy—who'd saved her from a foster home—had let her help with some important project of theirs.

But he'd said . . . "*One* of your foster mothers?"

He put down the pot of yellow flowers he'd been inspecting and muttered, "I had a few."

Raised in foster homes. From what age? Was that upbringing partially responsible for whatever criminal behavior had landed him in court?

She realized Jesse had walked across to another table, and she trailed behind, still musing. But the sight of the plants on the table wiped everything else from her mind. "Geraniums." The word burst out spontaneously, with a childlike excitement that embarrassed her.

He gave a sardonic grin. "That's one for you."

She flushed. "We had a housekeeper when I was a little girl who kept a couple of pots of geraniums on the kitchen windowsill."

"Mmm."

She remembered Mrs. Eggleston fondly. The housekeeper had worked afternoons. Maura's newly acquired adoptive parents had spent long hours at the university, and Mrs. Eggleston had been the one to pick her up from school when she was in grades one through three. They'd sat together in the kitchen with milk and digestive biscuits, and Maura had chattered about her day. It had felt homey. Not as good as being with her real parents, who she still missed like crazy, but definitely one of the best things about her new home.

Then, when Maura was in grade four, Agnes and Timothy sent her to an after-school academic enrichment program and she hardly ever saw Mrs. Eggleston anymore.

"We should get some geraniums," she told Jesse.

"Sure. They'd be good there. They like sun."

Didn't all plants like sun? She brushed the thought away. "How are we going to do this? We really should make a list."

"Nah, I'll figure it out in my head. We'll order the plants and get most of them delivered this afternoon. Take a few with us to keep me going." He headed inside, passing under some lushly overflowing hanging baskets.

Maura stopped, entranced. "Jesse? These would look good by the front door."

He came back, looked up. "Pick the two you like best. I'll take them in and pick up plant hangers."

She deliberated for some time, looking at the baskets from all sides. Her first impulse was to go with a delicate pink and white one, but remembering what Jesse had said about the residents liking something lively, she instead chose ones with a mix of vivid colors. When she pointed them out, Jesse raised an eyebrow and she sensed an "I told you so" coming, but he held his tongue.

He stretched up to hook the baskets down, and the tank top pulled out of his jeans. There was a smudge of dirt on the brown skin of his back, just above his waist. At some point, he must have used a grubby hand to tuck his shirt in. She imagined her hand, sliding down inside those jeans, and had the most outrageous thought. What kind of underwear did he wear?

Did he even wear underwear?

Surely he must. It would be uncomfortable, that rough denim against sensitive naked skin. Wouldn't it?

For a moment, she closed her eyes, wondering what that naked skin would feel like. Firm, definitely. Velvet skin over solid muscle. Warm, because he gave off heat she could feel even when she stood a foot away.

Except . . . that heat had disappeared.

She opened her eyes. No Jesse.

Oh, there he was, inside the building already, plunking the baskets she'd chosen on the floor by the cashier's counter.

A blond woman in a green apron was helping a customer, but she favored Jesse with a big smile.

He began to roam about the store, collecting mysterious bags and bottles.

Maura gazed up at the baskets again. It would be nice to have one on the balcony of her apartment. And a geranium for her own kitchen window.

On her way to the geranium section, a fresh, tangy scent made her pause at a display of herbs. She read the names, rubbed a leaf of rosemary between her fingers and inhaled, then picked up a pot of basil. She loved those Italian caprese salads with basil, tomatoes, and bocconcini cheese. Some Thai dishes used basil, too. And here was parsley for garnish. Mint for her peas, or maybe to go in a glass of club soda.

She found a cardboard flat and began to fill it with little pots.

When she was finished, she put her box down under the hanging baskets and reached up to the one she had decided on. It was heavy and she was afraid she might drop it, so she glanced inside to enlist Jesse's help.

He stood at the cash register, laughing with the blonde. And Blondie—who was older than Maura by more than a few years, and looked a lot like Cameron Diaz—was smiling and laughing like he was the only man in the world. Jesse was flirting, when he was supposed to be working. And no, of course she wasn't jealous, just annoyed.

He turned and caught her watching. He beckoned her over. "Need your card."

Oh, fine, now he needed her—for her money. She handed him her notebook. "Are you sure you've got everything on the list we made yesterday?"

"Yup." He handed it back unopened.

She ground her teeth and gave the Cherry Lane credit card to the cashier. When the blonde handed her the slip, she saw that the total wasn't as high as she'd feared. With relief, she signed her name. "We'll need most of this delivered. Today, if possible."

The cashier smiled brightly. "Jesse and I've got that all arranged."

Maura would just bet that wasn't all they'd arranged. The cashier knew his name and he likely had her number, in more ways than one. Of course it was none of Maura's business if this middle-aged woman made a fool of herself with Jesse.

She remembered her own agenda. "Jesse, could you get another basket down for me? I want to take one home."

" 'Kay." He followed her over and unhooked the one she pointed out.

When she picked up the flat that held her own herbs and pink geranium, his mouth kinked up at one corner. "Kitchen windowsill?"

She shrugged. "I couldn't resist."

He gave her a warm smile that went a ways to restoring her good spirits, then carried the basket over to the blonde. When the woman began to ring up the purchases,

Jesse said to Maura, "Give me the key and I'll start loading the van."

Give the key to a man who'd been in trouble with the
law?

Their gazes met, a challenge in his.

She reached into the side pocket of her purse and
handed over the key, which he took with a nod. Likely
he knew this didn't mean she trusted him, only that she
didn't believe he was idiot enough to make off with the
van.

He squatted beside a couple of big bags of fertilizer, getting his arms around them. His butt pressed tight against
his jeans until Maura wondered if the ancient seams—or
her own blood pressure—might explode. Then he stood,
and his shoulder muscles strained as he balanced the
weight, one bag on each shoulder. Maura tried to imagine
Edward Mortimer lifting even one of those bags, and suppressed a giggle.

The giggle died abruptly when she turned back to the
counter and realized the cashier had been watching her
watch Jesse.

There was amusement in her eyes. She was probably
thinking how pathetic it was for a woman like Maura to
ogle a guy like Jesse. Fortunately, when she spoke she was
businesslike. "This stuff goin' to the same place? That seniors place?"

"No, this is just for me."

The woman gave her the total, and Maura paid with her
credit card as Jesse collected more of their purchases.
When she followed him to the van, it looked cheerful
with colorful blossoms from the hanging baskets poking
out here and there.

She climbed into the driver's seat and he jumped in beside her. As he reached close to her to fasten his seat belt,
she noticed that his skin glowed with a sheen of sweat. She

hadn't seen as much sweat in her entire life as she had the last two days. The men in her life simply didn't sweat. She didn't recall either of her two lovers breaking a sweat, even when they made love. Nor had they raised one from her, when it came to that.

In bed with Jesse Blue, a woman would sweat. Maura was sure of that. In fact she was beginning to sweat right now, just thinking about it. She rolled down her window and pulled off her cardigan, then fastened her seat belt. She was about to turn the key in the ignition when her cell phone rang.

Jesse watched Maura fumble in her bag for her phone— a different cell this time. "Good timing," he told her. She'd scared him earlier, when she put them in danger of being sideswiped by a semi.

She answered, then said, "Oh! Cindy, I didn't expect—"

He heard an animated female voice break in, but couldn't make out actual words. Should he get out of the van, give Maura some privacy? Nah. If she wanted him to, she'd say so. He leaned back against his open window and watched her out of the corner of his eye. She was acting flustered and he was curious.

"Oh," she said, "didn't I send that in?"

Her right hand clenched on the steering wheel. "Well, actually, I'm not sure I can. My schedule's pretty busy and—"

The other woman sure wasn't letting her finish a sentence. Though he still couldn't hear actual words, he got the impression of a high-powered sales pitch.

"No, I realize a lot of planning's gone into it," Maura said, finally managing a complete sentence.

Aha. Yet another person was issuing her an invitation she didn't want to accept. Earlier, he'd almost felt sorry for the poor schmuck Edward whom she'd rebuffed. But what a loser, asking her to a dull lecture when she was used to champagne and dancing.

He glanced at the long slender fingers tapping the steering wheel, the long shapely legs. He'd bet she was a fine dancer . . .

He flashed back to what he'd imagined last night, him and Maura dirty dancing. The kind of dancing that was like fucking standing up. His dick stirred to life and he shifted uncomfortably.

Maura glanced his way and he dropped an arm across his lap.

She refocused out the windshield. "Cindy, this isn't a good time."

A pause, then, "I do not have my head in a book. I'm with someone and—"

Her back went ramrod straight. "No, not my parents. As a matter of fact it's a man."

This time he caught the other woman's words, because they pretty much screeched out of the phone. "A man?"

"Yes, a man." A muscle twitched in Maura's cheek. "A very attractive man, in fact."

He started with surprise.

Her cheeks deepened from pink to red, all those cute freckles hidden by her blush now, as she stared straight ahead, listening. "Maybe I will," she said. The muscle twitched again. "Fine, I'll be there." A moment later, she exclaimed, "Yes, put me down as a plus one!" She slammed the flip-phone closed and buried her face in her hands.

Jesse had no idea why she was upset, but it was weird seeing his usually poised boss lose her cool. Cautiously, he said, "Sorry for eavesdropping, but did you just make me your plus one?" He must've got things wrong.

She raised her head and stared at him, face on fire. "I'm sorry. I shouldn't have said what I did. I . . . well, yes, I used you. I was so annoyed at Cindy. "

"Yeah. I got that." He was pretty sure she didn't really mean for him to be her date, but did she really find him attractive, or had she just said it to piss off this Cindy person? "Hey, it's okay." With a hint of sexual innuendo, he said, "You can use me anytime you want."

Her eyes widened, then she gave a splutter of laughter and banged her forehead with her fist. "I can't do anything right today. I can't even apologize properly." Her cheeks were still rosy, her eyes gleamed with humor, and he wanted to grab her face and plant a kiss on those smiling lips.

Fortunately, before he gave into the impulse, her lips straightened and she frowned. "Boy, have I got myself into a mess."

Should he ask? "Yeah?" he ventured tentatively.

"It's so silly. There's a high school reunion. It's next weekend and Cindy is calling all the people who haven't RSVP'd. I really don't want to go."

"So don't go."

"I told her I would."

"Got the impression she was pretty determined, but why'd you agree?"

She dropped her head into her hands again and groaned. "She goaded me. She basically implied . . ." Her voice dropped, and it was so muffled he didn't catch what she said.

"What?"

Her head jerked up and she glared at him. "That I couldn't get a date."

Cindy was crazy. He frowned.

Maura groaned again. "See?"

"Uh, see what?"

"You agree with her!"

He shook his head, baffled. How come women never

made sense? "That plus one thing? You, uh, didn't really mean that you wanted me—"

"Oh, Jesse, no! I'm so, so sorry."

No, she'd never want a guy like him taking her to her high school reunion. He'd known that—and he'd hate an event like that—so he shouldn't feel pissed off.

"It was a spur of the moment thing," she was saying, "and I know better. I should always think things out ahead of time and have a plan, not leap impulsively."

"Sounds like a recipe for a boring life," he snarked.

Another groan. "And that's the whole problem, isn't it?"

"Uh . . . You lost me."

"You know who I was in high school? President of the History Club. My adoptive father—he's a history professor—was so proud. At the prom, my date— No, forget that, I'm not telling that story. Then I went to college and you know what I studied? Accounting and business admin. And where do I work? With a bunch of senior citizens. There's not a single interesting thing about me!"

Somewhere in the middle of her rant, his mouth had fallen open.

The wind teased a tendril of fiery hair free from its knot, and it danced beside her delicate ear. Her blue-green eyes were huge and intense. Her breasts rose and fell against a light green blouse. Her neck was pale and slender and begged to be touched.

He shook his head. Was she having him on? Was this some bizarre kind of game? No, wait, women did this stuff all the time. Like, they'd say they were too fat, and you were supposed to say they looked great. Okay, he knew what she wanted. "There's nothing wrong with you or your life." Aside from her being uptight and snotty, but he knew better than to say that.

"You just implied I live a boring life, and you're right."

Did she mean that, or was it another "tell me I'm not fat" game. Cautiously, he asked, "Your job is boring?"

"Not to me. I think it's great. But anyone else would find it boring."

"Why?"

She raised nicely arched eyebrows. "I'm an accountant. Working with numbers isn't most people's idea of fun."

"Numbers are good." Jesse liked numbers. They didn't give him the same trouble that letters did. Somehow, they kept their shape and stayed in place; they didn't get all jumbled and distorted. The only subject he'd ever done decently in at school was math. He'd even helped girls with math—and other, more fun things—in exchange for their help with essays.

"Numbers are good?" she echoed. Then she flicked her head. "Oh, I get it. You're kidding."

He shrugged, not wanting to explain. "Bet you're good with them." She liked things to be orderly. "And there's more to your job than numbers. You've got a way with folks like Virginia. You make them feel good. That's important."

Her face softened and she was truly beautiful. Not just striking, not just sexy, but totally beautiful. "Jesse, I think that's the nicest thing anyone has ever said to me." She leaned toward him, her lips parted.

He stared at that mouth. Peachy-pink lips, a glimpse of white teeth. Last night, when she'd almost bumped into him in the hallway as he was leaving, he'd stared at that mouth, thought about kissing her. Had known it was a bad idea. Same thing earlier, when she'd been all flushed and laughing.

It was still a bad idea. Very bad.

His body had other ideas. He leaned forward so that his lips brushed hers. God, she was soft.

He hardened instantaneously, but forced himself to go

light on the kiss, to test and see how she responded. Not much pressure. Lips, just lips, nothing more.

Her eyes had slammed shut and she was so still he wasn't sure she was even breathing. She didn't respond, but she didn't draw away.

Then, a little sound seeped out. Part moan, part whimper, part sigh. Her lips softened, then she was kissing him back, but not totally into it yet.

He caressed the crease between her lips with an experienced tongue, back and forth, trying to persuade her.

Her lips quivered, then opened for him.

Before she changed her mind, he dipped his tongue into wet, honeyed heat. Jesus, she was sweet. Her mouth tasted as lush as it looked.

She made that sound again, reached up to thread her fingers through his hair, and finally she was with him, totally with him. Lips, tongue, all raw and hungry like she was as hot for him as he was for her.

His dick pulsed with need. Either it had been way too long since he'd had sex, or there was something special about this woman. Oh, hell, of course Maura was special. He'd known it when he first laid eyes on her.

He deepened the kiss, wishing she'd open her eyes so he could see their amazing color. He slid his hand down her shoulder and across to the soft curve of her breast. Cupping it, he felt the hardness of her budded nipple through thin layers of fabric.

And now her eyes did open—to widen in what looked like horror. She jerked backward.

Chapter 8

Maura gaped at the man beside her. Was this another of her crazy fantasies? "Jesse! Oh, my God, tell me that didn't really happen."

"What're you talking about?" He stared at her like she'd gone crazy. Which maybe she had. "I kissed you. You kissed me."

Her hard nipples and the ache of need between her legs could have come from a dream, but her lips felt swollen and tender. From his kiss. "You did," she murmured, still finding it hard to believe. "You really did."

He shouldn't have. She shouldn't have responded. It was all wrong. But . . . did he really want her? Find her attractive? That was so hard to believe. "Why did you do it?"

He made an untranslatable masculine sound. "You're hot."

Hot? *Hot?* No, she definitely wasn't. That must be the standard line he fed every gullible woman, every woman who made the mistake of thinking she was special to him. What he really meant was, she had lips and breasts—albeit small ones—and they were there, available—or so he thought—so he just took them. Kissed her, invaded her mouth, then groped her. And then he had the audacity to say she was *hot*? "Don't insult me," she snapped.

He heaved himself back in the passenger seat, arms

crossed over his chest, and she could feel the tension radiating off him. "It's a fucking insult to kiss you?"

"What? You think every woman should be flattered if you kiss her? And don't swear. Macho crudeness doesn't impress me."

"Nothing impresses you, lady," he growled. "You're so damned high and mighty."

"I am not!"

"And you know what?" He slanted a glittery-eyed gaze in her direction. "You kissed back."

She closed her eyes briefly, remembering those minutes of bliss. Then she shoved the memory away, shaking her head. "I did, but it was wrong. All wrong. You shouldn't have, and I shouldn't have."

"Yeah, I'm getting that message."

"You didn't even really mean it." Or at least, it hadn't mattered that it had been her. Any female would have done.

"Mean it? Jesus, were you there for that kiss? I sure as hell meant it."

He wasn't getting her point, and she didn't feel like elaborating on her own undesirability. "Yes, fine, I'm female and you're a red-blooded male with instincts. Physical ones. But we're completely different. We're from different worlds."

His jaw looked so tight that she was surprised he could actually speak. "Sure as hell are."

"We're opposites."

"I get it," he ground out.

And that wasn't even the worst thing. "I supervise you. That kiss was completely unprofessional. It was stupid." It could cost her her job, much less the promotion.

"Stupid. Yeah. That's for sure. It won't happen again."

Of course it wouldn't. It had been some silly, mood-of-the-moment instinct on his part. She'd only responded because, inexperienced as she was, for a moment she'd confused fantasy and reality. Now, though, she was firmly grounded.

They sat in silence for a few minutes, him still with his arms crossed over his chest, her upright in the driver's seat wishing she could take back the past ten minutes of her life. Although . . . would she really give up that kiss? It had only lasted a minute or two, but it had been the hottest, sweetest one of her life.

Jesse cleared his throat. "Look, about my community service . . ." The gravel in his voice was more pronounced than usual.

"Yes?" She glanced over.

Challenge in his hazel eyes, he asked, "You going to kick me out?"

She pressed her lips together, considering. "You want to stay?"

His jaw worked. "Need to."

He didn't want to work with her, but he needed to complete the community service assignment or he'd go to jail. Well, she didn't want to work with him, either, and maybe she had the perfect excuse to throw him out. She sighed. "It wouldn't be fair to kick you out. We both did something we shouldn't have, and we both regret it. Right?"

"Hell, yeah."

Of course, for him that kiss had been completely unmemorable. "Then perhaps we can try to forget it." No, she could never do that. "I mean, pretend it never happened."

His gaze fixed on her mouth for a long moment, then he turned his head to stare out the windshield. "Forget it. Sure."

"And we'll continue with the community service just as before."

The muscles in his throat rippled as he swallowed. "Thanks."

She sensed how hard it was for him to speak that single word. "You're welcome. And, uh, Jesse, neither of us will say anything about this, right? It wouldn't look good for either of us."

He didn't turn to look at her. "It didn't happen."

"Right." *Of course it did!* "Thank you."

She started up the van and drove toward Cherry Lane, even more cautious than usual because she was upset. Neither of them said a word until she pulled up in the front loading zone and they climbed out.

He swung open the sliding side door and reached inside. Pulling out two hanging baskets, he said, "I'll put these up, then get going with the fertilizer before the bedding plants come." He paused, holding the heavy planters as if they weighed nothing, then added, "If that's okay with you, Ms. Mahoney?"

Ignoring the edge in his voice, she nodded and focused on being a supervisor. "That's fine. And be sure to take a proper lunch break, too."

She turned to head inside and heard "Gee, thanks" in that same sarcastic tone.

Oh, great, now he was going to give her even more attitude. Maybe he realized that the kiss gave him a certain power over her. If he let something slip to Gracie or one of the residents, Maura could be in serious trouble.

Why on earth had she kissed him, rather than slapping his face and ordering him to back off?

Once in her office, she glanced out the window and saw Jesse bend to set down two heavy bags of fertilizer, then straighten again and stretch his back in one of those natural, catlike movements. He sauntered in his easy, long-limbed gait back across the garden to the door.

The man radiated sex appeal. That was why she'd kissed

him. She was weak. Ruled by hormones. She'd been off balance, off guard; too many disconcerting things had happened.

She'd even been silly enough to agree to go to that stupid reunion, and now she had to find a date. Perhaps she could invite Edward. He was male, intelligent, and more than passable in the looks department. Her parents would be thrilled. And, even if he wasn't exactly dazzling, at least she'd prove to the Cindys in her class that she could get a date.

Maura pressed her fingers to her forehead, feeling guilty for thinking this way about Edward, when he'd only been nice to her. He was perfect in so many ways. She should see him again, be more open-minded. Stop comparing him to a player like Jesse Blue.

Now, if she went to the reunion with Jesse . . .

He'd actually wondered if she wanted him to take her. Of course she didn't. It would be all wrong, just as that kiss had been all wrong.

Except, the kiss had been so wonderful. Leaning back in her chair, Maura closed her eyes for just a moment and let herself remember it . . .

So sexy, sweet at first, then rapidly becoming raw and passionate . . .

Raw . . . Jesse was raw, edgy . . .

What a tantalizing, wicked thought, that she might go to the reunion with him. She could just imagine . . .

The doors to the high school gym flew open and they rode in on Jesse's shiny black bike. Heads turned, people gaped, all conversation ceased.

Everyone was in evening dress, but none came close to touching Jesse when he slid off the bike in his tux. He looked as dashing and sexy as Sean Connery's Bond. He bowed slightly in her direction and held out his arm so she could slip her hand through it.

She inclined her head and accepted the invitation, and they swept forward. She wore a red off-the-shoulder ball gown that swished with each step she took, and killer heels. As tall as she was, Jesse was even taller.

"Is that Maura Mahoney?" she heard Cindy say. "I can't believe it!"

"Who's that man she's with?" someone asked.

"He's a movie star, isn't he?" another answered. "He's the most handsome thing I've ever seen."

"He's pure sex, walking," an awed voice whispered . . .

"Maura? Maura? Ms. Mahoney?"

Maura started, and opened her eyes to see Ming-mei standing in her office doorway. She bit her lip. *Pure sex, walking*. Had she really dreamed up those words? Such perfect words. An erotic tingle rippled through her aroused body. Somehow, she managed to say, "Sorry, I was deep in thought. Yes, Ming-mei?"

"There's a truck outside and a man asking for Jesse Blue."

"That must be the delivery from the garden center. Tell them to bring the plants into the courtyard and to try not to make a mess."

Ming-mei was shaking her head. "It's not the garden center and there aren't any plants. It's a . . ." She shrugged helplessly. "Maybe it's a friend of his?"

Why hadn't Ming-mei asked? The young woman could definitely show more initiative. "I'll come and talk to him."

At the entrance, Maura stared out past the frame of two new hanging baskets toward a battered blue truck parked in the loading zone. Then her gaze shifted to a question-able-looking character who squatted under a cherry tree, smoking. Greasy hair pulled back in a ponytail, T-shirt full of holes, weight-lifter muscles. And that was just his back.

She was beginning to sympathize with Ming-mei. "Hello?" she called.

He rose to his feet and tossed the cigarette onto the boulevard, making her grimace. He was short and stocky, a bit bow-legged as he ambled toward her. His face was pocked with old acne scars and his arms were adorned with tattoos. She saw a skull before she dragged her glance back to his face.

"Yo," he said. "Lookin' for Jesse Blue?"

"So I heard. Why?" If her community service project thought he could invite his deadbeat friends to Cherry Lane, he had another very big "think" coming.

"Got somethin' for him." He gestured toward the truck, where she saw a huge cardboard box in the back, secured haphazardly with some kind of ropes or cords.

"What is it?"

"Swing set."

"Swing set?" The words didn't match up with this man in the least. "You mean, children's playground equipment?"

"Nah. Like . . ." He gestured aimlessly, and his face bore a tortured expression as he searched for a description. He glanced at the old wooden benches that sat on the porch and his face brightened. "Kinda like that, but it swings, you know?"

She had no idea what he was talking about. "What's your name?"

"Beater."

As in an old car, or a man who beat others up? Or maybe it was his real surname.

"Please wait here for a minute, uh, Mr. Beater."

Although it was a sunny day and normally they left the front door open, now she closed it firmly, shutting him out on the porch. She stalked toward the courtyard.

Jesse was in a shady corner spraying one of the shrubs, which he'd trimmed back considerably. "Jesse?" she called.

"Yeah," he said over his shoulder, not bothering to look up much less stop work.

Wait a minute, what was he doing? "I thought you were spreading fertilizer."

Holding the spray bottle, he turned around. "Decided the sun's too hot. I'll do it later."

"Oh. All right." As she walked toward him, her nose twitched. "What's that smell?"

"Soap."

"Soap?"

"Natural insecticide." His voice and expression were flat. Civil, but no more.

"Oh." Remembering why she'd come, she said, "There's a man outside named Beater. He's brought something for you."

Jesse's expressionless face split in a sudden grin. "Awesome!"

"Would you mind telling me what this is all about?"

"It's one of those old-fashioned swing things. Wooden frame, bench-type seat."

"And so . . ."

"I'll put it near one of the cherries. The old gals'll like it."

Her mouth opened in a silent "oh." Yes, they would. She imagined a swinging seat under a cherry tree. With a view of Jesse Blue gardening. Oh, yes, the "old gals" would be in seventh heaven. On the other hand . . . "You can't just go and order things. Didn't I tell you we're on a very tight budget?"

"You don't have to pay."

What? He couldn't mean . . . Was she receiving stolen property? "What do you mean?" she demanded.

He was shifting from one foot to the other, obviously eager to go. "Gave Beater a call last night. He said he thought he could rustle one up. No charge. Be nice if you offered him a cold drink, though."

She was supposed to offer a cold drink to a thug named Beater to thank him for bringing stolen property to Cherry Lane.

And then she thought of Virginia Canfield and Hilda Jenssen, swinging under the cherry tree. Jesse was walking past her. Without thinking, she reached out and touched his arm. "Wait."

His skin was hot and damp, his arm firm and vital. Ripples of shock and pleasure surged through her. She snatched her hand back. "I need to know where it came from."

He scowled. "We didn't steal it."

"I . . ."

His eyes met hers, challenging her to trust him.

"All right," she muttered. "Go ahead and bring it in." She wasn't happy about the way Jesse had arranged this, but he must realize his every move was under scrutiny. He wouldn't be so foolish as to do something illegal right under her nose. As for Beater, she wasn't so sure.

She followed Jesse back out, determined to keep a close watch, and was in time to see a navy-blue BMW pull up.

Her mother got out and Maura walked toward her. "Agnes? What are you doing here?" She could count on one hand the number of times either of her parents had come to Cherry Lane, and have fingers left over.

Her mother opened the passenger door, took out a capacious canvas tote-bag, and pulled Maura's black pashmina shawl from it. "You left this at the restaurant last night."

"Oh, thanks." She'd taken it in case there was chilly air-conditioning, then forgotten it in her haste to get home and watch *Breakfast at Tiffany's*. "You didn't have to come by to drop it off."

She waved a dismissive hand. "I was driving in this direction for a meeting. It was no trouble." Then she frowned at the blue truck. "What on earth is going on?"

Jesse and Beater had wrestled the huge box so that it stuck three-quarters of the way out of the open truck bed.

"Need a fucking dolly," Beater said.

"Don't have one," Jesse said.

"Fuck, man, this thing's heavy."

"Should've brought a fucking dolly then," Jesse returned.

Despite the proliferation of F-bombs, the two men sounded relaxed and easy together.

Jesse studied the giant box. "Could unpack it, take it in pieces."

"Shit, it's not that heavy."

And they proceeded to strong-arm it off the truck and onto their shoulders. With Jesse in the lead, they lurched toward the front steps.

"Maura? What's that all about? Who are those men?"

Not about to tell Agnes that one was some kind of petty criminal doing community service, and she didn't have a clue who the other was, she said, "They're delivering a hanging swing set, which we'll put up in the courtyard for the seniors."

Agnes frowned. "I don't think much of the company you bought from, if they use delivery men like that."

And she wouldn't think much of her adoptive daughter if she knew that, only an hour ago, Maura had been kissing one of those men. "I should go in and supervise."

"You certainly should. You don't want men like that roaming around this place."

That was exactly how Maura felt about Beater, and it was clear that Agnes viewed the two men identically. "One of those men works here," she found herself saying. "The tall one, with no tattoos. And he's proven to be efficient and responsible, and very good with the seniors."

"Really?" Agnes's tone dripped disbelief.

Silly to have defended Jesse—it's not as if he and her mother would ever meet. Maura felt one of those twinges of acid in her stomach, the kind she always felt when she disagreed with her parents. Still, she said, "Yes, really."

"Hmm. His appearance certainly leaves something to be desired."

Maura refrained from saying that was a matter of opinion.

"I should go and let you get on with your work." Agnes walked around the car and opened the driver's door. "If I don't talk to you before, I'll see you at the reunion."

"What? Do you mean the Academy reunion?"

"Of course. Timothy's still on the Board."

"But you don't usually go to those events, do you?"

"No, but this time it's your class's reunion. We wouldn't miss it." Her mother gazed at her across the roof of the car. "Who are you going with?"

"I, uh, haven't decided yet." Her cheeks heated at the thought of that crazy fantasy about riding in with Jesse on his motorcycle. Her parents would disown her. And, even if the other women found Jesse attractive, he wouldn't fit in. Wilton Academy was an elite school; its graduates and their significant others would have multiple university degrees.

"I'm sure Edward Mortimer would be happy to accompany you."

Aagh. Maura must be slow on the uptake today. Of course that was why Agnes had made this rare visit. "Mmm."

"Maura, the two of you are very compatible. He's an excellent match for you."

Or for Agnes and Timothy. "I'll think about it." She should call him back anyhow, to apologize for being abrupt. Perhaps he was more interesting than she'd given him credit for last night.

"You do that," Agnes said, climbing into her car.

Maura hurried into the building and out to the court-yard, where Jesse and Beater had set the big carton down on the lawn. "Well, thank you for this," she said, a little dubiously, to Beater.

"No sweat."

Remembering Jesse's suggestion, she said, "That's hot work. Would you like a cold drink?"

"Sure." Beater grinned, revealing crooked teeth. "Got a beer?"

"Uh, no, sorry." In fact, they did have a liquor license, but served alcohol only to the residents.

"I'll pass then."

"I'll take a Sprite," Jesse said, "if you're offering."

Oh, great, now she was supposed to play waitress for him? Still, he had managed, by whatever means, to get a swing set for the seniors. "I'll just walk Mr., uh, your friend to the door."

The two men slapped each other on the back, ex-changed a few more F-laden remarks, then Maura es-corted Beater, in mutual silence, to the door. She thanked him, watched him walk toward his truck, then went to drop her pashmina in her office and get the soda for Jesse.

When she returned to the courtyard, he was extracting various components from the carton and laying them out on the grass. He took the cold can she handed him. "Thanks. Got a screwdriver?"

"Yes, I'll get it."

She found it, and this time when she came back, he was sitting cross-legged on the grass, his worn jeans taut across his thighs and crotch.

He pulled open the plastic top of the screwdriver, selected one of the gizmos inside, and screwed it in place. Next, he began to pick up the various pieces of wood, holding them this way and that, obviously trying to decide how they fit together.

She noticed a book of instructions lying on the lawn and leaned down to pick it up. "Wouldn't it be easier to use this?"

He glanced up, said, "Nope," and went back to work.

She flipped open the booklet and looked at the first page. Maybe Jesse was right. The author certainly had a limited command of the English language. She tossed it down again. "I'll leave you to it."

He'd gotten her thinking, though. When she went inside, she headed to the reception desk and said to Ming-mei, "The home center in the mall must sell garden furniture. We'll need a couple of tables and eight or ten chairs. Not too expensive, but durable enough to stay outside."

Ming-mei frowned at her. "You want me to . . ."

"Go over, choose something appropriate, and arrange for delivery."

"But . . ."

"I'll authorize two hundred dollars. Take it from petty cash. If you need more, check with me."

A smile tugged the corners of Ming-mei's mouth. "You trust me to choose?"

Maura smiled back. Maybe all the young woman needed was a little responsibility. "Just bear in mind the age and health of our residents."

Her delicate forehead creased in a frown as she considered that, then she said firmly, "Padded seats."

"Yes, exactly. You've got the idea."

Back at her desk, Maura glanced out the window and saw that the swing set was a magnet. Half a dozen elderly men had congregated in the courtyard. They stood in a circle around Jesse, pointing and talking with great animation, obviously all offering advice—differing advice, from the gestures they made—on how to construct the swing.

Jesse listened, nodded, and kept on with what he was doing.

She chuckled softly, less and less concerned about having him interact with the residents. So far, he'd always been polite with them, and considerate.

He got along better with them than he did with her. To him, she was . . . what? An annoying supervisor? A plain woman who had enough pride to not fall for a player's attempt at seduction?

And yet, she remembered the moments before that kiss. The compliments he'd given her about her job. It was as if he really understood the pleasure she took in her work—something her parents had never grasped. She had felt seen, understood, even appreciated.

By a man she supervised, who came from a completely different world, who would never in a million years fit into hers.

Thanks to his "assistants," it took Jesse way too long to get the swing assembled, but he didn't mind. Seemed they were having fun, and that made it fun for him, too. Finally, the half dozen old boys gave him a thumbs-up, patted each other on the back, and headed in for lunch.

All except Fred Dykstra, who said, "You haven't forgotten, have you, Jesse?"

Jesse stretched. "Nope. You still wanna do this?"

"I've been looking forward to it. You brought another helmet?"

"Sure did. Let's go."

Yesterday, the old biker had asked for a ride. Jesse'd figured, what could it hurt? He'd go slow and make sure Mr. Dykstra hung on tight. The man might walk with a cane, but he wasn't exactly doddery.

As they walked down the corridor to the entrance, Jesse asked, "How did you like the movie last night?"

Fred shook his head. "Hoo boy, that young woman sure was mixed up, but I guess she found what she was looking for in the end. I'm glad my daughter's happily married and not traipsing all over the world by herself."

"Does your daughter live here?"

"Yes, she and her family live in town. She's a teacher; her husband's a vet. They have twins, a boy and girl, heading into their teens now. Good kids. My son-in-law will be picking me up later. I always go over for Sunday dinner."

"Sounds nice." A nice, normal family. He could only imagine it.

As they passed the front desk, Fred handed his cane to Ming-mei, the very polite young Asian woman who'd greeted Jesse when he arrived. "Hold on to this for me, Ming-mei."

"Certainly, Mr. Dykstra, but . . ."

"I won't be needing it for a while."

Jesse held out an arm, but Fred waved it away. "I'm feeling young today, Jesse." They walked together to the entrance, and he said, "I was thinking, I might ask my daughter to invite Lizzie for next week."

Jesse winked at him. "You and Lizzie hittin' it off, are you?"

Fred winked back. "A man doesn't kiss and tell."

"Ain't that the truth." A truth that, unfortunately, made him think about Maura.

So she wanted to pretend that kiss had never happened. How the hell could he forget her honeyed mouth now that he'd tasted it?

Why had he kissed her? It wasn't just those sexy lips, it was that she'd loosened up, stopped being so snotty, seemed approachable. Seemed to almost be inviting a kiss. And yeah, she'd been into it, until she came to her senses and realized just who she was kissing. The guy from the wrong side of the tracks. Crap, she didn't know the half of it. He could just imagine her expression if she found out he'd never graduated from high school and couldn't even read the instructions for putting together that swing set. He gave a snort of disgust.

"Jesse? Something wrong?"

He shook his head as they approached the Harley and forced Maura out of his brain. "Nah, I'm good." He handed over one of the helmets. "You've ridden before. Not much has changed. Lean into the curves, right?"

"I remember."

"And hold on tight. No macho no-hands stuff, okay?"

He showed Fred how the helmet fastened, then climbed onto the bike and waited for the old man to mount up behind him. He started the Harley, revved the engine a few times, and they were off.

He cut through a residential area, then steered onto a country road with little traffic. Fred was doing fine, keeping his balance like a pro. Jesse opened her up just a little and heard a whoop in his ear. He laughed and let out a whoop of his own. The speed was pretty wimpy, but the old guy's enthusiasm was contagious.

Last night he'd fantasized about Maura riding behind him on the bike. Nope, that'd never happen.

Maura's phone buzzed again. This time Ming-mei said, "I thought you'd like to know that the garden center truck is here. Also, I bought tables and chairs and they'll be delivered this afternoon."

"Thank you, Ming-mei."

"Maura, do you know where Mr. Dykstra was going at lunchtime?"

"No idea. Why?"

"He went out almost an hour ago with Jesse Blue. He left his cane at my desk."

Maura frowned. "Maybe they went across to the mall for lunch. But he shouldn't go far without his cane."

Troubled, she walked out to the entrance. She had to smile at the sight of flats of bright flowers being unloaded from a green van. The van was spotless and bore the Sunnyside Nursery logo, and the young men unloading the plants wore tidy jeans and green Sunnyside smocks. Yes, her mother would approve of the professionalism of this delivery.

The delivery men had just taken a load into the building when the rumble of an engine drew her attention. Jesse's bike skimmed down the driveway. There were two people aboard. Maura stopped smiling. She walked toward the parking lot as Jesse pulled into it. Surely he wouldn't have . . .

Fred Dykstra clambered awkwardly off the back and almost lost his balance as he tried to stand. Maura ran toward him, but Jesse had already steadied the man. The same way he'd steadied her, a couple of times.

"I'm all right, I'm all right," Fred said. "Just stiffened up a little." He beamed at Maura, his whole face one giant smile. "We went for a ride."

"I see that." She bit her lip. She wanted to yell at the pair of them, but she couldn't bear to wipe the grin off the old man's face. She'd discuss it with him later.

As for Jesse Blue . . . She trailed behind as he walked Fred inside, steadying him until he retrieved his cane. The two men shook hands and Fred hobbled away.

When he was out of hearing, Maura told Jesse, "I want to talk to you. In my office, now." She marched away.

Chapter 9

When Jesse followed her into her office, Maura shut the door and demanded, "What did you think you were doing?"

He folded his arms across his chest. "He asked to go and I figured it wouldn't hurt." There was no hint of apology in his voice.

"It wouldn't hurt? What if he'd fallen off? He could have been seriously injured. Not to mention the fact that Cherry Lane could have been liable. Our residents are required to sign waivers when they go on outings."

"Lawyer stuff," he said disparagingly.

She was far too close to him. His body gave off a kind of heat, a magnetism, that made it hard to concentrate on what she was saying. She retreated behind her desk and sat down. "Yes, it is lawyer stuff, as you so elegantly put it. We're legally responsible for the people who stay here, and we have to take that seriously."

He flopped down in a guest chair, uninvited. "But . . ." He frowned. "I don't work here. This was just a guy thing. I've got a bike, he wanted a ride, I took him."

It took her a moment to translate that. "You're suggesting it really didn't have to do with Cherry Lane, it was personal. Hmm. That's a good point, but . . . Look, the fact is, he met you here, the two of you left from here, it

was the middle of a workday. Cherry Lane agreed to have
you work here, so I'm pretty sure we're legally responsible for your actions while you're here." And she was the
supervisor, so it was her responsibility. Thank God nothing had happened, or she'd have lost all chance of that promotion.

He was sprawled back in the chair, his knees bent and
legs spread, looking as hot as ever. She couldn't believe she
and this man had kissed. Maybe it really had been another
of her hormonal fantasies.

"It was just a bike ride," he said.

He honestly didn't seem to understand what he'd done
wrong, which made it hard to remain mad at him. It was
also next to impossible to avoid staring at his crotch,
which was aimed in her direction. Close to where the two
seams crossed, she could see a distinct bulge in the worn,
faded fabric. Testicles, she thought. What an odd, clinical
word. The slang term, "balls," seemed more appropriate.
What would it be like to cup their soft weight?

"It's fun," Jesse said.

"What?" She knew another of those embarrassing
flushes was brightening her cheeks.

"He's a good rider. Didn't come to any harm."

"Thank heavens for that." She hoped he would attrib-
ute her flush to annoyance.

Jesse's lips curved up. "You oughta have heard him
whoop."

Maura grinned spontaneously, then straightened her
lips. Having Jesse Blue around was anything but boring.
Still, she couldn't let him distract her. *Be thorough in formu-
lating your plan, and disciplined in carrying it out.* "No more
rides," she said sternly.

He rolled his eyes.

"Jesse, I mean it. I'm your supervisor, and that makes
me responsible."

Humor glinted in his eyes. "Ought to come for a ride, then. See how safe it is."

"Don't be ridiculous." A fast, throbbing machine under her, her thighs spread wide around Jesse's denim-clad hips, her arms wrapped around his hot, muscular torso . . . Yes, it was totally ridiculous that the idea should be appealing. Besides, he didn't really mean it; he was just trying to get to her.

He said something under his breath. It sounded like, "Chicken."

She was, if that meant a person who avoided taking risks. She preferred to think of herself as sensible. And the sensible thing to do now was to ignore his provocative remarks and get back to her point. "No rides. Not with any of the residents. Is that understood?"

He heaved a disapproving sigh. "If any of them ask, I'll tell them to talk to you." He shoved himself to his feet. "I'll go plant the flowers."

"You haven't had lunch."

"That was my lunch hour. I'm okay." He opened her door and sauntered off.

She hadn't eaten lunch, either, so she headed toward the dining room to grab a snack to hold her until teatime with Virginia. On the way, she popped her head into the kitchen and said to Felipe, one of the cooks, "There's a man working in the courtyard. Would you mind taking him a sandwich and a cold drink when you get a chance?" She thought about the size of Jesse Blue and the energy he expended in the garden. "Better make that a couple of sandwiches."

Then she settled down with a group of residents and listened as they dissected last night's bridge game. There, for probably the first time today, she could relax. At least until Sophie Rudnicki pushed back her chair and stood up, saying, "I want to see what's happening in the garden."

Hilda Jenssen promptly followed suit. "There's always

something new, isn't there? Makes life interesting these days."

"It certainly does," Maura said dryly.

"That gardener you hired is doing a fine job," Mrs. Jenssen said. "You're to be commended, my dear."

"Actually, it was Louise who, uh, hired him. But yes, he's doing a good job."

"Brightens up the scenery, too," Mrs. Rudnicki said. "Don'tcha think?"

"I really didn't notice." Lying again, but what else could she say?

Mrs. Rudnicki snorted. "Open your eyes. Single girl like you, I'd think you'd be paying more attention."

Mrs. Jenssen gave a tinkly laugh. "Oh, Sophie, what are you thinking? Maura date a gardener?" She cocked her head in Maura's direction. "No, I see you with a professional. You know, my niece is a paralegal in a law firm. I wonder if there are some nice single lawyers there."

"Mrs. Jenssen, please." Maura held up both hands. Now that she was thirty, was everyone going to try to matchmake her? "In fact, I met a very nice man last night. A university professor."

"I hope it works out, dear. It's fun to be single when you're young, but there comes a time when it's more rewarding to share your life with a partner."

Oh, great, now she was no longer *young*.

"Especially if you find a partner who's fun," Mrs. Rudnicki chimed in. "A girl's got to let down her hair sometimes, doesn't she?"

Those words sent a small shiver through Maura. Her grade twelve friend, Sally, always used to say, "Come on, girlfriend, loosen up and let your hair down." Sometimes, Maura let herself be persuaded, and often they'd had a great time. But not on prom night . . .

"That Jesse looks like a whole lot of fun," Sophie Rudnicki was saying. She started to walk away, saying over her shoulder, "You coming, Hilda?"

The two elderly women bustled away, arguing over what kind of man made the best husband.

Maura knew the answer to that question: The man you were most compatible with.

She took her leave of her other lunch companions, musing about whether she was totally uptight and stodgy. She had fun, didn't she? She watched old movies, cooked nice meals, enjoyed a glass of wine, and she had a pink geranium to put on her windowsill. Or, if those things were her idea of fun, did that just go to prove how stodgy she was? She had a feeling that was what Sally would say.

People who take risks are simply foolish, and poor planners. That's what Agnes and Timothy always said. And they were right that avoiding risks was wise, and letting her hair down had proved to be a bad idea. Still, a woman shouldn't let herself be crippled by inhibitions.

She was glad when, as she passed the reception desk where Lizzie Gilmore and Virginia Canfield were talking to Ming-mei, Lizzie flagged her down and interrupted her train of thought. "Have you seen the furniture Ming-mei picked out?"

"No. Has it arrived?"

She followed the two older women to the courtyard door and gazed after them as they went outside. A couple of old dears swung happily on the new swing set and half a dozen others—including Sophie Rudnicki and Hilda Jenssen—sat in green chairs with colorful padding. Various coffee cups and glasses littered two green tables. The courtyard was a completely different place than it had been a day ago.

One thing she'd say for Jesse, he didn't let the visitors keep him from his work. He kept planting flowers while the old-timers chatted. He looked up when Lizzie and

Virginia joined the group and said something that made them laugh.

Maura went back to the reception desk. "Good work, Ming-mei. The furniture looks great and our residents are enjoying it."

The young woman flushed. "Thank you, Maura."

Maura felt a warm glow as she walked back to her office. Maybe she wasn't so awful at human relations after all. For some reason, Jesse's presence, disturbing as it was, had made her more sensitive to the people around her.

It was such a lovely day that she eased her window open. When she got back to work, she was aware of the buzz of conversation and the occasional laugh. It was companionable, and it lifted her spirits.

Jesse was used to working with a construction crew. Having a bunch of seniors hanging around was different, but he kind of got into it. They didn't really interfere with his work, just occasionally told him what plants should go where. It was a kick to hear them laughing together.

He eyeballed the bedding plants that remained unplanted, then glanced up at the sun. Must be around two thirty. Setting up the swing set, then the new tables and chairs, had set him back. He'd hoped to finish the planting and also fertilize and water the lawn today, but that wasn't going to happen. At least he ought to be able to get all the young plants in the ground if he stayed a little late.

"Jesse?"

It was Maura calling him. He glanced around, seeing that she'd shoved her office window wide open and was beckoning him. He peeled off his gloves, wiped a hand across his sweaty brow, and headed over.

"You're making good progress," she said.

"Thanks." He was glad she'd gotten over being mad about the bike ride.

The windowsill was only a couple of feet high. Inside, she sat sideways on it, swinging those slim legs to one side so her skirt rode up a little. He lounged against the wall of the building, checking out her fine knees and bare forearms.

"I was thinking about what we should line up for your next job." She sounded excited, which brought his gaze to her face in a hurry. Her eyes were sparkling.

"Yeah?" It was nice talking here, just the two of them, rather than in the middle of a bunch of seniors.

"You know that pool I mentioned? The waterfall and so on?"

"Yeah."

"You said you'd be able to do the work."

"Sure. But I thought you didn't have the money."

"When the Board discussed the idea, we figured we'd have to pay for a landscape design person and the labor, as well as the supplies. If you can do the work . . ." Her head was tilted to one side, her face glowed with enthusiasm, and the sun shot sparks off her hair. She made such a damned pretty picture that he had trouble concentrating on what she was saying.

"Sure can. And you don't need a designer." You looked at a piece of land, thought about the sun and shade, considered who was going to use it, then the pictures formed in your head. "We can figure it out."

"Really?"

"Maybe ask Virginia, too. She's got some real good ideas. Used to have a huge yard. And volunteered at one of those botanical gardens."

"I do remember her saying that. So, how much do you figure the materials would cost? And the plants and so on? I can run some numbers and present a proposal at the next Board meeting."

"Depends on what we're talking about." He turned and

studied the courtyard. "It'd help if I could sketch something out."

"Just a minute." She hopped off the windowsill into her office, rummaged around in a cabinet, and returned with a pad of paper and one of those click-click pens she was so fond of. She handed them through the window.

He accepted them willingly. He was fine with sketching, just so long as he didn't have to write any words. "Wanna come out and talk about it?"

It wouldn't have surprised him if she went standoffish again, but instead she looked pleased. "All right." She began to close the window.

A devil—the same one who'd invited her on a bike ride—made him say, "Why take the long way?" He reached for the window frame and tugged it in his direction. She'd turned down the ride; how would she react to the window?

She stared at the frame, her eyes glazing over the way they sometimes did.

He glanced down, too, to see what she was looking at. His big brown hand rested close to her pale, delicate one. The contrast was startling and pretty much illustrated the difference between the two of them. But it was sexy, too . . .

Her skin looked so feminine, so tempting . . .

If he moved his hand just an inch, he would touch her. His vision blurred . . .

His dark hand stroked the back of hers, soft as a flower petal. Unable to stop, he traced a path up her bare arm, to her shoulder. Somehow her blouse had disappeared. He spread his hand across her throat, feeling the fine bones just under that creamy skin, the pulse beating wildly. Beating for him.

Boldly he moved down to where the skin was even paler. No camisole, no bra to hide her small, lovely breasts.

The top curve of her breast was so soft, yet so resilient under his fingers. Her nipple was rosy. When he touched it with his rough finger, he tried to be gentle. It tightened, formed into a pebbly bud. She moaned softly.

His hand splayed open, covering that whole creamy breast now. A brown starfish on a white beach. He stared mesmerized at the picture the two of them made together, himself and Maura. She looked down, too, and murmured his name . . .

"Jesse? Jesse, are you all right?"

He jerked, and his vision cleared. Staring down, he saw their hands, close to each other on the window frame. Man, he'd gone off into one of those sex dreams.

"Did you get too much sun?" she asked anxiously. "Maybe you should come inside."

Too much sun? Oh, yeah, he was hot, very hot. But not from the sunshine. "I'm fine," he said gruffly.

"If you're sure."

"Yeah. Let's get on with this planning stuff. Come on and hop out."

"I don't hop out of windows," she said stiffly.

"Let down your hair for once. Maybe you'll like it."

Her eyes widened in surprise and her cheeks colored. He wondered if she was remembering that kiss. She'd liked it—he was sure of that—before she'd decided it was a stupid idea. She muttered something under her breath. He didn't quite catch it, but it sounded like she'd said, "Liking it's the problem."

Then, surprising him, she shoved the window wide.

He stood back. She was wearing a skirt. This should be fun.

She sat down with those long legs tucked neatly together. Then she kinked them sideways, still together, straightened them and swung them over the sill, bumping one knee against the window frame. Yeah, she was klutzy, which was kind of cute for such a classy, buttoned-up woman.

He offered his hand, then realized it was a dumb thing to do, considering how grubby he was.

For a moment, she just stared at it.

He was about to pull it back when she reached for it.

Her slim, cool, elegant hand slid into his rough one, and he felt a shock of awareness. Awareness of her as a woman, and awareness that she was consciously, voluntarily touching him. She didn't need his assistance, but she was accepting his gesture.

She stood up and gently tugged her hand out of his. "Thank you," she said, not looking at him.

He cleared his throat. "Welcome." Then he said, "Virginia's over there on the swing. Want to get her opinion?"

"Why not?" She sounded almost reckless. "Let's talk to all of them. It's their garden, after all."

Together they walked over to join the group of seniors. Maura said, "Jesse and I have been talking about doing some more improvements to the garden. Don't get too excited because I'll need to draw up a budget and get Board approval, but we'd like your input. Jesse, why don't you tell them what we've got in mind?"

Another surprise, her treating him with respect. He squared his shoulders, determined to prove he deserved it.

Half an hour later, they had a plan. He'd drawn out a sketch, and Maura—wearing her sexy glasses, damn her— had made a list of the things they would need. "Now you can call the garden center and get a quote," he told her.

She took off her glasses and tucked them in her pocket. "Would you talk to them? You're so much more knowledgeable."

"Glad to."

He was amused that she led the way back across the grass to her office window, not to the door that led into the building. Awkwardly she swung over the sill and turned around just as he began to follow her.

He was nearly on top of her before he could stop his forward momentum. He lost his balance and she raised her hand, catching his upper arm, steadying him. He sensed the gesture was automatic. If she'd had time to think about it she probably wouldn't have chosen to grip his sweaty arm, but he had to admit her hand felt good there. Far too good.

"Thanks," he muttered. Then, "Sorry."

"It's okay." Her hand lingered and her eyes glazed over.

Suddenly he wondered if she, too, had steamy fantasies about the two of them.

"Ms. Mahoney?" he said softly.

She jerked, gave a gaspy little breath, and broke the contact. Turning her back on him, she walked over to her desk and took the chair behind it, gesturing him to one across from her. Putting the desk between them. Reminding him—and maybe herself?—of the nature of their relationship.

He had to remember, if things went wrong with Maura Mahoney, he'd blow his community service and end up in jail. Lust was lust, and he could fucking well control it.

She clicked a few keys on her computer. "I'm looking up the phone number." She frowned, muttered, "Can't see a darned thing," and slipped her glasses back on her nose.

He'd pretty much figured out by now that she really did need the glasses; she wasn't deliberately trying to torture him. The effect was the same, though. His jeans were getting uncomfortably tight.

He sat forward in his chair and rested his elbows on her desk. Could a guy get fired if his boss found out he got a boner most every time he looked at her?

"All right, here's the number," she said, reaching for her phone. A moment later, she spoke into it. "This is Maura

Mahoney from Cherry Lane. We're a seniors residential facility. I bought some things there this morning, and we're thinking about doing some more elaborate landscaping. I'm looking for a quote to present to the Board. Let me put you onto our, um, gardener, and he can tell you what we're looking for."

She handed the phone to Jesse and he took it, playing it safe and making sure their hands didn't touch. "Hi," he said. "Who'm I talking to?"

"Jesse, is that you? It's Chris."

"Hey, Chris." He'd gotten to be friends with her and her family over the past year or so. "Twice in one day, huh?"

"The plants get there okay?"

"You bet. So listen, let me tell you what we're thinking of."

Maura shoved her notebook across to him and he saw another of her lists. He ignored it and leaned back in the chair, his body back to normal now that he was concentrating on business. "Lookin' for one of those premade pools that you sink into the ground. Want to set it up with a little fountain, recirculating water, you know the kind of thing."

Maura watched as Jesse talked to the blonde named Chris. Twice in one day. Would they be adding a third time, tonight? Just what had Chris said to elicit Jesse's enthusiastic "You bet."

Still, he was sticking to business and seemed to know what he was talking about. He had a great memory, too, never needing to refer to her list.

"Well, that's great, Chris," he said. "Really appreciate it."

The woman said something that made him laugh and duck his head. "Oh, don't go saying stuff like that."

Maura gritted her teeth and reminded herself it was no concern of hers. When he hung up, she said coolly, "You got a quote?"

He told her the figure and she wrote it down. "That doesn't sound bad at all." She was astonished it was so low.

A knock sounded at the open window.

Jesse got up and ambled over. "What's up, Fred?"

Fred Dykstra peered in. "We've been talking."

Maura went to join them.

"About this garden we're planning," the old man clarified. His phrasing made her glad she'd included the residents in the planning session. She had Jesse to thank.

"Go ahead," she told Fred.

"It's likely to be pretty expensive."

"Jesse just got us a quote and it's not too bad. The Board may go for it."

"Got a better idea." He grinned at her.

"What do you mean?"

"Some of us have a little money we'd like to put into it."

"But . . . Cherry Lane pays for repairs, maintenance, improvements. Your money is for you, for whatever you want to spend it on." Most of the residents were far from wealthy.

"Like a fine garden to sit out in."

"I can't let you—"

"Listen to the man," Jesse said.

Since when did he issue the orders? Still, she owed Fred the courtesy of listening. "Go ahead."

"I'm doing just dandy when it comes to money. Some folks here aren't, but lots of us have a little extra. There's only so many ways to spend it. Now we've got this garden happening. We've helped plan it and we'd like to help pay for it."

"But . . ."

She jumped when Jesse touched her arm. "Don't have to decide now," he said. "Let's everyone think about it for a day or two."

She frowned. She wasn't going to change her mind. But

his hand was still there, resting on her forearm, and her brain was turning to mush. "All right."

Fred tipped an imaginary cap. "Good advice, young man. Now I must go and have a little nap so I'll be fresh for dinner with the kids. It's been a fine, busy day!" He whistled as he walked back across the grass, leaning only slightly on his cane.

Maura turned to Jesse. "I can't . . ." But his hand was on her bare arm, and his body, all that virile masculinity, was just inches away from her. Her mind stalled. What was it she couldn't do?

Oh, yes, she couldn't lean toward him, press herself up against that hard, muscled body. Run her finger through the rip that exposed a section of brown chest. She really couldn't touch the bare thigh, revealed by another rip that had expanded since morning. Run her finger up his inseam to explore . . . "I can't," she murmured again.

"You can," he said in a rough voice. "You know you want to."

That was the truth. But wait.

She forced her gaze away from his thigh and up to his face, where she saw an expression that a more experienced woman might have been able to read. What were they talking about?

He cleared his throat, glanced away, took a step back. "They want to do it," he said. "It makes them feel like the garden is really theirs."

Garden. Oh, yes, the garden. He was still talking about it, while she'd gone off on a flight of fantasy.

She replayed his words. Was her brain completely addled or did they make sense? "There's no precedent for this," she said in a worried voice. "I don't know what the Board would say."

"Don't tell 'em."

The notion was absurd. She aspired to be general manager. She wasn't about to go behind the Board's back. "You don't understand how things work. For example, there will be legal implications to consider."

He snorted. "A lot of legal hassle that only makes lawyers rich. These folks know what they want to do. So, let them."

If only it were that straightforward. "I'll think about it." But she'd only proceed if she had the Board's approval and all the I's had been dotted and T's crossed.

Jesse's disregard for lawyers made her remember that she still didn't know what offense he'd committed. Despite his whole James Dean, Rambo vibe, she was having increasing trouble imagining him as any kind of criminal. But he was, or he wouldn't be here.

She hadn't wanted his lawyer, or Jesse himself, to know how unprepared she'd been for his arrival, but now she needed to hear, from Jesse's own lips, how he'd landed in trouble.

She went behind her desk, sat down, straightened her spine, and clasped her hands atop her desk. "Jesse, I need to ask you something."

"Yeah?" He settled himself on the windowsill, only three or four feet from her, like a big cat lounging there. A black cat that just might be a panther.

"Tell me about the offense you committed."

His body tensed, and in that moment he became the panther. He narrowed his eyes and the insolent expression was back. "You've read my file, Ms. Mahoney." The way he said her name was a sneer.

"Actually, I haven't," she said, keeping her voice steady.

She read surprise on his face before he swiped a hand across his jaw. After a moment, he measured out the words, "I beat a guy up."

A brawl. Yes, she could imagine that. It wasn't a stretch to believe that violence might lurk close to the surface in

Jesse, and be easily stirred. She imagined him and some anonymous man in a bar, drinking too much. Trading insults. Moving to fists. Jesse probably hadn't started it— unless he'd been getting too friendly with the other guy's girlfriend.

She nodded. It was bad—she abhorred even the idea of violence—but it could have been worse. "There will be no violence here, you understand?"

He raised an eyebrow; it was another sneer. "You figure I'd beat up on a guy like Fred?"

"I have no idea what you'd do. And watch your attitude, Mr. Blue."

His eyes blazed, his nostrils narrowed, and muscles in his jaw twitched.

Maura wanted to spring out of her chair and take a step backward, but refused to let him know she was afraid. If he had a violent temper, there was no knowing what he'd do. But she needed to find out. If he could control that temper, he could stay. If he lost it, he was out of here immediately, no matter how handy he was in the garden.

"I hear you," he muttered, lowering his eyes. "I'll get back to work now. If that's all."

"That's all."

He was over the sill and across the garden like a spring that's been confined and then released. The truly frustrating thing was that, no matter how ticked off she was with him, Maura found herself at the window, watching him walk, noting the animal power of his stride.

She was losing her marbles, to be attracted to a man like that. Or, she reminded herself, it was some kind of hormonal thing. She needed to do some research on . . . what would the topic be? Female sexuality?

Chapter 10

After an enjoyable tea with Virginia and a stimulating discussion of *The Time Traveler's Wife,* Maura returned to her office and closed the door.

Using her Internet browser, she searched for "female sexuality."

"Aagh. Five *thousand* hits?"

That was way too intimidating, and she didn't know the right terms to narrow her search. Sometimes, there was nothing like the good old-fashioned method: a book. She accessed the online catalog for the branch library in the mall across the street and wrote down a few call numbers. No way was she walking in and asking a librarian to direct her to the section on female sexuality.

Not, of course, that sexuality was anything to be embarrassed about.

She even had a fair bit of knowledge about it. Agnes and Timothy had occasionally had discussions about human sexuality, from an archaeological or historical perspective, and Maura adored romantic novels and movies. The trouble was, her knowledge fell into two categories: academic and fictional. Neither provided much help when it came to her own sexual issues.

She headed out, her purse tucked inside a practical canvas tote bag that was a near replica of her mother's. "I'm going over to the mall," she told Ming-mei. Normally, she always added, "You can reach me on my cell phone if anything comes up." But Ming-mei was perfectly aware of that. This time, Maura said, "I'll leave you to hold down the fort." For the second time that day, she saw a flash of pleased surprise in the young woman's eyes.

Maura walked out into the sunshine, passed Jesse's huge black bike, and crossed over to the shopping center. The neighborhood was a good one, and the mall attractive and busy on this Sunday afternoon. As she made for the library, she glanced into store windows. In front of a lingerie shop, she stopped dead. There was the peach-colored bra she'd dreamed about. With a lacy matching thong—though her dream hadn't gotten that far before the radio-alarm woke her.

Actually, she could use some new underwear. Not peach lace; how impractical. Instead, she went in and studied the sale table of cotton bikini panties and hipsters. Three for twenty dollars. She chose flesh-colored, the most practical shade.

"Can I tempt you with anything else today?" The saleswoman was blond and wavy-haired, as fresh and pretty as Amanda Seyfried in *Mamma Mia!* and with a similar engaging smile.

"I don't think so."

"Oh, come on. Every woman deserves a treat now and then."

Maura glanced around, noting all the tempting concoctions of silk and lace. She wasn't about to say that her idea of a treat was pj's, hot chocolate, and an old movie. She might as well just announce "I'm a middle-aged spinster" and be done with it.

But she wasn't. Thirty was not middle-aged, despite Mrs. Jenssen's hint that Maura was no longer young.

"You have a peach bra and panties in the window," she heard herself say.

"They're just lovely, aren't they? They'll be perfect with your coloring. Now, I'm guessing you're a 36B, and a medium for the thong?"

Before she knew it, Maura was in a change room staring at her own ivory-skinned body decked out in peach lace. She shook her head critically. She was tall and gawky. She was pale and plain. She looked ridiculous in lace. The lingerie, on the other hand, was lovely. It deserved a woman like the salesgirl.

The lace was kind of scratchy. Not the most comfortable thing, but so feminine. Like the ruffled party dresses she'd worn before her parents died. The kind that, as an older girl, she'd gawked at in stores while her adoptive mother insisted on buying her something simple.

A tall girl should dress in clean, classic lines and understated clothing. Agnes had said that, and Maura believed her. After all, bright colors and trendy styles would only call more attention to her beanpole figure.

Maura closed her eyes and ran her fingers over her lace-clad breasts, across her tummy. Now, without her reflection to contradict her, she could feel feminine and pretty, the kind of woman any man would be attracted to. Even an outrageously handsome, sexy man like Jesse Blue.

Earlier today, he'd touched her breast through her clothing. It had felt so shockingly good . . .

Her hands cupped her breasts, remembering his touch . . .

Her body arched, pushing her breasts forward, imagining his hands caressing her . . .

He ran a thumb over the lace of her new bra. His thumb, the lace, both abraded her nipple ever so slightly, bringing it to instant attention.

He leaned down to press a kiss to the top of her breast, where it was framed so prettily by the scalloped edge of the bra. Then he skimmed back the lace and kissed underneath, trailing his tongue between the bra and her flesh.

Suddenly she wanted to be rid of the bra, to have no barrier between their two bodies. She opened her mouth to tell him that it opened at the front, but his fingers were already on the clasp, flipping it expertly.

He held the bra together with his hand for a moment, then slowly peeled back the two halves, revealing her skin inch by inch. "So beautiful," he murmured. "Perfect . . ."

Perfect? Her eyes snapped open. Even in her wildest fantasy, she couldn't imagine a man calling any aspect of her appearance perfect.

Look at her now, in the mirror, her chest and cheeks suffused with color, her hands clutching the bra against her chest. She looked . . . Hmm. She dropped her hands and studied her reflection. She actually wasn't a total beanpole. The sides of the thong called attention to the gentle swell of her hips, and she filled out the bra well enough to have a little cleavage.

When was the last time she'd really studied her body?

"How are the sizes?" the saleswoman called.

"Good. Fine." Hurriedly, Maura stripped off the peachy garments.

When she emerged from the fitting room, the saleswoman said, "Don't you just love them?"

Maura smiled. "They're beautiful." She handed them over, giving the lace a last caress. She meant to say, "But they're not for me." Instead she heard a voice say, "I'll take them."

"Excellent!"

What had happened to her mouth? It wasn't taking directions from her brain. Not wanting to admit she'd made a mistake, she passed over her credit card. And found herself smiling.

When Maura walked out of the store, a little pink bag with gold handles dangling from one fingertip, she felt like Julia Roberts when she'd finished her shopping spree in *Pretty Woman*.

She glanced in a store window and caught her own reflection. Reality check. She was plain, gawky Maura, on her way to learn about her own sexuality. Any other thirty-year-old woman would already know; trust her to have to research it in a book.

Inside the library, she browsed surreptitiously, feeling as embarrassed as if she'd walked into a shop full of sex toys.

She selected a book that had been published recently, seemed more practical than academic, and was written by a husband and wife. The photo on the back cover gave her a moment's pause. The fair-haired woman simply glowed, and the dark-haired man gazed at her adoringly. They looked like the kind of people for whom sex came naturally.

And yet this book was more than three hundred pages long, and contained topics like physiology, sexual changes with age, how to achieve orgasm, sexual dysfunction, and many, many more. Who knows, maybe Mr. and Mrs. Sexually-Fulfilled were the "after" picture, and had started out with some problems of their own.

Blessing the automated self-checkout, Maura completed the transaction as quickly as possible and buried the book deep in her tote bag. She tucked the lingerie bag in there, too.

Her secrets safely concealed, she made her way back to Cherry Lane and chatted for a few minutes with the residents who clustered around the door, waiting to be picked up for Sunday dinners.

Inside, Ming-mei greeted her with a smile. "Did you get what you needed?"

"Mmm-hmm." Or at least so she hoped.

Back in her office, she checked the garden. The residents had gone in, leaving only the furniture and Jesse. He had planted three of the borders and was bent over the fourth, working industriously. The sprinkler tossed water on one of the newly planted borders. She glanced at her watch. It was five thirty. He had put in his hours for the day.

Didn't he realize that? He didn't wear a watch, and he showed no sign of quitting work.

Yesterday, they'd got off to a late start so it hadn't bothered her that he'd stayed late, but she was determined this arrangement be administered fairly. She should inform him of the time. She glanced at the window. She could open it and hop through, or at least call him again, but that seemed too informal, given the sour note their last discussion had ended on.

She could buzz Ming-mei and ask her to tell Jesse the time.

"Oh, grow a spine, girl!" Her back ramrod straight, she strode out of her office, down the corridor, and into the courtyard. Jesse didn't look up even when she stood right over where he crouched, tucking plants into the soil.

Trying not to think of the kiss, and her little fantasy in the lingerie shop, she said, "Jesse?"

Now, finally, he glanced up. "Yes, ma'am?"

Oh, great, now he was ma'am'ing her. And not with a mocking gleam in his eye. His usual spark, that vital sense of energy, was missing. Was he worn out from a long day, mad at her for warning him there'd be no violence at Cherry Lane, or worried that she might terminate his community service?

"It's half past five," she said. "You've put in your time for the day."

"Wanna finish these." He kept right on working.

"But you're only required to put in seven hours."

"They'll dry out."

"What? Oh, the plants will dry out if you don't plant them? Hmm, maybe there's some place we could put them."

"Easier to just plant them." Which he was doing, doggedly.

"All right, but keep track of how late you stay and you can get off early some other day."

He didn't reply.

Earlier, they'd worked together easily, talking to the seniors and planning the garden. They'd pretended the kiss had never happened. Well, *she'd* pretended; perhaps *he'd* already forgotten it. Now, she hated that things were awkward again.

If she was more skilled with people, she'd know how to handle this. But today, with Ming-mei, she'd learned a lesson about human relations. People liked being given responsibility, and credit. So she said, "Thanks for what you've done today, Jesse."

His hands stilled.

"You've worked really hard."

His head lifted and he gazed at her, his face expressionless.

"I appreciate your ideas on the landscaping, and getting that quote from the garden center." She hated confessing her imperfections, but something made her add, "I'm hopeless with this kind of thing myself."

His eyebrows rose.

She forged ahead. "And thanks for being so considerate of the residents. A lot of young people think that . . ." She shrugged.

Jesse spoke, finally. "That old folks don't count for much?"

She nodded.

"Guess they count for as much as anyone else."

"Yes, they do. Thanks for understanding that."

Finally he gave her a smile. It wasn't one of his dazzling grins, but it seemed real. "You're welcome."

She smiled back. "Good night, Jesse. See you on Tuesday."

"Night, Ms. Mahoney." This time there was no sneer in his voice.

She should have told him to call her by her first name. The staff at Cherry Lane all did. At first, she'd used the formality to remind him she was his supervisor. Now, she had to confess, she just liked hearing him say her name.

The way he drawled it now sounded almost like a caress. A caress that made her skin tingle and a pulse beat between her legs.

When Jesse finished in the garden, he tidied his tools into a corner. He could ask Maura about putting them back in the storage locker, but he kind of liked the way they'd left things when they last spoke.

Whistling, he left the building. The receptionist, the bitter-faced woman with gray hair he'd seen last night, glared at him suspiciously. He nodded; kept whistling.

Man, a shower was going to feel fine. His back and legs ached from hunching over, but he never minded a hard day's work. Made him feel like he was good for something. Like he counted.

Maura'd said some people didn't think seniors counted for much. People had said that about him, and a lot worse, when he was young. The way he saw it, everyone was different. Some folks were smarter, some were younger, but everyone counted and had stuff to contribute.

He climbed onto the bike and put on his helmet. He could go for some real speed, a road with lots of twists and turns, him nudging the bike deep down into the curves. A road that would make him work at it, take his mind off his crazy boss, who alternated between snotty ice queen, steamy fantasy, and sometimes a woman who actually seemed pretty nice.

God help him if he began to like that woman, as well as lust after her. She did control his future. Twice today, she'd been thinking of cutting him loose: after that kiss, and when she'd asked him about his attack on Pollan.

Shit, he'd have to watch himself. Didn't want to end up in jail. His grip tightened on the handlebars and he revved the throttle.

Over the next hour, riding hard and fast, his tension dissolved in the sheer joy of operating the powerful machine. Finally, starvation had him turning back. He could have beer and a burger at Low Down, or Con would take him in if he showed up. That nice Mrs. Wolchuk had invited him to the Polish Community Center. All good options, except he wasn't in a mood for company.

He did need food, though. It was a lot of hours since he'd eaten ham and cheese sandwiches in the garden.

Nice of Maura to give him lunch, especially when she was pissed that he'd taken Fred for a ride.

She'd smiled, though, when he told her about the old guy whooping his head off. There was a spark of fun in the woman, under that straightlaced exterior.

He thought of how he'd last seen Maura, out in the garden tonight. Her pretty green sweater had been buttoned all the way from neck to hem. All those buttons, they gave a man ideas . . .

Button, unbutton . . .

He stopped at a red light.

Her sweater had about a million of the things . . .

Little green ones that matched the soft wool, small enough to challenge big hands like his. But man, he wanted to unbutton her, to get inside that sweater, to make her open up to him . . .

His hands were clumsy as he fumbled with those buttons. He could have stripped the sweater over her head, but there was something sexier about undoing her, a button at a time. He leaned down to nip her collarbone.

"Jesse," she protested.

He nipped again, then moved to the other collarbone. She sighed.

As he worked down the front of her sweater he resisted pulling the edges apart. Prolonging the anticipation.

Wondering about what lay beneath. Firm breasts—curves his knuckles nudged against as he worked the buttons. Breasts confined by a bra, but what kind?

With each button he undid, his dick pulsed and thickened.

When he reached the ones that held the sweater closed across her stomach, he thought about that stomach, a pale curve of soft flesh under her skirt. He bet himself what kind of panties she'd be wearing. Simple, practical, expensive, he figured.

That was fine by him. Anything would be sexy, on her.

Very slowly, he peeled the edges of the sweater back, starting at the neck. His pulse thudded as he revealed the pale top curves of her breasts and—

A blast of horns brought him back to reality. Now he ached in two places: his stomach and farther south.

He could fix one of the aches easily. He swung into a parking lot. The Colonel would deal with his hunger pangs. As for his lust pangs . . . He was on his own there.

Maura Mahoney was his fantasy, and she'd never be a real part of his life.

In reality, she wouldn't climb on the back of his Harley, visit with Con and Juanito, stop for a beer with the guys, shoot a game of pool, pick up pizza or KFC to take home for an evening in front of the TV—much less let him un-button all of those buttons.

Oh, hell, she wasn't the only female in the world. He could phone someone. There'd been women he hooked up with, who just enjoyed a good time. Hadn't seen any of them in a while. Nah, none of them appealed.

Tuesday he'd see Gracie and ask her out. She was pretty, sparkly, and he could see her fitting into his world.

He picked up three pieces of extra-crispy and large orders of fries and slaw, and rode back to his apartment. There, he peeled off his dirty jeans and tee. Dinner first, shower later. He cracked open a beer and settled in his battered leather recliner, clad in black boxer-briefs. The joys of living alone. No one to care how he looked or smelled.

Who needed women anyhow?

Maura lugged the heavy hanging basket out to her balcony and gazed up. No hook. Oh, well, she was off tomorrow so she'd have a chat with the building manager. He was an older man, a widower, and enjoyed doing fix-up tasks for the residents.

She set her pink geranium and herbs on the windowsill and smiled. The kitchen looked much cheerier. Why hadn't she thought of this years ago, when she moved out on her own? Maybe next, she'd get a bird.

Now, before she did anything else, she had to phone Edward. Had it just kept skipping her mind, or had she been putting it off? She checked her cell for the number he'd called from.

When he answered, she said, "Edward, it's Maura. I'm sorry for being abrupt this morning. I'd pulled off on the side of the highway and it was too dangerous to stay there."

"No problem. I'm sorry you can't attend the lecture tomorrow."

It would be good to spend time together, if she was considering inviting him to the reunion. She opened her mouth to tell him her plans had changed, when he said, "Fortunately, your parents and one of Timothy's colleagues decided to come along."

"Oh. Well, that's good then." No, she didn't want to hang out with that group. What should she say now? "You're enjoying your visit here?"

"Yes, though it always takes a while to get the feel of a new place."

"You've traveled a lot?" She'd never had anyone to go with, and exploring a new place on her own didn't appeal.

"My father was in the military. Then I did my post-secondary schooling at four different universities, and I'm still on the move."

"That's unusual for an academic, isn't it?"

He chuckled. "You're right. You can't get tenure when you don't stay in one spot. As your father's been reminding me."

"I guess all professors want tenure."

"I'm not sure I'm there yet. But who knows, this may be the place I want to settle. I do want a family, and I suppose that'll mean landing in one spot. It's tough on a spouse and kids, always moving around."

Hmm. Edward was more interesting tonight, talking just to her, not getting caught up in her parents' intellectual discourses. They chatted for a few more minutes, and she liked that he didn't go on and on about himself, but asked her about her job, and whether she enjoyed travel.

"Well, I'm afraid I must go," he said finally. "One of the professors has invited me to his house for dinner. But Maura, I've enjoyed talking to you. Since tomorrow night doesn't work for you, is there some other time we could get together?"

"I'd like that. I'm working most evenings." Her schedule was crazy, what with filling in for both Louise and the general manager, not to mention supervising Jesse. "I'll be free on Friday." And, hopefully, the Board would approve her budget at the afternoon meeting and she'd be in a good mood.

"Then it's a date."

She'd see how things went, then decide about the reunion. As she hung up the phone, she felt optimistic.

Quickly she tossed together a chicken and veggies stir-fry, using some of her fresh herbs, and ate it at the kitchen table along with a glass of a BC Ehrenfelser wine that she loved. After tidying up, she took the library book to her reading chair. She needed to find out why she'd gone from pretty much frigid to having hotter-than-sin fantasies, virtually overnight.

Her best guess to explain her odd sexual urges and fantasies was a hormonal change related to turning thirty, so she turned first to that section of the book.

Hmm, yes, there could be hormonal changes, it said, like loss of testosterone, and that could lead to . . . lowered sex drive? Well, that certainly didn't apply to her.

Maybe this next part did. She read that many women in their thirties felt more sexual and enjoyed their sex lives more, because—oh. Those women were more experienced, more confident, more knowledgeable about what turned them on. Maura snorted. That sure as heck didn't apply to her, either. What turned her on seemed to be fantasies about a completely inappropriate man.

When it came to the men she'd dated, including her two lovers, her sexual response had been lukewarm. Was there any hope she'd ever be aroused by a suitable man— a man like Edward?

Sighing, she flipped to the chapter on sexual dysfunction, including frigidity.

To her surprise, she found that she wasn't alone. The

book said that a lot of women didn't have orgasms, and many considered themselves frigid. Her eyes widened as she read on. Often, it was because their partners didn't have much of a clue how to arouse them. Nodding, she tapped her pen against the book. Yes, that did apply to her lovers and dates. Jesse, though . . . Oh, my, the touch of his hand, even the sight of him, made her body tingle and yearn.

He was experienced, sexually confident, very physical. He must have some special knack that the men she dated hadn't. With a lover like him, surely any woman would experience sexual bliss.

He could teach her . . .

No, that was ridiculous. Not only was he all wrong for her, but she certainly wasn't going to risk her job for the sake of a sexual experiment.

She turned back to the book and read on. The authors said that women often didn't know their bodies well enough to know what aroused them, so they couldn't guide their partners. Although Maura couldn't imagine telling a man what to do to please her, the truth was that she'd have no idea what to say.

The book used the M word. The word that was never actually said in that "master of my domain" Seinfeld episode about the contest where the characters challenged each other to see who could go the longest without masturbating. Maura had never been able to relate to that episode.

The book said women should experiment with their own bodies to understand the process of orgasm and how they best achieved it. It said most girls did this in their teens and it was perfectly natural.

So, in this area of her life, her development was stunted. Yes, a few times while watching a particularly sexy movie, she'd touched herself, but she'd always stopped. The thought of trying to manipulate her own body to pleasure just made her feel more deficient. Pathetic. Besides, she'd had no reason to believe it would work.

Still, the authors stressed the importance of this kind of experimentation. They recommended that women overcome their inhibitions, and they'd learn a lot.

Inhibitions. There was that word again. She thought of herself as practical—like when she avoided social situations where she knew she'd just feel uncomfortable and not make friends. But sometimes did she cross over the line to being inhibited and repressed? Had that held her back from having fun—and great sex?

The authors of this book seemed positive that inhibitions were more of an obstacle to a satisfying sex life than frigidity. So perhaps she ought to . . . loosen up. Often, she heard her parents' voices in her head, but now there was a different chorus: her old friend Sally, Sophie Rudnicki, Jesse.

Let down your hair, Maura.

In the safety of her own home, what would it hurt?

She reached up and began to pull the pins from her hair as she read on. The authors said that, to break through the barrier of inhibition, a woman had to relax and open herself to the possibility of orgasm. The possibility of being a sensual, sexual creature.

The authors had recommendations, like wine and candlelight, a bubble bath. Maura made a list, then began to work through it.

She found candles on the top shelf of the hall cupboard, red ones left over from a holiday dinner. Not scented, but she'd sprinkle perfume in the bath water. Though she rarely wore perfume, there was an unopened bottle that had been an impulse buy, like the orchid in her office. The scent made her think of sultry southern nights. Gardenia, she read on the bottle.

She didn't have bubble bath, so instead used a milk bath

Aunt Evelyn, her dad's sister, had given her. What would her prim and proper unmarried aunt say if she knew how her gift was being used?

For music, Maura chose an album of light jazz with lots of saxophone, music that matched the sultry gardenia scent. Next on the list was wine. Supposedly a relaxer of inhibitions, which was why she rarely had more than one glass. Tonight, she poured a second glass of Ehrenfelser.

Then, leaving her glasses on so she'd be able to read, she stripped off her clothing and stepped into the heated water, book in hand.

Relax, the book said. *Savor all the sensations, concentrate on each sense individually, and then let them all slip together into one overall feeling of sensuality.*

Okay, the senses. Sight. She squeezed her eyes shut, then opened them again, and focused, moving the book aside. Oh, yes, she enjoyed the mellow flicker of the candles, that creamy glaze on the top of the water, the sparkles of gold as the light caught tiny bubbles. She lifted one knee, noting how the milky surface parted and the bubbles drifted away. Water ran down her leg and her skin looked satiny and slick.

Moving on to another sense, she touched her leg, smooth and slippery from the milk bath. What else did her sense of touch tell her? That the tub was hard under her bottom and the angle of the back put a strain on her neck. She pulled a towel off the rack and folded it under her neck, which felt much better.

Stretching back, she closed her eyes and felt her muscles relax. The air smelled flowery in a way that made her think of Elizabeth Taylor with a creamy gardenia tucked into her dark hair, sultry and, yes, sensual.

With her eyes closed, she could almost imagine she was in a swimming pool with gardenias floating on the top. Mmm-hmm . . .

Floating in silky smooth water, with that exotic scent making her feel all sultry and feminine . . .

A pity she was all alone in this pool . . .

But wait, the flowers were bobbing up and down, stirred by some kind of activity in the water. "Maura Mahoney," Jesse's voice drawled in that sexy way of his.

And then he was there in front of her, his face illuminated by moonlight. Drops of water gleamed on his bare shoulders.

She should have felt embarrassed because she was naked, but somehow it didn't matter. Maybe it was because, under the water, she was invisible. As was he.

She was treading water, and so was Jesse. His leg brushed hers and slipped away. Then his hands clasped her waist, tugging her body close to his. Those hands were so strong, yet so gentle against her bare skin. Stunned by sensation, she lost her sense of balance and reached out for him. One arm grazed his hip. A naked hip.

Heavens, he was as naked as she was.

He pulled her closer, and her breasts pressed against his chest. Their legs, as they treaded water, touched and then moved away, touched again, and still he pulled her closer. Her hips were gliding through the water toward his, and any moment now, she would be pressed against—

"Aagh!" Maura made a quick grab for the library book as it began to slip from her fingers, catching it just before it hit the water.

She shook her head impatiently. Must Jesse Blue distract her from everything she tried to do? She couldn't even conduct this experiment without drifting off into thoughts of him. But, hmm . . . She squeezed her thighs together, feeling an ache between them. Maybe the experiment was working.

She straightened her glasses and stared at the book. Where was she? Oh, yes, concentrating on each sense.

She'd done sight, touch, and smell, which left hearing and taste.

The jazz, muted as it drifted in from the living room, was as sultry as the scent of the moist, warm air. As for taste, she picked up her glass and took a sip, then another. A generalized fruity taste, kind of tropical, a little citrusy. Delicious, and definitely one of her favorite wines. She remembered that this was her last bottle, so picked up her notebook, turned to the page with her current shopping list, and added wine.

A yawn snuck up on her. The tingle between her thighs had faded, and soon the water would cool off. She'd better hurry up.

She ran a finger down the page of the library book. Then she wrinkled her nose. Of course she'd known this part was coming. She was supposed to touch her own body, all over. Run her hands across her breasts, tease the nipples between finger and thumb, experiment to find the kind of touch that caused the most pleasant sensations.

She gazed down at her breasts, partially submerged in water. It wasn't that she never touched them. She did a thorough self-exam once a month. She shouldn't be squeamish about this.

Chapter 11

Holding the book in one hand, Maura ran the other cautiously over a breast. Nothing happened except that she felt silly. She tweaked a nipple. Ouch. Too hard. She tried it more gently, repeating the motion until her nipple began to bead up. This was odd. Her breast was reacting but she felt nothing that she'd label arousal. Nothing like she felt just looking at Jesse Blue . . .

"Concentrate," she chastised herself.

She was supposed to caress her arms very slowly, feeling the softness of the skin and the firmness underneath. Then go back to her breasts. Then slide her hands down her rib cage, marveling at the structure of the bones beneath the skin. Then to her waist and hips, reveling in the feminine curves.

She obeyed the instructions, though she had some trouble with the idea of "reveling." She just wasn't getting the hang of this. Her body felt fine, there was nothing wrong with it, but it wasn't exactly responding to all these caressing touches. She persisted, stroking her legs, her thighs. And now came the part she felt especially squirmy about. After a hearty slug of wine, she blew out the candles.

Remembering what the book had suggested, she gingerly pressed a palm between her legs, which at least had the virtue of feeling warm. But the sensation wasn't one she'd call arousal. She tried long, slow strokes with one finger, varying the pressure. Her finger got tired but that was all that happened. She went exploring for the famed clitoris that was supposed to be the center of sensation. She knew the darned thing was small, but hers must be absolutely minuscule. Hmm. Maybe that was the problem. She was anatomically deficient and that's why she'd never been aroused during sex.

Men could have penile implants. Was there a comparable procedure for a woman?

Now she was supposed to insert a finger inside her body. She tried, but her opening was tight. She poked, maneuvered. How did her doctor get a speculum in there? How had her lovers ever . . . As for a man built like Jesse, would it even be possible?

Drat, she was freezing to death and this whole experiment was horrible. She'd proven that she was frigid, just as she'd suspected. Resolution was supposed to be a good feeling, but she felt rotten.

She sat up, pulling the towel from behind her head. But wait a minute. If she was frigid, why had she been having those weird steamy thoughts about Jesse Blue? The book said sex was a complex thing, relying on mental and emotional factors as well as physical ones. So it seemed her mind could get aroused, and sometimes her body would even tingle and ache in a needy, pleasant way . . .

She flipped to the next page in the book. And now they told her that for a lot of women, the masturbation experiment wouldn't work the first time. Their recommendation was to have fun with it, and keep trying.

Fun. No, it didn't compare to a good novel or movie.

She put on fresh pajamas, tidied the bathroom, and brushed her teeth. It had been a stressful day, and she was exhausted.

Yawning, Maura slid under the covers and turned out

the light. The sheets felt smooth and slippery, like the water in her last little fantasy. She could even smell gardenias. She lifted an arm and sniffed languidly, then closed her eyes and yawned again . . .

Lazily, she stroked a hand down her arm. Her skin felt silky, soft . . .

Just as it had in the gardenia pool . . .

That seductive scent teased her nostrils . . .

She and Jesse were still languidly treading water, his hands at her waist.

He let go with one hand and reached out to touch her shoulder, then he slid his hand down her arm in a long, lingering caress that ended at her fingers. He entwined his hand with hers and held them together, looking down at them.

She gazed down, too, and saw how pretty they looked in the moonlight, his large brown fingers alternating with her slender pale ones.

He released her hand and began his journey back up her arm, moving on across her collarbone, framing her throat for a moment, then slipping down the center of her body.

She sucked in a breath when he cupped one breast, lifting it, pressing it upward. He ran his palm back and forth, his touch gentle, yet provocative.

Her nipple tightened. A lick of heat raced down her body in an arrow from her breast to the place where her legs came together.

It was an odd, achy, enticing feeling, one she'd never felt before. She wanted to concentrate on it, but now he'd taken her nipple between his thumb and one of his fingers. He squeezed and released, squeezed and released, and more of those flames sparked through her body.

She heard a moan and realized it had come from her.

Jesse leaned forward to capture her lips. First he nipped the bottom one, then he ran his tongue around the edge of her mouth, first her top lip and then her bottom one. Her lips were parted slightly, but he didn't invade them; he just ran his tongue sideways across the space between them, stroking top and bottom lip at the same time. Back and forth. Mesmerizing her . . .

His hand was moving from her breast, gliding down her body. Across her stomach, down farther into her wet tangle of curls, and down even farther.

She gasped, and his finger began to take up the same movement as his tongue, stroking back and forth at the opening to those other lips. His finger glided slickly, easily. Her body quivered with sensation, all centering around that amazing finger dancing over her intimate flesh.

"Maura," he groaned, "you drive me wild."

He was driving her wild, too, though she barely had the ability to form the thought, much less say the words. His finger, that daring finger, was flirting with the opening of her body, dipping in and retreating, then dipping back, farther each time. Stroking inside her, exploring secret places she'd never before been aware of, teasing and tantalizing her.

This was all so delicious and so new. Instinct told her to tighten around him, and her body began to move rhythmically, matching its tempo to his as he slid in and out of her. There were two fingers now, she realized. And his thumb was joining in, rubbing gently against the place where all that fiery sensation was pooling. Her clitoris.

"Oh, Jesse." She was begging for something and didn't even know what it was. She'd never experienced this overload of sensation, this agony of expectation. She couldn't take it any longer. Something had to happen.

It was like being so happy that you'd burst if you couldn't laugh out loud. And Jesse wasn't letting her laugh.

"Now?" he asked.

"Oh, yes," she answered, not knowing what he was offering.

His hand went away and she moaned her displeasure. This wasn't what she'd meant.

But then he was back, probing at the entrance to her body, where she wanted him, but not with his fingers this time. My heaven, he was so big she could never . . .

But she did. He eased inside and her body opened itself to him.

"You feel so amazing," he told her.

"So do you."

Again he created a rhythm for them, and her body followed willingly, knowing he was leading her somewhere she very much wanted to go.

His lips sealed themselves to hers, kissing her the way those gorgeous actors and actresses did in movie love scenes. Romantic, passionate.

As he kissed her, he began to move more quickly and she squirmed, pressing harder against him, the tension within her almost unbearable—yet, oh, so pleasurable.

He pulled back slightly and slid his hand between them. Unerringly he found that little nub, her magic button, and began to rub it.

Her back arched and she cried out, feeling something inside her begin to come apart. He thrust harder, faster, taking her, possessing her, as she dissolved in surging waves all around him. Tremors rocked her body, and she almost sobbed from the sheer joy of the experience.

And Jesse, he . . .

He . . .

Where was Jesse?

Maura woke, one arm wrapped tight around the spare pillow. Her other arm stretched down her body, and her hand was deep inside her twisted pj's, buried between her thighs. Her whole body was limp, pulsing with satisfaction, throbbing as if . . . as if the dream had been real.

Had she really . . . ? My gosh, could you bring yourself to orgasm in your sleep?

Good heavens, she really had learned how to do it. The M word. She pressed her palm gently against the damp folds of flesh, feeling her body begin to settle. Then she giggled, as a realization hit her. All those techniques in the book were wrong, at least for her. The trigger that loosened her inhibitions and freed her sexuality was the thought of Jesse Blue.

She grinned. Whatever the trigger, she wasn't frigid. Definitely not. In fact, she might even be . . . hot. She giggled. A hot babe. Who'd have ever known that meek and mild Maura Mahoney had this astonishing capability for great sex?

What had she learned from this? Should she turn on the light and make notes?

No, she just wanted to fall back asleep and dream.

Maura woke up feeling almost aglow. She might be a late bloomer, but she was a sensual woman and one day she'd find the right man. Maybe, now that she'd awakened her sexual side, she'd discover new feelings for Edward on Friday night. Perhaps those exquisite tingles of arousal would dart through her. A girl could hope.

In her robe, she had breakfast at the kitchen table with the balcony door open to a fresh morning, and made her list for the day. Normally, she had Sundays and Mondays off, spending them on chores, reading, and enjoying her afternoon tea with Virginia Canfield. She'd lost her Sunday free time, what with Jesse Blue and the budget, and today she had a pile of chores to catch up on.

After showering and dressing, she got a load of laundry

going, then she cleaned the week's accumulation of odds and ends out of her purse.

The receipt from Sunnyside Nursery was there. She glanced at the total again, and it did seem amazingly low. Her accountant's brain had taken note of the prices of several of the plants, and she remembered them as being more expensive than shown here.

She dialed the number shown on the receipt.

"Top of the morning," a cheery female voice said.

"I was in yesterday and just reviewed my bill. Is there someone I could talk to?"

"Oops, did I mess up? It was busy yesterday."

"Oh, are you . . ." Maura broke off before she said "Blondie." Remembering the name Jesse had called her on the phone, she finished, "Chris?"

"That's me."

"Well, my bill looks a bit low."

"Low? You're calling because your bill's too *low*?"

Maura shrugged. It was a pity if honesty was such a rare occurrence. "Yes. I'm Maura Mahoney from Cherry Lane and . . ."

"Oh, yes, Jesse's friend."

Maura opened her mouth, then closed it again. It would be pointless to explain. "I was in with Jesse Blue, yes."

"I gave you a deep discount. Same on that quote for the pool."

Maura frowned. Why on earth would she have done that? Unless . . . "Because of Jesse?"

"Uh-huh."

Aagh! Maura—Cherry Lane—got a deal because a middle-aged blonde had the hots for Jesse Blue. She ground her teeth. "Did you get that approved by your employer?"

Chris chuckled. "I *am* the employer. My husband and I

own this place. As for the discount, Jesse's helped our boy a lot and we're happy to pass on the favor."

"Helped your boy?"

"Danny's sixteen, kind of wild. The first day Jesse was in here—he came in with a landscape designer he was working with—Danny and his dad were getting into it. Shouldn't have had the argument here at work, but you know how stuff happens. Danny, who never has time to work here, comes in asking for some money, and his dad lights into him over how he's spending his time, hanging out with a bad bunch of kids to all hours.

"It's getting pretty heated," she went on, "and then Jesse asks Danny, all casual, if he's interested in basketball. Suggests Danny drop by these Monday and Friday evening pickup games at Delancey Secondary."

"Really?" Maura asked, fascinated. So that was why Jesse couldn't work at Cherry Lane those nights.

"Yeah, and Danny thinks Jesse's cool so he goes. Since then, he's cleaned up his act. He's working here on weekends—he's one of the guys who delivered your order. He doesn't see his old gang nearly so often and has some new friends we actually approve of though we don't let on. You know how that goes."

"I guess." Not that she had experience with kids, or with friends for that matter.

"So, anyhow, we owe Jesse. He said your seniors place doesn't have a lot of money and the old folks would really appreciate a nice garden, so I figured I could do my bit to help."

"That's very kind of you. Jesse didn't tell me."

Chris laughed. "He's a man of few words. Let us know if we can do anything else for you."

Maura promised to send her a tax receipt, then hung up, shaking her head.

As she switched laundry from the washer to the dryer,

she mused over what she'd learned. So Jesse helped troubled kids as well as being nice to seniors.

And, completely unknowingly, he'd helped her, by serving as the unlikely spark to the steamy fantasies that had
awakened her dormant sexuality.

Yet he had, as he'd admitted himself, beat a man up. He
had that bad boy edge, and she'd seen things in his face that
troubled her. Things that excited her, too, but that was a
whole other issue.

For two days, she'd been his supervisor, she'd let him
mingle with the seniors, but she didn't really know what
kind of man he was. She had assumed Louise Michaels
wouldn't let a hard-core criminal do community service at
Cherry Lane, but maybe Jesse's lawyer had put a spin on
the story. Maybe Louise had been distracted by her and
Don's efforts to adopt.

Suddenly, Maura had to know the full truth about Jesse.
Besides, if Louise and Don really were new parents, she
wanted to offer her congratulations.

She dialed Louise's cell phone. "Hi, it's Maura. I hope
this isn't a bad time."

"No, it's fine. And it was only Braxton Hicks contrac-
tions yesterday, or I'd have called with the news. But it
could happen any moment now. We're with Brittany now,
and we're all so impatient."

"I bet."

"We met the dad, too. He's a good boy. They're still
dating, but no way do they want to settle down at their
age. Thank heavens for us!"

Maura was about to tell her how happy she was for
them when Louise rushed on. "Did I tell you the baby's a
boy? The four of us all talked about it, and we agreed on
the name Jeff. With a J not a G. Well, Jeffrey, actually."

"It's a great name." Maura wondered if—hoped that—
one day she'd be doing this herself: choosing a baby name.

This morning, she felt more hopeful about marriage and children. She was a sensual woman and on Friday she had a date with a really nice guy. "I'm so happy that it's working out for you."

"So am I. Oh, gosh, so am I." Louise's voice sounded teary.

They were both quiet for a moment, then Maura said, "I hate to bother you, but I've got one quick question."

"Oh! Oh, of course. I forgot all about Cherry Lane. How are things going? How are all my sweeties?"

"Everyone's great. It appears that Fred Dykstra and Lizzie Gilmore may be an item."

"Aw, good for them."

"And we're getting a garden in the courtyard."

"What! You don't say. The Board approved it?"

"I haven't had to go to them yet because so far the expenses are low, and within our budget. I put your community service project to work."

"Great idea. What's he like?"

"Uh, he's—" *Pure sex, walking.* Maura cleared her throat. "A hard worker, and he gets along well with our residents." She wouldn't mention Fred Dykstra's motorcycle ride; she'd handled that problem just fine. "The only trouble is, we can't find your file on him."

"Oh, really? Let's see, I would have labeled it with either his name or 'Community Service.' "

"So we figured, but Gracie looked in your filing cabinet—"

"Wait! I know where it is. Oh, no, I can't believe I did this. There's a stack of stuff on the credenza in my office. Things I was dealing with just before I left. You'll find the file there, and would you mind taking a look at the other things, too? I think there's something I wanted Gracie to do, but beats me if I can remember now. My brain's so focused on the baby. And, Maura, those are HR files and should be locked in the cabinet. Please do that right away, or get Gracie to."

"I will." She'd drop into Cherry Lane while she was out grocery shopping. Gracie, the only other person with authority to deal with confidential files, wasn't working today. "By the way, do you recall why you agreed to have Jesse Blue do his community service with us?"

"Let's see . . . His lawyer, Barry Adamson, and I are friends from Toastmasters and I often talk about Cherry Lane. About how great our residents are, and all the life lessons they've learned and are willing to share. Barry mentioned this client of his, who could stand to learn a lesson or two." In the background Maura heard what sounded like a knock.

"Do you remember what offense Jesse was charged with?"

"It was assault. I know that sounds terrible, but Barry told me the whole story and assured me this young man would never endanger our residents or staff."

Assault. So Jesse hadn't lied to her. "The whole story?" she echoed, encouraging Louise to go on.

"Let me remember. There was a girl, and she—" She broke off.

In the background Maura heard a high-pitched female voice squeal, "The baby's coming!"

"Are you sure this time?" Louise asked, her own voice excited.

"My water broke!"

"Gotta go," Louise said into the phone, then hung up before Maura could wish them all luck.

Quickly, Maura hung up the clothes from the dryer, then headed for her car.

When Maura entered Cherry Lane, Ming-mei was chatting with one of the physical therapists, a pleasant young woman her own age. It looked like the shy receptionist was making a friend.

"Maura," Ming-mei said, "what are you doing here to-day?"

"I need to do a couple of things." She paused and said to the two of them, "By the way, cross your fingers for Louise. The baby's coming, and it's for real this time." She knew that Louise, who was much more sociable and popular than she was, would love to know everyone was rooting for her.

In Louise's office, Maura found a stack of files and papers on the back corner of the credenza. "Aha!" Halfway down the pile was a folder neatly labeled JESSE BLUE.

She sank into Louise's chair and began to read. Halfway through, she gasped and clutched at her chest. Yes, he'd beaten a man up, as he'd told her. But she'd imagined a bar brawl, a few punches thrown. In fact, the man had broken ribs, an injury to his spleen, a broken arm, several broken fingers, and a broken nose. There were no pictures in the file, thank heavens, but Maura's imagination supplied an image of the poor victim, Gord Pollan.

Hands shaking, feeling nauseous, she dropped the file on the desk. How could the Jesse she knew have done such a thing? This was . . . sheer violence. It was inhuman.

When she regained her composure she read on, but the file was too brief to provide much illumination. Louise had said a girl was involved. Jesse had beaten this man almost to death over a girl?

She locked up all Louise's HR files and wrote herself a reminder to go through them when she was in tomorrow, then went to her own office and found Barry Adamson's card. The receptionist at his firm put her through to his voice mail. She gnashed her teeth, left her cell number, and asked him to call her as soon as possible.

Maura hurried through her grocery shopping, then headed home. Working methodically through the chores on her list, she tried hard not to imagine Jesse, his face flushed with anger, punching and kicking another man.

It was noon when Barry Adamson phoned. "Sorry I missed your call, but I'm in court today. Is there a problem with Jesse?"

"He nearly killed a man."

"What?" he bellowed. "Who?"

"No, no, I didn't mean that. I'm referring to Gord Pollan." That name was etched in her mind.

"Huh? You already knew about Pollan, from the file. I'm not following."

"I didn't know about him. Louise did, and obviously the two of you discussed it, but she didn't have a chance to fill me in. I've only just seen the file, and I have to say, I don't understand what you were thinking, you and Louise. This is a seniors facility. These are gentle old people. We don't want someone violent here."

"Oh, uh, Jesse hasn't been violent, has he?" he asked cautiously, confirming her fear that Jesse very well might be violent.

"Not yet," she said darkly. "But that doesn't mean it won't happen."

"I doubt that. I mean, the fact pattern certainly isn't going to repeat at Cherry Lane. It was a very unusual one."

"What, exactly, *was* the fact pattern? That wasn't in the file. I gather a girl was involved?" Sometimes Maura wished she were more attractive to men, but she'd never *ever* wished that two would fight over her.

"This jerk Pollan was harassing a friend of Jesse's. An ongoing pattern of abuse. So Jesse, uh, put an end to it." To her astonishment, the lawyer sounded admiring, like a little kid looking up to a hero—except in this case his hero was the playground bully.

Men! Honestly. Okay, maybe the fight hadn't been over

a girl, in the sense she'd first thought. Jesse had apparently thought he was protecting a friend. But what a stupid, caveman way to go about it. "Violence is hardly the way to put an end to abuse."

"Well no, not usually, but . . . Oh, sh-oot, I've got to get back into court."

He hung up on her.

Maura buried her face in her hands and rubbed her forehead with her fingertips, realizing she had a headache. Jesse Blue had distracted her from her schedule all weekend, and now he was ruining her one day off. But the fact was, she couldn't get the picture out of her head: big, strong Jesse using those very masculine hands to attack another man. To beat him to a pulp.

No way would she ever fantasize over Jesse Blue again.

All afternoon, the knowledge of Jesse's crime was a dark cloud hanging over her. When she made a tomato bocconcini salad for dinner—using her own basil—it seemed flavorless and she shoved it away unfinished. Even her wine didn't taste the same as usual, and she took no more than a couple of sips.

This was ridiculous. She was in charge, not Louise. If she was going to ban Jesse from Cherry Lane, then she should *just do it*! She could leave a voice mail for Barry Adamson and never have to see Jesse again.

The idea of not seeing Jesse again made her stomach feel hollow. No, that must just be hunger. She'd barely eaten a thing all day. Yet she had no appetite.

Gather all the information and weigh it carefully, and never act on impulse. Right. That advice had always served her well.

The facts set out in Jesse's file were horrendous, but the judge hadn't locked him up. Louise and Barry believed it would be all right for him to work at Cherry Lane. Louise had contemplated that he would interact with the residents.

How could an almost-killer be trusted to interact with frag-ile seniors and learn life lessons from them? And what was the unusual fact pattern the lawyer had referred to?

Tomorrow morning, she'd phone Barry again and try to catch him before he went into court.

She paced around her apartment, straightening things she'd already straightened. "Aagh! I have to see Jesse."

She had to know now, from him not from Barry Adamson—to ask him to his face, and this time not let him get away with an evasive answer. And she was pretty sure where he was tonight. Chris at the garden center had told her.

It took only a few seconds to find the address of De-lancey Secondary.

The school was in a part of town she didn't know, so she let her Smart Car's GPS guide her there. She pulled into the parking lot next to a basketball court where a bunch of teenage boys, young men, and two or three girls were running around. Pulling down the sun visor, she hid be-hind her sun glasses, feeling like a spy.

Jesse was the biggest, the most mature, by a long stretch. And he looked quite breathtaking in another of those holey tank tops and a pair of baggy shorts. He had fabu-lous legs, strong and well-shaped, sprinkled with dark hair. The kids were a mixed bag, from skeletally thin to chubs, shaven heads to long dreadlocks. Black, white, Hispanic, Native American, Asian.

She didn't know anything about the game of basketball except that the objective was to get the ball through the hoop, but she didn't care. What caught her interest was the conversation that carried through her open car windows, and the group dynamics. Some of the kids were confident and others not; some were buddies and some were loners.

The tension that had gripped her all day eased a little as she watched and listened.

The kids were getting a workout, developing their skills and learning how to be part of a team. Learning how to respect each other rather than to grandstand. Jesse was a natural leader. He was as good with these young people as he was with her seniors.

He'd beaten Gord Pollan close to death, yet he used his spare time to coach troubled teens. His fists had shattered human bones, yet she remembered the gentle way he'd taken Virginia's frail hand to help her out of the swing. Jesse Blue was an enigma, and she needed to know his secrets. For the sake of her seniors, of course.

Surely he couldn't have done what he'd been charged with. There must have been some mistake. That's why he hadn't been sent to jail. She would wait until the game was finished and the kids had headed home, then she'd talk to him.

She watched him run around and leap up to make baskets. Every now and then he lifted the hem of his tank top to wipe his face, giving her a brief, tantalizing flash of brown torso. She wondered what he wore under those baggy shorts. A jock strap? She had only the vaguest notion what a jock strap looked like, but figured Jesse would be the perfect choice to model one.

Eventually one team was declared the winner, and a lot of hand-slapping occurred. The kids began to wander off, alone or in small groups. Maura opened her car door.

"Jesse! Hey there, hon." It was a female voice, and Maura quickly eased the door closed again.

A curvy, Latin-looking woman—a woman who bore an amazing resemblance to Salma Hayek, though Maura wasn't sure the actress would choose this woman's tight pink skirt and top—bustled toward Jesse on stiletto heels. The owner of the cheap scent on Jesse's leather jacket, Maura was sure of it. Surprisingly, the woman's hand was linked with that of a boy, seven or eight years old.

The woman greeted Jesse with a big hug, and he was in no hurry to extract himself. When they broke apart, he picked up the boy, hoisted him high, and twirled around with him until the boy squealed with laughter, then put him down again. The three walked away with Jesse in the middle, one arm around the woman's waist and one around the boy's shoulders.

Maura sat, so stunned she could do nothing but gape. His wife and son? Why had it never occurred to her that Jesse might be married? That he might have a child?

He'd kissed Maura. He had a gorgeous wife and a sweet little boy, and he'd kissed Maura. The total bum! Loyalty was huge to her, and she couldn't abide cheaters.

Did his wife know that he spent his days coming on to every random female who crossed his path?

Shaking her head in disgust, Maura started up her car. Tomorrow, she'd talk to Jesse. She'd give him a chance to state his case. But she couldn't imagine anything he could possibly say that would make her keep him on at Cherry Lane.

When Jesse finished work at the construction site on Tuesday, he figured the sensible thing would be to grab a snack and head straight over to Cherry Lane. He wasn't due there for an hour, but he could put in his three hours and finish up early. Wasn't much point changing, since he was only going to be doing more hard labor. At least he assumed he was. He'd finished up the planting on Sunday, so Maura would likely get him started digging out the pond.

He knew what he wished she had in mind for him. He'd been fantasizing dozens of different scenarios since he'd last seen her. What he should be doing was thinking about taking Gracie out, but instead he couldn't get Maura off his mind.

Instead of heading toward Cherry Lane, he realized he'd pointed the Harley in the direction of his apartment. Okay, he'd shower and change. It was what Barry would tell him to do. But, as he stood under the cascading water with another hard-on, he knew he was fooling himself. He wanted to look good, to impress the damned woman.

Like there was any fucking way. A guy who'd dropped out in grade ten? Yeah, maybe she gave him credit for knowing about gardens, but that was a long way from seeing him as the kind of guy she'd invite into her bed.

He really should ask Gracie out.

He didn't get that chance, though, because when he entered the building, it was the sour-faced woman on the reception desk, not the bubbly redhead. That shower and change of clothes had made him late enough that Gracie'd left for the day.

"Ms. Mahoney in?" he asked the scowling receptionist.

"You're Jesse Blue." She said it in the same tone she might've said, "You're a cockroach." He'd heard that tone a lot when he was a kid, and it always riled him.

He nodded.

"She left instructions with me." The woman tapped a piece of paper on the desk in front of her.

Crap. Had Maura gone for the day and left him one of those lists she was so fond of? "Yeah?" He'd have been able to sweet-talk Gracie into reading him the list, making a game of it. He was an expert at tricks like that, but this woman didn't seem like the type to play along.

"She wants to see you in her office."

"Oh." His heart quickened with relief and anticipation. "Thanks."

The woman's eyes glittered unpleasantly, and she sounded almost gleeful when she said, "She didn't sound happy."

What? He'd thought they'd actually been getting along on Sunday evening.

Chapter 12

As Jesse walked down the hall, he remembered countless walks to the principal's office when he was in school. He'd learned not to care. Either he'd get lectured, punished, or expelled. Water off a duck's back.

But now he was nervous. As he walked down the hall, he tucked his T-shirt—a relatively new one—into his clean jeans.

He paused in Maura's doorway. Her head, with the fiery hair tamed as usual, was down as she concentrated on some papers in front of her. She had her glasses on.

"You wanted to see me?" he asked.

"Oh!" Her head came up. She was wearing a tailored white blouse today and looked tired and stressed, though a flush crept across her cheeks. "Nedda was supposed to buzz me when you arrived."

He shrugged. Didn't surprise him that she hadn't. That Nedda woman struck him as the kind who loved to make trouble, then play innocent.

Maura yanked her glasses off. One day he'd figure out if she was sexier with them on, or off.

There was a new scent in the air, something barely there, but he had a great sense of smell. It was flowery, kind of exotic. He liked it.

"Close the door, come in, and sit down." Her voice was

controlled, but it was obvious she wasn't pleased with him. What had he done now?

He obeyed her instructions, tossing his leather jacket on the spare chair, and waited, putting a name to the faint scent. Gardenia. Made him think of sultry nights in Hawaii, where he'd gone once on vacation.

A flowery lei around Maura's neck, draped over creamy shoulders that were bare in the moonlight. Her face turned up to his, her eyes sizzling with desire—

She shoved a file folder across the desk toward him. Okay, Maura in a crisp shirt that bared only an intriguing triangle of throat. Maura, whose blue-green eyes were narrowed as she frowned at him.

He raised his eyebrows.

"I've read it," she said. When he didn't reply or reach for the folder, she said impatiently, "Your file. I've read your file."

"Oh." The word dropped heavily. It hadn't been enough for her, him saying he'd beaten someone up. She had to go read the file, learn the gory details. Now she figured he wasn't good enough to be around her precious old folks. Around her. He had half a mind to just get up and leave, but he was damned well going to make her say it.

Instead, staring at him with that frown line creasing her forehead, she said, "Tell me about it, Jesse. Who was Gord Pollan, and why did you beat him so badly?"

Last time he'd told the story it was on the stand, so the judge could decide whether or not she'd approve the community service arrangement Barry had worked out with the prosecutor. The judge had read him the riot act, but she'd endorsed the deal. Maura Mahoney would be harder to impress.

But he found himself wanting to try. For some crazy reason, he wanted her to understand. Was there any hope of that?

"I've got this friend, Consuela," he said slowly. "We've been pals since high school. I was new at school and she was nice to me." And she'd stayed nice, even when she found out he wasn't so bright, even when he dropped out before they could expel him.

Maura was still frowning.

He went on quickly. "She was dating this guy, Rico. He was an assh— A real jerk. He beat on her, just like her stepfather had. She got pregnant in grade twelve. They split before she had the baby, thank God. It was a boy, Juanito; he's eight now."

Maura's face lit with something that looked like understanding. "Are you married?"

"Huh? You mean to Con? Or at all? No, neither. Con's like a sister. But what does that have to do—"

"Nothing," she broke in. "Sorry. Go on."

Women. Why couldn't they think in straight lines? "A while later she hooked up with this loser, Pollan. He was nice to her in the beginning, but then he started beating her up, too. She lied about it, didn't want people to know. Kept hoping things would work out. I didn't see her much those days, figured she was busy with her guy."

Jesse had basically been screwing his brains out with a succession of hot girls, and he'd been stupid enough to believe that Consuela had found a good guy. "I should've known," he said bitterly. "Should've checked on her."

Maura's expression showed no judgment; she just listened in silence.

Jesse took a deep breath, hating to remember this shit, then let it out. "One night she calls me from the hospital, needing me to come pick her up. Her face is black and blue, like he used her as a punching bag. I get her, we pick Juanito up from kindergarten, and I take them back to my place. Con finally tells me what's been going on. She says she's had enough and is leaving the guy."

Maura gave one firm nod. "Good for her."

"Didn't work out that way," he said bitterly. "Pollan apologized, pleaded, and she went back to him. Next time, he cracked a couple of her ribs. She left him again. This time she went to a shelter, quit her job and got a different one, tried to hide from him. But he found her. When he apologized and pleaded, she said she wasn't going back. He beat her up again. She talked to social workers, a lawyer. Got a restraining order saying he couldn't go near her."

"But he did?"

"Broke her arm that time. Went to jail for it."

Maura's pale face had gone almost white, and those ocean eyes were huge. He felt sorry, a sheltered woman like her hearing a story like this, but she'd asked. Besides, that flicker of hope said she just might understand.

"When he got out, he found her new apartment and beat her up real bad. She had to have surgery. Could have died." He wouldn't tell her that Pollan had kicked Con so badly in the belly that she'd needed a hysterectomy. He wouldn't violate his best friend's privacy, even if it would make his case stronger.

Maura's face looked frozen when she said, "So you . . ."

"Did the same to him."

"But he would have been put back in jail."

"And got out again. Found her again."

"She could have . . ." Her voice started out strong, then drifted away. She was frowning again.

He let her think about it for a few minutes, wondering if she'd come up with a solution that he hadn't thought of.

"She could have left town," she said hesitantly.

"Why the hell should she have to? 'Sides, Pollan said that if she ran, he'd find her. Age of technology, right? People can't just disappear."

A deep groove carved Maura's forehead in half. "Do you honestly think you solved the problem?"

He nodded firmly. "Told him if he so much as laid a finger on Con or Juanito, I'd kill him."

Her mouth opened in a big circle. He'd been honest, but for her it was too much. Once she got her breath back, she'd kick him out. So much for that flicker of hope.

She leaned forward, across the desk. "You can't take the law into your own hands."

He snorted. "The hands it's in sure didn't help Con. I only made one mistake, and that was waiting so long to do what I did."

She shook her head vigorously.

He wasn't about to argue. He couldn't win. She believed in society's rules and he didn't. Lucky her if those rules had protected her. They hadn't done much for him or Con. He and Maura'd always be on different sides of the tracks, like he'd known all along.

He studied her squinted eyes and creased forehead. She was trying to analyze him. Shouldn't be having such a tough time doing it. He was the simplest guy in the world.

"So do I go or stay?" he asked, pretty sure what the answer would be. Shit. Was he heading for jail?

"You . . ." She rubbed her forehead. All that frowning and analyzing must be giving her a headache. "Are you telling me the truth?"

He nodded. Lying was something he'd done as a kid, along with acting out and generally being a dick-head. "Yeah."

"And will you tell me the truth if I ask you something?"

Insulted, he grated out the word, "Ask."

"Can I trust you to never, ever, no matter what the circumstances, lift a finger against any of the residents here?"

He thought it over. Knew the answer she was looking for, but wouldn't lie to her. "Nope."

She gave one of those growly sounds of exasperation. "You would actually use violence against a senior citizen?"

"Yeah. Like, if one of the men hit one of the women, you bet I'd stop him."

She opened her mouth and closed it again. After a few seconds she said, "How would you stop him?"

He leaned forward and glared at her. "You mean, would I beat him within an inch of his life? Jesus, woman, what do you think I am?"

"You tell me." Now there was fire in her voice and it warmed his heart. She hadn't judged him yet; she wasn't giving up on him. She tapped the folder on her desk. "What I've got is a file that says you *did* beat a man within an inch of his life. Yet I've seen you with the residents and you've got a real empathy for them."

Bracing her elbows on her desk, she leaned forward, too. "So tell me, Jesse, can I trust you?"

He'd go to jail if she kicked him out, but that was less important right now than convincing Maura Mahoney that he wasn't a total asshole. "With the old folks? Yeah, you can trust me."

She stared intently into his eyes, and he met her gaze.

A few long minutes passed.

Then she nodded. "All right then. Let's talk about what work you should do next."

"What?" Man, that'd caught him off guard. "I can stay?" She believed him. Trusted him. He wanted to laugh, jump up, and give her a big smacking kiss on the lips. He resisted that impulse but couldn't hold back a giant grin.

"You can stay. I believe you, Jesse." Slowly, she smiled, too, and it lit her eyes.

Shit, he really, really wanted to kiss this woman. "Thank you, Ms. Mahoney."

"Call me Maura."

In his mind, in his fantasies, he'd said her name so many

times, but now, for the first time, he tasted it on his lips. "Thanks, Maura."

Her cheeks were coloring. "Well, there's work to be done." The pink deepened, eating up her freckles one by one. "I didn't order supplies from the garden center for the pond project because I wasn't sure . . ."

"Whether you'd let me stay."

She nodded. "We can phone now."

"You got approval from your Board?"

She wrinkled her nose, looking embarrassed. "I'll have to talk to them about how to handle the legalities, but they won't have to approve a budget. Fred Dykstra persuaded me to let the residents contribute, and that's covered all the anticipated costs."

"Cool. Bet they're happy."

"Yes. Yes, they are."

She made the call to Sunnyside and told him the pool would be delivered tomorrow, Wednesday.

"I'll do the lawn tonight," Jesse said. "Mow, seed the bare patches, fertilize, water. Then I'll start digging the hole for the pond."

"That sounds good. I'll be here, so if there's anything you need, just let me know."

"D'you usually work evenings, or are you doing this because of me?"

Her cheeks flushed even brighter. "Because of, uh, your community service, you mean? Don't worry about it. I'm filling in for a couple of other people, and that means longer hours. It's good experience, because I've applied for the general manager job here."

"General manager. Wow." Oh, yeah, their worlds were different. "Well, good luck."

"Thank you."

"But, uh— I thought you liked the job you've got."

"I love it. But I have a master's in business administration and I'm not using all the knowledge and skills I learned. I've been in this job four years now, and it's time to be more ambitious."

Ambitious. Must be nice to have all that education, to be able to be so ambitious. But he still figured the most important thing was finding a job you enjoyed. Speaking of which, pushing a lawnmower around on a warm April evening didn't sound half bad to him. He shoved himself to his feet. "I should get to work."

He'd just wheeled the lawnmower out to the garden and was going to start it up when Fred Dykstra came along. They shook hands and Fred said, "Maura Mahoney had a talk with me about our bike ride."

"Yeah, she was on my case, too."

"She was pretty upset."

"Seems to me it's your business if you wanna go for a ride." He hated the idea of old folks being treated like babies, being told what they could and couldn't do.

"She's concerned about liability."

Jesse snorted. "You gonna sue someone if we tip over?"

Fred laughed. "Not likely."

"And I got no plans to tip over anyhow. But . . ."

"Maura doesn't want us doing this."

"Guys like us, we oughta be able to ride a bike if we want. If you weren't living here, she'd have nothing to say about it."

"But I am. And she does. Don't you agree?"

Not so much. But on the other hand, he knew this was important to Maura. Tonight, she'd shown trust in him. He couldn't go behind her back and take Fred out on the Harley. "Shit. Guess it's off then. That blows." Then he said, "Sorry, shouldn't be using language like that."

But the older man didn't look offended. Instead, humor

lit his blue eyes. "You see things too black and white. Ever heard of compromise?"

Jesse shook his head. "When folks talk about compromise, what they mean is you're going to lose and they're going to win."

Fred reached up and patted Jesse's shoulder, almost as if he were still a boy. "You're a cynical fellow, and maybe you have reason to be. As for me, I don't believe in condemning someone until I've given them a chance."

"No, sure. But Maura—Ms. Mahoney—had a chance and said no."

"I'll talk to her again. If she agrees, you'll take me out?"

"Yeah, but she won't."

Fred Dykstra shook his head. "Just get on with your mowing, Jesse."

Jesse shrugged and obeyed.

In another twenty or so minutes he turned off the engine again, seeing Fred and Maura walking together across the grass. Below her tailored white shirt, she wore slim-fitting beige pants, and those legs of hers went on forever. All the way up to the place where her thighs joined.

"Here's the deal," Fred said.

Jesse, who had forgotten he was there, gaped at him.

"I wanted to get the two of you together," Fred said.

Oh, yeah! That was what he wanted, too. But wait, Fred couldn't mean *that*!

"To make sure everyone's on the same page about this," Fred said.

Oh. The bike ride thing. Jesse glanced at Maura, who seemed to be battling a grin. He frowned. What had Fred said to her?

The old man went on. "Cherry Lane has legal obligations to the residents and has to be concerned about potential lawsuits. They have liability insurance, of course, but they don't need a lawsuit or any unfavorable publicity. Therefore, Maura will contact the lawyer tomorrow and ask him to draft a waiver that will cover bike rides. I'll sign it. Once it's signed, we can go riding."

"Sounds like a hell of a lot of fuss over a simple ride," Jesse grumbled.

Fred raised his eyebrows. "To me, it sounds like a fair compromise that takes everyone's interests—and responsibilities—into account. Not to mention, it protects you, young fellow, from being sued for any damage that might result from a ride. Not only would Cherry Lane be liable, but you could be personally liable. You wouldn't want me suing you, and making you sell that bike to pay damages, now would you?"

Jesse gave a token roll of his eyes, knowing Fred would never do that. All the same, this did sound like a reasonable solution. He hadn't even realized he might be liable if something went wrong. Still, there was one flaw to the plan. "Lawyer'll take forever drafting the damned thing."

"I'll ask him to make it a priority." Maura spoke for the first time. "I know how much Fred enjoyed the ride on Sunday."

Well, how about that? Jesse grinned at her. "Cool."

She smiled back, and his heart began to thud.

Her mouth straightened like she'd gone serious again, but her eyes twinkled and squinted up at the edges. "Jesse, do you know what Fred did before he retired?" She was trying to keep her voice level, but he could tell she had a surprise for him.

He shook his head.

She produced her surprise with a flourish, and another grin. "Hostage negotiator."

"No shit. I mean, uh, wow." That was a damned serious job. He realized why Maura was laughing and gave a chuckle. "Hey, Fred, I guess Ms. Mahoney and I were pretty easy, after some of the guys you've dealt with."

"Feels good to exercise old muscles."

"Stick around us, we'll give you a workout." He said it unthinkingly, then wondered if Maura'd think he was being disrespectful.

But no, she was laughing, her cheeks glowing in the evening light.

He closed his eyes for a moment. Dusk, Maura with laughing eyes, that scent of gardenias. Sometimes life was damned fine.

She left, of course, but he got a lot of pleasure out of unashamedly ogling her ass as she and Fred walked back across the courtyard. When she wore a skirt, he got to admire her shapely legs, but pants showed off her butt. She did have a truly fine one, curvy and firm. Not one of those little ones that looked like a boy's, but not one of those big pear-shaped booties, either. On a scale of one to ten, this ass was a twenty.

This ass didn't belong to an accountant or a general manager. It definitely belonged in a lingerie catalog.

She and Fred stepped inside and the door closed.

Jesse gripped the handles of the lawnmower, thinking that he should start it up again. Maura was out of sight now, walking down the hall to her office.

The scent of gardenia lingered in the evening air, and the memory of that sweet, curvy ass lingered in his mind. He closed his eyes for a moment . . .

Imagined her walking into her office . . .

Imagined following her . . .

Maura stood with her back to him as she searched for something in a filing cabinet. When he reached out and put one hand on either side of her waist, she gave a little gasp. She held absolutely still and didn't look over her shoulder. "Jesse," she said, and it wasn't a question.

"Maura." He bent down to drop a kiss on the side of her neck, above the collar of that white shirt, and she shivered.

Then he leaned forward, pressing his body against hers. Resting his cheek against the top of her head, he closed his eyes, the better to savor the full contact. Her fine-boned shoulders nestled just under his own broader ones; his chest arched around her back.

His pelvis pressed against her curvy ass, and he was growing harder by the moment.

She squirmed backward against his hard-on. He gripped her waist tighter, forcing her to hold still, and he found her exact center, the split between those two sassy curves showcased by her clingy pants. He thrust hard, lodging himself firmly against her, and she gasped his name.

Then he reached around her with one hand, tracing the line of her fly down across her stomach and past. He cupped her pussy with his palm, and she moaned and began to squirm again. He pressed harder against her ass while his fingers began to stroke her through the thin fabric of her pants.

"Oh, Jesse," she moaned, then—

"Jesse? Jesse?"

What? No, she wasn't moaning his name, she was calling across the garden from her office window, which was behind him. And he was standing there gripping the handles of a turned-off lawnmower. He himself was very turned on, sporting a boner that was about to explode out his own fly.

He looked over his shoulder. No way was he going to turn to face her. He could only hope none of the residents were looking out their windows.

She had the window open and was leaning through it. "I forgot to ask, did you get any dinner?"

"Yeah, I grabbed something on the way over. Thanks."

Before she could ask anything else, he bent painfully to pull the cord that started the engine. Then he pushed the mower away from her, walking slowly. By the time he turned to head back in her direction, his body was under control and her window was closed partway.

He glanced at that window many times over the course of the evening, but she remained inside as he sowed grass seed and spread fertilizer.

Several of the old folks came to visit, including a few he hadn't met before. A couple had already heard that some of the residents were making financial contributions and were checking out "the investment," as they phrased it, so he tried his best to explain, be polite, and listen to their opinions.

Virginia Canfield brought a couple of white-haired ladies who she said had wanted to meet him and hear about the garden, so he chatted with them, figuring he'd stay late to dig the hole for the pond. These old folks had to go to bed soon, didn't they?

But when her two companions went inside, Virginia remained. She tilted a rather mischievous grin up to him. "We ladies have been speculating about you, Jesse Blue. A fine young man like you—and don't think that just because we're old, we don't appreciate a fine figure of a man—we've been wondering if there's a special lady in your life."

"Nope, no one special." He wasn't seeing anyone now, and in fact, while he'd had fun with lots of women, none really stood out. None had taken over his thoughts and fantasies the way Maura had.

"Now that's a real pity." Virginia studied him a moment longer, then said, "What kind of water plants are you thinking of for the pond?"

Glad she'd changed the subject, he asked, "What would you like?"

"Pink water lilies. I've always loved them. They're strong and they're feminine. It's a good combination."

"Yeah, I guess it is." In women, too. Women like Maura.

"I think Maura would like water lilies. Don't you?"

"Yeah. She likes pink." He'd seen that when she chose her own hanging baskets.

"You're getting to know her. That's good. She's a lovely woman, isn't she?"

At least when she wasn't being all prissy and judgmental. "Yeah."

"A special one." She said those words like they had particular meaning.

"Uh, yeah. She is." For a moment, he wondered if she really had changed the subject, or if she was still talking about his dating life. But no way would Virginia think a tool-belt guy was a good match for refined Maura.

The elderly woman gave a small, self-satisfied smile. "Well, I'll say good night and let you finish up here. It's getting dark."

He escorted her across the lawn and safely inside, then got back to digging the hole. The glow from Maura's window told him she was still there. Other windows were lit around the courtyard, and they provided enough light for him to keep going until he finished the hole.

It was time to pack it in. He glanced toward Maura's window again. Should he tell her he was going? The golden glow drew him. First, though, he washed his face and hands under the tap.

When he approached her window, open just a slit now, she was at her desk, scribbling away with one hand while the other toyed with a curl of hair that had come loose from the neat knot at the back of her head.

On, he thought. She was sexier with the glasses on.

He wanted to keep watching, and knew she couldn't see

him out here in the dark garden, but he was no peeping Tom. "Maura," he called softly, and tapped on the window frame.

She jerked upright and stared in his direction, then yanked her glasses off.

Maybe she was sexier with them off.

She came over and shoved the window wide open. "I didn't realize it was so late. You've put in extra time, as usual."

He leaned a shoulder against the outside wall. "Wanted to finish digging the hole, but people kept coming out. Hope it's okay that I talked to them."

She smiled. "I never anticipated that being part of your job. Never realized how interested the residents would be in the garden. But it's lovely for them to be so involved. And guess what? I had three more people come in this evening and make contributions. They told me how helpful you'd been, answering their questions. You handled it really well. Thank you."

He could feel the smile growing huge on his face and was about to respond when a phone rang.

"I should get that." She crossed quickly to her desk and picked up a cell. "Maura Mahoney." Then, "I'm glad you enjoyed the lecture."

It must be Edward, the guy she'd blown off before. She'd given him another chance.

Seemed like every time he felt a real connection between him and Maura, something happened to ruin it. Maybe that was a good thing.

Figuring he'd been dismissed, he began to close the window.

Listening to her mother on the phone and seeing the window begin to slide shut, Maura couldn't bear to see Jesse go. She lifted a hand, beckoning him to come inside.

He paused—darn it, what was she doing? he probably wanted to rush off to meet a date—then stretched the window wide again, climbed through, and took one of the vinyl guest chairs. He settled his body, his long legs sprawled out in front of him. Every move he made was graceful, in the way that a lion was graceful.

Maura tried to interrupt as Agnes raved about a recipe, but she couldn't get a word in. She was having trouble figuring out who her mother was, these days. As a child, she'd wished her adoptive mother was home more, that she was more domestic and maternal like her real mom had been. Now that Maura was grown up and Agnes was making fewer trips and involving herself more in her daughter's life, Maura found herself—guiltily—wishing the opposite. She loved Agnes and Timothy and still craved their approval, but it was easier to win approval when they were less involved in her life. Now her mother was saying she wanted to try the recipe on Friday, and Maura should come over.

"Not Friday, I have plans." Apparently Edward hadn't mentioned their date. Points to him, and Maura sure wasn't going to bring it up and have Agnes gloat, and get her hopes up.

Now Agnes was on about the dratted Academy reunion.

Maura gazed at Jesse from under her eyelashes. His jeans fly was pointing right at her again, making it impossible for her to not notice the bulge beneath.

When he'd first come to her office tonight, he'd obviously been only a few minutes out of the shower. Damp hair, clean clothes. Now his clothes were grubby and there was a smear of dirt on his arm. His face was clean, though, and she realized that the dampness on it, and in his hair, wasn't sweat but water. He'd washed up before coming to see her. For all his rough edges, he could be considerate. And, clean or sweaty, he was the sexiest man she'd ever seen.

Agnes was rattling on. "Why don't you and your date"—a blatant pause while she waited for Maura to supply a name, then a sigh—"whomever that might be, get together with us for dinner first, then we can all go together."

Edward would probably be happy to do that, if Maura did invite him to the reunion. Her, not so much. She played back her fantasy about attending with Jesse Blue, and stifled a grin. If either Agnes or Jesse knew what she was thinking, they'd be appalled.

"Thanks," Maura hedged, "but I'm not sure that would work. I'll let you know next week." She was a big girl. Why did she always feel a sour twinge of guilt at disappointing her parents? And why did they so often ask things of her that she really didn't want to give?

"You do that." It sounded like an order, with only one possible outcome. Then Agnes said, "Now, as for that recipe I want to try, how about this Thursday?"

"Sorry, I have to work then." Jesse would be here on Wednesday and Thursday. Technically, Maura could probably let Nedda record his time. He would put in more than his required hours whether she was there or not. He wouldn't hurt anyone unless he had a very strong reason, and the seniors sure weren't likely to give him one. Still, she wanted to be here when Jesse was working, for reasons she didn't want to analyze.

Right now, she was holding him up. He probably wanted to hurry home for a shower, then get together with a girlfriend. "Speaking of work," she said into the phone, "there's someone in my office now, Agnes. I have to go."

She hung up, noting an expression of surprise on Jesse's face. "Sorry about that," she said. "I swear, she thinks I don't have a life."

"Thought you were talking to that lecture guy," he said. "Uh, who's Agnes?"

"My mother."

"Oh." He digested that, then said mildly, "Seems to me you're old enough to be running your own life."

She squinted at him. "If that's your way of saying I'm almost middle-aged . . ."

He gave a surprised laugh. "Middle-aged? You kidding?"

"Oh! Well, thanks." His comment had sounded spontaneous and genuine, and she felt her cheeks growing rosy. "My parents don't really try to run my life." Except that they'd wanted her to choose one of their professions, they'd put a stop to her friendship with Sally, they'd made her feel so guilty about watching movies that she hid it like an addiction. "Well, of course they've always, uh, offered guidance on the important things, but mostly they were too busy to care about the rest."

And now they were match-making and Agnes wanted to try out recipes on her. "It seems they have a belated urge to do some parenting, for whatever reason."

He tilted his head questioningly. "A belated urge?"

It dawned on her that they were having a pretty personal conversation. She'd opened the door to that. This probably wasn't appropriate between supervisor and . . . whatever he was. Besides, he couldn't really be interested in her boring little life. "I shouldn't keep you. I'm sure there's someplace you need to be. A girlfriend waiting for you?" Now why had she asked? It was none of her business.

Chapter 13

Jesse shrugged casually. "No girlfriend these days. And nope, nowhere I need to be. So go on, tell me about the parent thing."

No girlfriend? Seriously? A guy like him? And did he actually want to have a conversation about her boring life?

Yet they had, more than once, kind of connected.

She studied him, lounging across from her. Purely masculine, infinitely sexy, and yes, he made her blood tingle and an achy pulse beat between her thighs. But, maybe even more than that, she was coming to like him. Hard to imagine they'd ever be friends—they were way too different for that—but moments like this were precious.

Wanting to prolong this one, she said, "They're my adoptive parents. My birth parents were killed in a car accident when I was six."

"Sorry."

"Me, too. They were great. I treasure the memories." She still felt the pain, too, though she'd learned not to show it. *A stiff upper lip, Maura, that's what's called for,* Timothy and Agnes had lectured. "They didn't have many relatives. My dad's uncle Timothy and his wife Agnes agreed to adopt me. They were considerably older than my parents, and their lives were already set."

"Set?"

She nodded. "He's a history professor and he was mostly at the university or hidden away in his den. She's an archaeologist, so she taught during the school year and was away on digs in the summer. They were so wonderful to squeeze me into their lives." They'd been the only ones willing to do so. But for them, she'd have ended up in foster care like Jesse. She'd always been totally aware of the debt she owed them and had tried so hard to live up to their expectations.

"An archaeologist and a historian? So conversation at your dinner table was about dead people."

She gave a surprised laugh. "I guess that's true." And it still was, unless they were nagging her about her career or single state.

His eyes gleamed wickedly. "You've come a long way, baby."

That "baby" made her heart clutch. No man had ever called her "baby," but she realized it was just a phrase. "A long way? How do you mean?"

"They work with dead people. Your people are alive, just pretty old."

She smiled. "I never thought of it that way." Following the natural progression of the idea, "And if I ever have a child, she'll probably work with middle-aged people."

"She?"

"Or he." Though she'd always envisioned one quiet little girl, a miniature of herself. But prettier, socially skilled, popular. The girl she wished she'd been—and might have been, had her birth parents not died.

Now, though, a foreign image flashed into her mind. A little boy with curly black hair, a real hell-raiser of a kid. Heat crept up her neck.

"*If* you have a kid?" he asked.

"I may not." Sad, but true—though her hopes were a little higher now, since that last pleasant chat with Edward.

Jesse cocked his head. "You don't like kids?"

"I do, though I don't know much about them. Our house wasn't exactly kid-friendly." Her adoptive parents hadn't had friends with children, and Maura hadn't made friends of her own. She'd rarely even felt like a kid.

An insight struck her: Agnes and Timothy had never wanted children and so when their sense of responsibility led them to adopt her, they'd tried to turn her into an adult. They'd put their needs ahead of hers. "If you're going to have children, you ought to do it right." The words flew out without thought.

Ashamed, she clapped her hands to her cheeks, feeling them heat. "No, sorry, I shouldn't have said that."

"Your adoptive parents didn't do it right." It was a statement, not a question, and there was sympathy in his tawny eyes.

"They did," she protested. Agnes and Timothy had given her everything. "Really."

"But?"

She shook her head vigorously.

"You're loyal. I get that." The corners of his mouth curved a little. "But there's a 'but.' Come on, spill."

An urge she didn't understand compelled her to tell this man—this utterly masculine, physical, sexy guy with the warm hazel eyes—things she'd never said before. "They took me when no one else would, and they really were good to me. But they hadn't wanted a child. I was an interference. They weren't parental, and they were too set in their ways to adjust. They wanted me to be a small adult, mature and self-sufficient. No dolls, no play dates, no tears over my parents' death."

Once she'd started, words she'd not even dared think

before spilled out of her mouth. "It seemed like they were never *there*. Even when Agnes was in town, even when Timothy emerged from his study, they weren't really there. Their heads were somewhere else, in ancient times."

"Sounds rough."

Those simple words brought her to her senses. Rough? She thought *her* life had been rough? "Oh, my gosh, I'm terrible. Being ungrateful to Agnes and Timothy, and complaining about my childhood when you grew up in foster homes. My home was great. I was always well fed, clothed, educated. I had academic enhancement classes, private school, a top-of-the-line computer, reference books, whatever I needed."

"Reference books." He grimaced. "What you wanted was their attention."

Embarrassed, she shrugged. "It's such a small thing to complain about."

He shook his head. "Kids should have attention. And love."

"Yes!" She nodded firmly. "I absolutely agree. But so many don't get either one." Warmth filled her. The way she and Jesse were talking, it was almost as if they were friends. This felt so good. It was much better than those bizarre sexual fantasies.

Though, even better . . . She imagined the two of them naked under the covers, satiated after wonderful lovemaking, having this kind of conversation . . .

"Did you ask for it?" His tone was mild, curious.

"Ask for . . . ?" Wonderful lovemaking? Now she'd lost the thread of the conversation. She was so bizarrely sex-obsessed these days.

"Attention. I'm guessing you didn't ask for it."

"I did, in my own way. I tried to be perfect: neat and tidy, quiet, obedient, top of my class. I wanted them to notice me, to tell me how good I was." To not regret taking her in. She'd have done anything to win a smile, a word of praise. Eventually, she'd come to understand that, in their fashion, they did care for her, but it wasn't in their nature to hand out words or demonstrations of love.

"Bet you were a good little girl. Me, when I first went into foster care, I was four. Even if I tried to behave, I'd forget in, like, a nanosecond."

"Four. Oh, Jesse." Her heart ached for the boy that he'd been. "What happened to your parents?"

A pause. "Never had a dad. My mom said he was just some Indian guy she met in a bar." Another pause. "She was an addict. Died of an OD."

"I'm so sorry." Her own birth parents had been wonderful. She'd had such a happy family for those six short years.

Jesse shrugged. "I went into foster care. And sometimes, I did try to be good. But you know what happens then, right? You become background. If you don't make waves, they don't see you. They take you for granted."

She nodded slowly. "You made waves." Remembering herself as a child, she tried to imagine what that little girl might have done to "make waves." Boy, she was so darned boring she couldn't visualize mischief, much less commit it.

"Oh, yeah, I acted out."

"How?" Jesse could tell her what childish mischief looked like.

"You really wanna hear this?"

"Yes." She wanted to know everything about him. He was the most fascinating person she'd ever met, and it went way beyond the fact that he was pure sex, walking. Or, at the moment, sitting. Sitting, talking to her like he was truly interested. Like she mattered. Warmth filled her—arousal, yes, but something else, too. Affection?

He shrugged. "You won't like it. I beat up on other kids, broke things, stole things."

Her mouth opened in a silent "O." That went way beyond mischief. And yet he'd done them so someone
would notice him. And also, she was sure—even if Jesse
didn't want to admit it—because he was frustrated and angry and hurt. Poor little boy. She really, really wanted to
hug him. "I imagine that didn't work, either. Yes, you'd
get noticed, but . . ."

"Yeah. As a troublemaker. They'd kick me out of the
house, back into the system. I'd get shuffled off to another
foster home." He sounded perfectly resigned, reciting the
facts of a childhood that horrified her.

He gave a rueful, twisted grin. "Kid like you, acts perfect, but no one notices her. Kid like me, acts out, gets
noticed—then gets booted."

Agnes and Timothy had never given her the easy,
demonstrative affection her birth parents had, but at least
she hadn't been booted—whether that was due to her own
good behavior or their sense of duty.

Studying Jesse, she thought that even though they were
so very different, she felt an amazing sense of empathy.
One that made her want to go over to him and take his
hand. If she did, he'd think she'd gone crazy. But she did
say, "When we first met, I didn't think we had anything in
common." A smile twitched her lips. "I wasn't even sure
you could communicate beyond single words or grunts."

Jesse sure as hell didn't talk this way with his guy
friends, but his longtime friendship with Con had taught
him that women wanted something different. Still, com-
municating had never felt so natural with his girlfriends as
it did with Maura.

He grinned back at her. "I thought you were a buttoned-up ice queen who—" Nope, he couldn't tell her
about his Victoria's Secret fantasy. "Didn't figure we'd ever
be talking like this."

"When I heard Louise had arranged community service, I expected a juvenile delinquent. You were a surprise. At first, I thought you were my worst nightmare."

"And now?"

Those blushes of hers were so feminine, so sexy. Man, he wanted this woman. It was all he could do to keep his body under control. Every time he was with her, he wanted her more. Tonight, she'd opened up. Shared parts of herself that he'd bet the reserved Maura rarely shared. The woman sitting across from him might have the buttons on her shirt done up and her hair pinned tight, but she wasn't acting like an ice queen.

"Now," she said softly, "I'm really glad you're here."

He wanted her, and for the first time he sensed she might be open to that. She didn't see him as a charity case, or some guy to fuck in secret. Maybe it was crazy to get involved with her, but hell, he'd never backed down from crazy.

He'd have told her he was doubly glad he'd whaled on Pollan since it had landed him here with her, but he figured that approach wouldn't go over so well. Instead, he gave her his best smile and said, "And I can think of places I'd rather be."

Hurt flashed in her eyes, and he quickly went on. "Like, on my Harley, with you on behind me. What'cha say, Maura Mahoney? Wanna come for a ride?" It was a test. She could back off, rebuild the walls between them. Put him in his place. He sure hoped she wouldn't.

The hurt vanished in an instant, replaced by a sparkle. "A ride? On your bike? Me?"

"You haven't lived 'til you've been on a bike on a warm summer night."

"Then I definitely haven't lived." Her words, which might have been teasing, sounded weighted, as if she really meant them.

He stood and walked with slow deliberation around her

desk. Looming over her, he held out his hand. "Then let down your hair and live a little."

She gazed up at him, expression unreadable. Then, also slowly and deliberately, she put her hand in his.

Feeling a sizzle of heat, a surge of elation, he gripped her slim fingers and tugged her to her feet. Trying to hide how much this meant—her acceptance of him and of this change in their relationship—he joked, "There's one thing you gotta do first."

She glanced around. "What?"

"Sign a waiver."

She gaped at him, then must've seen the twinkle in his eyes, because she laughed. "I think I'll just trust you. I'll put myself in your hands."

He grinned. "I'm good with my hands."

Her cheeks went pinker, but she came back with, "I've noticed that."

Hell, yeah, she was into him, just like he was into her. This was going to be one fine ride.

As she collected her purse, he got his jacket. When he'd arrived at Cherry Lane, he'd just tossed it on the spare chair, but she'd draped it neatly over the back.

When she walked toward the door, he rested a confident hand on her lower back.

She jumped like she wasn't used to a man's touch, then gave a tiny, approving sigh. But then she gasped, stepped away, and turned to face him. "No, wait. What are we thinking?"

He was thinking of her on the bike behind him, arms wrapped tight, body plastered against his. Of riding into the night, finding a place to stop, kissing her in the moonlight and seeing where that led. His blood pulsed and his groin ached at the thought. Tonight, maybe one of his sex dreams would become reality.

But it seemed Maura was thinking something very different, from the shocked expression on her face. "We can't do this," she told him.

What the fuck? "Are you on about liability again?"

"No, it's not that." She shook her head vigorously. "I mean, yes, it is, but not that way."

For a while there, he'd thought they could communicate just fine. Now he didn't have a clue what she was talking about.

"I'm supervising your community service," she said.

"Yeah. So?"

"It wouldn't look good."

Her dating the gardener. That's what she meant. Heat—and this time not the heat of arousal—rose in him. Pissed off, he snapped, "Then just forget it."

Her eyes narrowed. "What are you mad about?"

Was she so high and mighty, she didn't even see that she'd just insulted him? "Who gives a shit about appearances?" He used the swear word on purpose.

"I do, because I care about my job and I've applied for a promotion," she said crisply. "And you should, because you don't want anything to jeopardize your community service." She gazed intently up at him. "You're impulsive, and that can be rather charming. But you don't always think through to the consequences. Like when you took Fred Dykstra for that bike ride."

"That's better than being so freaking obsessed about consequences you never have any fun at all."

"There's a difference between— No, wait." She took in a breath, let it out. "Before we need to call Fred to negotiate, might I suggest there's a middle ground?"

He took a breath, too, remembering what the older man had said earlier. "A compromise?"

She nodded. "There's virtue to your position, and to mine. I do want to go for a ride with you, Jesse. But that's personal. It's separate from our work here."

He liked how she said "our work," as if they were a team. "What are you saying?"

"We leave separately." She considered. "You go first, and ride your bike over to the mall parking lot. I'll come along five minutes later and drive over to meet you."

She didn't want anyone to know she was seeing him *personally,* which still pissed him off. But he heard what she was saying about her job and his community service. If he thought about what Barry Adamson would say about Jesse coming onto his boss . . .

"Okay, Maura, it'll be our secret." And in a way, that made it even sexier.

Maura darted to the ladies' room, where she splashed cold water on her face and hands, trying to cool the heat that raced through her. It was a bike ride. Not a date. Jesse'd never want to date a woman like her. Would he? And of course she didn't want to date a man like him.

A virile, skilled, hot-as-sin man.

No, a man who was her opposite, who didn't even like to read, whom Agnes and Timothy would hate.

Jesse had kissed her. But just because she was there. Not because he was attracted. Right? And she'd kissed him back because she was surprised and, okay, attracted, but only in a hormonal way.

He'd touched her lower back when they were leaving her office. To her, it had felt intimate. But for him, it was probably just a habit. He did it with all the women he . . . what? Dated? But this wasn't a date.

He'd asked her for a bike ride because . . . Well, maybe because they'd been getting along, almost like friends. Or because he thought she was overreacting when she insisted on waivers and he wanted to prove that it wasn't dangerous.

Dangerous. Hopping onto a huge, black, throbbing Harley, behind Jesse. That sounded plenty dangerous to her, and it had way more to do with the man than the motorcycle.

She brushed her teeth, took her hair down and combed it, then pulled it back up, and brushed on a touch of brown mascara and a thin coat of pink lip gloss. Afterward, she looked exactly the same as when she'd started.

Still, some purely female instinct had her dabbing gardenia perfume at her throat and into the small amount of cleavage created by the peach bra that, for some silly reason, she'd worn under her tailored shirt.

"Aagh," she muttered to her reflection. "You're hopeless. It's not a date."

All the same, it was personal, not business, and it was the first time in her life she'd had a personal engagement with a totally hot man.

By now Jesse should have a good head start. She hurried toward the front door of the building, anticipation quickening her step. A hot man, a motorcycle—this was shaping up to be the most exciting night of her life.

She rounded a corner, entered the reception area, and—"What?"

The disagreeable Nedda was at the desk, avidly watching as three other people conversed. Fred Dykstra and Lizzie Gilmore stood hand in hand, talking to Jesse. Jacket hooked casually over his shoulder, he was laughing at something one of them had said, and didn't look in any hurry to leave.

What part of leaving separately had he failed to grasp?

Squaring her shoulders, she marched toward them. "Good evening, everyone."

"Hey, Ms. Mahoney," Jesse said, that wicked gleam in his eye. "I was just heading out when Fred and Lizzie came in. They were telling me about their dinner."

"We taxied to the waterfront for a seafood dinner," Fred said, "and ate outside. It's a lovely evening."

"Indeed it is," Lizzie said. "You young people should get out there and enjoy it." Her gaze flicked between Maura and Jesse.

Maura noted Jesse's spontaneous grin, then glanced past him to see Nedda staring with unabashed interest.

"An excellent idea," Maura said briskly. "I'm heading out now."

"Jesse," Fred said, "you walk the girl out. Make sure she gets to her car safe and sound."

"Somehow I manage on my own every other night," she said dryly.

"Don't argue with a hostage negotiator," Jesse said. "Come on, Ms. Mahoney." He gestured toward the door.

Huffing a little, not sure whether to be amused or annoyed, she said, "I surrender."

They all said their good nights, and she and Jesse walked away in silence.

Outside, the night air was soft and scented, the street silent. He said quietly, "You really want to meet at the mall?"

She was deliberating, when he moved closer and again rested his hand on the dip of her lower back, just above the waistband of her pants. Even through a layer of silk, she could feel his heat and it made her own skin tingle. "Uh . . ."

"Let's just hop on and ride." His hand left her back and she felt the loss, then a moment later he grasped her hand.

His action had the effect of banishing all rational thought. Jesse Blue was holding her hand—and not just to steer her to his bike, or he wouldn't be linking his fingers through hers and squeezing gently. Sexy warmth pulsed up her arm and radiated through her body. Was this really happening?

When they arrived at his Harley, she realized something. "Oh, no. We can't. I don't have a helmet." She should have known this was too good to be true.

"You sure do believe in following the rules, Ms. Mahoney," he teased, giving her hand another squeeze.

"But it's not safe," she protested. "And it's illegal. And—Oh," she said as he reached over to the far handlebar and unhooked a second helmet. "You brought an extra?"

"A guy can hope. And look where it got me."

What had he hoped? That he'd find a woman who wanted to ride with him? Or that . . . Had he actually hoped to take her, Maura, out on his bike?

He stowed her purse in a container on the bike, then held out his jacket. "This'll keep you warm."

She'd never in her life worn a guy's jacket, or shirt, or anything else. "But won't you be cold?"

He shot her an outraged look that had her smothering a giggle, then held out the jacket so she could slide her arms into it.

She wrapped the oversized leather around her, reveling in the thought of his body inside it. "Thank you."

"Looks good on you." He ran a finger over her cheek, his rough skin making the caress even more sensual. With a sexy smile, he went on. "But then, most things would."

The sheer ridiculousness of that compliment made her finally realize what was happening. This was another of her sexy fantasies.

Don't let me wake up!

"It's a great jacket," she told him. "Beautiful leather."

"I've got three possessions that matter: my bike, my jacket, and my giant TV. That first day, I liked how you treated my jacket."

She ducked her head and smiled, remembering how she'd smelled it. Hmm. In a fantasy, she could be bold. And so she slanted a teasing smile up at him. "That first day, I smelled your jacket."

"You what?"

"You know. Smelled it, so I could smell you."

Something flared in his eyes. "And now it'll smell like you. Gardenia. You didn't wear that perfume before."

"No, I didn't."

"Wonder what got you wearing perfume," he teased. "Couldn't have had anything to do with me, could it?"

She punched his arm. "Arrogant." She'd done it for herself, like wearing the peach lingerie, because it made her feel feminine and sensual. But yes, Jesse had been in the back of her mind, the way he always was. "Actually," she said airily, "I was hoping to win Fred Dykstra away from Lizzie Gilmore."

He chuckled. "That first day, I never guessed you had a sense of humor."

"That first day, I probably didn't." In fact, the real her, as compared to this Maura-in-a-fantasy, probably still didn't. "Now, didn't someone promise me a bike ride?" She couldn't wait to climb up on that throbbing machine and wrap her arms around Jesse. She wanted to cram as much as possible into this fantasy before she woke up.

He passed her a helmet and helped her do it up, his fingers lingering on her skin. Then he put on his own, climbed onto the bike, and waited for her to swing on behind him. How silly to have worn pants in this fantasy. If she'd been in a skirt, she would have hiked it up her thighs, her naked flesh sandwiching Jesse's jean-clad hips and thighs.

"You're into rules," he said, "so here they are." He reached back to find her hands, where they rested on her own thighs, and tugged her arms around him.

Oh, yes, this was good. She felt his heat, his solid muscles, through his tee. And as she leaned closer, she caught the erotic scent of fresh-cut grass and hardworking male.

"Keep your arms around my waist," he said, "and hang on tight."

"Ooh, there's a tough one," said the Maura-in-a-fantasy

woman, tightening her grip and pressing her breasts shamelessly against his back.

He sucked in a breath and growled, in a fake grumbly tone, "Damn it, stop distracting me."

She had the power to distract him? But of course she did. She was sensual Maura, wearing peach lace lingerie and gardenia perfume.

"Here's the other thing to know," he said. "When we take a curve, the bike'll lean over, into the curve. Your body will want to lean in the other direction, to counter-balance it."

She nodded. "That seems logical."

"Maybe, but it's wrong. You lean into the curve."

"Lean in?" What did he mean?

"Just plaster yourself to my back and follow where my body goes."

"I can do that." And what woman wouldn't be thrilled to bits to follow that rule?

Jesse could hardly believe that the prissy woman who'd looked down her nose at him was now twined around him. That she was as into him as he was into her.

That she'd smelled his freaking jacket.

Thank God he'd driven this bike so often he could do it in his sleep, because Maura was one giant distraction. At first she'd been a "little old lady" rider, stiff and cautious, but by the time they got out of the city and onto a country road, she'd loosened up. She pressed the fronts of her thighs into the backs of his and squished her breasts against his back. Her hands rested just above his belt. If she moved them down a couple of inches she'd realize what she was doing to him. But hell, she probably knew anyhow.

Now, he wanted to make her whoop. He wanted to hear the classy Ms. Mahoney let out a whoop. Knowing this road was almost always deserted at night, he whipped the bike along the straightaways and curled it deep into the curves.

She clung tight as a burr, leaning into the curves right along with him. Her helmet clunked against his as she said something he couldn't catch. Was she asking him to slow down? "Louder," he yelled at her.

"Faster!" she hollered back.

He laughed and the wind snatched the sound from his lips. There was a hill coming up and if he popped the bike over the top, it would fly a few yards. And so he made it happen.

Maura whooped like a banshee, and he let go with an answering one as her arms crushed his stomach. Man, he was glad he'd met this woman.

The road got twisty then, and he had to slow down. They were nearing a place where there was a pretty meadow by a stream. All you had to do was hop a wooden fence. It was someone's private property, but no one would be hanging around at this time of night. When he got Maura in that meadow in the moonlight, he'd do his best to make his fantasies come true.

Oh, yeah, it was going to happen. The more he slowed the bike, the more touchy-feely Maura got. Her hands were roaming his chest, exploring his anatomy. Then she headed south again, resting one hand on his belt buckle.

Yeah, baby, go for it, he urged her silently, slowing the bike even more.

One finger ventured to the top of his fly. Another joined it, then the first one moved down farther. The fingers stopped. She had touched the tip of his erection.

He held his breath. The woman sure knew how to torture a guy.

As if she'd suddenly made up her mind, she moved her whole hand and cupped him with her palm.

He sucked in another breath.

She squeezed experimentally and he smothered a groan.

She took her hand away and he breathed again. Then she ran a fingernail down his fly and up again.

"Oh, Jesus," he gasped.

She stopped. "Sorry." Her lips were so close to his ear he felt her warm breath. Teasingly, she said, "My hand slipped."

"Then let it slip again, would you?" He grabbed her hand and placed it, palm-down, against him.

He imagined her sliding down his zipper, extracting his dick. The cool night air, her hot hand pumping him—

Jesus Christ! Now there was a recipe for an accident. She was doing a fine job of making him lose his concentration. Regretfully, he eased her hand to safe territory, and a few minutes later he pulled off on the side of the road.

When he shut off the engine, Maura slid off, stumbling a little. He caught her arm, steadied her, then climbed off, too. He took off his helmet, experiencing the usual jolt of going from noise to silence. Although, as his ears adjusted, of course the night wasn't silent. Leaves rustled; an owl hooted.

Maura took off her helmet, too. "Why did you stop?" Her voice sounded loud against the stillness. She hushed it down to almost a whisper. "We're in the middle of no-where."

"There's a place I know. Think you'll like it." He took both their helmets, then pushed the bike off the road and hid it behind bushes.

She stood by the side of the road, stretching. Her neatly tucked hair had gotten messed up by the helmet and, without asking, he pulled out the pins until it all tumbled down in a soft, tangled mass.

She finger-combed it. "I must look a total mess."

Out here, there was no city light in the sky, just moon

and stars. Her pale face with its perfect features glowed, and her tousled hair gleamed, more silver than gold tonight. "You look beautiful."

She ducked her head, then suddenly flicked her hair and looked back up at him. Staring straight into his eyes, she said, "So do you."

Oh, man. Not that he liked the idea of being beautiful, but he got what she meant and loved that she'd said it.

She gazed expectantly at him, and he knew she was waiting for a kiss. And he needed to give it to her. But not here, on the side of the road where someone might come along. Not here, when what he really hoped was that once they got going, they wouldn't want to stop.

"Come on." He held out his hand.

She slipped hers into it like it belonged there. "Come where?"

Come all around me. And then, just when you start to relax, I'll make you do it all over again.

Chapter 14

Struggling to control his body, Jesse said, "We're gonna hop a fence."

"We're trespassing?"

"Got a problem with that?"

She reflected a moment, then gave a soft giggle. "Not if they don't catch us."

"I've created a monster. What happened to Ms. By-the-Book?"

"I'm reading a different book tonight."

And it was the only book in the world that he'd ever liked.

He started to tug her in the direction of the fence, but she pulled back, stopping him so he turned to look at her. "Maura?"

"Jesse?" Her eyes were huge, almost pleading. "This is a fantasy, right?"

A fantasy come true. "Damn right."

"You won't let it end too soon?"

God, she really was into this, as turned on as he was. "Hell, no."

This time, when he tugged her hand, she hurried along beside him. He clambered over the fence, then helped her over. The meadow was as pretty as he remembered, the grass as soft. "Kick off your shoes," he said, unlacing his sneakers and pulling them off, then stripping off his socks.

She slipped out of her shoes and wriggled her toes sensuously in the grass. "Oh, heaven. That feels so good. Oh, yes, I know this fantasy." She glanced around and murmured something that sounded like, "But where's the cat?"

He was about to ask her to repeat what she'd said, when she crossed to the bank of the stream, dipped her toes in, then quickly pulled back. "Too cool for wading."

"I didn't bring you here to go wading."

"No?" she teased. "Then what did you bring me here for?"

"Oh, you know. To sit and talk," he teased back.

"Talk?" She wandered back toward him, looking puzzled.

"You know when a guy says 'talk,' he really means other stuff, right?"

"Men do have their own mysterious language."

He chuckled. "Take off my jacket, Maura. I'll keep you warm."

While she obeyed, he stripped off his T-shirt.

She gaped, then said breathlessly, " 'Talk' means taking your clothes off?"

He spread the T-shirt on the grass. "Don't have a blanket." He beckoned for her to hand him the jacket, and spread it, too.

Her gaze roamed all over his torso, and he could tell she liked what she saw. Women always did, but tonight Maura was the one who counted. In fact, since he'd met her, she was the only one who counted. Was he crazy to think there might be something real, something special, between them?

Jeez, what was wrong with him? He was out here alone with a gorgeous woman—a woman who'd told him not to let the fantasy end too soon, which meant not before she climaxed. And he was going all girly, thinking about *feelings*?

He plunked himself down on the grass and patted the cast-off clothing.

She eased herself down, looking nervous now, like he'd thrown her off balance by whipping off his shirt. But hell, if she wanted an orgasm, they had to get naked.

Still, Maura was different from other women he'd known. He knew she had a passionate side, but sometimes she seemed almost innocent. She dated guys who took her dancing and gave her champagne, yet it seemed she didn't trust a man to give her great sex, to make her come. *Don't let the fantasy end too soon.* And he'd promised it wouldn't.

He wasn't a champagne kind of guy, but he did know about sex. He'd make this good for her.

Despite the way she'd groped him, now she was giving off signals that said she didn't want to be rushed. So, not touching her, he said, "I'm glad you came out with me tonight."

"It's been wonderful. I was wrong about bike riding." The tip of her tongue licked her lips. "And wrong about you."

He separated a strand of her wavy hair and curled it around his finger. Then he tugged her toward him, and she came.

He touched his lips to hers. God, she was sweet. He wanted to dive in and devour her, but forced himself to ease back. "I can't believe you don't have a serious boyfriend."

"The men I meet are perfectly nice, but . . ." She shook her head. "And you, Jesse? There's really no special woman in your life?"

Virginia Canfield had asked him the same question earlier tonight. The truth was, the only woman he'd really thought of as special was Maura. He shook his head. "No. I've dated—"

"I bet you have," she broke in.

He shrugged. "Yeah. But just casually. And no one in the last two or three months." He framed her face with his hands and leaned closer.

She gave a little sigh and leaned forward, too, resting her hands on his chest.

The scent of gardenia teased his nostrils with its sultry fragrance as he pressed his lips to hers, more insistently this time. He nibbled her bottom lip, sucking bits of it in and out of his mouth and pressing his teeth gently into her flesh. And then, when his tongue licked the crease between her lips, she parted them and opened for him.

He slid his tongue inside and hers met it, hesitantly at first, then eagerly, passionately.

Instantly, he was hard.

And harder still when her soft hands began to explore his naked torso. Shoulders and upper arms first, then growing bolder, her fingers tangling in the wiry hair on his chest, rubbing over the nubs of his nipples. Not squeezing, just brushing over tentatively, the way she'd first touched his fly. Getting the feel of him?

When he touched the button at the neck of her blouse, she didn't stop him, so he slipped it through the buttonhole. She was sitting upright, leaning slightly toward him with her legs tucked together to one side, a little prim despite the heat of her kisses, despite the erotic scent of gardenia.

He was in charge and she was waiting to see what he'd do. Though his body urged him to move this along, he needed to bring Maura with him. To give her pleasure.

She sat very still as he continued to undo buttons. He didn't mean to touch her naked flesh, not yet, but his thumb grazed her stomach and she shivered. When all the buttons were undone, he slowly parted the front edges of her shirt, sliding them back to reveal the woman inside.

His breath caught in his throat. She was wearing a bra

straight out of Victoria's Secret. Lacy and sexy as all get-out. Her skin was ivory and the bra was a couple shades darker. Pale pink, maybe. He couldn't tell in this light, and who cared anyway?

"Lie down." His voice came out huskier than usual.

Silently, she obeyed. She didn't touch him, just gazed up, looking nervous and expectant.

He bent to drop a kiss on her lips. Then he kissed the hollow of her throat, the ridges of her collarbones, the soft flesh just above the cups of her bra.

"It opens . . ." Her voice squeaked. She cleared her throat and began again. "It opens in the front."

Thank God. She wanted him to open it. He flicked the clasp, took an anticipatory breath, then spread the bra apart. Her breasts were as beautiful as he'd fantasized them: small, firm, rosy-tipped, with taut nipples. He palmed one breast in each hand, cupping them reverently. Maura, this was Maura, her nipples all beaded up just for him.

He bent to breathe air on one of those buds, then moistened it with his tongue. He licked, sucked, trying to be gentle.

Her body shifted and she pressed up against his mouth, silently asking for more.

He gave it to her, then turned his attention to the other nipple, cupping the first breast warmly in his hand as he teased the other with his mouth.

She moaned and he returned to her mouth, to kiss her as passionately as he knew how, and she kissed him back fervently.

When he touched the waistband of her pants, she didn't stop him, so he undid the button and slid down the zipper.

She lifted her lower body so he could slide the pants down, and he carefully pulled them all the way off, leaving tiny panties. Her legs were long and lovely. Even her feet were elegant. One day he would massage them, nibble them, see if he could bring her to orgasm just by playing with her feet. Not tonight, though. There were more important body parts to explore.

He trailed his fingers up the inside of her legs, heading for, but just bypassing, the triangle of lace covering her sex.

"Wait a minute," she murmured, then she sat up and peeled the blouse and bra off her shoulders.

When she lay back down, all he could do was stare. Naked but for the triangle of lace, she was a moon goddess. His goddess, to worship.

Sex had always seemed easy to him, lusty and natural. His partners were always satisfied. But now he felt such a strange mix of feelings. He wanted to bury himself deep inside Maura and have mind-numbing sex, yet he wanted to caress her tenderly, let her know how much he cared for her. Yes, he cared. Cared for the woman inside, as well as the perfect body. But he couldn't tell her. This was too new, and they were too different. He had no idea what tonight meant—for either of them.

Enough, for now, that they were here, like this. That she wanted him.

"You're so beautiful, Maura. I'm scared to touch you."

"Oh, Jesse, touch me. Please."

To have Maura aroused and begging his touch made his swollen dick pulse. "Where?" he murmured. "Where do you want me to touch you?"

"Everywhere."

He stretched out beside her, leaning across her body so his chest just touched her breasts, and he slanted a kiss across her lips. His erection was painfully hard, escaping his cotton boxer-briefs and pressing against coarse denim. But he didn't want to rush things, didn't want to be selfish and leave her behind.

He concentrated on her face, kissing her eyes until they

closed, then watching them pop open again as he tickled her eyebrows with his tongue. He traced the line of her nose, stroked across her lips, nibbled that stubborn jaw. Slid down and flirted with her nipples again, watching as her pelvis began a dance that told him, clear as words, what she was feeling inside.

His tongue traced the center of her body down to her navel, circled it, slid down again, to the edge of the lacy band of her one remaining garment. He took her waist in his hands, using his thumbs to caress downward, sliding along her hips, then across the lacy triangle of her panties. He felt the springy curls of hair, the firm mound underneath. His index finger trailed farther, to the damp silky strip that ran between her legs.

She started, then subsided, but he felt the tension in her body. This time it wasn't the tension of arousal, he thought, but of anxiety. Didn't she want him to do this? Was he moving too quickly, or not quickly enough? Not touching her in the right way? He'd promised her an orgasm, and he'd always cared about pleasuring his partners, but never before had it been this important.

He stroked cautiously along the strip of fabric, and suddenly her muscles relaxed and she moaned. She began to move against his hand, her body telling him exactly how she wanted to be touched as she squirmed and pressed against him.

God, he wanted to be inside her. But he was fascinated by her body, by her reactions, and he sensed she was close. He couldn't leave her now, not while her body cried out for release.

He glanced at her face, saw her eyes squeezed shut and a look of intense concentration. Her thighs were spread wide, and she pressed upward against his fingers as he stroked a little harder now, a little faster. Through drenched silk, his thumb found her swollen nub and teased it.

Her hips moved in a private rhythm, and little moans came out of her mouth.

Then, "Oh, Jesse!" and her body froze for a second. Froze, then surged against him, bucking and throbbing. He nestled his palm close, holding her through the spasms.

Jesus, but he wanted to come, too. Just watching her, touching her, feeling the moist heat of her crotch as she throbbed against his palm, had brought him so close to the edge he could barely hold on.

He became aware he was sucking in air in great panting breaths, just like she was.

"Jesse?"

"Yes?"

"That was amazing. But . . ."

"What?"

"Don't you want . . . I mean, don't you want to uh, take off your jeans and . . ."

"Oh, yeah."

"What's keeping you, then?"

He gave a ragged chuckle. "God knows." He sprang to his feet, wrestled the button through the buttonhole, and hauled down the strained zipper. He struggled to get his legs out of his jeans and realized she had sat up and was staring up at him, her eyes huge. He glanced down, saw the huge erection busting out of the top of his underwear.

Should he strip off his boxer-briefs, or would that be rushing things? Hell, he was supposed to be good with his hands; he was supposed to know what he was doing. It wasn't like he'd never had sex before. But this, it was different. Maura was different, and that made things great, but a hell of a lot scarier.

She was sprawled across his T-shirt and jacket, so he sank down on the grass beside her, feeling its soft tickle against his bare skin.

When he leaned over to kiss her, her hands gripped his shoulders and moved down his back.

He slid his body over hers, taking his weight on his knees yet letting their bodies touch. His chest to her breasts, his belly to her soft, flat tummy. Her hands continued their journey and reached his buttocks, squeezing and pressing him close. Her hips rose, grinding that lacy triangle against him, and he thrust against her, unable to stop himself.

"Wouldn't it be better . . ." She murmured something he didn't catch.

"Hmm?"

"Could we take off our . . ."

Thank God. He rolled off her quickly, yanked off his underwear, then eased hers down her legs. He wanted to stare spellbound at the beauty he'd just revealed, but his body was demanding action. Very, very soon. He grabbed at his jeans, fumbled his wallet out of his pocket, and found a condom. His hands were shaking so badly he could barely get the damned thing on.

When he did, he again covered her body with his. She raised her knees, cradling him between them. Her eyes, dazzling in the moonlight, gazed straight into his.

And suddenly, despite the urgent need in his body, the world stopped spinning and stood still. "Maura," he breathed.

Her smile was the loveliest thing he'd ever seen. "Jesse."

It could have been seconds, minutes, even hours that they stared straight into each other's eyes. He had the strangest feeling of connection, like nothing he'd ever experienced before. He'd fantasized plenty about Maura Mahoney, but tonight was a whole different thing.

He had to join with her, couldn't stay separate from her any longer. Reaching between their bodies, he touched her with his fingers, stroking, circling, making sure she was ready.

She wriggled against him, making those sexy little moaning sounds. "Please, I need you."

He parted those damp silky folds, then eased the tip of his dick inside her. She was hot, tight, and he was scared he was going to hurt her. Then she did two things, at once. She squeezed his buttocks just as she thrust upward, encompassing him.

His body went crazy on him. He pumped into her like a madman, and damned if she didn't grab his butt even tighter. He'd only managed four or five strokes when he knew the dam was going to break. Fortunately, he heard her cry his name, felt her body spasm around him. "Jesus, Maura," he cried as he thrust one final time, letting everything pour through him and into her. He couldn't stop pumping, but each successive thrust was weaker until finally he collapsed on top of her.

Her tummy fluttered under him; her breasts pushed up as she took deep breaths.

His head was crammed into the space between her neck and shoulder, where he inhaled gardenia and something even more sultry and sexy. Maura's arousal; her satisfaction.

Not wanting to crush her, he tried to take some weight on his knees, but they felt like jelly. He touched her skin with his tongue, tasting salt, pressing little kisses into her until he had the strength to lift his head and look at her face.

His moon goddess's grin nearly split her face. He realized he was smiling the same way. "Wow, that was something," he said.

"It's not just your hands you're good with, Mr. Blue."

"Oh, man, I can do way better than that. I acted like a high school kid."

"You mean you can last longer than three seconds?" she teased.

"That sounds like a challenge." He touched her lips gently with his. "God, but you're hot. And sweet."

Except, Maura didn't feel hot. Cold was seeping into her bones. She moved away from Jesse, sitting up and wrapping her arms around herself, suddenly self-conscious. This wasn't how a sex fantasy was supposed to go. Shouldn't the scene shift, and magically they'd be in a nice cozy bed, with rose petals strewn across the sheets and a crackling fire to warm her?

It had to be a fantasy, though. For perhaps the dozenth time she told herself that.

The real Maura Mahoney would never have wild sex with a man she'd known only a few days—a man who could cost her her job. And Jesse Blue wouldn't look at the real Maura like she was the loveliest, most sexy woman in the world.

It couldn't be real.

It had felt real, but so had last night's gardenia pool dream.

Except, tonight had felt more real—as if the details she'd skimmed in novels, the ones she'd incorporated in previous fantasies, had come blazingly to life.

She'd read, once, that a person couldn't know what the ocean was like from just reading about it and seeing pictures. They couldn't understand until they'd waded in, felt waves caress and suck at their ankles, smelled that crisp, tangy scent, heard the roar of waves and the cry of gulls.

Tonight, for the first time, she understood sex: the physical sensations, so intense and exquisite; the incredible feeling of having her empty, needy, most intimate places filled by a man; the emotion of joining, sharing, merging; even the less romantic aspects like the chilly ground and watching Jesse strip off the used condom. She would never have fantasized that last detail.

Oh, my God. This was real!

Hurriedly, she grabbed up her shirt and pulled it on, not bothering with her bra.

Jesse sat up, too. "Maura?"

She ignored him until her fingers, clumsy with nerves, managed to get the buttons done up all the way. Once she was covered from shirt collar to the shirt tails tugged down to cover the tops of her thighs, she finally turned to him. "We shouldn't have done this."

Oh, God, they shouldn't, for so many reasons. Why had she let this happen? She'd been totally irresponsible, wanting so badly to be with Jesse—to be wanted by Jesse—that she'd fooled herself into thinking this was a fantasy.

"What the hell?" He gaped up at her.

She scrambled to her feet, holding the tails of her shirt in place, and pointed to his T-shirt, crumpled in the grass where she'd been sitting. "Get dressed. Please."

When he stood, she picked up her thong—disgustingly damp; no, this was no romantic, sensual fantasy—and, shuddering, tugged it on under her shirt, followed by her pants.

"What the hell's gotten into you?" His voice was rough with frustration.

Cautiously, she glanced over her shoulder. Then, seeing that he was dressed, she turned around. Oh, my, he was so handsome, his long black hair rumpled, his T-shirt creased, and those old jeans clinging to his muscular legs.

She'd had sex with him for real? He'd wanted to take her for a bike ride, wanted to make love—no, she corrected herself—have sex with her?

"Jesse, I got carried away, and it was wrong. You see, I've been having some fantasies and dreams, and—"

"When you go into those little trances."

Feeling foolish, she nodded. "And when I'm asleep."

"Me, too," he said. "I've had them, too."

"About us?" Her voice squeaked in disbelief. "You and me?" She was hardly the stuff of fantasies.

He nodded. "Since I first saw you."

"Me?" she asked again. Pleasure and pride warmed her.

"Figured it'd never work out with us, but tonight I realized I was wrong."

His words sank in and she pressed her hands to her cheeks. "No! No, you were right." Sex between them was wrong. Very wrong. She took a step back, tripping over his jacket. She'd have fallen if Jesse hadn't caught her arm to steady her.

But his touch didn't steady her. It made her want him, but wanting him was stupid. She stepped away again, this time more careful about her footing. "Tonight, I fooled myself into thinking this was just another fantasy. But it's real, and it's wrong."

Scowling, he said, "Jesus, we already went through this. You said your personal life was your own business."

She had said something like that, before they left Cherry Lane. "I was talking about a bike ride. Just a harmless ride. Not sex!"

"What's the difference?"

Aagh. For him, clearly there wasn't one. For her, sex was special. She'd only ever made love with two men before, and then after they'd dated for months and months. Sex was intimacy; it meant a relationship; it was—well, obviously, a totally different thing for her than it was for him. He'd probably been to bed with dozens of women.

It was one of the many, many differences between them. Insurmountable ones.

And even if all of that wasn't true, one cold, hard fact remained: she was his supervisor. She could lose her job over what to him was a quickie fling.

"Maura, don't make such a big deal out of it."

She realized she was shaking her head, back and forth, like she was trying to deny that this had ever happened.

Except, no, upset as she was, she couldn't totally regret it. Couldn't regret feeling his caresses, experiencing the kind of sex she'd never even imagined.

Finally, she managed to stop shaking her head and regain control. Chin up, she stared at him. "You're right. It was one night. No big deal. But no one can find out."

He rolled his eyes.

"I mean it! My job's at stake, and your community service." Sleeping with his supervisor, even if it was consensual, surely could get him into big trouble. Didn't he realize that?

"Yeah, fine," he said coolly. "Whatever."

"We have to go back. I'm cold and I want to go home." Actually, she wanted to be home now, cozy and safe in her own warm bed. She hated the thought of retracing the starlit journey that had, at the time, seemed so sexy and exciting. Now, all she could think of was how cold she was, and how wrong she'd been. She should have heeded the lesson she'd learned on prom night a dozen years ago: letting down her hair could get her in serious trouble.

Jesse picked his jacket off the grass and handed it to her. This time he didn't offer to help her put it on.

Before, she'd been thrilled to snuggle up inside his leather, but now she'd almost rather freeze. That would be foolish, and she'd been foolish enough tonight. Briskly, she pulled it on, slid her feet into her shoes, and began to walk toward the road.

Jesse's hand caught her elbow.

She jerked away. "I can manage on my own."

"Road's that way." He pointed in the opposite direction.

Wordlessly, she turned and again began to walk.

He paced beside her with his long-legged stride and

watched silently as she struggled over the fence, this time not offering his hand.

She waited while he pulled the Harley from its hiding place.

He pulled something from his jeans pocket and handed it to her. "Might want that."

Her bra, crumpled into a little ball, still retaining the heat of his body. She thrust it deep into her pants pocket.

When he climbed onto the bike, she reluctantly got on behind him. This time, when she put her arms around him, she couldn't enjoy the warm solidity of his strong body.

Tomorrow, he'd show up at Cherry Lane to do his work. He'd be there for weeks, months. Could they pretend this had never happened?

How could she ever look at him again without remembering the amazing feeling—physical and emotional—of joining with him?

Of course Jesse dreamed about her after he got home Tuesday, in between tossing and turning and trying to figure out what the fuck had gone wrong.

He couldn't believe Maura regretted the sex—what woman in her right mind would regret two bone-shaking orgasms?—but after she'd let down her hair, she'd pinned it right back up.

Her and her stupid rules. In her book—the old one, not the one that put her on the back of his Harley—she figured that having sex could get them both in trouble. She said she'd be risking her job and that promotion he couldn't figure out why she wanted, and he'd be risking his community service.

But hell, he wouldn't slack off on his job because he was sleeping with his boss, and he knew Maura'd always take her duties seriously.

She was blowing the whole thing way out of propor-
tion. And he was losing sleep, which was something he'd
never done over a woman, except when Pollan was caus-
ing trouble for Consuela.

With Con and Pollan, Jesse'd found a solution and made
it happen.

As for Maura, she was complicated and high maintenance. Normally, he'd walk away from a woman like that.
When she'd blown him off last night, that was what he'd
figured on doing.

The thing was, she was worth it. He wasn't going to
walk, and he wasn't going to let her do it, either. Satisfied,
he turned his pillow over to the cool side one more time,
punched it into shape, and finally settled down to sleep.

The next day, Jesse worked his construction job in high
gear, as if that could make the time pass more quickly.
Then he whipped home to shower and change, and rode
over to Cherry Lane.

Fact was, he liked Maura. More than he'd ever liked another woman. She liked him, too. She'd shared personal
thoughts and shared her body. She wouldn't give either
one lightly. And he didn't take them that way.

She was special, and he wasn't going to let her stupid
rules get in the way. Of course he didn't want to cost her
a job or a promotion, and he sure didn't want to end up
in jail, either. But it was no one else's business what the
two of them did in their free time.

They could see each other, and no one at Cherry Lane
needed to know anything about it.

Maybe she'd have thought things over, too, and come to
the same conclusion. If not, he'd persuade her.

Charged up, he parked in the parking lot, hooked his
helmet on the handlebar beside the spare one Maura had
worn last night, and strode toward the door.

Inside, he walked straight past that nasty receptionist, Nedda, and down the hall to Maura's office.

When he stepped through the door, she was at her computer. Her hair was more tightly pinned than ever, and she wore the gray shirt he'd first seen her in. Even so, she was stunning.

He'd stripped her naked, kissed far too few inches of her naked body, and made love to her. Looking at her now, it would've been hard to believe, but for the color that flooded her cheeks when she saw him.

"Jesse." Her voice squeaked.

He wanted to pull her into his arms, tug the pins from her hair, unbutton that shirt, feel her melt into him. "Hi, Maura." He closed the door behind him and walked toward her.

She jerked to her feet, and he saw she was wearing her gray pants as well. Rather than come to meet him, she stood behind her desk, hands flat on it, arms rigid like they were bracing her. "No, don't close the door."

He stopped.

She wasn't smiling; in fact, her face was strained and almost fearful. Her arms looked like two bars she'd erected to keep him away. "There's nothing more to say," she said stiffly. "We resolved things last night." Her voice lowered on the last two words so that he could barely hear them.

Shit. "No, we didn't." Again, he started toward her. If he touched her, just to stroke her cheek or take her hand, she'd soften.

She held up a hand. "Jesse, no. Didn't you hear me last night?"

"Yeah, but I thought it over. We can keep seeing each other, and no one here needs to know."

Her taut face softened. "You want to keep seeing me?" She said it almost like it surprised her.

"Hell, yeah."

Her lips trembled in a half-smile. "That's really nice." Then they straightened. "But we can't," she said firmly. "There's too much at stake. And, Jesse, I don't like dishonesty."

Dishonesty? "You mean not telling people? That's not lying. It's none of their business. Personal, like you said last night."

She winced. "I was talking about a motorcycle ride. And I know you don't see any difference between that and sex . . ." She paused.

Personal was personal. Bike ride, lovemaking, whatever. He shrugged.

Her chin firmed. "But I do."

"I don't get it."

"I realize that," she said, sounding annoyed. "But I'm the acting HR manager, responsible for supervising you. Cherry Lane's Board of Directors would see all sorts of potential problems if you and I, uh, have sex."

At least she wasn't saying she'd hated the sex or that he wasn't good enough for her. "Having sex wouldn't affect how we do our jobs."

She tilted her head and studied him for a long moment. "No. Maybe it wouldn't. But it's still not right. And speaking of work, we both need to get back to it."

He'd run out of arguments and thought best when his hands were busy. Later, when the place was quiet and evening had settled, he'd come back and try again. "Okay, but this isn't over, Maura."

Sad-eyed, she said, "It has to be. But I hope we can still be . . ." She trailed off.

"What? Friends?"

She nodded, looking tentative.

Hell, he wanted a lot more from her than that. "We'll see," he growled, and strode away to the garden.

Chapter 15

Jesse had just started work setting the prefab pond into the hole he'd dug, when Fred Dykstra showed up. The older guy was smart, so Jesse said, "You've got all this hostage negotiation experience." Maura'd be pissed if he shared their secret, so he kept things general. "Got any techniques for persuading somebody who's got the wrong idea in their head?"

The corner of the elderly man's mouth twitched. "Well, I'm guessing to them it may not seem wrong."

"Yeah. So how do you make them see sense?"

Another twitch, a moment's reflection. "You told me about that lady with the little dog."

"Mrs. Wolchuk?" How did she come into this?

"Most folks would say the sensible thing would be for her to sell her ramshackle house before the roof falls in on her, and move here. Right?"

"I guess. But she's got that dog, and she loves the house."

Fred smiled. "You see her side of things. That's the first step in any negotiation. If you tell someone what they should do, they get their back up. You need to understand their side and let them know you understand."

"Huh. I guess that makes sense."

"And have you heard of the term 'subtlety'?" Fred's mouth was twitching again.

"You're saying I shouldn't be too, uh . . ."

"Heavy-handed in your approach?" He nodded. "Especially if you're dealing with the fairer sex. Which I'm guessing you are."

"Maybe."

"Their logic is sometimes different than ours, and they make decisions with their hearts, not just their brains."

Not Maura. She was so determined to be in control, to be professional. But she did have feelings. She'd shown him her vulnerable side, talking about her adoptive parents, and even about that stupid Cindy woman and the silly reunion.

Maura wanted a date, and she wanted to be friends with him. Jesse sure wasn't a champagne kind of guy, he didn't even own a suit, and a high school reunion sounded like sheer hell. But caring about someone meant that you did stuff you didn't really want to, just to make them happy. Con and Juanito had taught him that.

"Sorry?" He realized Fred had said something that he'd missed.

"Just wished you good luck. Hope you work things out with this special woman of yours."

Special woman? Had he told Fred that? Now his own lips twitched. "Guess you were pretty good at your job."

"Guess I was."

Maura stayed out of the garden that evening but couldn't resist frequent peeks out the window. A number of seniors were out there chatting with Jesse and each other, but he kept working steadily.

He'd installed the ugly black plasticky-looking pond, and she tried to picture the final effect the way he'd described it to her. Rocks casually placed, a miniature waterfall, and a pebbly shore at one end. Ornamental grasses, a leafy red Japanese maple, and lovely pink water lilies. Orange and gold koi swimming around. It amazed her that he could make all that happen.

She'd never been good with her hands. Never been a physical person.

Except in her fantasies, and last night under the stars . . .

No, she wouldn't let herself drift off into another fantasy. At home in bed, maybe, but not at work. She shouldn't allow herself to be distracted by the man. Even though they'd had sex. Amazing, world-shaking, multi-orgasmic—

No, she had to stop thinking about it. What mattered was whether he'd agree they could be friends. Jesse wasn't a man who thought of women only as sex objects; he'd been close friends with Consuela for years. He saw her like a sister, and she was gorgeous and sexy. It should be easy for him to view Maura platonically—which was what she wanted, so why did the idea hurt?

And could she ever look at him without wanting him?

She'd have to learn.

When he climbed through her office window at the end of the evening and sprawled in one of the vinyl chairs like he belonged there, it wasn't with a mere friend's eyes that she appreciated the masculinity of his craggy features. The ripple of muscles when he lifted an arm to brush tousled hair back from his face. Not to mention the power of his jean-clad thighs and the seductive bulge beneath his fly. She'd cupped that bulge last night, felt him harden under her touch.

Last night, he'd been inside her. For real, not just in a fantasy. Her body heated and moistened, and it was all she could do to keep from squirming.

She cleared her throat. Not having the nerve to come right out and ask how he felt about being friends, she figured she'd just see how things went. "You've made good progress tonight."

"Thanks. By the way, Virginia asked if she could come to the nursery this weekend, when we go to buy the maple tree and pond plants. What do you think? Is that one of your liability things?" He actually sounded serious, not as if he was mocking her.

"No. We do take the seniors on outings in the van. Our insurance covers that." She smiled at him. "But thanks for thinking of that, and for checking with me."

"Guess I'm learning," he said wryly, making her chuckle. "She said her daughter's family's coming for a visit," he said. "That'll be nice for her."

"It will. Her daughter's a writer, her son-in-law's a foreign diplomat, and they travel a lot. They stay in touch regularly with e-mail and Skype, but Virginia doesn't get to see them often."

"Too bad."

"It is. But Virginia says, you raise your children with love and effort and hope, then you set them free to chart their own course through life."

"Bet she was a good mother."

"I'm sure of it." Their gazes met across her desk, and she knew they were both wishing they'd had a mom like Virginia. Immediately, she felt guilty. Agnes had done her best, and Maura owed her so much.

"Lucky kids," he said in his gravelly voice, "the ones who get born to the right parents."

She nodded. "Parents like you and I would at least know some of the mistakes to avoid." Then, realizing what she'd said, Maura clapped her hands to her cheeks. "I didn't mean . . ." The two of them together, having a baby—a cute little hell-raiser of a boy, or a spunky little girl . . . No, of course not. Surely he knew that.

"I mean," she hurried on, "if you get married to someone and have kids, and if I get married to someone . . ." She broke off as his eyebrows rose higher and higher.

"Didn't figure you were proposing," he said, an edge to his voice. "Not when you won't even go out with me."

Actions have consequences, her parents had taught her. *Always consider those consequences before you act.* She couldn't risk her job on a short-term thing, which was all it could ever be. Likely, she intrigued Jesse because she was different from the women he usually dated, but the novelty would wear off quickly. Perhaps it was the same for her. He'd no more fit into her life than she would in his.

She decided not to re-open the discussion of whether they should see each other. Her decision was made. Instead, she said, "As for marriage, I don't see you doing that any day soon." Not only was he a player, but he was young, a fact that she'd noted in his file. "You're only twenty-seven."

He shrugged, looking uncomfortable for some reason. "A person's as old as they feel, as old as they act."

She took a breath. If she hoped to be his friend, she should be honest. "I'm thirty, and I look and feel all of it." Even down to that newly awakened sexuality.

"Hmm." He studied her appraisingly, a twinkle gleaming in his eyes. "I dunno what thirty's supposed to look like but . . ."

Unwise to ask, but she couldn't stop herself. "But what?"

"Seems to me, it's a pretty good year."

She flushed. "Well, thanks."

"And I'm almost twenty-*eight,*" he said firmly, as if that fact mattered.

She'd mentioned his age, called him young. Did he think she figured he was immature?

Did she? She pondered that for a moment. Physically, Jesse Blue was most definitely a man. She flicked a glance through her eyelashes, to verify that fact. Oh, yes, he was the most "man" she'd ever met, not to mention the hottest, most virile, sexiest, most tempting—

Aagh! She took a deep breath and tried to slow her racing pulse.

As for his work, he was as skilled and responsible as anyone she'd ever seen. Being able to conceive of a garden landscape and implement it was thoroughly impressive. When it came to dealing with the seniors, he was respectful and considerate. Yes, even if Jesse had some opinions that troubled her, such as his disrespect for the rules, there was no question he was mature.

"I wouldn't mind being twenty-eight again," she mused. "Thirty seems like such a big number. It feels like suddenly things are supposed to change."

"Such as?"

"Oh, well." Why did this always happen? She found herself revealing more to Jesse than she really intended. "Like, I should have a more impressive job, not let my education go to waste. And my parents think it's time I got married."

"Do you?"

"Not unless I find the right man. I'd never get married just for the sake of being married. I like my own company."

"I like your company, too." He said it simply, without a teasing grin or mischievous twinkle in his eye to turn it into something suggestive, and that made the compliment even more special.

She realized that he'd accepted her offer of friendship, and her heart warmed. "Thank you. I like yours. Strange as it seems, given how different we are, I feel like I can be myself with you." More than she could with her adoptive parents, in fact. How very peculiar that the person she felt most comfortable with in so many ways was also the one who made her tingle from just being in the same room.

His smile widened. "I hope so."

They sat in silence for a minute or two, one on either

side of her desk. Oddly, the silence didn't feel awkward. Or, at least, it didn't if she kept her mind off sex, which was, admittedly, difficult to do in his presence.

"So," he said quietly, "you got a date lined up for that reunion thing? Did you take pity on that lecture guy?"

A strange question, yet it did kind of flow from what they'd been saying, about marriage and finding the right man. She wrinkled her nose. Look at her. She couldn't even find the right man for one night, much less a lifetime. "Not yet. I can't decide whether it's better to go with Edward or go alone. I keep hoping . . . oh, that my appendix will burst or something."

He gave a surprised hoot of laughter, and she found herself chuckling along with him.

"I'll keep my fingers crossed for you," he said, and they both laughed again.

Then he said, "I wondered," just as she started out, "Have you," and they both broke off. "You first," he said.

"Have you gone to a high school reunion, Jesse, or hasn't your class had one yet?"

His face sobered instantaneously. He stared at her for a long minute.

For some reason, she felt tension in the silent air between them.

Then he said, "Don't have a class."

"What do you mean?"

"Didn't graduate high school." He flung it out like a challenge.

"You're kidding." Yes, he'd been in foster homes, had a tough upbringing, but in this day and age, surely everyone at least finished high school.

He shook his head.

Oh, my. She'd known they were different, but had no idea how huge that difference was. "But a high school education is so important. Your job opportunities will be so limited." No wonder he worked jobs like construction; he had no other options. The man had so much potential; it was a darned shame to waste it.

He shrugged. "Whatever." His leg jiggled up and down restlessly.

"I know you were shuffled around to different foster homes," she said, thinking it through. "And you don't like books."

His leg jiggled faster.

"I'm sure you didn't like being cooped up in a classroom. I can see why you'd have dropped out. But Jesse, you're twenty-seven." Mature, she'd thought a few minutes earlier. "Why on earth didn't you get your GED?"

He rose to his feet and glared at her. She'd often thought of him as an animal, a panther or a lion, and he was definitely one now—one full of barely caged anger. "Why do you think? Because I'm a fucking idiot!" He turned on his heel and stalked out.

When she managed to close her gaping mouth, she said, "You are not!" But he was already out the door.

Too stunned to follow, she slumped back in her chair. After a few minutes, she realized she was shaking her head. Jesse wasn't an idiot. He was organized in how he approached tasks, he had a flawless memory, and he could do calculations in his head. He was a creative landscaper and he'd drawn an accurate, beautiful sketch of the courtyard garden. When he chose to, he could be perceptive and sensitive in dealing with people. He most definitely wasn't stupid.

But he hadn't finished high school. Had he hated it so much that he dropped out, or been such a hell-raiser he got expelled? In either case, the more significant question was why he hadn't gotten his GED.

He couldn't hate books that much, could he? Enough to limit his career options for the rest of his life?

He certainly did seem to avoid the written word, and . . . Wait. Yes, he really did. He refused to read to the residents, yet was happy to talk to them. He ignored her lists, wouldn't make one of his own, yet he retained information accurately in his head.

Maura pressed a hand to her chest, where her heart was fluttering wildly.

He couldn't read. Was it possible?

She felt like a detective, chasing down the clues to solve a mystery that was, for some reason, incredibly important to her.

If he wasn't stupid, and he couldn't read, then . . . Did he have some kind of disorder or disability, like dyslexia?

She sprang to her feet, determined to know the truth.

After looking up Jesse's address, she headed for her car, almost running down the deserted hallway, passing Nedda without a word.

She was halfway down the block before she remembered her seat belt, then she came as close as she'd ever come to exceeding the speed limit.

The GPS took her straight to his place, which she saw was a second-floor apartment in an old wooden house, not far from the school where he coached basketball. His motorcycle was outside, the lights were on, but when she took the wooden outside stairs and knocked on the door, there was no response.

She peered through the window beside the door, into a tiny kitchen. There was a beer bottle on the counter, but no other sign of life. She knocked louder.

"Hang on, I'm coming."

She heard his voice first. Then, when she saw him, the sight took her breath away. He'd been in the shower. His black hair hung wet and tousled, drops of water beaded on his bare chest, and a navy blue towel wrapped around his waist. Bare torso, bare legs, bronzed skin. Too much naked Jesse for her to take in. Beautiful, utterly gorgeous, naked Jesse.

Pure sex, walking. Walking right toward her. Every hormone in her body fired to life. She jerked her head back from the window but knew he'd seen her from the stunned expression on his face.

He threw open the door. "What are you doing here?"

She should say something polite, ask to come in, but she was so stunned by his appearance that all her brain could come up with was, "Can you read?"

His body froze, then he blinked once.

He was blocking the doorway, but she moved past him, into the kitchen that seemed minuscule when filled with one large, dripping, almost-naked male. A muscular, sculpted, very masculine male whom she'd had multi-orgasmic sex with.

She stared at him, trying to keep her eyes on his face, but her peripheral vision was good enough to send her hormones into overdrive. Tingles raced through her—hot or cold, she couldn't tell—but the heavy pulse of arousal between her legs was definitely hot.

He reached past her and his arm grazed her shoulder. Burning it, even through the silk of her shirt.

She jumped back, banging her hip on the edge of a small wooden table.

He had grabbed the beer bottle and now held it to his mouth, taking long gulps.

He put the bottle down with a bang and she jumped again.

Trying to ignore her overstressed hormones, she focused on the reason she'd come. "You're not stupid, Jesse. I know that for a fact. I'm guessing you have a problem like dyslexia that prevented you from learning how to read or write properly. If I'm wrong, then I apologize and I wish you'd forget I ever said anything. But if I'm right, then it's the school system, your foster parents; they're the ones who are stupid, for not diagnosing it."

He dropped onto one of the two wooden kitchen chairs.

She glanced down as he sat and saw the towel split at the front, revealing a goodly part of a very fine thigh, where drops of water beaded in the wiry black hair. Her fingers itched to stroke his naked flesh. To part the towel farther.

How could she think about sex at a time like this?

She forced her gaze back to his face, but it was hidden, cradled in his hands as he leaned his elbows on the table.

He hadn't said a word. He hadn't denied it. She knew she was right. As she'd driven over, the whole picture had come clear in her head.

She sat down in the other chair and told him what she saw. "You changed schools and foster families so often, no one picked up on it. Kids called you names and you struck out at them. The only way you could best them was physically, so you beat them up. But they won in the end, because you believed them. They're the ones who were ignorant, but you accepted the labels they gave you."

He had dropped his hands and was watching her now, expressionless.

She went on. "And you discounted all the things you do well. I'm an accountant, but I can't do calculations in my head as quickly or accurately as you do. You're great at organizing and planning things, and that sketch you made of the garden was brilliant. A landscape architect would have been proud of it."

His face with its striking, utterly male features was immobile, but his hazel eyes gleamed with some emotion. Was it hope?

"I've learned things from you, Jesse. I'd never have involved the residents in planning the garden. That was your idea, and it was a great one. Now it's everyone's project and they're feeling alive, involved, excited. Not to mention, they actually had some wonderful ideas that you and I wouldn't have come up with. And you were right about letting them contribute financially. There's absolutely no reason they shouldn't, if it's what they truly want. You've only been at Cherry Lane a few days, and you've made things better for all of us."

His face twitched and his eyes glittered golden. He rose quickly and moved past her, to the fridge. The shower water was drying now. There were only a few drops left on that wonderful brown skin.

She longed to reach out and stroke him. Anywhere. His arm, shoulder, leg. Instead she clasped her hands tightly together.

He pulled out two bottles of beer and twisted the cap off one.

She didn't drink beer; still, she reached for a bottle when he offered it. Their hands touched and for a moment both of them held still.

For Maura, the tension was electric. It was sexual, it was emotional. Jesse had every right to be angry at her for interfering, but he hadn't denied a word she'd said. He hadn't tossed her out on her ear. He had handed her a beer. She wanted to grin with excitement, yet the moment was too solemn for that.

He leaned a hip against the table, opened his own beer, and took a long swig.

She lifted her bottle to her lips and sipped cautiously. The beer was kind of bitter, but not bad. She took another sip. She was drinking beer in Jesse Blue's kitchen. And he, more than half-naked, was within an arm's reach.

"I can read some things." The words came slowly and his voice rasped. "If I concentrate real hard. I know some words really well. They make pictures in my head."

She nodded, holding her breath, immensely flattered that he was sharing this with her. She was right. Oh, God, she was right. And she was sure that, if he wanted, there were ways of helping him.

He met her eyes. "When I try to read a book, I can't . . . put all the pictures together. With long sentences, by the time I make it to the end, it doesn't make sense."

She nodded. "It's probably dyslexia."

"It," he repeated, passing a shaky hand across his jaw. "Just calling it *it* makes me feel so different. An *it* is . . . a problem that's, uh, outside me, in a way. It's not *me* who's stupid, there's this *it* thing that's a problem. Does that make any sense?"

She had to touch his hand, where it rested near her on the table. It was firm, warm, as strong as he was, this man who'd survived a terrible childhood and made something of his life. She wanted to leave her hand there forever. "It makes perfect sense. Oh, Jesse, the teachers should have caught it. There are programs for dyslexic children, different techniques for learning how to read. Dyslexics aren't stupid, in fact many are really smart. They're just different."

"Guess I've heard of dyslexia. Never paid much attention."

"Because people called you stupid and made you believe it. Damn them! Why couldn't they see who you really were?" Her voice broke. She never swore, but this was so *damned* unfair.

He moved abruptly and her hand fell away.

She barely had a moment to feel the loss before he gripped her shoulders, hard, pulling her up from the chair until she was standing in front of him. She gazed up at him, blinking away the moisture that glazed her eyes.

"You see, Maura." His voice was soft, husky, intense. "You're the only one who really sees me."

His hands branded her, and the heat seared its way through her body. She couldn't say a word. She couldn't do anything but gaze spellbound into his glowing eyes. Her fingers were numb, and she barely managed to place the beer bottle on the table without dropping it. Unaccountably dizzy, she swayed toward Jesse, dropping her head, closing her eyes.

Her cheek brushed his shoulder and he was fiery hot. The man always gave out so much heat, so much magnetic energy. His pulse thudded as fast as her own was racing.

He pulled her tighter.

Her hands were trapped, resting in loose fists between her breasts and the firm hairiness of his chest. Her hips shifted forward, brushed the towel, and she felt an erection swell and lift behind it.

She pressed closer, her body craving the sweet pleasure he could give her, and her panties grew damp.

Jesse made a sound. A groan? Then his body tensed, he shifted, and he drew away.

She sighed her disappointment and gazed up—in time to let out a surprised squeak as one of his arms came under her bottom and the other around her back, and he scooped her up as if she weighed nothing at all. Cradled in his arms, against his bare chest, for the first time in her life she felt small, almost delicate, and very definitely feminine.

But there was no time to savor the sensation, because he strode quickly down a short hall and lowered her to his bed. Normally, she'd have been curious about his bedroom, but right now she couldn't peel her gaze off Jesse.

Somewhere along the route, the towel had fallen off.

She barely had a chance to register the sight of all that stunning masculine nakedness, especially the forceful jut of his substantial erection, before he lay above her, his legs on either side of hers so she felt the hard press of his sex against her belly.

Why were her clothes on? He should have taken them off so they could be naked, his hard, demanding flesh meeting her moist, needy flesh. She squirmed under him, but, even with most of his weight on his knees and elbows, he pinned her firmly.

He cupped her face between his hands. "Maura." Then he kissed her forehead, once, in a soft, lingering caress. Her nose, once. And finally, his lips met hers and she sighed with relief and hunger.

His kiss started out slow, even tender, but as she answered him with her tongue, as her hands stroked down his bare shoulders and back to squeeze the firm muscles of his behind, and her pelvis ground against his erection, the kiss grew fiery and intense.

Finally, his breathing labored, Jesse broke away, rolled off her, and started to undo her buttons, fumbling in his haste.

She batted his hand away, to work the buttons herself, and he promptly went for the waistband of her pants. Clothing went flying every which way until she was as naked as he.

He pulled her into his arms, his body heat sending fire racing through her veins, thickening her blood, making her soften and melt.

Oh, this was good. So good. A fantasy come true, just like last night.

Except . . . No, wait. Last night she'd decided . . .

What had she decided?

"No, Jesse!" Though it took every ounce of strength she possessed, Maura broke away and sat up.

His eyes, glazed with passion, blinked. "What?"

She shook her head. "We can't do this."

He blinked again. "What the hell?"

She reached for the closest bit of fabric—her shirt, as it turned out—and held it in front of her body. *Déjà vu.* She'd done this last night.

Being together was wrong. She knew it. How could she have let herself get carried away like this?

Jesse's appeal, their heightened emotions, his nakedness but for that towel . . .

Excuses. Good ones. Still, this was wrong.

He sprawled beside her, naked, unmoving.

She shoved at his shoulders, strong shoulders that didn't budge, heated brown shoulders that she'd much rather caress. "I have to go."

"Jesus, Maura, what the—" Frustration glittered in his eyes, and she was positive he'd been going to swear before he broke off. His chest heaved as he took a few deep breaths.

Chapter 16

Jesse stopped himself before he could demand what the fuck was going on. That wasn't going to win him any points with Maura.

He sucked in air as his racing heart began to slow, and tried to think.

What had Fred told him? Be subtle rather than heavy-handed, and try to understand where she was coming from.

To give her a little space, and to help himself cool down, Jesse rolled away and sat on the end of the bed. He even picked the towel off the floor and draped it over his now-wilting erection.

Okay, what was Maura's concern? She'd told him, so he said, "I get it, that you're worried about your job."

The two of them ought to be able to figure out a solution.

He glanced over his shoulder. Tonight, she hadn't forgotten to put on her bra. He saw the white fabric as she did up the buttons of her shirt. When they were fastened, she looked at him. "Yes, I am. And about your community service. There's too much at stake, Jesse."

Pissed off, he wanted to snap that there was something else at stake. Their relationship. Didn't she see that?

Yeah, she had to. Moments earlier, they'd been all naked

and sweaty together. What she meant was that her job was more important to her. That hurt, more than he'd have believed possible.

On the one hand, she saw him, understood him, better than any woman ever had. She talked to him like he was a friend, respected his skills. She was hot for him. But none of it was enough. He wasn't important enough to her.

He rose abruptly. The towel fell and he didn't give a damn. "I get it," he said bitterly, stalking across to the dresser. "Took me long enough. Seems I'm an idiot after all."

"Jesse . . ."

Her pleading tone made him turn. She was crouched at the end of the bed, her flushed cheeks and vivid tumble-down hair a contrast to the drab gray buttoned-up shirt.

"What?" he demanded.

"You're not an idiot. I do want this. I mean, you and me, like this." Her cheeks grew even brighter. "Well, not like this, but the way we were."

"You're not making sense." He turned to take fresh boxer-briefs from the drawer.

"I know. Sorry. What I mean is, I like being with you. But I'm practical. I love working at Cherry Lane. I could see staying there a long time. I don't want to lose that chance, just for a few nights of fun with you."

"Fuck." Was that all he was to her? He slammed the drawer shut and turned in time to catch her wince.

"We're different," she said. "Such different people. And for me, sleeping with someone is serious. For you, well, you're into casual relationships. Which is fine," she added quickly. "I'm not judging. But a short-term fling isn't worth risking my job, and it's not worth you taking the chance of going to jail. Right?"

Looking at her earnest face, her tousled hair and lovely

ocean eyes, those long, slim legs beneath the tail of her shirt, the answer didn't come easily. "I guess," he said slowly, but immediately the words were out, they didn't sit right. He and Maura, yeah they'd only known each other a few days, but right from the beginning she'd been special. Already, she was much more than just "fun." She mattered.

But how much?

He wanted a family and home, but a big part of him figured he'd never make that work. He'd screw it up, the way he always used to. To even think that a grade ten dropout who'd been in trouble with the law could make it long-term with a classy lady with an M.B.A. . . . Well, it was just plain crazy. Wasn't it?

"I don't want you to be mad at me," she said softly.

He realized that, while he'd been musing, she'd climbed off the bed and finished dressing. Now that she was standing, he saw her shirt was buttoned lopsided.

He walked over.

Her body quivered, but she held her ground.

Gently, he reached out and unfastened a button.

She started to pull back. "No, Jesse, I don't want—"

"You did them up crooked," he broke in.

"Oh." She stilled and let him undo all her buttons, then do them up again. "Thank you."

She should've been in his bed, naked and hot and sweaty. He probably could've seduced her back there, but that wouldn't have been fair. Yeah, Fred was onto something, with this stuff about understanding where the other person was coming from.

Didn't mean Jesse had to like it.

"I hear what you're saying," he said. He just needed more time to think about it.

"We can still be f-friends?"

It seemed that word was hard for her to say. He realized

that she'd never mentioned friends. Did she have any? "Yeah. I like us being friends." Not having Maura in his life seemed pretty much unthinkable.

A smile trembled into life. "Me, too. So, I'll see you tomorrow."

"See you then." He watched her walk away.

He heard his apartment door close and went to the kitchen to look out the window. She got into one of those tiny Smart Cars and drove away.

Shaking his head, he sat down at the kitchen table in his underwear to reflect.

He'd drained his beer, but Maura had taken only a few sips of hers. He lifted the bottle, put his lips where hers had been, and swallowed lukewarm liquid.

With just a few words, she'd changed his world. Dyslexia, not stupidity.

He thought about things he could do that others had trouble with, things he'd always taken for granted. He thought about the jobs he'd lost or walked away from because he refused to read instructions or write reports. He'd always preferred to be labeled a troublemaker than a dummy.

Yeah, he really was an idiot. An idiot for not realizing he wasn't stupid.

Maura had given him options for a different future. He could get his GED. Maybe even study landscape design.

But at the same time, she'd taken away another option: the one of the two of them being together.

He went to the fridge and got a fresh, chilly beer. No, he was seeing things in black and white, as Fred had termed it. And he was thinking short-term, the way he'd always done.

He needed to change his perspective. He'd be working with Maura, seeing her almost every day, getting to know her better. Yeah, he'd sure as hell miss the sex, but they'd figure out how they felt about each other. Patience wasn't his long suit, but he could learn—with the right incentive.

One day, he'd no longer be working at Cherry Lane.

One day, there'd be nothing at stake but their hearts.

Jesse had barely slept, his brain was so filled with ideas. Some were hugely ambitious, like being a landscape architect, and like him and Maura maybe getting serious one day.

But one was more straightforward. He made a quick trip during lunch break, then talked to his construction boss and got some more information. He'd have to run his plan by Maura. She might see some angle he hadn't considered, not to mention some liability issue.

Or maybe that was just an excuse to see her as soon as he possibly could.

Unfortunately, his day job went overtime. Not only didn't he get a chance to clean up before riding over to Cherry Lane, but he was ten minutes late. At least that Nedda person wasn't there to scowl at him. Instead, it was Ming-mei, who gave him a friendly smile.

"Ms. Mahoney in?" he asked, enjoying the taste of her name on his tongue. Ms. Warm Honey . . . oh, yeah, she sure was.

"She is. Go right ahead. I'm sure she'll want to see you."

He sure hoped so.

When he glanced through Maura's open door, she was staring straight at him, like she'd been waiting. Her words confirmed it. "Jesse, you're late. Is everything all right?"

No criticism, just concern and a warm smile.

He smiled back, enjoying the sight of her in a tailored blue shirt with two buttons undone at the collar. Much prettier than the dull gray she'd worn yesterday. Man, he wished he could round her desk and give her a big kiss.

Friends for now, he reminded himself. They'd see where that took them. "Hi, Maura. Yeah, everything's fine. Sorry, we had to work late on the construction job. Didn't have a chance to change before I came over."

Her gaze scooted over him, and he wished there weren't rips in his jeans and tee. Or maybe he didn't, because her cheeks flushed as she studied them. "There's no reason to, when you're only going to get dirty again. Come in, sit down. Did you have time to get dinner?"

When he shook his head, she said, "I'll have the kitchen send you a couple of sandwiches when the rush dies down."

He smiled with pleasure, as much at her thoughtfulness as at the idea of food. "Thanks."

Color tinting her cheeks, she said, "You thought about what we talked about last night? I mean"—she flushed brighter—"about being dyslexic?"

"Sure did. I want to find out what kinds of programs and courses I could take."

"I hope you don't think it's presumptuous," she said hesitantly, "but I did a little research."

"No, hey, that's great. Thanks."

Her smile flashed, and he wanted to hug her. Then kiss her. Then unbutton her and lick the sweet curve of her neck, all the way down to other sweet curves, where he'd— He forced himself to stop imagining.

This business of just being friends was going to be tough.

"I talked to a social worker today, Jesse." She picked up her pen, clicked the top, opened her notebook, and studied it. "I made a list." Then she glanced up at him and grinned. "Which I need, because my memory's not as good as yours."

He liked how she said that, not rubbing his nose in the sorry truth that he'd have trouble reading her list. Yeah, he had a great memory. It was one of the ways he survived in a world that was so reading-oriented. "Tell me what you found."

She put on those sexy glasses and recited the details of half a dozen different programs. "The social worker recommends the one offered through the education department at the university. Several of her clients have had great success with it."

"University. Seems like a strange place for someone who never finished high school." And intimidating as hell.

"They specialize in adult learners. Some students will be older than you. But it's your decision, Jesse. Call the ones that interest you, and get more details."

Yeah, it was his decision. And maybe he was man enough to handle a university program. "I'll call the university first, and see how that sounds."

When she recited the name and number, he committed them to memory. "Okay, got it. I'll call tomorrow." He smiled at her across the desk as she took off her glasses again and put her notebook and pen down. "Thanks for doing this. Thanks for everything, Maura."

Had he once thought her blue-green eyes were chilly? Now they were as warm and inviting as a tropical ocean, as the faint scent of gardenia that perfumed the air.

"You're very welcome. That's what friends are for."

He couldn't look away from those mesmerizing eyes. He wanted to see them widen as he leaned in for a kiss, glaze over with passion . . .

Heat surged through him and his body tightened. Nope, better not go any farther down that road.

Remembering the idea he'd wanted to run by her, he said, "By the way, is it okay if I take a couple hours off on Saturday? I'll make up the time."

She nodded. "Of course. You've already put in extra time. Do you want to come in late, or leave early?"

"Need to check with her first."

Her face tightened. Because he'd said "her"? Oh, man, she was jealous. Cool.

"Mrs. Wolchuk," he clarified. "The one with that little white dog?"

"Boopsy?" There was a smile in her voice now.

"Yeah, Boopsy." They both chuckled.

"What on earth are you doing with Mrs. Wolchuk? Jesse Blue, you aren't taking her for a bike ride, are you?" Her tone was teasing.

He laughed again. "No, there's only one lady I want to take riding. Thought I'd do a little work on her house. I went by and talked to her. Roof's got some pretty bad leaks, and she's got a lot of other stuff that needs fixing."

"I thought she couldn't afford repairs. Did she have a big win at bingo?"

"Nah. I just figured I'd do it for her."

She tilted her head. "For free."

He shrugged. "My boss says I can take some leftover stuff like roof shakes from the job we're working on now. And use his business discount with suppliers. He's a good guy."

"And so are you, Jesse. That's really sweet . . ." The way her voice trailed off told him she'd thought of one of those angles he hadn't seen.

"So what's the 'but'?" Were they going to need their hostage negotiator to sort this one out? "Are you mad that it'd cost Cherry Lane a new resident?"

"No, of course not. But . . ." She sighed. "It's so kind of you, but it's just a Band-Aid, isn't it?" Her voice was sad. "She'll need more repairs over the years. You're only delaying the inevitable."

He nodded. "Sure. But it could buy her another few years. In her own house, with Boopsy."

This time neither of them chuckled when he said the name.

Maura brightened. "You're right. It's a good idea, and a generous one. She'll be so grateful. It's sad how many people are in her situation. I could name a dozen Cherry Lane residents who came here before they were ready, just because they couldn't keep up their homes."

"There ought to be an organization that does that kind of thing."

"Yes, there should."

They were both silent a moment, then he said regretfully, "I should get to work."

"Want to go this way?" She gestured toward the window, which was already open.

"Maura Mahoney, have you been hopping in and out through the window?"

"Mmm-hmm." Her eyes sparkled. "Oh, Jesse, more and more residents are enjoying the garden, and a few more have donated funds. There's a heated discussion going on about the type of fish to get for the pond. And Virginia says we need a compost heap."

"Good idea. It's great seeing folks getting involved."

As he stepped over the high sill, he thought about how, when he'd first come here, Maura had wanted to shut him into the courtyard and keep him out of her office. When she'd ventured out herself, she'd been uncomfortable. Now, both of them were moving back and forth.

Between two worlds, he thought. The barriers were coming down. They were friends now. They'd been lovers, and he really hoped they would be again. Trying to be "just friends" with Maura was going to make for an ongoing case of blue balls.

He got to work and stayed at it while almost a dozen residents wandered out to visit. All the time, he was aware of Maura's open window.

Dusk fell, her window glowed golden, and eventually the seniors went inside.

Jesse leaned against the rough trunk of one of the cherry trees to take a breather and wondered what Maura was doing. Maybe she was enjoying a break, too. Leaning back in her chair, brushing that fiery hair . . .

Long strokes, all the way from the roots to the ends . . .

He imagined standing at the window, watching her brush with long, sensual strokes, the way he'd seen her doing it before . . .

Her back was to him. Jesse pushed the window wider and stepped silently over the sill. Her hand paused. He guessed she was aware of his presence, but she started brushing again.

"Want a hand with that, Maura?"

She swiveled her chair to face him. "I want more than your hand." Her tone was seductive, matching the gardenia scent in the air.

He gulped. Her hair was down around her shoulders, and she'd unbuttoned another button on her blue blouse. How come he hadn't noticed before that the fabric was almost sheer? Through it he could see lace covering the soft swell of her breasts. Maybe the same bra she'd worn when they made love in the moonlight.

Slowly she stood and moved the few steps toward him. She placed her hands on either side of his waist.

And he realized that somehow his grubby work clothes had disappeared and he was wearing nothing but a towel. A towel that lifted at the front like it had a life of its own.

"You're glad to see me," she murmured throatily.

"Oh, yeah!"

"Do you want me to touch you?"

"Jesus, yeah."

She flicked the towel open and there was his hard-on, standing up and begging for a treat.

She reached out one of those slender, delicate hands and closed it gently around him.

He'd been wanting this for so long, he groaned with relief, with pleasure.

She slid her hand up and down slowly, experimenting,
testing his reactions. "Do you like this?"

"Oh, yeah." His knees were so weak he could barely
stand up. He plunked his butt into the vinyl-covered guest
chair he always sat in.

She kneeled in front of him, stroking up and down his
shaft. Her hair swung forward, brushing his chest with
fiery fingers, and then down his belly, his thighs.

"I'd like anything you did to me, Maura Mahoney."

"Anything?" she purred.

Her index finger was circling the head of his dick. Even
so, he took a moment to think about her question. "Anything," he confirmed. She could tie him up and torture
him, and he'd be in heaven.

But what she was doing right now was just too good,
and his arousal was so damned intense, he had to stop her
before he embarrassed himself. A guy was supposed to
have a little self-control.

So he gripped her wrist and eased her hand away. "My
turn." He unbuttoned her blouse, whipping through the
buttons, then undid the one at the waistband of her pants.
When he slid down her zipper, she stood and let her pants
slip down until they hit the floor. She stepped out of them.
She still had her shoes on—strappy sandals with heels. And
a lacy bra above a tiny triangle of lace, neither of them doing much to conceal the beauty underneath.

He was so hot, he couldn't hold back. He slid his hand
between her legs.

She gasped, then clenched her thighs around him. The
silky fabric was wet. Thank God she was ready for him because he was so ready he was going to burst.

He stroked her a couple of times, just to make sure, and
she writhed and moaned, "Oh, Jesse."

"You want me, Maura?" he growled.

"Yes!"

He grabbed her thong and yanked it down her legs. He hadn't planned on waiting for her to step out of her panties, but this was Maura. She wasn't going to make love with underwear tangled around her ankles.

She rested her hands on his shoulders for balance and, one foot at a time, carefully freed herself. Then she gazed at him with those vivid ocean eyes and said, "Where?"

Was she thinking he could produce a bed out of thin air? All he cared about right now was getting inside her. That would be plenty special for him. But no doubt she wanted something fancier.

Her desk was tempting—he'd love to shove all those file folders and papers aside—and screw her brains out right beside that silly little clicking pen. But the wood surface looked awfully hard. He didn't want her to get hurt.

"Jesse?"

"Right here. Sit down."

"What?"

He grasped her at the waist and she gave one of her cute little squeaks as he hauled her down on his lap, facing him.

"Oh," she murmured, gazing down at his dick, standing tall between them.

He grabbed her butt, dimly aware that those creamy curves deserved better treatment, and lifted her. Then he eased her down and she gasped when the head of his dick probed her wet folds, seeking entry.

He gritted his teeth, holding back, not wanting to hurt her.

"Jesse, yes." Her stunning eyes, flushed cheeks, swollen lips were only inches away. "I want you. Now."

"Oh, yeah, Maura."

He gave a giant thrust and she hollered—

"Jesse? Are you still out there?"

What? What the fuck? Slowly, he came to his senses.

Jesus Christ, he was humping a cherry tree and he was about to explode inside his jeans. Shit. Anyone could be watching. No, it was too dark for them to see anything, thank God. He struggled for control.

"Jesse?"

"I'm here," he croaked.

"Oh, good. Would you mind coming to see me before you leave?"

"Sure."

"Are you all right? Your voice sounds strange."

"I'm fine," he bellowed, frustration fueling his voice.

He was more than halfway tempted to yank down his fly, stick his hand inside, and finish the job. No one could see. He'd be the only one who knew. But with her inside her office across the courtyard, it didn't feel right.

So he stuck his hands under the garden tap, washed them, and splashed cold water on his face. If only he could pour a bucket of it down his jeans.

Eventually, his hard-on subsided and he was left with nothing but an ache. He tidied up the garden and walked to her window.

She'd said she fantasized about him, too. He wondered if she was still doing it, now that she'd decided they could only be friends. He sure hoped so.

Right now, she had her head down and was clicking her pen. Good. That was the one thing she did that annoyed him. It'd keep him from drifting off into any more steamy fantasies. He knocked on the frame of the open window.

She looked up with a smile. "Come in, Jesse."

He stepped over the sill. "Hi, Maura."

"Have a seat." She gestured toward his usual vinyl chair.

Nope, he wasn't going to sit there again, not after what he'd just been imagining. He plunked down in the other one.

"I forgot to tell you," she said. "Cherry Lane's lawyer has drafted a waiver. So the next time you want to take Fred—or one of the others—for a ride, please make sure they sign the form first."

"You bet." He wasn't surprised Maura had moved quickly on this, but he'd figured a lawyer would take days messing about. "And I'll make sure they're fit enough, and tell them how to ride."

Mischief tilted her lips. "The same rules you gave me?"

He chuckled, glad she was no longer trying to pretend—or forget—that they'd had sex. "Maybe phrased a little different."

"I certainly hope so," she said with mock primness. Then her eyes started to glaze, and he guessed she was re-membering. Perhaps drifting off into a fantasy.

She gave a little jerk and clicked her pen a couple of times. Briskly, she said, "Also, I was thinking, if you find a reading program and want to get started, you don't have to wait until the community service has ended. We can adjust the schedule so you work here fewer hours, but for a longer period of time."

"Not sure that's a good idea."

"Staying here longer?" She frowned, looking disap-pointed. "You don't want to?"

Only long enough to figure out how he felt about her. If they were just going to be friends, they could see each other away from Cherry Lane. If he wanted to talk about long-term and she wanted to listen, then the quicker she stopped being his boss, the better. He couldn't exactly tell her all that stuff. "Want to get the community service fin-ished and clean up my record."

She nodded quickly. "Of course."

"But thanks for the offer. If we can juggle the schedule so I can take courses and work longer hours some days to make up the time, that'd be great."

"You're going to be a busy guy. Your job, your work here, helping Mrs. Wolchuk, and taking courses."

He shrugged. "It's good to be busy."

She was studying him again, this time not like she was going into a trance, but with narrowed eyes. Now what was on her mind?

"Something wrong?" he asked.

She bit her lip. "I'm not sure if I should say this."

"Go ahead."

"You mentioned your record. And now that I'm getting to know you, now that we're friends"—she colored slightly—"I really have trouble imagining you beating up that man."

Was this another reason she didn't want to get involved with him? Did she have a picture in her head of him with bloody fists, beating up Gord Pollan? Well, it was true. That was part of who he was, just as much as the part that wanted to help old Mrs. Wolchuk keep her house and dog.

"I did." How could he make her understand?

He thought about a movie he liked, that he'd watched again a few days ago. "There's this movie. Near the end, this bad guy attacks a couple of kids. They're in the woods, all alone. He's maybe going to kill them. But this other guy, I think he's kind of been looking out for the kids, and he comes along and—"

"Are you talking about *To Kill a Mockingbird*? I love that movie. I just watched it again last week."

"Yeah, me, too." So they'd both been alone, watching that movie. Like in *When Harry Met Sally*. It'd be way more fun to watch together. They were friends now. They could do that. Except, if he watched a movie with her, he wasn't going to want the night to end with the movie.

Then he remembered something. "Hey, I thought you didn't like movies."

Her cheeks flamed. "I lied. I'm sorry."

"Huh?" Maura, who hated dishonesty, had lied about whether she liked movies? "How come?"

"My parents think movies and TV—except documentaries—are a waste of time. They were banned in our house. But I always had a secret craving, and when I moved out on my own I indulged it. I know there's really no reason to be embarrassed about it but yet . . ."

Her parents really had done a number on her, but he understood why she'd always tried so hard to please them. "*I'm* not gonna criticize. I love 'em, too."

She gave him a big, warm smile. "Thanks."

"Anyhow, so Boo Radley kills that bad guy Ewell, right? He saves the kids. It's not like he has time to call the cops."

Her face went serious. "No, but he shouldn't have killed him. I doubt he needed to do that. Still, Boo Radley wasn't, well, normal. He probably had a mental illness. That's why the sheriff ended up protecting him and saying Mr. Ewell fell on his own knife."

"Yeah. And Ewell was a bad guy. Boo wasn't. He was protecting the kids. That's all he cared about, and he did it in the only way he knew how."

She gazed at him across the desk, her eyes troubled. "And you protected Consuela in the only way you knew how."

"Yeah." He studied that pure, perfect face of hers. "And I did it better than the cops or lawyers had been able to."

"It's so wrong that the justice system couldn't help your friend."

"Yeah, it is." He leaned forward and rested his arms on her desk so that his dark, bare forearms brushed her crisp blue shirt. "Maura, it's not like I wanted to beat up on Pollan. I had no choice."

"Some problems don't have easy answers," she said slowly.

"You got that right."

She pressed her lips together, then released them. "If I was in Consuela's situation, I'd want a friend like you."

Warmth rushed through him. He knew that was a big admission for her. Gruffly, he said, "And you'd have one." And now he really had to kiss her. He leaned forward.

"Jesse," she breathed, and he read uncertainty on her face.

Before she could decide how to respond, a knock sounded on the open door and Ming-mei's voice said, "Maura, I— Oh, sorry, I didn't mean to interrupt. I thought Jesse was out in the garden."

He sat back in his chair as Maura cleared her throat and said briskly, "That's fine, Ming-mei. What is it?"

"Mrs. Davidson's daughter is here, and I know it's past visiting hours but there's a family crisis."

Maura glanced over at him. "Thanks for giving me your report, Jesse. I won't keep you any longer." Relief and regret mingled in her eyes.

"I'll be going." He stood and headed for the door, not the window.

"Oh, Jesse," Maura called, and he turned back as she went on. "Tomorrow night, you're not coming in, right?"

"That's right."

"I'll see you Saturday then."

A day without seeing her. Maybe that was a good thing. The situation with Maura was complicated, and he wasn't good at complicated. They could probably both use a breather.

Chapter 17

Friday evening, Maura sat across the table from Edward Mortimer in her favorite French bistro, a neighborhood restaurant where she often dined by herself. When he'd asked her to suggest a place, it was the only one that had sprung to mind.

It felt strange to be here with him. The hostess had given them Maura's usual table, in a quiet corner where there was enough light to read a book while she ate.

Tonight, she was reading a menu she knew by heart. When Edward said, "What would you recommend?" she listed a few things she enjoyed. For appetizers, they decided on mussels for him and endive salad for her, followed by rosemary rack of lamb for him and coq au vin for her.

Surreptitiously, she checked her watch. That discussion had taken all of five minutes. What now? She was such a clumsy conversationalist, never sure what topics would interest people. When in doubt, it was always safe to ask about their work, but she'd heard—or, rather, daydreamed through—enough of that at her birthday dinner.

"You mentioned you grew up in a military family and traveled a lot," she said. "What was that like?"

"There was good and bad. The best part was seeing so many interesting places. It gave me a real travel bug."

"And the worst?"

"I'd make friends, then either my family would leave or theirs would."

"That does sound difficult." But at least he'd made friends, which was more than she had, except for Sally. "Where was your favorite place?"

"Hmm, that's a good question."

She'd asked a good question? All those talks she'd had with Jesse must have improved her conversational skills.

But she shouldn't be thinking of Jesse. Shouldn't be missing him and wishing he was across the table from her, rather than coaching basketball. Did he like French food? Maybe they'd have gone for pizza instead, then debated what movie to watch, or whether to make love before or after the movie—or maybe both.

The appetizers arrived and Maura gave herself a mental slap on the wrist. She was with Edward, who was a very nice man. Jesse was her friend, which was all he'd ever be, whereas Edward had potential. He wasn't a player, and he did want marriage and kids. If she was going to date any man, it would be Edward, not Jesse.

He lifted his glass of red wine toward her. "Thanks for coming to dinner with me."

She clicked her glass of white against his. "Thanks for inviting me."

"When I asked you to that lecture, I got the impression you weren't interested in me."

She'd been driving with Jesse, totally distracted by him—and no, she hadn't been interested in Edward. "You caught me at a bad time and I wasn't in the mood for attending a lecture. Not that I don't enjoy them, but I've been to so many over the years. It's nice to have a change. Like tonight."

He nodded. "Hard to talk to each other at a lecture."

She stifled a grin. Given her questionable social skills, that was one of the things she actually liked about lectures.

They tasted their food and he said, "The mussels are great. Thanks for recommending them." He asked her how her week had gone, and she told him about being extra busy since she was filling in for Louise.

He asked good questions himself, and drew her out. She was actually surprised when, as they finished their main courses, she caught sight of her watch and realized an hour had passed. When Edward suggested sharing dessert, she agreed, and they had crèpes Suzette with Grand Marnier sauce, flamed at the table.

As she savored the decadent dessert, Maura gazed across the table at him. He was probably the nicest man she'd ever gone out with. Intelligent, interesting, considerate, and pleasant looking. Whether by accident or design, her parents had done a good job this time. A month ago, she'd probably have been delighted.

Now, she wished for sparks of arousal. Surely Jesse couldn't have ruined her for being happy with an appropriate mate.

Her library book talked about the different ways attraction and love could grow. Initial sparks could be simply lust, and fizzle. Love could grow from proximity, common interests, shared responsibilities, mutual respect. That often happened in arranged marriages, and then the love ignited into genuine passion.

She studied Edward over the rim of her coffee cup. Could she ever feel passionate about him? Or did her newly awakened libido have the hots for only one man?

She'd get over it. Jesse would get a new girlfriend and stop shooting her those heated gazes that got her blood roaring. And Maura would seriously consider dating Edward.

In fact, she should invite him to be her date for the reunion. Surely that would be better than going alone.

And yet, she couldn't form those words. Not while they

discussed their favorite desserts. Not when he drove her home. And not when he walked her to the door of her apartment building and said, "I had a lovely time, Maura. I'd like to see you again."

Instead, she said, "I had a lovely time, too. Why don't you call me next week?"

Would he try to kiss her? Did she want him to? If he did, would she feel tingles, sparks?

The last time she'd been alone with Jesse, he'd leaned across her desk, intent clear in his eyes. She'd wanted so badly to kiss him but knew she shouldn't.

She wouldn't have. Even if Ming-mei hadn't interrupted, she wouldn't have.

With Edward, though . . . Oh, for heaven's sake. She was a sexy thirty-year-old woman, learning about her own sexuality. She leaned over—because, with Edward, she didn't have to go up on her toes like with Jesse—and rested her hands on his shoulders. "Thanks for tonight, Edward." Then she touched her lips to his.

It took him a moment, but only a moment. His arms came around her and he kissed her back, his lips moving softly against hers. His breath smelled pleasantly of orange brandy; he exerted just the right amount of pressure, and though he flicked his tongue against the crease between her lips, he didn't press for entry.

She responded in kind, thinking that he was really a very nice kisser. And yet, she felt no sparks.

After ten or twenty seconds, he eased away, smiling. "I'll talk to you soon. Sleep well, Maura."

"You, too."

She held back a sigh until she'd gone inside and closed the door. That experiment hadn't been a dismal failure, but it certainly hadn't been a roaring success. Still, if she got to know Edward better, maybe love and passion would grow.

It was still fairly early, but the week had been tiring, so rather than watch a movie, she curled up in bed and let her tired lids droop. Tomorrow, she'd see Jesse again.

Tonight . . .

She shouldn't dream about him. But she hoped she would.

Partway through the Friday night basketball game, Jesse noticed Consuela and Juanito watching. Afterward, they came over to say hi.

"Got any plans for the night?" Con asked.

He shook his head. "Want to go to the park for ice cream?"

"Yay!" Juanito put in his vote.

They made their way to the park they always went to, the mom and son in Con's old car and Jesse on his bike. Once they'd bought cones, Juanito ran off to play with another boy, and Con and Jesse found an empty picnic table and sat on either side of it.

"You know that guy?" she asked.

She could be talking about any man in the world, but he guessed who she meant. "The one from Monday?" He licked melting chocolate ice cream. "You see him again?"

"Yeah." She twirled her raspberry sorbet cone between her hands, then finally captured a drip with her tongue. "He's a jerk."

"Jesus. What'd he do? He didn't"—he glanced around to make sure her son was out of earshot—"hit you, did he?"

"No. He took me to a movie and was too touchy-feely, then he took me home and wanted to have sex. I said no way, and he kept pushing. He said I looked so hot, he couldn't believe I wouldn't put out."

"Asshole."

"Yeah. Why don't guys respect me? Do I have to dress like a librarian?"

He laughed. "What do librarians dress like?"

"I don't know. Conservative. *Tasteful,*" she said sarcastically.

Like Maura, he figured. "Well, guys would probably see you differently, but seems to me you ought to be able to dress however you want to." He studied her, tonight in frayed jean cutoffs and a bright pink top, both of which hugged her curves. Her wavy black hair was pulled up into some kind of fluffy ponytail, and her lipstick and nail polish matched her top. She looked as vivid as a hot-pink geranium. "You look great."

"Thanks, hon."

They licked their cones for a few minutes in silence. Across the park, Juanito had finished his. He and the other boy were running around with a yappy little terrier.

"Friday night," she said, "and neither of us has a date." She tilted her head and stared at him. "I know my reasons. How about you, Jesse?"

"There's only one woman I've met lately who I like, and she won't go out with me."

Her dark brows rose. "She won't? Jeez, what's wrong with her?"

"Long story."

"Aw, come on. I told you my story." A teasing glint lit her dark eyes. "You finally meet a girl who's immune to your charm?"

Maura definitely wasn't immune. "Nah, but she says it's a bad idea. She's my supervisor at that seniors place."

"Say what? Jesse, seriously?"

He nodded.

"What's she like?"

"Pretty, smart, thoughtful, generous. Well-educated. Kind of ambitious, I guess. There's this promotion she wants, to general manager."

"General manager? Of the whole place?"

When he nodded, she said, "Wow."

"She says if we got together, her Board of Directors would be pissed off. It could cost her the promotion, and maybe even the job she has now." He'd been thinking hard about asking his lawyer if they could find some other place for Jesse to do community service. He liked Cherry Lane, but he really wanted to ask Maura out. Now, not three months from now.

Con studied him some more, frowning. "Look, Jesse, hon, you know I love you to bits. You're fantastic. But a woman like her . . . I mean . . ."

"What does she see in me?" he asked, kind of disappointed but not exactly surprised.

"Well, yeah. I mean, not that there isn't a whole lot to see, but she just sounds like such a different type of person than you. Than us."

"She is, in some ways. But still, we kind of, you know, connect."

"Have the hots for each other."

"Yeah, but more."

"Huh."

He'd finished his cone and she handed hers over, half-finished. He began to lick raspberry sorbet.

"Seems to me," she said, "if I found a great guy, that'd be more important than my job."

Would he give up his job for a woman? Yeah, maybe, but . . . "You or me, we could get other jobs. You'd easily find another salon. I could find another construction job. Maura's, like, part of Cherry Lane. She loves the seniors and they love her. They're friends, you know?"

"I'm friends with the other girls at the salon, and with my clients. And you're friends with the guys on your crew."

"Yeah, but there's something different about Cherry Lane." He felt it, too, almost like he was becoming part of a big family. For Maura, who had issues with her parents and didn't seem to have a lot of other friends, he could see why the place was special to her. "And there's the promotion she's going for."

Con shrugged. "It's still just a job. Life's about other stuff." She gestured toward Juanito, who was throwing a stick for the terrier. "Stuff like my kid. I'd give up any job—give up anything—for him. So would you."

He licked the last drops of melting sorbet and crunched the cone as she went on. "Look at you, Jesse, you'd have gone to jail to protect me. That's what's important in life. The people you love."

"Won't argue with that." And when he did find the right woman, she'd feel the same way.

"I'm just saying, it's safer to stick to your own kind. Remember Snotty Sybil, the one who drove the Jag? The one who tried to give you that Rolex watch?"

Jesse winced. He'd thought he and Sybil liked each other, but he'd found out she saw him as her sex toy. Good enough to screw; good enough to boast about to her girlfriends at lunch—he knew, because she'd told him. But not good enough that she'd have lunch with him, out in public, when he invited her.

"Maura's not like that. Besides," he added wryly, "she refuses to sleep with me."

"Okay, that's good."

"Matter of opinion," he grumbled. Though Con was right. At least he knew Maura was interested in him for more than sex.

Consuela chuckled. "Yeah, good point. But she works at that seniors place, and she's got you doing community service. Maybe she's the do-gooder type, and she looks at you as her little charity project. Acting all nicey-nicey, but feeling all smart and superior. Like Nurse Nancy, a few years ago."

Did Con remember every woman he'd ever dated? "She's not like that, either."

"Okay. But I still think it's safer to stick to your own kind. Less chance of getting hurt."

Like Con was the expert on how not to get hurt. Still, what she said was the same thing he'd thought many times himself. It was good advice. He probably shouldn't talk to his lawyer about changing his community service, not until he knew Maura better.

Saturday, when Jesse rode his bike up the cherry-lined driveway to Cherry Lane, he thought what a difference a week made. Last week, he'd been dressed in fresh new clothes, feeling resentful about having to do community service.

This week, he was a couple of hours later because he'd been working on Mrs. Wolchuk's roof. His clothes were already grubby, the taste of Mrs. W's fresh poppy seed cake was sweet on his tongue, and he was hungry to see Maura.

When he got there, a smiling Gracie—had he actually once planned to ask her out?—greeted him. "Hi, Jesse. Maura has a couple of meetings today, so she can't go to the garden center with you. But she left these." She handed over a set of keys and a charge card. "She added your name to the list of drivers who're insured to drive the van, so you can take Virginia to the garden center. Put everything on Cherry Lane's card."

"Okay. Thanks." He was happy Maura trusted him, but why wasn't she there? Had she decided it was better to stay away from each other? "Meetings?"

"Legal stuff, can you believe it, on a Saturday?"

More waivers?

"She said she'll catch up with you later this afternoon."

He grinned. Sounded as if Maura wasn't avoiding him, just busy.

So he got busy, too, collecting Virginia and heading off
to shop for plants and fish.

Midafternoon, Jesse looked up from his work to see
Maura coming across the lawn. Today she wore a choco-
late-brown skirt and a filmy blouse the color of ripe
peaches. A feminine blouse, not like her usual starchy shirts.

She greeted him with a big smile and sparkling eyes, but
talked only about the garden—until she ended with,
"When you're done for the day, would you come see me?"

"You bet." It was hard not to let his grin slant into a private one, but as usual a group of seniors was hanging
around, listening to every word.

Later, after a few more hours' work and a dinner made
up of Polish goodies Mrs. Wolchuk had packed for him,
Jesse was building a natural-looking rockery to house the
fountain. Maura came out again, this time almost running.

He dropped the rock he was holding and rushed to
meet her. "What's wrong?"

"There's a burst pipe in Mr. and Mrs. Trotter's bathroom and it's flooding their apartment."

He wiped his hands on his jeans as the two of them hurried back across the courtyard. "You turned off the taps?"

"Yes, of course."

"Under the sink?"

"Yes, but the water's still pouring out."

So a pipe must be broken behind the taps. "The shutoff
valve for the apartment? Out in the hallway somewhere?"

"The what?"

"Get the tool kit from the storage room. I'll go turn off
the valve. Which apartment?"

"It's two oh three. Take the stairs at the end of that hall."
She pointed.

"Right." He took off at a run while she headed in the
other direction.

A couple minutes later, he'd shut off the water and was taking off his shoes at the open apartment door. "Ms. Mahoney sent me," he told the anxious-faced elderly pair who greeted him. "I've shut off the water and I'll fix you up as soon as I can."

A few steps in, the living room carpet squelched under his sock feet, so he stripped off his socks as well. "You weren't home when the pipe burst?"

Mr. Trotter, who had his arm around his wife, said, "We went down for dinner. When we came back, it was like this."

In the bathroom, Jesse saw that the cabinet top was littered haphazardly with cartons, bottles, and assorted crap that likely normally lived below the sink. Inside the open cabinet doors was another jumble of stuff, soaked now. Squatting, he located the broken pipe just beyond the cold water shutoff tap.

He went back to the living room as Maura arrived with a big red tool kit. "It's pipe fatigue," he told them. "Got some old pipes there, and you shoved a lot of stuff under that sink. Pressed up against the pipe, bent it; eventually it broke."

"Told you you shouldn't put so much stuff in that cabinet," Mr. Trotter grumbled to his wife.

"And I told you we needed to buy a wall cabinet, but did you listen?" she returned.

Jesse stifled a grin and caught Maura doing the same. "Best thing to do," he said, "is replace all the piping under the sink. Home center across the road should have all the stuff, and I can do it in an hour or so. But your carpet's soaked. Need to get that dried out."

"How?" Maura asked.

"Rent two or three industrial dehumidifiers. They suck out moisture big-time. But they're really noisy and they'll

make the place hot and humid and smelly. Be best if you
didn't stay here tonight."

"We'll put you up in a hotel," Maura told the Trotters,
"at Cherry Lane's expense." She picked up the phone and
booked them a room at an inn by the water, then Jesse
told her who to call about dehumidifiers.

As he put on his shoes to go to the home center, she
said, "When you go past reception, would you ask Nedda
to send someone to mop the bathroom floor?"

"Sure."

Nedda. That was the sourpuss who alternated with Gracie and Ming-mei on the reception desk. The one who
seemed to have a grudge against the world. When he re-
layed Maura's message, the woman's gaze was suspicious
and she didn't even nod.

If she'd worked for him, he'd have fired her long ago.
When he'd said that to Maura, she'd told him the woman
was related to a Board member, so they had no option.

When he got back with the piping, the rental company
had arrived with the dehumidifiers. The Trotters had
gone, the bathroom floor was clean and dry, and Maura
said, "I'll get out of your way. But thanks, Jesse. I don't
know what I'd do without you."

He gave her a teasing grin. "You just keep thinking
that."

Their gazes met and her cheeks colored. Then she
pressed a hand to her cheek. "Oh, in all the excitement I
forgot. There's something I want to talk to you about.
When you've finished here, could you lock up, then tidy
up whatever you were doing in the garden and come see
me?" The sparkle he'd seen earlier was back in her eyes, so
the something must be good.

Had she maybe got the Board's okay on the two of
them going out? That'd be about the best news he could

imagine. Waiting, being patient, didn't suit him one bit. There might be no hope, long term, for a guy like him with a woman like Maura, but he needed to find out.

Whistling, hopeful, he went about his work.

After he'd cleared up the garden, he didn't go knock on Maura's window but took the time to wash up in the men's room, with hot water and soap. Then, blood humming with anticipation, he headed to her office.

He stepped inside and closed the door behind him. Man, she looked great in that peach-colored blouse. All soft and approachable. He ached to cross behind her desk and kiss her. What would she do if he did? "You talk to the Board of Directors?"

"What?" Her puzzled expression told him that wasn't the *something* she'd had in mind. "Oh, yes, we had the Board meeting, and they're fine with everything."

His heart leaped. "Everything?"

"What we're doing with the garden, and letting the residents contribute. They even told me I'm doing a good job, so I'm winning brownie points toward that promotion."

"Great. And?"

"Well, they approved my budget."

With a sense of letdown, he sank into a vinyl chair. Not *the* chair, the one from his fantasy, but the other one. "Guess you're happy about that."

"I'm even happier about other things." She smiled, all sparkly eyed again. The smile tipped into a grin, like she had the secret to end all secrets. "Jesse, you know how we were saying there should be an organization that looks after people like Mrs. Wolchuk?"

"Yeah, sure."

"I think there is."

"Hey, cool. But I still don't mind doing the work for her."

"Maybe you could work for the organization."

That was what had her so excited? "Sounds complicated."

"I know you don't like complications and rules and paperwork. That aspect could be minimized."

"But why do I have to go through some organization? Oh, is it a liability thing? If I do it myself and something goes wrong, I'm personally liable. But if I do it through an organization, then I'm covered, and they have insurance?"

"You're a quick learner, Jesse Blue."

Okay, so sometimes rules had purposes. Resignedly, he asked, "So what's the name of this organization?"

Her eyes were absolutely glittering. "You tell me."

"Huh? I've never heard of it."

"That's because it's brand new. It's not registered. It doesn't have a board of directors or a charitable tax number or even a name. Doesn't have any funding or any employees, either." Ms. By-the-Rules Mahoney sounded as proud as if she was describing a Fortune 500 company.

"Not following you." He felt the way he so often used to: stupid.

"It needs a director. He could work part-time until the Board and the funding sources are organized. It would be a start-up operation."

"How long's that going to take?" There'd be paperwork, legal stuff, lots of complications. "I told Mrs. Wolchuk I'd come by for a few hours every week."

"I understand. But let me tell you the kind of things the director would do," she went on. "He'd assess repair projects, find sources for construction and garden supplies at rock-bottom prices, and in the beginning he'd have to do most of the work himself."

Things Jesse could do in his sleep. If someone had diagnosed his dyslexia when he was a kid, he could be this fancy director. "Uh-huh."

"Of course there'd be an administrative side, too. The kind of work that I do here at Cherry Lane. Accounting, budgets, reports to the Board, funding proposals."

He grimaced. Even if he'd had a better education, he wouldn't want to do that. He was a man of action.

"That would be a different person, though," she said. "And just a few hours a week."

He shifted restlessly. Maura'd probably be mad if he went ahead with Mrs. W's work, but he hated to start a job and quit in the middle.

"I foresee that the organization will grow," she went on. "The director will have to hire staff and direct them, but from what I've seen the guy I have in mind is excellent with people."

"The guy *you* have in mind? You're involved in this organization?" Maura really did confuse him sometimes. "Why didn't you mention it the other night?"

"Because I didn't know about it." Her eyes gleamed with excitement.

"Okay." Just like with his dyslexia, she'd done some research and found out about this organization. It did sound cool. He'd like to work for them when they got going, but right now, he wanted to help out Mrs. W.

"This director," she said, "he'll have to do some project management and supervision, but I think he'll still want to be hands-on most of the time." Her eyes had an I've-got-a-secret sparkle and the corners of her mouth twitched like she was fighting back a smile. "Right, Jesse?"

"If he's like me he would."

She was losing the battle with her smile.

And then it hit him: something that would explain the sparkly eyes and secret smiles. But no, he was a laborer who couldn't read properly. He couldn't be the director of some fancy foundation. Could he? Wondering if he was making a total fool of himself, he asked, "Are you talking about me?"

"Well, duh," she said. That un-classy word, coming from Maura's mouth, was almost as much a shock as what she'd been saying.

"Duh?" he repeated as a laugh built inside of him.

"Duh." Her smile had broken through and her eyes glittered with a fierce joy.

His mind couldn't process this. "What're you talking about?"

She leaned forward. "As we said, there's a need for an organization like that. So I figured, let's create one. You would be the perfect director. I'll serve on the Board and do the paperwork. I met with Cherry Lane's lawyer today, and their firm will help us pro bono. No charge. Mrs. Wolchuk can be our first client. Oh, Jesse, don't you think it would be wonderful?"

He did. But he was too stunned to take it in.

Her eyes widened and she rose, looking uncertain. "Are you okay? Oh, gosh, I've gone off like . . . a runaway horse and I've probably got it all wrong." She started to round the desk, cracking her hip against a corner. "You probably love your job, and I'm sure it's got job security and great benefits." She stopped a couple of feet away from where he sat.

Now, finally, his brain was working again. "Yeah, my job's good. Great boss, good team, but it's just building stuff like apartment buildings. It's not helping anyone. You know?"

She nodded vigorously. "That's why I thought this would be so perfect for you."

The idea was sinking in. "We could help all those old people like Mrs. Wolchuk." He and Maura together, working as equals.

"Exactly."

Excitement surged through him. He sprang out of his chair and pulled her into his arms.

She gave a shaky laugh and then threw her arms around him, not seeming to care that his clothes were grubby from a hard day's work. She gazed up at him. "You really think it's a good idea?"

"It's a fantastic idea. God, lady, did anyone ever tell you how smart you are? And how caring?"

Her body stiffened and her eyes widened again. "No, never." She burrowed her face into his shoulder. He felt moisture against his neck.

"Jesus, Maura, are you crying?" He tried to pull away from her so he could see her face.

She just clung tighter. "Happy tears," she choked out.

Well, okay. She was happy, and he was holding her. He was so damned happy, he'd have waltzed her around the room if he had any clue how to waltz. Gently, he rubbed her back. "Hey, it's okay," he soothed.

His body finally cottoned on to the circumstances and arousal surged through him.

Chapter 18

Now, there was a cure for sloppy, sentimental tears: the press of a growing erection against her belly.

The whole week had been so stressful, like nothing she'd ever experienced before. Highs, lows, uncertainties. Fantasy, reality. Sex. Decisions. Always, in her life, Maura had strived for control.

Right now, nothing seemed to matter except the warm, hard man who held her. A man who'd told her she was smart and caring. A man who saw her the way no one else ever had.

A man who wanted her, who thought she was sexy. The hard evidence thrust insistently against her.

She leaned back in Jesse's arms and gazed at him, blinking moisture from her lashes.

He smiled down at her. But not all that far down, even though he was inches over six feet. She was used to being more or less on eye level with men, which she'd never liked. What man found a skinny beanpole attractive?

Jesse did.

He tilted his head and his lips touched hers.

Oh, yes. Pure bliss. Firm lips caressing hers, that uniquely Jesse scent in her nostrils, his strong, muscular body and the erotic thrust of demanding male flesh, confirming how much he wanted her.

Just as much as she wanted him.

How could anything that felt this good possibly be wrong? How could she resist a man who made her feel this way? Being together might not be wise, but it was *right.*

And so she surrendered, flirting her stomach sideways against the bulge in his jeans. It was the first time in her life she'd wished she was taller, because then she'd have been able to press her crotch right against his erection.

As if he'd read her thoughts, he grabbed her buttocks and lifted her off the ground, that extra few inches she longed for. And there he was, thrusting against the very part of her that most longed for him. She moaned.

"Oh, yeah, Maura, let me hear you. Let me feel you."

She closed her eyes as she pressed and wriggled against him, trying to achieve the impossible task of surmounting several layers of clothing.

This time it was Jesse who moaned. Then his mouth captured hers again, and this time his lips were hard and his tongue demanding. Maura responded eagerly.

Her head reeled, the pleasure was so intense. Their mouths pillaged each other, their hips ground together, and inside her belly that amazing sensation was building. Pleasure, anticipation, growing in intensity. Now that she'd finally experienced orgasm, she wanted, needed—

He grabbed her hips and thrust her away from him.

Her eyes flew open and she whimpered with disappointment.

He stepped away from her and locked her office door. Then he strode to the window and lowered the blinds.

Oh, my gosh, this was like a fantasy. But even better, because the sexual passion between them was fueled by caring, connection, a— "Oh!" she gasped as he grabbed her roughly at the waist, then his lips took hers urgently.

One quick, ravishing kiss, then he broke free. "Now, Maura. I need you now."

"But . . ." How? Here, in her office? "I need you, too," she confessed.

Boldly, she pressed a hand against the hard column of flesh inside his fly, his heat scorching her through the denim.

"Unzip me." His gravelly voice rasped.

Somehow, it was unbearably arousing to have him command her. Especially when he was telling her to do the exact thing she most wanted.

Hands trembling, she forced his jeans button through the hole. She grasped the tab of his zipper and worked it down. As she unzipped him, his erection filled the open space and she stopped to enjoy the sight of all that naked masculinity distending the front of his underwear and poking out the top.

"Maura, you gonna finish the job?"

"Mmm." She resumed work on the zipper, then began to slide his jeans down, hooking her thumbs under the elastic of his underwear and taking it along, too. She peeled him inch by inch until he gave an impatient exclamation and took over, shoving his clothing down.

His erection sprang free, jutting demandingly from a nest of dark curls.

Her pulse raced. It throbbed so wildly at her throat that she had trouble catching her breath, and so demandingly between her legs that she ached to have him inside her.

As she stared, a drop of moisture beaded at the head of his penis.

"Take off your skirt and panties," he said.

Breathlessly, she undid her own button and zipper, let her skirt drop, then sent her panties skimming down on top of it.

By the time she'd finished, he'd pulled his T-shirt over his head, found a condom, and sheathed himself.

Not taking the time to free himself from battered running shoes and the jumble of jeans and underwear at his ankles, he sat on one of the vinyl chairs. "Now, Maura. Come here and kiss me."

His body was so beautiful, all ripply bronze muscles, springy dark hair, and that tantalizing erection.

Clad just in her blouse and bra, she moved toward him and leaned down to kiss him.

Their tongues had just touched when again his fingers stroked the folds between her legs—quick, a little rough, teasing her needy flesh. Then he caught her by the waist, both hands gripping tight, and eased her down to sit straddling his thighs.

His penis rose in front of her, and she pressed against it, tilting her hips to rub their bodies together.

One of his hands was inside her blouse, not bothering with the catch on her bra, just shoving the fabric up so he could cup her breast. He rolled the nipple between his thumb and finger, sending a fresh surge of pleasure to her groin.

She arched into him, her head going back, and caught a glimpse of her purple orchid curving above them, the sensual flower faces smiling approval.

His free hand grasped her bottom, lifted her, the crown of his penis probed between her legs, and she forgot all about the orchid. In one quick thrust, he was deep inside her and she whimpered with shock and sheer pleasure. "Oh, yes, Jesse."

"God, you're hot. You drive me crazy." His head was back, the planes of his face rigid. "Don't move. Just hold still."

She did, savoring the feeling of him filling her, so hard

and so deep. He felt so good, and she was all hot and squirmy and needy. No, she couldn't keep still any longer.

She lifted up a little, sliding up on him the way she slid her mouth up a Popsicle. And then down again, because it felt so good when he was all the way inside her and their pelvises pressed together. She leaned forward slightly, gripping his shoulders for balance, and changed the angle. Up, down, a little twist this way, and oh, my, what delicious pressure against her sensitive flesh, both inside and out. Fascinated, she gazed down, watching as their bodies joined.

Yes, she'd read descriptions of lovemaking, but words, no matter how well written, couldn't capture the immediacy, the intensity. The sight of his firm shaft, wet and gleaming, sliding in and out of her; the sexy coarseness of his dark, curly hair rubbing her most intimate flesh; the fierce bite of his fingers gripping her waist and her own digging into his shoulders; the wet, slippery sounds of their bodies joining and the rasp of their labored breathing.

The amazing bliss of being with this man, in the most intimate of all acts.

"Oh, Jesus," he groaned, then his lips captured hers.

She kissed him back just as fiercely. His eyes were open now, tawny gold, staring into hers. In their depths she read passion, yes, but more. It was like he saw into her soul, saw all her frailties and all her strengths, and wanted to claim her as his woman.

He set the rhythm of their lovemaking now, a driving rhythm that with each upward stroke lifted both their bodies off the chair.

Need spiraled inside her, centering, growing until it consumed her. She swiveled her hips, tightened around him, moaned with need, gazed deep into his amazing eyes, and— "Oh!" She shuddered as waves of pleasure rolled through her.

She was still climaxing when Jesse jerked upward, deep into her core, and his orgasm caught her up and swept her under again.

When finally it was over, she felt boneless. She sagged against him, her arms loosely circling his back. When she could finally speak, she said, "I could never have fantasized anything like this."

He hugged her close. "Me, either. Being with you is incredible."

For long minutes, Maura surrendered to sheer bliss. Then a sound in the corridor outside—a cough?— brought her back to reality.

She pushed back from Jesse so she could see his face. Wonderingly, she said, "This wasn't supposed to happen."

"Always thought your rules were crazy."

Her rules. She knew she'd had good reasons for them, but the allure of Jesse was just too strong.

Actions have consequences. Always consider those consequences before you act.

And she always had. But now she didn't want to. Rather than listen to her parents, she'd take a page from Scarlett O'Hara's book, and leave that for tomorrow. Then, perhaps she'd remember the rules and regret this.

No, she couldn't regret this. It felt so perfect to be with Jesse.

What had she told herself last night? She was a sexy thirty-year-old woman, learning about her own sexuality. And what better teacher than Jesse? For now, she'd think only of tonight.

"There's one thing I'm sorry about," he said, tawny eyes gleaming.

He had regrets already? "What?"

"Taking it so fast. When I'm with you, I lose control."

Oh, my. How flattering. As her parents had taught her, she'd always believed strongly in control. Now, with a sense of discovery, she said, "There's such a thing as too much control."

"There's such a thing as long, slow, thorough lovemaking."

Yes, toes could actually curl. Heat licked through her. "Are you offering to demonstrate?"

"That's my plan." He stood, dumping her onto her feet. "But not here. Let's go to my place. Or yours?"

"Mine," she said immediately. Jesse in her bed, creating memories she'd always treasure.

As they dressed, he said, "Come with me on the bike?"

She stepped into her skirt. "I'm not dressed for it."

He grinned lasciviously. "You can hike it up. It'll be sexy."

Oh, yes, it would, just like she'd imagined the last time she rode behind him. She was sorely tempted. But then the early shift staff would see her car in the parking lot, and there'd be questions. "Better not. We should leave separately, too."

"Tried that before," he reminded her.

"Tonight, it should work. It's late enough, no residents are likely to be around, wanting to chat."

"So this is gonna be our secret?"

She nodded. "It has to be."

He studied her for a long minute, but just said, "Okay."

When Maura parked by her apartment, Jesse was already there, standing by his Harley. He came over, took her hand, and dropped a kiss on her lips like those were the most natural things in the world to be doing.

When they went in, she clicked on a light, nervous about his reaction.

He glanced around the living room. "Nice. Looks peaceful."

She had chosen neutral colors—lots of shades of beige with occasional accents of blue, green, and brown—and furniture with simple lines. She looked around critically now. There should be plants. Maybe he'd help her pick some out.

He took off his shoes and left them by the door, then padded behind her in sock feet to the kitchen. "Flowers and herbs look good."

She glanced toward the windowsill. "They do." The room felt so much homier. She opened the fridge. "Would you like a glass of wine?"

"Don't suppose you've got any beer."

"Sorry, just wine."

"That'll be good."

"A snack? I didn't get much dinner tonight." It was true, but she was also way out of her depth, having a man—a lover, a sexy hottie like Jessie—here in her apartment. They'd both come here for sex. She knew that. Yet she couldn't just dive into it.

Not the way she had back in her office. What on earth had got into her?

Well, Jesse of course. She smothered a giggle and set about putting out Camembert and water biscuits, and pouring Ehrenfelser.

They sat at the kitchen table, her in her customary seat on one side, with the view out the window, and him at one end, close to her. When he told her about the work he'd done at Mrs. Wolchuk's, and the home baking she'd given him, Maura began to relax. Yes, this felt right, too. They were friends. They could talk about things.

Hopefully, when their fling was over, that friendship would remain.

They moved on to the subject of the new nonprofit society and tossed around names: No Place Like Home, Home Sweet Home, House Keepers.

Now, both of them finished with the cheese and crackers and sipping a second glass of wine, he began to touch her—brushing her arm, caressing her thigh, dropping a kiss on her nose or cheek. Making her totally aware of him and getting her stirred up.

So she did the same back, slipping a finger inside a rip in his jeans, toying with his earring and taking the opportunity to caress the lobe of his ear. "I like your earring. It's sexy."

His finger tapped her cheek softly, here, there, and across her nose. "I like your freckles."

"Oh, no, seriously? I've always wished I didn't have them."

"They're cute, and then you blush so pink they disappear."

"I hate blushing, too."

"It's sexy. Everything about you's sexy." He reached over and took her glasses from her shirt pocket. "Especially these."

"Now I know you're joking. I should get contacts, but they bother my eyes and—"

"No! Don't get contacts. Jesus, Maura."

"What?"

"You'll spoil my fun."

Her nose wrinkled in perplexity. "What fun?"

"It's this game that drives me crazy. Whether you're sexier with them on, or off." He sounded dead serious.

"You are the strangest man."

"Yeah, but you like me."

She chuckled. "Yes, I do."

Their gazes caught and held again. "And I like you back," he said quietly. "You're a special woman, Maura Mahoney."

Stunned, she couldn't find words to respond.

Jesse shifted, looking a little embarrassed. He reached over to twine a curl of her hair around his finger. "Your hair's tousled."

"Is it?" She'd forgotten to straighten it before leaving Cherry Lane, she'd been in such a daze.

He tugged out a hairpin. "It wants to come down."

Now he was back to his teasing ways, and she felt more at ease. "Does it now?"

One by one, he pulled out the pins, and curl by curl her hair tumbled past her shoulders. When every strand had been freed, she leaned back and shook the heavy mass.

"Hair brush?" he asked.

Her mouth made an "oh." He wanted to brush her hair? She couldn't imagine a more seductive form of foreplay. "Bathroom counter." She pointed down the hallway.

A moment later he was back, pulling up a chair behind her and sitting where all she could se. of him was his reflection behind hers in the kitchen window.

She lounged blissfully as he worked out a few tangles with his fingers, then eased the brush through her thick hair, moving from roots to ends in long, sensuous strokes.

It felt almost sinful to be enjoying herself this way. Especially when her gaze caught on the plate of leftover cheese and crackers on the table. "I should put the cheese back in the fridge."

"You should relax and enjoy." He parted her hair at the back and teased the nape of her neck with soft kisses and little licks.

"It'll go stale."

"The world won't come to an end. Let go of those rules every now and then, Maura. You don't always have to be perfect." His tone was teasing.

She gave a wry chuckle. "I'm far from perfect."

"Perfect would be boring."

But she *was* boring. She'd always thought that about herself, except in grade twelve with Sally. And ultimately, that had gone so wrong. "I believed it was better to be a boring good girl than a bad girl who got in trouble."

"Makes sense." The brush kept moving, long past a hundred strokes. "You were that little girl who lost her parents, thought no one wanted you. Got taken in by folks who didn't know how to care for you, or care about you. You had to be perfect. Probably, some survival instinct said that if you weren't, they'd toss you out."

A survival instinct. The most primitive, fundamental instinct in the world. "Maybe so." She studied his vague reflection in the window. Jesse Blue, hot motorcycle guy and amateur shrink.

"But you're grown up. You don't have to be that kid anymore."

"I . . ." Was that why she was so rule-bound, why she didn't make waves, why she hated to disappoint Agnes and Timothy, and everyone else in her life? "That sounds kind of messed up," she said slowly. "I should have gotten past the issues that affected me as a child."

His hand stilled for a moment, then he went on brushing. "Yeah, and I should've figured out I wasn't stupid. That there was some other reason I couldn't read."

"When you were a child, no one gave you reason to believe in yourself. And kids form strong beliefs." She thought it through as she spoke. "Subconscious ones. We don't always realize why we behave the way we do, so we're not likely to change."

"But when we realize what we're doing . . ." He put the brush on the table and, standing, took her hands and pulled her to her feet. Voice low and husky, tawny eyes warm, he said, "You helped me see myself in a different way. See things I didn't even realize were holding me back."

"Yes," she breathed. "That's it. That's what you're doing for me."

His hands framed her face, scooping the long hair back from it. "Seem to recall some talk about long, slow lovemaking."

That memory was vivid. "And thorough. Don't forget thorough."

"Not a chance."

He put his arm around her waist and guided her out of the kitchen.

She flicked off the light but left the scraps of cheese and crackers lying out on the table.

In the bedroom, candles left over from her bath experiment sat on the dresser and she lit them, rather than turn on the lights. They, together with ambient light coming in the window, would provide enough illumination.

When she turned from the dresser, Jesse held out his hands to her and she went to him. He kissed her forehead, her nose, her cheeks, then finally her lips, each touch sending sparks of arousal darting through her. "Thorough," he murmured. "Have to get every freckle."

Thorough and naked would be even better. She eased back in the circle of his arms and brought her hands to the bottom of his T-shirt. She peeled it upward until his hands took over.

He pulled it over his head and tossed it to the floor. His torso was perfect: strongly muscled, with those sexy curls of dark hair, those cute dark nipples.

Glancing below his belt, she saw he was already aroused. She ran her finger down his fly, pressing against the bulge inside, hearing his quick intake of breath.

"My turn," he said, and started working on the buttons on her blouse.

She blessed the feminine instinct that had made her put on her peach lingerie this morning, and blessed it again when he unfastened her skirt and let it drop.

He scooped her up, carried her over to the bed, and put her down.

She tossed back the duvet and had barely stretched out

on the ivory sheet before he'd stripped off the rest of his clothing and was following her down. He blanketed her with his body, hard where she was soft, and gave her one intense, toe-curling kiss. But then he eased away.

When she made a sound of complaint, he said, eyes dancing in the candlelight, "Thorough."

He began to kiss her, starting at the hollow in her throat and working his way down until he suckled her nipple through the softly abrasive lace of her bra. The only part of her he touched was that one nipple. When she'd played with her nipples in the bath, she'd thought her breasts were unresponsive, but, oh, how wrong she'd been. Tingly heat radiated out from her nipple, and her lower body clenched and twisted with need.

Relentlessly, Jesse carried on, teasing her other nipple, then unhooking her bra and starting all over again with the first nipple.

What delicious agony.

Finally, he gave her a respite when he carried on, licking a teasing trail down over her ribs and belly, then circling the dip of her navel. He toyed with the lacy band at the top of her thong but didn't peel it down. Instead, he breathed hot air through the skimpy fabric.

She shivered, guessing where his mouth was heading.

And yes—oh, yes!—now that seductive mouth was kissing her intimately through the narrow band of the thong. His tongue licked, probed, sucked, and she pressed herself demandingly against it.

But he moved away, kissing inner thighs, nibbling and licking her damp flesh, heading toward but just avoiding the places she really wanted him to touch. She squirmed, twisted, moaned her frustration.

He peeled her thong off and tossed it away, then finally he was back where she needed him, laving her swollen lips with his tongue, flicking gently at her clitoris—and yes, she most definitely had one and it was joyously operational.

But then he backed off again, not touching her but blowing air across her wet, swollen flesh.

He came back, retreated again, and each time he returned, the sensations were more intense, the need coiled higher and tighter inside her.

"Jesse!" she pleaded, unable to stand it any longer.

Now he swirled his tongue around her clit, flicked it, sucked it gently between his lips. She held her breath, and this time he didn't leave her, he kept sucking until her body exploded with pleasure.

Thorough. Oh, yes, there was a lot to be said for thorough.

When the ripples of climax faded, she knew what she wanted next: to explore Jesse's body.

She forced her limp body into a sitting position and, trying to sound confident, said, "Lie down for me."

He cocked an eyebrow but obeyed, settling on his back with his head on a pillow. He was so dark against her ivory sheet and pillowcase, with his beautiful brown body and the shiny black hair tangled around his face. He looked exotic, almost dangerous—yet, he was Jesse. Her friend; her lover.

Experimentally she ran a hand over his chest, felt the crispness of his chest hair, the bead of his nipple. Would he like it if she suckled his nipple, the way he'd done to hers? She leaned over and gave it a try, and he moaned in response.

This was good information for future reference, but at the moment her mind was pretty much one-track. Her hand drifted down toward his lean belly. His erection was a solid baton of flesh lying flush against his stomach, right straight up the middle all the way to his navel. It was a bit intimidating and she could hardly believe that all of that . . . masculinity had been inside her body.

It was exciting, too. The throbbing between her legs had started up again.

"Won't break if you touch it," he drawled.

He must think she was so naïve.

She summoned her courage and grasped him in her hand, wrapping her fingers all the way around his shaft, about midway down.

He sucked in his breath and she held still. Then he slowly let out his breath, and she began to move her hand, pumping up and down a few times. Next, she circled the head of his penis with a gentle finger, amazed at how velvety smooth his skin was there. She cupped his testicles one by one, surprised at how furry they were.

Jesse made encouraging sounds, little moans and purrs of satisfaction.

Her own body was growing more aroused, just as if he'd been touching her. But he wasn't. This time he was leaving it up to her.

Emboldened, she bent down, her hair streaming across his belly, and licked him.

His hips jerked and he groaned, sounding like he was in pain.

Quickly, she lifted her head. "Am I hurting you?"

"Oh, yeah, you're killing me."

"Oh, Jesse, I'm sorry."

He gave a ragged chuckle. "Killing me with pleasure, Maura."

"Oh! Well, that's . . . good." She went back to what she'd been doing, licking every inch of him, then closing her lips around him and sucking. His musky, purely masculine scent was a potent aphrodisiac.

He caught a handful of her hair and tugged. "Come here and kiss me."

She stretched over him, blanketing him, wriggling up his body for that kiss.

His mouth took hers, fiercely, and his hands grasped her buttocks, holding her tight against him. She wriggled some more until she was perfectly positioned on top of him.

His tongue thrust in and out of her mouth, in a rhythm that mimicked sex.

She sucked it.

He groaned again. "I need to be inside you."

"Oh, yes."

"Got protection?"

Condoms? He thought she was the kind of girl who kept condoms beside the bed? Actually, that was pretty flattering. "I don't. You do, right?" He must. They couldn't stop now.

"In my wallet."

She scooted off the bed, found his jeans, and brought his wallet to him. He extracted the little package, tossed his wallet onto the bedside table, and handed her the condom.

Startled, she almost dropped it. He wanted her to put it on him? She'd never done that. Her two lovers had always taken care of this aspect of the process, and she had averted her eyes discreetly.

Inspired, she leaped off the bed and hurried to the kitchen, where she grabbed her glasses. Perched again on the bed, she slipped them on.

Jesse's eyes widened. "Holy shit. I've never seen you with your hair down and your glasses on. God, woman, that's sexy."

She smothered a satisfied grin and said demurely, "I have to read the instructions." That was true, but he'd think it was sex play.

She scanned the instructions and opened the wrapper,

then, with her glasses still on, fumbled to roll the condom onto his erect penis.

He groaned and rasped out, "I should've done it."

"Am I doing it wrong?"

"You're doing it so right, it's driving me crazy."

She grinned smugly. "That's okay then."

The moment she'd secured it, he sat up, pulled her into his arms without giving her a chance to take off her glasses, and rolled so she was on the bottom. He rose above her and an instant later surged inside.

Oh, yes! That felt so very good, the way he filled every empty, needy bit of her.

This time, though, it wasn't a quick race to the finish line. They kissed, they caressed, he shifted pace from fast to slow. He rolled again so that she was on top, then again so they were on their sides facing each other. Sometimes, he slowed so that he moved just the tiniest bit, rubbing some secret spot inside of her that had her gasping with pleasure, then crying out as orgasm rolled through her.

Then, finally, he rolled atop her again, caught her hands, and held them above her head. Gazing straight into her eyes through her glasses, he drove them both to the peak and over the top.

They hung there together for long moments, then as her muscles began to relax, he eased down. After dealing with the condom, he settled on his back, his arm around her, tucking her into the curve of his shoulder. She finally took off her glasses so she could nestle closer, and wrapped a leg over him.

Lazily, he stroked her shoulder and arm, and ran his fingers through her hair, which was now hopelessly tangled. "When you went down on me and all this gorgeous hair tumbled across my belly and cock, it was a fantasy come true."

She smiled into his eyes. "You make all my fantasies come true."

"I'd like to do that, Maura. You mean a lot to me."

"And you to me."

"You're not going to start quoting the rule book and saying we can't keep seeing each other?"

"I'd decided to think about that tomorrow."

He cocked his head toward her bedside clock. "And it is."

She glanced at the time. Yes, it was past midnight. "You want to keep seeing me?"

"Yes." One simple word, spoken firmly, with no hesitation.

For how long? But she couldn't ask that. He'd told her all his relationships were casual. This was the guy who viewed sex and bike rides as equally significant. Soon there'd be another woman on the back of his Harley and in his bed.

The thought shouldn't make her heart ache. It was naïve and stupid to care too much for a man who was a player, a man she'd known from the beginning couldn't possibly fit into her world.

Yet, somehow, it was impossible not to care for Jesse. Surely, when their affair had run its course, she could shift that caring into pure friendship. "I want to see you, too," she told him. They'd be careful, make sure no one else found out. He knew that was one rule she wouldn't break.

Jesse studied her unblinkingly, then he swung off the bed. "Back in a minute."

What? Had she said the wrong thing?

Cool without him there, she pulled the top sheet and duvet over her and sat up to await his return.

When she saw the two glasses of wine in his hands, she breathed a sigh of relief.

He handed her a glass and swung into bed beside her, propping pillows behind his back. He clicked his glass to hers. "To us, Maura Mahoney."

Happily, she replied, "To us, Jesse Blue." As lovers, friends, business colleagues. She hoped Jesse would be in her life for a long time.

"About that reunion of yours," he said slowly.

The reunion? *Aagh.* Why did he have to spoil this perfect moment by reminding her of the reunion? "No appendicitis yet," she tried to joke. "Guess I'll have to go." And go alone, too. There was no way she could invite Edward now.

"If you wanted"—Jesse sounded as if he was struggling to dredge up words—"I could go with you."

Jesse? Her date for the reunion? She squeezed her eyes shut and a scene she had imagined before flashed into her head.

The doors to the high school gym flew open and they rode in on Jesse's shiny black bike. Heads turned, people gaped, all conversation ceased.

Everyone was in evening dress but none came close to touching Jesse when he slid off the bike in his tux. He looked as dashing and sexy as Sean Connery's Bond. He bowed slightly in her direction and held out his arm so she could slip her hand through it.

She inclined her head and accepted the invitation, and they swept forward. She wore a red off-the-shoulder ball gown that swished with each step she took, and killer heels. As tall as she was, Jesse was even taller.

"Is that Maura Mahoney?" she heard Cindy say. "I can't believe it!"

"Who's that man she's with?" someone asked.

"He's a movie star, isn't he?" another answered. "He's the most handsome thing I've ever seen."

"He's pure sex, walking," an awed voice whispered . . .

"Maura?" Jesse's voice broke in. "Are you all right?"

Her eyes flew open, to see him beside her in bed, the sheet draped carelessly across his hips.

He'd offered her her fantasy.

But . . .

Obviously, they couldn't ride into the gym on a bike. And Jesse likely didn't own a suit, much less a tux. The girls from her class would be impressed by his looks, but they'd ask what he did, what post-secondary degrees he'd earned. It was Wilton Academy, for heaven's sakes; everyone would have graduate degrees and impressive jobs.

But the capper, for her, was imagining the shock and disapproval on her parents' faces. And if they found out he'd dropped out in grade ten, that he couldn't read . . .

"Maura?" Impatience edged his voice.

Why did she care what people thought? Jesse was special, a really great guy.

She should be ashamed of herself for thinking that way. And she was. But even if she put all the rest aside, she couldn't go out in public with Jesse. "I, uh, really appreciate the offer." She struggled to find words and couldn't meet his eyes. "But everything I said before is still true. About my promotion, and your community service. We can't risk them both, not for my silly high school reunion."

"I get that."

"You do? Then why—"

"Thought we could tell my lawyer the garden's done and you don't have any more work for me. He'd have to find me someplace else to finish my community service."

She'd been planning to move Jesse into doing repairs, but he was right. It was a plausible story to tell his lawyer. And if Jesse wasn't working under her supervision, the two of them could be together. But for how long?

"So, what about that reunion?" he asked.

Chapter 19

Maura's face wore a deer-in-the-headlights expression. And it sunk in. Deep and hard.

He'd actually been stupid enough to buy all that crap she'd been spouting about her promotion.

He'd realized he cared for her, a lot. That he was falling, head over heels, and liking it. He'd thought she felt the same, and so he'd found a way they could be together without it hurting her career.

And yeah, her career mattered to her, but that wasn't the real reason she'd been putting him off. He should've known better, a guy like him dreaming of a future with a woman like her.

"So I'm good enough to fuck," he spat out, "but that's it. I'm your dirty little secret."

Her "No, that's not it" came several long seconds too late.

He leaped out of bed and yanked on his underwear.

"Jesse, no. Wait."

His back to her, he ignored her. What an idiot he was. Damn it, he knew better. He'd been wary in the beginning; Con had even warned him. And still, he'd been stupid enough to believe Maura was for real.

"Jesse, let's talk about this."

He zipped up his jeans. Even that shit about dyslexia

and the repair service for seniors, it wasn't because she cared about him. She *saw* him, but not as a man, as a charity project.

"As for your stupid nonprofit society, I don't need your fucking charity."

"It's not charity. It's a worthwhile project and you'd be great at it."

He pulled his tee over his head and turned to look at her, sitting upright in bed with the duvet pulled tight around her shoulders. A do-gooder, trying to remake his life into some image she had in her head. Because he wasn't good enough for her.

"I'm happy doing what I'm doing," he said heatedly. "I don't need you messing around with my life."

"I was just trying to help," she said softly.

"Don't you get it? I don't need your help." He stalked out of the bedroom, down the hall, and out of her apartment, slamming the door behind him.

Con was right. People like them should stick to their own kind.

Blood boiling, he cranked over the engine on the Harley. He'd head over to Low Down, shoot some pool with the guys, and drink enough beers to drive Maura Mahoney right out of his mind.

If there was that much beer in the world.

Maura awoke to the insistent ring of the phone. She forced open eyes swollen by hours of tears—tears of self-pity, and of guilt—and glanced at the clock. It was ten. She never slept that late, but then she never cried until dawn, either. Her head ached fiercely and she longed to put it back on the pillow.

The phone rang again. Could it be Jesse? What would she say to him? She'd hurt him last night. She hadn't meant to. She'd thought he knew as well as she that they were too different; she'd thought he was a player who'd never care enough about one woman to give her the power to hurt him.

She'd been wrong. Wrong in so many ways.

Ever since she'd met him, she'd kept messing up.

She was a horrible person. And yet, the bottom line was still true: her world and his just didn't match. He'd realize it, too, when he thought things through.

But she'd hurt him. She felt awful for hurting him. And, selfishly, her heart would break if she'd destroyed their friendship.

Another ring. She was tempted to ignore the phone, but that would be breaking the stupid rules and she'd done enough of that. She grabbed it and said, tentatively, "Yes?"

"Maura? Oh, thank God!" It was Ming-mei, and the panic in her voice had Maura swinging out of bed.

"What's wrong?"

"There's been a robbery! Mr. and Mrs. Trotter came back from the inn where they spent the night, and her jewelry's gone."

"Oh, no!" Mrs. Trotter had several very expensive pieces. The recently retired general manager of Cherry Lane had advised the woman many times to keep them in safe storage, but she said she liked to look at them, and to wear different items when the mood struck her. "They're really gone? She didn't take them to the inn with her and forget she'd done it?"

"I asked. She says she was so upset about the flood that she forgot all about them until this morning, when she wanted to wear a special brooch to church."

"Still, things were pretty crazy last night. She could be confused. Or maybe she or her husband hid them away somewhere before they left?"

"Mr. Trotter is positive her jewelry was in its usual place when they left: an inlaid jewelry box on top of the dresser in the bedroom."

"I'll come in right away." Maura pulled underwear from a drawer, pants and a shirt from her closet.

"Thanks. The police are on their way, too. Mr. Trotter called them. Should I call Louise?"

"No. We can handle this."

Maura had showered sometime in the small hours of morning, so now she just flung on clothes. She didn't even bother to pin up her hair, only ran a brush—the brush Jesse had used last night, but she wasn't going to think about that—through it and yanked it back with a clip. Ouch. No, that made her headache worse. She released the clip and gulped a couple of aspirin and a glass of cold water.

Then she raced out to her car and pushed the edge of the speed limit. Scenarios ran through her head. First, in hopes this was a big mistake, she'd search the Trotters' room and phone the inn herself. If the jewelry really was missing, could Jesse have forgotten to lock the apartment door? But most Cherry Lane residents left their doors unlocked during the day, and if any of the seniors or staff had wanted to steal Mrs. Trotter's jewelry, they'd have done it before.

What about the rental company that delivered the dehumidifiers? Maura'd been with the delivery man the whole time, hadn't she? And Jesse'd been the one to set up the machines in the living room, bedroom, and bathroom, and get them running.

By the time she turned the corner to drive down the lane of cherry trees, she'd returned to her original thought: this had to be a mistake.

A police car was parked in front of the building.

Maura rushed inside. Ming-mei, at the reception desk,

said, "I'm so glad you're here! This is terrible, just terrible!"

A group of seniors clustered around, and several of
them began to talk at once.

Maura took a deep breath, wishing her head would stop
pounding. To the seniors, she said, "We'll get this sorted
out. Why don't you get on with your day?" And to Ming-
mei, "Let's go talk in my office."

"The police asked me to send you up to the Trotters'
apartment."

"All right, I'll go talk to them."

"They asked who was on duty last night, and I said you
were here working late and Nedda diFazio was on the
desk. They had me call her, too, and she should be here
soon. Should we let the Board of Directors know?"

"No, not yet." Oh, great. Just after impressing the
Board at the last meeting, now she might have to report
that a theft had occurred while she was in charge. "We'll
wait until we find out what really happened."

As Maura turned to go to the Trotters' apartment,
Nedda rushed through the front door. "There's been a
theft?" She was more animated than Maura had ever seen
her.

"We don't know that yet," Maura said.

"The police want to see you, too, Nedda," Ming-mei
said.

"Of course they do," the woman said. "I see what goes
on in this place." She shot Maura a nasty look.

In silence, the two of them paced down the hallway and
took the elevator to the second floor. The door to 203 was
closed, and Maura knocked.

A brown-skinned young woman in police uniform
opened it.

When Maura introduced herself and Nedda, the officer
opened the door wider. "I'm Constable Singh. Come in."

The apartment was hot and humid, as Jesse had warned, and the fanlike noise of the dehumidifiers aggravated Maura's headache. The Trotters sat side by side on their couch, holding hands. A beefy, fair-haired male police officer sat in a chair opposite them, holding a notepad and pen.

Constable Singh introduced Maura and Nedda. "This is Constable Meyer."

Maura nodded. "Thanks for coming. But I have to ask, Mr. and Mrs. Trotter, are you absolutely sure you didn't hide your jewelry, or take it with you last night?"

"We've checked that, ma'am," Constable Singh said. "I searched the apartment and phoned the inn to have them check the room. The jewelry box is still on the dresser, but it's empty and—"

"I know who did it," Nedda broke in eagerly.

They all turned to gape at her.

Meyer turned to a fresh page in his notebook. "Go on."

"It was that shady character who's been working in the garden. Jesse Blue." She shot a triumphant look at Maura.

Maura shook her head firmly. "No, that's not possible. Jesse would never steal."

"He's a criminal! He almost killed someone, and that's way worse than stealing!"

"You read his file!" Maura stared accusingly at the woman. "HR files are confidential and they're kept in locked cabinets."

She shrugged. "I went into Louise Michaels's office looking for something, and there was a stack of files out. If they were supposed to be confidential, she shouldn't have left them there."

Maura'd always known the woman had a nasty personality, but she'd never guessed she was such a snoop. "They were labeled."

"How'm I to know how you people label your files? I'm just the receptionist."

Seething, Maura turned back to the two police officers and tried to keep her voice calm. "Mr. Blue came to us to do community service. It was arranged by Ms. Michaels, the HR manager. She's on maternity leave and I'm filling in for her."

"The man's an attempted murderer?" Constable Singh asked disbelievingly.

"No, of course not. Mr. Blue did assault a man, but his reasons were good enough that the court didn't send him to jail. He's not a violent man, and he's been a hard worker, responsible, and excellent with the seniors."

"Excellent with the seniors," Nedda parroted in a snarky voice. "Sucking up to them, so he can rob them blind."

Infuriated, Maura snapped, "That's not true!"

"Ladies," Constable Meyer broke in, "thank you for this information. We'll need to get statements from both of you. We'll start with Ms. diFazio. Got an empty office we can use?"

"Ms. Michaels's," Maura said.

To the Trotters, Meyer said, "I have everything I need from you, except for that jewelry schedule on your insurance policy. But don't get it out of the dresser until we dust it for prints. Best thing for you now is to go downstairs and try to relax."

They all left the apartment. For Maura, it was a relief to get out of the noisy, humid place, but she was still seething over Nedda's false accusation. Surely, when the police interviewed her, they'd realize she was just a bitter, spiteful woman, making up a story.

Maura went with Nedda and the police to Louise's office and made sure the desk and credenza were bare of files and the cabinets and drawers were still locked. "I'll be in my office when you're ready for me," she told the officers.

First, though, she got the Trotters settled in the lounge,

where they were immediately the center of attention. It was unavoidable, but Maura hated knowing that Nedda's lie would soon be spread among the residents.

In her office, she rested her head in her hands and was rubbing her fingers into her aching temples when Constable Singh stepped through the door, followed by Constable Meyer.

"Headache?" the woman asked sympathetically.

"Yes. This has upset me." And that was no lie, even though the original source of her headache had been a night's worth of tears and guilt. She stood. "Shall we go to Ms. Michaels's office?"

"Here will do fine," the male officer said, plopping down in the chair Maura and Jesse had occupied last night.

Battling a flush, she said, "Fine," as Constable Singh took the other chair.

Both pulled out notebooks and pens as Maura seated herself again.

"Let's start at five last night," the male officer said, "and you tell us what you were doing."

Maura told them about the flood, regretting that her story established that she and Jesse were the only people, other than the Trotters, who had been in the apartment bedroom. "I know I didn't take the jewelry," she said, "and I'm sure Jesse didn't. There has to be some other explanation."

The two officers exchanged glances, then Constable Singh asked, "What's the Trotters' financial position?"

"They're not wealthy. Few of our residents are. Are you suggesting they'd fake a theft and claim the insurance money?" She shook her head. "She loves that jewelry, loves wearing it, showing it off, telling about when her husband gave her each piece. Besides, they were too upset about the flood to plan anything like that."

"Uh-huh," the male officer said noncommittally. Then,

"Tell me about Jesse Blue, and Ms. diFazio's allegation that he attempted murder."

Ms. diFazio is a nasty snoop. Pressing her lips together to hold the words back, Maura unlocked her filing cabinet and handed over Jesse's file. "This is what it says on paper." She went on to tell him about Consuela's situation. "You can speak to his lawyer, Barry Adamson. As for Jesse's time here, he's been skilled, conscientious, he puts in more than the required hours, and he really is great with the seniors. Ask them, they'll tell you."

"Uh-huh." He glanced at the file, then up at her. "Ms. diFazio says you're defending him because you're having an affair with him."

"What?" Her heart lodged in her throat and her mind raced. What did that nasty woman know? Nothing. She couldn't. Should Maura admit it? It would make both her and Jesse look bad. It might not actually violate the terms of his community service, but she wasn't positive. As for her, likely the Board would find out and she'd lose the promotion.

"You seem surprised," Constable Singh commented.

"I am." She shouldn't lie to the police. Only an hour ago she'd vowed not to break the rules.

Okay, then she'd go by the letter of the law. The male officer had asked a question. Trying not to blush frantically, she repeated his words back, "No, I am not having an affair with Jesse Blue." They'd had sex a couple of times, and now . . . now, he hated her, and maybe she deserved that hate. They'd been becoming friends, and now even that was gone. She was definitely not having an affair with him. It was the absolute truth. Surely Jesse would say the same thing, even if he was mad at her.

"But I have come to know him," she went on, "during the week he's been here, and I don't believe he's a thief."

"Uh-huh." Constable Meyer made a note.

That was so aggravating, that bland "uh-huh."

"You say he came to your office after he finished work, to report in. Was that your routine?"

"Pretty much. Since he started work, I tried to be around when he finished." She'd loved their talks, the growing friendship and intimacy. Trying not to flush, she said, "It's my responsibility to record his hours and keep track of his progress."

"So, he reported in. That took what, a couple minutes?"

"A bit longer." She'd answered the question. She wouldn't add that they'd had sex, but should she mention the repairs for seniors idea they'd discussed? It would make the two of them look awfully chummy, considering their relative positions and the fact that they'd only met a week ago.

"Then you both left. Together?"

"No. He left, and I tidied up a few things before leaving. His bike wasn't in the parking lot when I went out." No, it had been racing to her apartment.

"What did you do then?"

"Drove straight home, and didn't leave until this morning, when Ming-mei called me about the robbery." Again, she was telling the truth.

"Anyone to corroborate that you were home alone?"

She couldn't tell them Jesse'd been there, not after denying they were having an affair. Avoiding a direct answer, she said, "I live alone, but what's this about? You consider me a suspect? That's ridiculous."

"Ma'am, everyone's a suspect. We're gonna need your prints, compare to what we find on the jewelry box."

"Fine." They'd be printing Jesse, too. But she knew he was innocent.

Innocent people didn't get convicted. Or at least they weren't supposed to. But as Jesse had shown her, when he'd told her Consuela's story, the justice system didn't always work.

Jesse awoke with a pounding head and a mouth that tasted like camel dung. Not that he'd ever tasted camel dung, but it couldn't be any worse than the inside of his mouth.

Dimly, he realized that the pounding wasn't just in his head. Someone was knocking on his door.

Maura? Come to her senses?

Fat chance of that.

He hauled himself out of bed, wincing at the sunshine outside his window. Should've pulled the blinds when he came in at dawn, but he'd been too shit-faced to do anything but fall into bed. In yesterday's grubby work clothes, he now realized.

Heading for the door, determined to silence that fucking hammering, he kicked something and his keys skittered across the floor. He froze for a moment. He hadn't ridden home, had he? No, he vaguely recalled one of his pals flagging down a cab for him.

Hadn't locked his door, though, he realized as he flung it open. "Would ya stop that damned—" He swallowed the last word at the sight of two cops, one male and one female.

"Jesse Blue?" the woman asked.

The distaste in her narrowed eyes told her he looked like crap, and a sexy smile wasn't going to work on her. "Yeah. What's up?"

"I'm Constable Meyer," the guy said, "and this is Constable Singh. We need to ask you a few questions."

Shit, what had he done last night? "About what?"

"It's in connection with a robbery."

"Huh? Who got robbed?" Or had he been robbed,

with his door unlocked all morning? He glanced into the little kitchen, but everything looked normal.

"A couple who live at Cherry Lane. Mr. and Mrs. Trotter."

"The Trotters?" He tried to make his hungover brain work. "Oh, hell." He'd been in their apartment, alone. If something had gone missing . . . "I didn't take anything." He hadn't even given in to the temptation to use their shower to clean up.

"We're not saying you did. But you were in their apartment yesterday."

"Yeah, fixing the pipes."

"So let's talk."

"Do I need to call my lawyer?"

The two officers glanced at each other, then the woman, Singh, said, "It's noon on a Sunday. I bet your lawyer has better things to do than sit around while we ask you a couple of questions. Of course, if you need him to look after you . . ."

A couple of questions. That didn't sound so bad, and he knew he hadn't stolen anything. He could handle this without bothering Barry Adamson—or running up another legal bill. "Nah."

"Okay if we come in?" As Meyer asked the question, he stepped past Jesse into the kitchen.

The woman cop followed. "Mind if we take a look around?"

His sluggish brain processed that. "Whatever was stolen, I'm not the guy who took it."

"So you don't mind?"

Barry'd probably say they needed to get a search warrant, but that'd just make Jesse look suspicious. "Whatever. While you look, I could use a shower."

He couldn't think straight, not all grubby and sweaty, with a pounding head and camel-dung mouth. In the bathroom, he swallowed a few pills and drank a couple glasses of water, brushed his teeth, then soaped a day's worth of sweat off his body in the shower, finishing off with cold water to jolt his brain to life.

Feeling marginally more human, he went into the bedroom. "Whoa," he exclaimed on seeing Meyer, his hand inside Jesse's underwear drawer.

"Got a problem?" the guy asked.

"Nah. Search away, you're not going to find it. But toss me a pair of briefs."

The cop chucked underwear in his direction. "You sound pretty sure we won't find anything. Does that mean you stashed it somewhere?"

Jesse pulled on boxer-briefs, then clean jeans. "Means I never took it. What the hell is it, anyhow?"

"Pull on a shirt and we'll talk."

A few minutes later, the three of them sat at his small kitchen table, him on one side, the two cops across from him, both taking notes. They asked him about the flood at the Trotters', and he went through the whole thing.

"What rooms did the dehumidifier guy go into?" Meyer asked.

"Just the front room. He delivered, Ms. Mahoney signed, then he left and I set up the machines."

"When you left, did you lock the door?"

"Yeah."

"With a key?"

"No, it's one of those knobs you press in on the inside. I never had their key."

"What then?"

"Went out to tidy up in the garden, then, uh, I reported in to Ms. Mahoney." Now, he was on less certain ground. What had she told them?

"Ms. Mahoney." Meyer flipped pages in his notebook. "She's the accountant and acting HR manager."

"Yeah."

"She's supervising your community service?"

"Uh, yeah." He shouldn't be surprised they knew about his community service.

"So, you say you didn't take anything from the Trotter apartment?"

"I didn't."

"Suppose you're going to tell me you're not sleeping with Ms. Mahoney, either."

"What?" The question caught him like a punch out of the blue. Maura wouldn't have told them. She didn't want anyone knowing. Shit. He'd figured all the cops would ask about was the Trotters' apartment, so he'd be in the clear if he told the truth. Now, what the hell was he supposed to say? He couldn't exactly lawyer up at this point. "Who the fuck told you that? Bet it wasn't Ms. Mahoney." Though some stupid bit of hope in his heart made him wish she'd owned up to it.

"She's an attractive woman," Meyer said.

"And you don't clean up too badly," Singh put in. "They always say that opposites attract. Is that right, Jesse?"

"That's not how it usually works for me." Maura was the sole exception.

"So," Singh said, "if Ms. Mahoney said you were having an affair, she'd be lying?"

Had she? Had she actually said it, on public record? No, he didn't believe that. "She wouldn't have said it."

"Yeah, you're right," Meyer said. "Guess guys like us only get to dream about women like her, huh?"

Guys like us. As if that was going to soften him up and make him confess to something he hadn't done. "Whatever. So where'd you get the idea we were sleeping together?"

Another bit of page-turning, then Meyer gazed across at him. "Ms. diFazio."

"Who? I don't even know a Ms. diFazio."

"Nedda diFazio, who works evenings on reception."

"Oh. That sour bitch." She might've seen him and Maura leave a time or two, just a few minutes apart, but she didn't know a damned thing.

"Her word against yours."

"And Ms. Mahoney's," he reminded them.

"She also says that, after Ms. Mahoney left last night, you came back to Cherry Lane."

"What? No, I didn't."

"You're sure you don't remember?" Singh asked. "You came back, wearing a black leather jacket, and said you'd forgotten something in the garden. You walked down the hall, out of Ms. diFazio's sight. When you came back five minutes later, your jacket was zipped up and it was bulging like you had something inside it."

"No! Fuck, no, I never went back." He'd ridden straight to Maura's and sat outside on his bike, waiting impatiently for her to get home. "That bitch is lying."

"She's not the one who's had a run-in with the law," Singh said calmly. "Why don't you tell us about that?"

He went through the story. When he told them what Pollan had done to Con, he saw Meyer's heavy jaw clench and anger flash in Singh's dark eyes.

When he finished, Meyer said, "That the only time you've been in trouble with the law?"

"Haven't you checked?" Aside from a few speeding tickets, he'd kept his nose clean since he was a teen.

Meyer shrugged. "You look to me like the type of guy who might have a juvie record. What you think, Singh?"

"Looks that way to me," she said.

Yeah, he'd shoplifted some stuff, stolen a bike, got himself into all sorts of trouble. But juvie records were sealed. "Gonna tell me what was stolen?"

"Happen to remember a jewelry box that sat on the dresser in the bedroom?" Meyer asked.

Jewelry. He'd noticed the flashy ring on Mrs. Trotter's left hand. Seems that wasn't all she'd owned. He recalled the bedroom: old double bed in a mahogany frame, little bedside tables and dresser to match. Paintings he didn't like, kind of dark and European looking. Clutter on the top of the dresser. "Yeah, there was a box there." He made a rectangular shape with his hands. "About this size. Is that what went missing?"

"Did you touch the box, Jesse?" Singh asked.

He shook his head. "Didn't touch anything in the bedroom, just set up a dehumidifier on the carpet between the bed and the dresser."

"So we aren't going to find your prints on that box?" she went on.

They had the box, which meant the jewelry inside it had been stolen. "Nope."

"Your prints are on file," she said. "As soon as the prints from the site are processed, we'll check them against yours."

"Good."

"Smart guy like you'd know not to leave prints, though," Meyer said.

Jesse was starting to get worried. What happened to innocent until proven guilty? That bitch Nedda had lied her ass off and it seems these cops had their minds made up about him. "It wasn't me."

"Then who?" Singh asked. "The only other person in that bedroom was Ms. Mahoney. Are you saying she did it?"

"Jesus, no. That's crazy."

"Why?"

"If you knew her, you wouldn't ask."

"Know her pretty well, do you, Jesse?" Singh asked in a suggestive tone.

Fuck. "I've seen her with the seniors. She cares about them. She'd never do anything to hurt them."

"Gotta be you or her," Meyer said.

"No." He thought quickly. Who else could it be? "Maybe Nedda diFazio took the stuff. She's trying to pin this on me, so I bet she did it herself."

"Her word against yours," Meyer said for the second time. "Guy who's been in trouble with the law, versus a woman who has no criminal record and is sister-in-law to the Chair of Cherry Lane's Board of Directors. Wonder who a judge would believe, Singh?"

"Seems pretty clear to me, Meyer."

There were people at Cherry Lane who'd vouch for him. Fred and Virginia, some of the other seniors. Maura? It seemed not. If she had, the cops wouldn't be harassing him this way. Okay, she wouldn't alibi him because that meant revealing that she'd slept with him, but she could've at least vouched for his character.

Last night, he'd realized she didn't think he was good enough for her. Today, did she believe he was a thief? That hurt like hell.

But this wasn't the time to worry about his fucking *feelings*. He was up shit creek.

"I want to call my lawyer."

Chapter 20

Maura wanted to close her office door, rest her head on the desk, and cry.

The Chair of the Board had phoned, having been alerted by Nedda, his sister-in-law. Maura had given him the basic details and said she was confident the police would resolve the matter.

Cherry Lane was buzzing. By the time lunch was over, everyone in the place knew Nedda had accused Jesse of theft, and Jesse and Maura of being lovers.

The latter part was embarrassing, though it was almost amusing to hear the varied reactions. Some people said it was impossible; they were too different. Others said it was a great match, but Maura was too much of a lady to have an affair with a man she'd known only a few days.

As for the accusation against Jesse, the residents who'd gotten to know him were talking about going en masse to the police station to tell them he couldn't have done it.

Maura picked up a fork, toyed with a piece of cucumber in the untouched salad in front of her, then dropped the fork when her phone rang.

"Maura?" It was Louise Michaels's voice. "What's going on?"

"Did someone phone? No one should have bothered you with this. It's under control."

"The Chair of the Board called. There was a theft?"

Maura gave her the short version. "The police took fingerprints. I'm sure they'll catch the thief."

"You don't need me to come in and help with anything?"

"Thanks for the offer, but I can deal with it."

"Good practice for being general manager," she said teasingly. "Doesn't the job look more and more attractive?"

"Not so much. But you're right, it's been good for me, filling in for you."

"And since the old GM retired, you're basically in charge of the place." She chuckled. "And to think I once had my eye on that job."

Louise had decided she'd rather have a regular nine-to-five job and raise a family. "How are things with you?" Maura asked. "And Don and baby Jeff?"

"Perfect. Fabulous. I couldn't be happier. Oh, Maura, this is a dream come true."

"I'm so happy for you. Just hearing the joy in your voice has brightened my day."

"You know, a couple of people said we should think twice about adopting, that it's not the same as having your own baby. But Maura, aside from not going through nine months of pregnancy, it's exactly the same. Jeff's ours. We couldn't love him any more if—" She broke off, sniffling. A moment later she gave a shaky laugh. "See, I'm even all emotional and hormonal."

"You go back to enjoying your baby, and don't worry even the tiniest bit about Cherry Lane. Everything here's going to be fine."

"Thanks, Maura."

She hung up, smiling. At least something was going totally right.

Her hand was still on the phone when it rang again.

This time a male voice spoke, sounding harried. "Maura, it's Barry. Barry Adamson. What's going on?"

"Barry? Why are you calling?"

"Got a call from Jesse. The police think he stole some jewelry."

She jerked to her feet, a hand at her throat where her pulse jumped erratically. "They've arrested him?"

"I don't know what's going on. I'm on my way now. Figured while I'm driving, you could give me some background info."

Yet again, she explained what had happened. "Jesse's no thief, but it's hard to come up with any other suspects. I can't see any of the seniors doing it, I can't imagine the Trotters committing insurance fraud, and I hate to think it could be any of our staff."

He huffed out a sigh. "Okay. Thanks. Gotta go, I'm here."

"Call me afterward, will you?"

"Sure."

Maura hung up and took a deep breath. As Louise had reminded her, she really was in charge here. The Board hadn't chosen to appoint an acting general manager, but in a situation like this, Maura was de facto it. Which meant she shouldn't be hiding here in her office, nursing her angst over what had happened. She needed to go out and answer questions, reassure people, and try to keep them occupied and happy.

A couple of hours later, Maura hurried to her office to take Barry's call.

"They haven't arrested him, but he's their prime suspect," the lawyer said. "I believe him, but that woman Nedda diFazio is adamant that he came back after you left last night, and he left with something stuffed under his jacket."

"What? No!" He'd been at her apartment.

"He says she's lying; he never returned to Cherry Lane. It's his word against hers, and the police don't believe him."

Jesse hadn't told the police he'd come to her place. He'd protected her, even though he hated her. And he was suffering badly for it. Worried and frustrated, she said, "I believe him, and so do you. Why don't the police?"

"Because they don't know him. They see his record and don't know who he is as a person. As for diFazio, she's never even had a parking ticket, and she's got the Chair of Cherry Lane's Board vouching for her."

"She's his wife's sister." Maura, who normally would never bad-mouth someone, went on. "I never liked Nedda. She's the wrong kind of person to be working here, but we can't fire her because the Chair got her the job, at his wife's urging. I don't care for his wife, either. They're both sour, bitter women."

"Which raises another point. The woman alleges that you and Jesse are having an affair."

"What on earth makes her say that?" Nedda couldn't know. Even if she'd listened outside the office door—a thought that disgusted Maura—at most she'd have heard a groan or cry, and those could have another explanation.

"She admitted it was circumstantial evidence. Being alone in your office for long periods, leaving at the same time, looking flushed and tousled when you left. Nothing of significance. But why would she say it?"

"Because she's a bitter, nasty woman with a vivid imagination?"

"Does she have a grudge against one or both of you?"

She reflected. "I can't see why. She just likes to stir up trouble."

"Jesse suspects she stole the jewelry herself."

"Oh! Oh, my gosh. That makes sense, doesn't it?" she

said excitedly. "The seniors go to bed early, and she was alone at the reception desk. She has access to the master key that unlocks all the doors. Everyone knew about Mrs. Trotter's lovely jewelry. And Nedda knew Jesse'd been in the apartment, that he could have left the door unlocked and gone back later. She knew about his record and that he'd be an easy person to frame. The police have to search her house."

"They don't have grounds for a warrant. They only have Jesse's accusation and no evidence to back it up." He sighed, sounding discouraged. "I'll keep you posted."

After he hung up, she sat there with her head in her hands. She could give Jesse an alibi.

Without it, he probably wouldn't ⎧ ˋ convicted, maybe not even charged, because there really was no evidence against him. The true culprit would surely be found.

And if she told the truth, she'd lose her chance at the promotion, maybe even lose her job. Maybe—or was this too far-fetched?—she'd face criminal charges for obstruction of justice.

Agnes and Timothy would be shocked. Disappointed. Furious.

Her parents. Did she even care about the promotion, except to make them proud of her?

But . . .

"Oh, my God." She sighed. How could anyone be proud of her? She was a terrible, horrible, awful person. How had she let her need to win her parents' approval lead her to be such a bitch?

She'd thought her parents wouldn't consider Jesse good enough for her. The truth was, she wasn't good enough for him. Jesse had protected her, even though he had good reason to hate her. He was an honorable man. In everything he did, he was an honorable man.

He'd told her she was caring, but she'd cared more

about herself than about anyone else. "I'm not like that," she murmured. "Not deep inside. I don't want to be like that."

This past week, she'd found out some things about herself, and now it was time to dig even deeper, to find out who she really was. To find out if she was a woman who could be proud of herself. And if she was, then it didn't matter what her parents thought.

If Agnes wanted to start being more maternal, then she'd need to learn that her daughter wasn't an obedient clone of her parents and had a mind of her own. Even if that mind led her places her parents would rather she didn't go.

Maura sat up straight and dialed the phone. "Barry, there's something I have to tell you."

Later that afternoon, she hung up the phone after talking to the Chair of the Board. Well, she still had a job, which was more than she deserved, and the police hadn't pressed charges against her.

Immediately after confessing to Barry, she'd talked to the police, and next she'd phoned the Chair and told him everything. She'd withdrawn her application for general manager, telling him she knew she wasn't the right person for the job. She'd also said that she would understand if the Board decided to terminate her completely.

He'd said he'd call an emergency Board meeting by teleconference and would get back to her.

Now, she had the verdict. It no doubt helped that the stolen jewelry had been found at Nedda's apartment. The Chair had also admitted he'd never liked the woman himself, but it was hard to say no to his wife.

Maura was still Cherry Lane's accountant. Unbeknownst to her, Fred Dykstra and Virginia Canfield had phoned the Chair that morning to discuss Jesse's situation and ask if there was any way the Board could help him. After Maura's confession, the Chair had contacted them again, and their strong support of both Maura and Jesse, combined with her own sterling record at Cherry Lane, had saved her job. It had also saved Jesse's community service, not that there was the slightest chance he'd still want to work here.

He probably never wanted to see her again. It would be easier to avoid him.

But no, that's what the old Maura would do. The Maura who took the easy route, who avoided risk, who didn't stand up for what she believed in. She'd been so busy being the little girl who wanted to please, she hadn't grown into a woman with a strong moral core. And that was her fault, not her adoptive parents'.

Feeling about a hundred years old, she left Cherry Lane and turned her car toward Jesse's apartment. Probably, he wouldn't be there. He'd be out celebrating with Consuela and Juanito, or with other friends. Jesse had friends. He was a good, strong, wonderful man who made friends. He, the man with a seriously disadvantaged childhood, had turned into a decent, well-adjusted person.

She, the one who'd been raised with all the advantages, was a selfish, inhibited weakling who didn't have friends because she didn't deserve them.

She was going to change, though. And if Agnes and Timothy didn't like it, then so be it.

Jesse's bike was parked below his apartment. Praying he was alone, she mounted the steps. The worst he could do—the thing he was bound to do—was tell her he hated her and never wanted to see her again. That would break her heart, but it was her own damned fault.

For once she'd do what was right, even if the consequences meant rejection and pain.

* * *

Jesse sprawled in a recliner, a cold beer in his hand. He was free. He should be celebrating, but he was too confused.

A knock sounded on his door. Con, probably. He'd had voice mail from her, asking him for dinner, and he hadn't replied. Soon, he'd tell her all that had happened today, but not right now.

The knock came again, louder, and he sighed and heaved himself to his feet.

When he opened the door, he almost dropped his beer bottle. "Maura?"

Her hair was down for once, tousled around a pale face that looked tired and strained, falling loose and free past the shoulders of a green shirt. Despite himself, his heart gave a skip of joy, before he remembered the way she'd rejected him.

She walked past him, into the kitchen. Uninvited, just the way the two cops had done earlier.

He hadn't expected her to come, but now that she was here, she could clear up some of his confusion. Keeping his distance, he leaned his hip against the counter. "You told the cops I was with you. Gave me an alibi. Why?"

Her shoulders straightened, like it took effort, and she stared across the room into his eyes. "Because it was the right thing to do. Because I finally stopped being a coward."

"Well, uh, thanks."

She shook her head impatiently. "You don't owe me any thanks. You've every right to be furious with me."

Furious. Last night, he had been. This morning, he'd been hurt and disappointed. Now, he didn't know how he felt. It had been easier when she wasn't there, but he couldn't be sorry she'd come. Man, he was one mixed-up dude. What was he hoping for from her?

"What happened about your job?" he asked. "That promotion you wanted?"

"I withdrew my application." She shrugged. "I only wanted it to make my parents proud. I'm happy being an accountant. I've been so mixed up about so many things. I don't even know who I am anymore."

Mixed up. That made two of them. "Uh . . . I guess I don't know who you are, either. I thought you were one person, then last night I found out I was wrong."

"You thought I was nice, and found out I'm a bitch."

Wow. That was pretty plain talk, not to mention language he'd never heard from Maura. "I found out that you think I'm good enough to fuck, good enough to play do-gooder with, but not good enough to take you to that reunion." And yeah, that did make her a bitch.

She nodded, not looking surprised or hurt. "Actually, I didn't think that. But I worried what my classmates, and especially my parents, would think. Which is just as bad. Maybe worse."

He nodded. Either way, she was a bitch. But why was she here?

She glanced at the beer in his hand. "D'you have another of those?"

Startled—Maura was full of surprises tonight—he got one from the fridge, cranked off the top, and handed her the bottle.

She took a sip, grimaced slightly, then had a healthy slug of it. "My drink of choice is Ehrenfelser. Yours is beer."

Yeah, they were different. He got that. "You like champagne, fancy food, dancing. I like beer and pizza."

"I never go dancing, and I like pizza, too. And beer's not so bad. And I like old movies. We're not so different." Then she shook her head, took a breath. "No, there's one big difference. You're a good person. And I'm not good enough for you."

Well, huh. That stunned him enough that he sank down in a chair.

She stood, staring down at him with huge ocean eyes. "But I want to be. I want to be the kind of woman who deserves a man like you."

He wasn't all that sure what she meant, but she seemed sincere. And his heart, which she'd pretty much trashed, was insane enough to start hoping again. "You can be any kind of woman you want to be."

A smile flashed, lighting her face. "Yes, that's what I finally figured out. I'm responsible for who I am. Not my parents, not Sally—"

"Sally?" he broke in, lost again. "Who's Sally?"

"A high school friend. She got me to loosen up, and got me in trouble. Or at least that's how I saw it—how my parents saw it—at the time. But she wasn't responsible. I was. It's up to me if I let down my hair, drink too much, watch TV. It's up to me what kind of career I want, and what kind of man I date."

"Well, yeah."

She gave a wry laugh, took another slug of beer. "You'd think it would be obvious, right? To anyone with half a brain? That just goes to show how stupid I've been." She swayed slightly and grabbed the back of a chair. "Wow, this stuff packs a punch."

She'd had two whole swallows of beer. "Have you eaten today?"

"I guess not."

"Sit down before you fall down."

Obediently, she slid into a chair.

Trying to process what she'd said, Jesse rose to take an open package of cheddar from the fridge and a box of crackers from the counter. He tossed them on the table along with a knife. "Eat."

For a few minutes, they were both silent as she sliced cheese and ate a few crackers.

As usual with Maura, he was confused as hell. Why had she come? What did she want?

Finally, she said, "I'm sorry. Sorry for everything. For not telling the police the truth right away this morning and for being so horrible last night."

He thought about that. It was an honest apology. It was childish to hold a grudge. "Okay."

Her eyes widened. "Okay?"

He shrugged. "You did something you feel bad about. You apologized. Okay."

"Does that mean you forgive me?"

He reflected. "You did fix things with the police."

"Is there any way I can fix things with you?"

He felt that tickle of hope again. But she'd hurt him before, so did he want to lay himself open to that again? "Fix things? How do you mean?"

"We were friends, and I didn't deserve your friendship. I want to try again." She reached out as if she wanted to grab his hands, then stopped herself. "Jesse, I truly do like you and respect you. I don't care what job you work at, I don't care how much schooling you've had or whether you read or not. You're the finest man I've ever known, and I want that man as my friend. Is there any hope of that?"

He wanted that, too. He wanted a lot more than that. But how about Maura? He still wasn't clear exactly what she had in mind. "Friends." His voice rasped on the word. "Guess we could try that."

Her face lit up. "And our nonprofit society? It's such a great idea. But it's up to you. I can't see it working with anyone else but you."

He had really liked the idea. Been excited about it, started imagining the possibilities. "We could talk about that."

"You can stay at Cherry Lane to do your community

service, if you still want to. Fred and Virginia talked to the Chair of the Board and went to bat for both of us."

"Nice of them," he said gruffly, touched by their kindness.

She lifted the bottle to her lips and took a long swallow. When she put it down, she looked scared, but determined. "There's one more thing."

"What?" he asked warily.

"I'd like to invite you to my high school reunion."

Just what did that mean? Had she decided that going with him was better than getting appendicitis? "As your friend?"

She shook her head. When she spoke, her voice trembled with nerves. "No, as my d-date. My b-boyfriend." Her voice speeded up as she went on. "Jesse, I would be so proud if you'd go with me as my date. I know you're not into serious relationships, but even if it's just a short-term thing—"

"What? What d'you mean I'm not into serious relationships?" The way he felt about Maura was pretty damned serious.

"You've never been with a woman for more than a few months."

"Yeah, but—"

"Which is fine," she said quickly. "I know you see bike rides and sex as pretty much the same thing and—"

"What?" he hollered. Sometimes this woman made so much sense, and sometimes she made no sense at all. "What are you talking about?"

She frowned. "When I said it was my personal business if I went for a bike ride with you, but sex was different, you said they're the same."

"Oh, yeah, right." He remembered that conversation.

"And for me, sex is something special. But that doesn't mean I'm asking for anything you're not willing to give."

Light was beginning to dawn. And this time, hope was more than a flicker; it was a steadily growing flame. "You thought I meant that sex with you was no more significant than a bike ride?"

She nodded.

He chuckled. "Jesus, Maura. I meant it was the same principle. If one thing is no one else's business, then I figured the other wouldn't be, either."

"That's what you were talking about?"

"Yeah. And yeah, I've never had a relationship that was serious. But things were different. The women were different."

"Different than what?"

Wasn't it obvious? "You," he said with exasperation. "You're special, Maura. Sex with you is special, talking to you is special, everything about you is special. I've never felt this way before, damn it."

Her lips twitched. "Damn it?"

"Well, hell, you've turned my world upside down. I'm trying to get my bearings."

This time, she did take his hands. Her grip was warm and firm. "Oh, Jesse, me, too. I've never met anyone like you and I've never felt anything like this before. I've messed up so badly, I'm such a terrible person, I can't believe you still think I'm special."

"Had my doubts for a while," he said gruffly, "but everybody makes mistakes."

"So you'll do it?" She squeezed his hands. "You'll be my reunion date?"

"On one condition."

"What's that?"

"You'll stop talking about short term. I've got a lot more than that in mind for you, Maura Mahoney."

"Oh, Jesse, I'll accept that condition with pleasure." Her face, her eyes, even her voice glowed.

Finally, he let himself smile. Really, really smile. It felt like his heart was opening up to her. Opening up in a way it had never dared do before. "Figure we ought to seal the deal with a kiss."

She let go of his hands and came around the small table to sit in his lap, her arms going around his neck. "You're one smart man, Jesse Blue."

Then her lips were on his and, as they kissed, he imagined a whole new, wonderful fantasy. Maura, as his woman, sexy and smart and sensitive, challenging him and loving him. With the two of them together, who knew what fantasies they could make come true?

Chapter 21

When Maura opened her door to Jesse in his tux, with tousled hair, carrying his bike helmet, he took her breath away.

The gay clerk at the tuxedo rental store had oohed and aahed and thoroughly embarrassed poor Jesse, but the result was a designer tux that looked like it had been made for his broad shoulders, slim waist, and long legs. The white shirt was crisp and the bow tie and cummerbund were a golden-brown that matched his tawny eyes.

"I feel like a teenager going to the prom with the most handsome boy in school." She winced. "No, bad analogy. Tonight will *not* end the way my prom did." Or at least she sure hoped it wouldn't.

His eyes gleamed as he took her in from head to toe: hair worn loose and free, scarlet dress—because fantasies could come true—and high-heeled red shoes. "You sure don't look like a teenager. You're all woman, Maura. A beautiful, sexy woman." He touched his lips to hers, careful not to mess up her red lipstick. "My woman," he added smugly.

"I love how that sounds."

"You and me both. Now, I want to hear that prom story. You started to say something that first day, after talking to Cindy, but you wouldn't finish."

"It's embarrassing."

"Tell me." His eyes were warm and sympathetic.

And so she did.

When she finished, he said, "If that guy Troy's here tonight, I'm gonna punch him out."

"You are not!"

He chuckled. "It's fun pushing your buttons. No, I figure Troy's already got his punishment. He missed out on being with the sweetest, sexiest girl in the class."

She melted into his arms. "You're the best. Have I told you that?"

He kissed her nose. "Tell me later, when we're in bed, Ms. Warm Honey. Now, you done stalling? Ready to face the music?"

The music. Cindy, all her former classmates, not to mention Agnes and Timothy. Maura'd told her parents she was bringing a date. She wouldn't ask them to accept him; she'd tell them he was her guy, and he was the smartest, nicest man she'd ever met. No way would she give up Jesse to please her parents.

"I'm ready." She slipped her arm through his.

They'd decided, for the sake of her dress and hair, to arrive by car rather than blaze into the gym on his Harley as per her fantasy.

When they walked in, their arrival had an impact even without the bike. Conversations stopped, and she heard people whisper, "Is that Maura Mahoney?" as she and Jesse strolled arm in arm toward the bar.

But then she heard, "Jesse Blue?"

She saw a man waving from across the gym. Was that . . . yes, it was Ernie Blair, from her high school class, just a few pounds heavier. But how did he know Jesse?

"Jesus." Jesse's hand tightened on her arm. "Maura, hell, it's the lawyer who prosecuted me. Christ, you're not going to impress anyone if they find out you're dating a . . . criminal."

She gripped his arm tighter and told the truth. "I'm proud to be with you and I don't care what people think. In fact"—she clung even harder and her voice trembled— "I l-love you, Jesse Blue."

He swallowed hard. "Maura, there's a place in my heart that's always been empty. That's always wanted a home, but doubted I'd find one. And that place . . . well, you've filled it. I love you, too."

Moisture glazed her vision. How could she possibly be so lucky?

Before she could respond, Ernie Blair came up to them, beaming. "Wow, look at you, Maura. I hardly recognized you. Jesse, I had no idea you knew one of my old classmates."

"Guess it didn't come up in conversation," Jesse said wryly.

Maura kept her hand tight on his arm, offering silent support.

Jesse stuck out his hand. "I want to thank you for agreeing to the deal Barry Adamson proposed."

Ernie took his hand and shook firmly, but shot a questioning glance at Maura.

"It's all right," she said. "I know all about it."

He nodded and turned back to Jesse. "No problem. Far as I'm concerned, you saved that young woman's life."

A pretty Asian woman came up to them and tucked her hand in Ernie's. "Going to introduce me, sweetheart?"

"Of course. Folks, this is my wife, Lisa. Lisa, this is Maura, a classmate, and Jesse, uh, a business acquaintance."

Maura glanced at Jesse. The lines of tension in his face were relaxing. Then she turned to Ernie, who gave them both a reassuring wink. She smiled gratefully.

A familiar voice squealed, "Why Maura Mahoney, is that really you?"

Resignedly, she turned around. "Cindy, how good to see you."

Jesse's body shook briefly and she elbowed him in the ribs. Cindy looked as glamorous as always, though Maura didn't remember her hair being quite that shade of blond.

Cindy was busy ogling Jesse and fluttering her eyelashes. "Well, hello stranger. Now where did Maura find you?"

"In her bedroom," Jesse said calmly.

Ernie and Lisa gave delighted chuckles, Cindy's mouth gaped open unattractively, and Maura began to smile for real. "Cindy Johnson, meet Jesse Blue."

Cindy bared her teeth in a forced smile. "So, what do you do, Jesse?"

"Jack of all trades," he said.

"Not to mention, director of a charitable organization," Maura added.

"That's interesting," Ernie said. "That's new since we last met. What's the charity?"

Maura opened her mouth but Jesse pressed her arm, silencing her. "It's called House Keepers," he said. "We assist seniors who don't have the money to keep their homes in decent repair but aren't ready to move to a residential or care facility. We provide the labor and materials free of charge."

"That sounds like a worthwhile cause," Ernie said. "My firm sponsors several organizations, and I'd be interested in looking into this further."

"Let me give you my card," Jesse said, patting his pocket.

Maura gaped. They didn't have cards yet. It was on her list.

Jesse shook his head. "Sorry, guess I forgot to bring them. How about I give you a call on Monday, Ernie?"

Maura smothered a chuckle. Not only did he clean up just fine, he was darned smooth.

Ernie and Lisa departed to greet a new arrival, and Cindy said she needed a drink.

Alone again, Maura told Jesse, "You were brilliant. Not only beauty, but brains." And this man loved her.

He threw back his head and laughed, and the female heads in the vicinity turned their way. He leaned close to her ear. "Did I tell you about this fantasy I've got? It's about you in those shoes and your glasses and nothing else."

A sexy shiver rippled down her spine. "I do believe that could be arranged."

Then she gave a completely different kind of shiver, catching sight of Agnes and Timothy standing on the other side of the room staring their way. Agnes raised her hand in a "come here" gesture.

"Jesse, we should introduce you to my parents. They're—"

A female voice interrupted, squealing Maura's name. She spun on a high heel. "Sally!"

A pint-size dynamo with a mass of curly black hair flung herself at Maura and wrapped surprisingly strong arms around her.

Perfectly aware that Agnes and Timothy were watching, waiting for her to come over to them, Maura deliberately hugged Sally back. Then they stepped apart to stare at each other. "I didn't know you'd be here," Maura said. "I heard you moved out of town."

"Just moved back last month. I was hoping I'd see you." Sally grinned impishly. "So how are your folks?"

Maura laughed. "Not running my life anymore." No need to tell Sally that it had taken her until she was thirty to grow up.

"Looks like you're doing a fine job all by yourself. You

look fabulous, girlfriend. Now who is this utterly gorgeous man?"

Maura made the introductions, then Jesse said, "Just bet
you gals are dying to talk about me. How about I get us
some drinks?" With a twinkle in his eye, he said to Maura,
"Champagne sound about right?"

"Perfect," Maura said. Champagne, and later they'd
dance together, and who cared if neither one of them
knew how to waltz? As long as they had their arms around
each other, she'd be in heaven.

The two women watched him walk away. Sally fanned
herself. "Now there's a hot man. Tell me, does he have a
brother?"

"Sorry, he's one of a kind. And he's mine."

Sally laughed. "Maura, darlin', the way he looks at you
leaves no doubt. But I swear, your Jesse's the kind of man
who'll be giving me wicked thoughts all night long."

"He'll be giving *me* a lot more than wicked *thoughts*!"

If you enjoyed BODY HEAT you won't want to miss
Susan Fox's deliciously sexy romance,

Yours, Unexpectedly

Read on for a little taste of this exciting romance.
A Brava trade paperback on sale now!

Absorbed in the slide show of images of me and my fiancé Matt in the digital photo frame on my desk, I took a moment to register the growl of a throaty car engine outside my open bedroom window. One glance and—"Oh my God!" I leaped to my feet. The yellow MGB convertible cruising to a stop was my sister Jenna's. Which meant that the hottie with windblown brown hair in the driver's seat was her man, come to make things right with her.

I flew out of my room and almost crashed into Jenna in the hall. My sister, now twenty-nine, had always been the gorgeous one in the family—in a totally natural way she took for granted. Nothing, not even the male-driven angst she'd been through in the past couple of days, could change that. Her blue sundress was perfect with her tanned skin, her hair tumbled in sunny curls over her shoulders, and even the shadows around her eyes brought out their dramatic greenish-blue.

"Jenna! That's your car!" And in it, fingers crossed, the cure for those mauve shadows. I'd always loved her—even despite her gorgeousness, her flakiness, and my issues with my sisters in general—but in the past days we'd grown closer and I really, really wanted things to work out for her.

"What?" She shook her head, frowning in puzzlement. "No, my car's in California. What are you talking about, Merilee?"

When her old MGB had broken down last week just as she'd started her journey home from Santa Cruz to Vancouver, she'd left it at a repair shop and hitched a ride with the man who'd turned her life upside down. And yes, the car outside was definitely hers, which meant this had to be *the guy*—the stranger she'd fallen for, broken up with, and been angsting over. "Look!" I grabbed her hand and dragged her over to the window.

Her ocean-colored eyes went wide, wider, and wider still as she stared out. "What?" She sounded utterly stunned.

"It's Mark, it's Mark! It is, isn't it?" He hadn't flown to Indonesia to start his marine biology project, he'd gone down to California to pick up her car. He'd come for her—a windblown knight in a butter-yellow MGB—and he was going to make everything all right. It was like the happy, tear-jerker ending of every romantic movie.

Finally, emotion flooded her face: hope, and a joy so powerful that . . . that I felt the sour tang of jealousy in my mouth. I was the one getting married in two days. *I* was the one who was supposed to feel on top of the world.

Ack! What was *wrong* with me these days?

Jenna dashed out my bedroom door and I ran after her, shoving aside my stupid, petty, irrational doubts and recapturing my excitement for her. In the hall, I yelled, "Theresa, Kat!"

Theresa opened her bedroom door. My oldest sister looked all fresh and pretty in shorts and an avocado-colored top that made green flecks dance in her hazel eyes. Frowning, she held up her cell phone. "What is it? I'm talking to Damien."

At least she'd only been *talking* to her boyfriend, who was on a book tour in the States. Not having phone sex, which from what she said occupied an awful lot of their time. I still couldn't get over the change in my up-tight professor sister since she'd hooked up with Damien. She'd always intimidated the hell out of me, but now she'd softened and was easier to relate to. Love had worked magic. Love and phone sex.

"Jenna's Mark is here," I answered, loud enough for Kat to hear too, in her bedroom where she'd holed up with her hottie from Montreal. Ms. Sociability, the girl who had a million friends but the worst luck when it came to love, had finally found herself a winner.

Theresa's face lit. "Seriously?" Into the phone she said, "Have to go, talk to you later, love you." She tossed the phone onto her bed, then faced me again, brow pinching. "That man better not hurt Jenna again."

Kat's bedroom door opened a crack and she stuck her head out, reddish-brown curls in disarray. "Mark's here? Really?"

"Outside, in Jenna's MGB." I turned to Theresa. "He won't hurt her." I crossed my fingers, hoping it was true. Yeah, maybe I was a teeny bit envious, but my sister—all my sisters—deserved happiness. "He's come to apologize. I'm sure of it."

Theresa's frown slid into a smile. "It is our summer for happy endings, isn't it? All of us Fallon girls."

Her, with her new love Damien, the thriller writer she'd met on the plane from Sydney. Kat, with the sexy photographer who'd won her heart on the train ride from Montreal. And me of course, marrying the boy I'd loved forever. Which was exciting. Of course it was. Along with kind of scary. And confusing. Which it shouldn't have been . . .

This wasn't the time to worry about it. Mark had come for Jenna, and I didn't want to miss a moment.

Kat said, "Gotta pull some clothes on."

So that's why she'd only opened the door a crack. "Ew!

TMI." It was squirmy enough to hear her gush and rave about Kama Sutra sex with the fabulous Naveen, much less know exactly where and when—like right now, across the hall—it was going on.

"Don't let anything happen without me," she called as she slammed the door.

Theresa and I darted down the hall and pounded down the staircase, then raced out the open front door of the family home. Halfway between the MGB and the steps, Jenna stood with her guy. His arms were around her shoulders and hers around his waist.

As Theresa and I went over, Kat and Nav hurried up behind us. Mom's Mercedes pulled up and she climbed out and walked briskly toward us in her business suit. For once, my lawyer mom who had to control the world didn't jump in with questions. She was so smart she'd have sized the situation up in a nanosecond.

As we all moved closer to Jenna, I figured Mark had to know we were serving notice that if he messed with her, he'd have us to answer to. Within the family, we might snipe and nag and bitch, but when it came to outsiders, we protected our own.

I sized the guy up: a rangy, well-muscled bod shown off by cargo shorts and a black tank, angular features, a tan that made his sky-blue eyes even more dramatic. Even rumpled and windblown, he was a total hottie. Was I disloyal to Matt, to think that? Of course my fiancé was handsome, but he didn't have Mark's intense, utterly masculine vibe.

Mark's piercing blue eyes took in our presence, then he gazed down at Jenna and, oh yeah, I was watching a romantic movie. He shut us out as if we didn't exist, and focused entirely on her with a passionate intensity that gave me shivers. What would it be like to have a man look at me that way? My guy was loving and considerate, but . . .

I brushed the thought away and listened.

Mark told Jenna he'd postponed his trip to Indonesia where he was scheduled to head a coral reef restoration project and had instead taken a red-eye down to California so he could bring her much-loved car back to her—because to her, that car symbolized freedom.

I nodded. Yeah, Jenna'd always been all about freedom.

Then he said, "I was wrong. I shouldn't have asked you to change. I fell in love with you just the way you are. You're a wonderful person."

A silent "Aw" rose in my throat. He was romancing her so absolutely perfectly. Again I wondered what that would be like. My Matt and I had been together since we were seven. He'd never had to romance me, never had to do something grand and dramatic to win me, because love had always been there.

I had always thought words like *radiant* and *glowing* belonged in ads, not real life. My sister's face proved me wrong.

Vaguely, I was aware of Dad driving up and coming over to join us, but I was utterly caught up in what Jenna was telling her lover. When she said she'd just asked a travel agent to book her a flight to Bali for right after my wedding, I barely suppressed a gasp. She said she had been afraid of commitment, but now she was ready to build a future with Mark.

It was her own grand, romantic gesture. Did he have any idea how huge this was for her?

Maybe so. The way he touched her cheek was so tender it brought tears to my eyes. "You mean you'd give up all the variety for one man, one cause?" he asked huskily.

"We'll create our own variety. Side by side, as partners. That'll be all the excitement I can handle."

"And it'll be more excitement and more joy than I'd ever hoped for."

"You and me both."

Excitement. Joy. Yes, I saw those emotions on their faces, along with tenderness and passion. I'd seen the same feelings shared by Theresa and her Damien, and Kat and Nav. Intense, sexy, and romantic.

When was the last time Matt and I had looked at each other that way? Or had we ever? Tenderness, yes, but passion? Excitement? Pure, blazing joy? All week, seeing my sisters come home one by one from all over the world, bursting with the excitement of new, passionate love affairs, I'd felt . . . What?

Kind of flat. Maybe even unhappy, a little depressed. Off. In the week before my own wedding, the wedding I'd dreamed of since I was a little girl, when I should have been brimming with excitement, I'd felt empty. Left out. Like everyone else was having all the fun.

That was childish. In this family, I should know I'd never be the center of attention, and just stop wanting it.

Except . . . Was that really all it was? Or did it go deeper? Was it about Matt and me? Though I was eleven years younger than Theresa, eight years younger than Jenna, I felt—okay, I felt *settled*. Settled into a comfortable relationship that never ignited the kind of sparks I now saw flying between Jenna and Mark as they kissed like they were merging their souls.

Well, shit. Comfortable, rather than exciting. Settled, at the ripe old age of twenty-one. This was bad. Definitely bad. For fourteen years I'd told myself I was the Fallon sister who'd found her soul mate, the perfect love, and now . . .

Pre-wedding jitters. Everyone has them.

Then why was my heart racing and why, even as I joined my family in clapping and cheering for Jenna and Mark, did I feel left out and envious? I was the one getting *married,* and rather than looking forward to my beautiful white wedding, I was wanting what my sisters had.

My heart lodged in my throat, beating so hard it threatened to choke me. I tried to swallow as Jenna and her guy eased an inch or two apart. "We belong together," he said with absolute conviction.

"We do. I've been falling for you since . . . oh, probably since the moment you ordered strawberry pie."

"I've been falling for you since I first looked into your eyes."

It was one of those *aw, isn't that sweet?* moments, but instead of enjoying it, my brain was spinning. That was how it had been for Matt and me, recognizing from the beginning that we were soul mates. M&M. Except we'd been seven. Children, not adults. We'd grown up together. He'd been at our house so often, Mom and Dad said it was almost like having a son. I'd never dated anyone but him. We'd fumbled through learning about sex together. And the sex was great. Tender and affectionate and really . . . comfortable.

I put a hand to my chest, over my racing heart, and pressed down, trying to calm it. What a bitch I was, being disloyal to Matt, my best friend, the one person in the world who'd always been there for me. Always put me first.

But . . . why did he never look at me with passionate intensity? Why did I never feel sparks flying, like he couldn't wait to be alone with me and strip my clothes off? Did he really, really love me or was it just *comfortable* being with me?

Oh shit, I couldn't seem to draw air into my lungs. Was I going to pass out?

As per usual, no-one was paying me the slightest notice. Things with my family had improved in the past week, but

I would never be the center of attention in a family where everyone else was, in their own way, larger than life.

I could have fainted dead away and no one would have noticed. They were all, "You'll stay for dinner;" "I've been on the road for the last two days without a shower or change of clothes;" "I'm sure Jenna will help you find the shower." Blah, blah, and they'd be having sex in that shower, too, and everyone knew it.

Hot sex. Steamy hot sex. Not *comfortable* sex. Matt and I had been lovers for five years now, and never once had we made out in the shower. What did that mean?

Yesterday, I'd visited Gran. I'd always loved her so much, and it broke my heart that now she had Alzheimer's and mostly was pretty out of it. Still, somehow that had freed me to pour out all the stupid, toxic shit I'd been feeling since my sisters arrived home. The crazy jealousy, the uncertainty, the fear that my future wasn't going to be the blissful one I'd always dreamed of.

She had stared out the window the whole time I talked, not saying a word. When I kissed her and said I had to go, she caught my hand and said, "Every woman deserves passion. Have you found yours?"

Did she even know it was me? Was this one of her lucid moments or was she just rambling?

I'd told myself that Matt, marriage to Matt, was my passion. But now . . . Why was I almost hyperventilating? What did this all mean? Ack! I was supposed to be getting *married*!

I managed to take a shallow breath and said, with certainty, "I have to see Matt." I didn't have a clue what I was going to say, but I could tell him anything, couldn't I? We'd figure this out together, like we sorted out every other problem in our lives. Surely he'd know why I had this strange ache in my chest.

Jenna, who was leading Mark inside, showed no sign of

having heard. Mom and Dad had their heads together dis-
cussing Mark, and so did Kat and Nav. Theresa glanced at
her watch, probably wondering if she could catch Damien
again. Nope, I might as well not have been there.

I went to grab my keys, not bothering to change out of
my old shorts and tee.

Not a soul was in sight when I started up the hand-me-
down Toyota Dad had passed on to me when I was sixteen. The car almost steered itself toward Matt's house, a
route I'd used to bike when I was younger. "The beaten
path," his mom called it. And that reminded me, Adele
would be there. A nurse, she worked some pretty weird
shifts, but she and Matt had agreed to spend one mom-son
night at home in the busy week before the wedding. She
was great, a loving, hard-working single mom, but right
now I couldn't face her.

I pulled over to dial Matt on my cell. The phone rang,
then rang again. "Damn it, Matt, where are you? I need
you." It rang again, then once more, and finally he answered.

"You're there." I exhaled in relief. "Are you with your
mom?"

"Hey, M. No, she just got home from work. She's having a shower then we'll get dinner going."

"I'm on my way over. Need to talk to you. Meet me at
your place?" When Matt and I were eighteen, we'd helped
his mom convert their two-car garage into a tiny apartment for him.

"Sure. What's up?"

"Uh . . . Jenna's guy, the one she met hitchhiking from
California, showed up."

"Hey, that's cool. And so . . ."

"I need to talk to you."

"Are you okay? You've been acting kind of strange the
past few days."

He'd noticed. I shouldn't be surprised; it went with that soul mate thing. "Just meet me, okay?"

Ten minutes later, when I drove down the back alley, I saw a car in the Townsend driveway—a sporty black convertible that definitely didn't belong to Matt or Adele. The top was up, drops of water glistened on the black paint, and a guy in shorts, flip-flops, and nothing else was leaning over it, rubbing the car's body with a cloth.

A hot guy. Momentarily distracted from my worries, I appreciated the view: great butt, muscles flexing under the lightly tanned skin of a buff back, water drops glistening on strong arms and legs. Wow. If this was a car commercial, women would sure be buying.

Curious to find out who he was, I pulled up behind the Miata.

The guy turned, smiled, grabbed a gray T-shirt, and pulled it over his head, and I realized it was Matt.

My Matt. The center of my life for the last fourteen years.

I blinked. That image of the hot car-commercial guy had been weird, almost like a hallucination. This was the old familiar Matt coming toward me as I stepped out of my car—casual in baggy cargo shorts and a loose, faded University of British Columbia tee, his dirty-blond hair showing a few summer-gold streaks. My girlfriends said he was hot, that he looked like a younger, lighter-haired Bradley Cooper. Sure, he was good looking, but to me he wasn't movie star handsome; he was just good old Matt, the boy I'd grown up with.

"Merilee?" He tilted his head quizzically. His blue eyes, the shade of well-washed denim—yeah, they kind of were the color of Bradley Cooper's—were warm with concern as he tugged me into a hug. "Are you all right?"

His arms had always given me shelter. When my family

ignored me or I was pissed off at my sisters, or when I was suffering the pain that had finally been diagnosed as endometriosis, he'd been the one to comfort and support me.

Yet, now, maybe for the first time ever, I didn't feel at home in his arms. Or perhaps I was tired of feeling at home and wanted something more. I pushed away from him, not knowing how to say what I needed to. Sensing that once I started, things between us would change forever.

Stalling, I said, "What are you doing with the car?"

"It was supposed to be a surprise. It's Leon's brother's and he loaned it to me. I'm washing and polishing it, then some of our friends are going to do the whole 'Just Married' thing with it, so we can drive it from the wedding."

Just Married. Not long ago, it had sounded like the best thing in the whole world, but now . . . "M, what are we doing?" The words burst out of my mouth. "Is this the right thing?"

"Doing?" He frowned, processing, then said, "You don't mean . . . getting married?"

I nodded.

His eyes widened. "You're kidding, right? I mean, I know you've been having some, uh, pre-wedding nerves, but that's normal, isn't it?"

"I guess." Everyone said so, but what I felt seemed stronger. Maybe I was wrong, though. This was why we needed to talk. "I don't know. Are you feeling any, you know, nerves? Doubts?"

He shrugged. "Not really. I mean, we're young like everyone keeps telling us, but I want to marry you. We've always wanted that. Moving up the date from next year—"

"Should we have?" I broke in. Maybe the timing was wrong. "We always said we'd get married after we got our

B.A.'s." And right before starting the year-long program to get our Education degrees. Then I was going to teach middle grade kids, and he'd teach high school.

That was something else we'd been planning for years. We really were *settled*.

"But then you were diagnosed," he said.

Matt had nagged me into asking a doctor about what my sisters and mom had for years blown off as being normal menstrual cramps. I'd had surgery for endometriosis a couple of months ago. The diagnosis had made Matt and I rethink things. We'd always wanted kids and never once imagined I might face infertility at the age of twenty-one.

"Yeah." I nodded, mentally retracing the steps that had led us to move up the wedding. "Then you saw that last-minute deal on the cruise." A Mexican Riviera cruise—a perfect honeymoon and pure R&R. After the surgery, recuperation, and being crazy busy catching up on missed coursework and exams, I was desperate to lie back and do nothing.

"It all came together," he said, "as if it was meant to be."

That was how it had felt. Yes, I remembered. But now . . . I squeezed my lips together, then parted them and heard myself say, "But maybe it wasn't meant to be."

He frowned. "What are you saying?"

Words poured out, giving voice to all the doubts and fears I'd been trying to ignore all week. "Maybe we shouldn't do it. Get married. Not now." Oh God, was I totally crazy? I'd loved Matt since grade two.

"Jeez, Merilee, you're talking crazy. We've loved each other since we were seven."

It was spooky how he so often read my mind, or our minds were on the same track. I didn't even have the privacy of my own thoughts. "I know that!" I snapped. "Do you think I don't know that? I still love you, M, but . . ."

His hands gripped my shoulders, hard. "Calm down, you're not making any sense."

"I can't calm down. I don't want to calm down. This is important." He had to see that. Maybe once I explained, he'd make everything right. He'd say something, sweep me off my feet, show me he really, really, totally and utterly loved me, and that we could be just as exciting and passionate as my sisters and their guys. He'd do that *thing*— that grand romantic thing like Jenna's man had just done—that would show me I was crazy to have second thoughts.

Fingers biting into me, pinning me down, he stared into my eyes. "How can you have cold feet about getting married Saturday, when we've been talking about getting married all our lives?"

"I don't know!" I wriggled my shoulders until he dropped his hands, then I took a step back, away from him. "Maybe *because* we've been talking about it all our lives." He was *still* talking, not *doing* anything. "Maybe because I've known you all my life." And because of that, I should know better than to hope for a dramatic, romantic gesture.

He shook his head, looking frustrated and pissed off. "I don't get it. You always said we're soul mates. We're M&M. A couple."

"I'm not sure this is the right time." The more he tried to persuade me, the more *sense* he made, the less right the whole thing felt. Instincts counted just as much as logic, and what my instincts craved was *not* a bunch of rational discussion.

"Everything's booked." He snapped out the words. "Theresa made that project plan and you and your sisters have put everything together in under two weeks. Location, minister, reception, food, music. We've had the damned stag and stagette."

He was right, and at first I'd been thrilled to bits about the wedding, but now I felt trapped. "Stop being so logical." Even that silly stagette had given me doubts, as I'd been showered with sexy, kinky gifts I couldn't imagine us ever using.

He strode a couple of paces away from me. I heard him take a deep breath, then he turned around and faced me, his expression one of strained patience. "What do you want, Merilee?"

I blinked. What did I want? What had I been hoping for when I came here? Did I want him to fight for me? To sweep me up in his arms and . . . do what? To find that perfect romantic thing, the way Damien had when he asked Theresa to stay over in Honolulu with him. The way Nav had, playing stranger on the train with Kat. The way Mark had, flying down to California to bring Jenna's car to her.

I didn't want *settled*. I didn't want *comfortable*. I wanted what my sisters had: a grand, romantic, larger than life love. Was there any hope Matt could give it to me?

Stunned, Matt Townsend stared at the girl he knew better than anyone else in the world, and felt as if he didn't know her at all. Had she lost her freaking mind?

He struggled to hold onto his patience. After all the initial excitement about announcing the wedding, she'd grown increasingly moody. He'd figured it was the sister effect as her older sisters—the three-pack, as the family called them—had returned to Vancouver one by one. The Fallon girls pushed each other's buttons, and it was especially bad for Merilee, the unplanned baby who'd come along eight years after Jenna. Rebecca and James Fallon and the three-pack hadn't rearranged their lives to make room for the newcomer.

That had always annoyed Matt. Merilee was such a sweet person, but her family was so self-absorbed they barely noticed her. He did, though. He noticed, he valued, he loved her. He looked after her.

And now he was pissed off with her. She was talking crazy, and couldn't even say what she wanted. "Merilee?" he prompted, struggling to keep his voice even, "you don't want to call off the wedding, right?" When he put it that bluntly, she'd come to her senses. She wasn't going to dump him flat on his ass two days before their wedding.

"I think"—she sniffled and swiped a hand across eyes the blue of a spring morning—"that maybe I do." Tears began to roll.

Her tears usually made him want to cradle her in his arms and make everything better. This time he just gaped at her. She hadn't really said that, had she? "Are you nuts?"

"Oh, Matt," she wailed, "try to understand."

"Understand?" Anger and hurt rose in him, and his voice along with them. "Shit, Merilee, what the hell's going on?" Trying to regain control—he was *not,* would never be, a guy like his dad who lost his temper—he paced jerkily across the alley, then turned to stare at her. He'd done everything for this girl, focused his life on her for fourteen years. She was *not* betraying and abandoning him. "Two weeks ago, you said getting married was your dream come true."

"It was." She stared back at him, eyes huge and drenched with tears. Her shoulders were rounded inside one of his old T-shirts and she looked small and forlorn. Her dark honey-blond hair lay in gleaming curls on her shoulders, incongruously bouncy, as if it hadn't gotten the message that she was miserable.

He had, and he was feeling pretty damned crappy. Except he still couldn't really believe it. "It was," he said harshly, "and now it isn't. What's changed?"

"My sisters came home," she said, so softly he could barely hear.

"Your family's trying to talk you out of getting married?" Shit. He'd always thought the Fallons liked him. He'd been at family dinners for the past week, and everyone had been friendly. They'd even been getting along better with each other, too. And now they'd stabbed him in the back.

"No." She shook her head. "No, it's not that. Oh, M, I don't know how to say this."

Insulted, he said, "You can tell me anything. You know that."

She took a deep breath, then words flew out on the exhale. "I feel middle-aged."

Relief sent him rushing over to grip her shoulders comfortingly. Now it all made sense. "Sweetheart, you're worn out." When her surgery was scheduled, they'd discussed her skipping a semester at university, but she'd wanted to catch up her courses and exams so they'd graduate together next year. Besides, once they were on their honeymoon, she'd have a week of total rest.

She closed her eyes for a long moment, then opened them and gazed up at him. "I am tired, but that's not what I meant. We're so, you know, settled and comfortable as a couple."

"Settled and comfortable?" Those didn't sound like bad things except for the tone of her voice.

"I mean, we're all stable and b-boring"—she ducked her head, again not meeting his eyes—"and there's no spark or excitement or p-passion."

His hands jerked off her shoulders as if she'd scalded him. She thought he was boring? That their love life sucked? Well, just *shit!* His hands clenched, unclenched, clenched again. Yeah, he wasn't the most exciting guy in the world. How could he be when his mom had told him, at the age of six, that he had to be the man of the house— then at age seven he'd begun protecting Merilee as well?

Through an effort of will, he straightened his clenched fingers. A good man didn't give in to anger. He didn't beat up on women, he protected them. Matt was *not* a temperamental, irresponsible, violent man like his father, the man who had finally—thank God—abandoned him and his mom when he was six.

Matt had thought his maturity and consideration were qualities Merilee loved. Jesus, she'd said so. He'd never had a clue she was unhappy. He wanted to yell at her, to shake her, but he fought to keep his temper in check.

She gazed up, cheeks flushing. "I didn't tell you all the things I got at the stagette."

"What?" Startled out of his anger, he gaped at her. She'd gone from dropping that bomb to talking about the stagette? Who was this girl?

"I was so totally embarrassed. Like, there were Ben Wa balls."

Balls? To play some kind of game? He scrubbed his hands roughly over his face, hoping this was all some horrible dream. "What are you talking about?"

"V-vaginal balls."

Vaginal balls? He gaped at her, his anger and frustration momentarily forgotten. "Seriously?"

"I mean, can you just imagine? That's not, I mean, we wouldn't . . ." She buried her face against his chest.

Oh yeah, he could imagine. Sometimes he'd wanted to try something a little kinky in bed, but he never said anything, afraid she'd think he was a perv. Afraid, too, of where it might take him. Of turning into a man like his dad.

Like that one time, after a night at the pub with their friends, she'd been giggling about being a naughty girl for drinking so much. He was horny and he'd had too much to drink too, and, joking around, he'd said naughty girls should be punished. She'd teased, "I dare you." Then he'd pulled the long scarf off her neck, tied her hands above her head, forced her on her stomach, and spanked her. He'd hit Merilee. Yeah, he'd only been fooling around, but he'd actually hit her.

Only when she'd cried out in pain had he come to his senses and stopped. Horrified, he'd sobered up immediately and untied her. The shock in her eyes was more than he could bear. He'd apologized profusely and she'd forgiven him, even promised to forget it ever happened, and after that he'd taken care to always be gentle with her.

Merilee was sweet and wholesome, not kinky or skanky. Some of his guy friends boasted about their girlfriends, and sometimes—yeah, he was a red-blooded male—he was envious. But often he just thought the behavior was slutty. Like sexting a crotch shot, or giving a bunch of dudes blow jobs at a party? No, thanks. Merilee had morals and he respected that.

He wasn't surprised those vaginal balls had embarrassed her. Yet she said she wanted more spark, excitement, passion. Things she didn't find with him. Yeah, that cut deep. There were different kinds of passion. Their love was like a steady golden candle, not sparks and fireworks.

They'd grown up together. Never even dated anyone else. Best friends who, yeah, were comfortable together. What the hell was wrong with that? Loving security was the most important thing in the world, as he well knew after having a dad like his.

As for sparks, how could he and M have ignited sparks? From the bits of girl talk he'd overheard with their friends, it seemed like sparks happened when you first met someone and fell for them.

And what was Merilee's idea of excitement anyhow? Going out dancing? A picnic on the beach? They did those things occasionally and he liked them too, but money and time were in short supply.

They'd always been so practical. *She* had too; it wasn't just him. If she'd wanted something different, why the hell hadn't she said so? She had no trouble deciding what movie to see, what kind of pizza to order. What kind of careers they should both have. Mostly, he went along because it all sounded fine to him.

But *this,* this business about calling off the wedding— no, it didn't sound fucking *fine* at all.

"Matt, are you furious? Hurt?" Warm breath brushed his neck. "Say something. Tell me how you feel."

"I feel . . ." Betrayed. Mad. Frustrated. Shocked. "Shitty."

She wound her arms around his waist and held him tightly. "I'm sorry, so sorry. I do love you, but over the past few days, it's just been feeling wrong."

It felt wrong to marry the guy she loved?

Her arms felt like a vice, so he shoved free of them. Those blue eyes welling with tears didn't match up with what she was saying. "Then if it feels *wrong,*" he said bitterly, "we'll call it off. We'll call the whole damned thing off." The words flew out of his mouth, surprising him.

Surprising her, too, from her expression. "The whole thing?"

"Us," he spat the word out. And now, all those crappy feelings taking over, he was on a roll. "We're *settled,* we don't have passion, we're *wrong.* Call it quits."

"I didn't . . . You aren't saying you want to break up?"

Break up. Break up with Merilee? Those words brought him back to reality. The idea was unthinkable. But so was her calling off the wedding. He shook his head, not knowing anything anymore. "I . . . I don't know." He hadn't felt so shitty in his entire life. "What are you saying?"

"Just that we shouldn't be getting married Saturday."

"But . . ." He tried to think it through. "Then what?

We're the same two people. Settled, comfortable, all those things you don't like. We're not suddenly going to get *exciting*, whatever the hell you mean by that word."

Expression stunned, she said, "I didn't think that far ahead."

When he tried to, he felt only a bleak chill in his heart. Pissed and hurt though he might be, he told her the truth. "I can't imagine life without you."

"Me either."

They stared at each other for a long moment. He felt like screaming, crying, punching his fist through a wall. The same shit his dad had done, except sometimes that fist hit his mom instead. When Matt was a boy, every time he'd acted out his mom had said he was behaving like his dad, he was breaking her heart.

Yeah, he could hold it together. "We're in no shape to decide the big stuff right now. We're both in shock. Let's take it one step at a time. First step's cancelling the wedding."

She blinked back tears and nodded. "Okay, yes, I can think about that. Though my family will be furious. The money they've laid out, all the planning. Oh Matt, I got Theresa and Kat and Jenna to come all the way here for nothing."

Nothing. Their beautiful wedding, the happiest day of their lives, had turned into *nothing*. In fact, maybe their whole fourteen year relationship was turning into nothing. Tears burned behind his eyes and he clenched his fists, hot tension vibrating up his arms and tightening his shoulders.

"I'll tell Mom," he said, his voice raw. For years, his mother had thought of Merilee as her daughter. "And I'll call the cruise lines."

"Theresa will draw up one of her project plans," she said bleakly. "To cancel everything else." She stepped away from him. "I need to go, so I can tell everyone and get things started."

"You shouldn't drive." Nor should he, and the last thing he wanted was to be confined in a car with her, but he'd always looked after her. "I'll give you a ride home."

She held up her hands. "No. Please. I'll go slow, but I need a few minutes alone."

Torn, he said, "Promise you'll be careful?"

"Promise." Her blue eyes were huge, wet, and swollen.

They stared at each other for long seconds, then she said in a plaintive voice, "Love you, M."

It was what they always said when they said goodbye. The only time he'd ever heard her say it so sadly was when the doctor had diagnosed her endometriosis and they'd realized they might never have the children they both wanted so badly. Yeah, they could adopt, but they'd had that soul mate thing going on and wanted to create their own babies. Maybe it had been a sign. A sign that they weren't soul mates after all.

But now, as he'd always done, he gave her what she wanted. "Love you, M." And it was true. She'd betrayed him, angered him, shattered him, but love didn't die in the space of minutes. Would it, though? For fourteen years, his future had been certain. Now . . . He couldn't think about it.

In the past, they'd always kissed goodbye. Today, he folded his arms across his chest.

Merilee turned and walked toward her car.

When she had driven away, Matt dragged his hands across his face. Then, because he couldn't help worrying, couldn't help caring, he called her house. He had ambivalent feelings about her family. They were good people, interesting ones, yet they rarely gave Merilee what she needed.

When her mother answered, he said, "Rebecca, Merilee's on her way home. If she doesn't make it, call me. And when she does, be there for her. All of you. She needs you."

"But, what . . . ?" Rarely was the high-powered litigator ever at a loss for words.

"It's her story to tell. Just, for once, would you put her first?"

"Put her first? But, we—"

He hung up, cutting her off. No, they didn't put Merilee first. He was the one who'd done that.

Everything in his life was based on being half of M&M, and now that was gone. He gave a choked sob, unable to hold back the tears any longer.